HOST SAGA BOOK 4
NEW HORIZONS

MICHAEL J. FARLOW

New Horizons
Host Saga Book 4
Copyright ©2018 by Michael J. Farlow
First Edition: December 2018

Wolf Press

ISBN-13: 978-0-9973121-8-8 – Trade Paperback
ISBN-13: 978-0-9973121-9-5 – eBook (ePub)
Library of Congress Control Number: 2018908691

Published by Wolf Press, LLC
San Antonio, Texas

Cover and Interior design by: Streetlight Graphics

For new books, blog updates and to sign up for the newsletter, please go to
www.michaeljfarlow.com

ACKNOWLEDGEMENTS

For helping me put things in order and to groom my art, my principal editor Tammy Salyer continues to be a godsend. And for a third set of eyes, many thanks to my readers Kevin Wolff and Mike Peterson. As I continue to say, writing is not a thing to be done alone.

IN MEMORY

This book and series is dedicated to the memory of Van Lee McCullough, fellow naval officer, pilot and my dear friend. To those familiar with the two of us, it is obvious that the name of the main character in this series borrows my friend's first name. Those who knew him, went to school with him and flew with him have the advantage of great memories that would be the envy of anyone.

PROLOGUE

V AN CHILDS AND GUARDIAN FORCE continued to prepare humanity (Earth and Zarminia included) for the eventual full-force attack of the ruthless and empire-building Arkon. Shipbuilding was still inadequate to meet their needs in time. Van hoped discovering the Zarminians would be the help he and humanity would need with shipbuilding and technology. But it wasn't enough. Using the *New Horizons* and its AI, Jennifer, both left to him by the Galactic Host six months earlier, Van and his force prepared to again go in search of help.

Harry, his AI companion and teacher, had been left on Earth by the Host to assist Van, the guardian, to prepare for the Arkon. Van had first discovered the Host technology in Arizona years ago and had since taken increasingly bolder steps in its use. Dr. Rosantina Ramos, the Guardian Force chief medical officer, had replaced his past paramour, Barbara Fuller. They thought they were keeping their growing relationship private, but everybody knew.

His old friend Dick Carson, and men and women from Dick's old security business, continued to assist Van in accomplishing his goals as Galactic Force grew in size. In the past months, the five Zarminian countries and colonies, along with the invited Guardian Force and the Carians, had formed the Zarminian Federation with the former president of Sonara as its first leader. The other former presidents and an elected member of the Carians now constituted the Zarminian Federation Consortium.

Guardian Force had met the Arkon three times and had, with help and luck, managed to escape complete destruction at the hands of the small Arkon forces encountered so far. But nobody expected that to continue, and they feared more friends would die.

The Galactic Host had revealed they were watching Van and his growing base of allies, but continued to keep away. They were building their own force to eventually join with Van and others to combat the Arkon in a final struggle.

CHAPTER 1

V AN JINKED THE SMALL ARMED shuttle *Enterprise* to the left and then the right as fast as he could, but the Arkon attack craft stayed on his tail, firing red plasma shots that looked the size of beach balls as they passed the shuttle's cockpit windows.

He tried calling for help, but the opening shot from the previously stealthy Arkon had disrupted all communications. Sweat rolled down his face and off his nose as Van strained to escape the trailing ship.

"This guy is good," Van said out loud. "I've tried tight turns, loops, and everything I can remember, but I keep coming up SOL." Then plasma shots went below him and above him.

"What the..." Van started when his small shuttle shook violently.

"Warning!" the ship's limited AI called. "Shields down to thirty percent."

"Thank you," he called out in frustration, "that really helps! How long have I been in this fight?" He looked at the clock on his flight panel, which read 10:15 GMT. "Only ten minutes!" he yelled in disbelief as he took more evasive maneuvers.

Then he remembered the pilot's trick he and Frank had learned in their military days. Reacting more than thinking, Van pulled back on the throttle and hit his forward thrusters.

Zoom, the trailing enemy swept past him as he reengaged his engines and started a chase of his own.

The *Enterprise* was armed with a single plasma cannon and no missiles. There was also an old leftover weapon, twin projectile-throwing 30mm cannons that were seldom used as Galactic Force got more sophisticated. But this old and reconstructed ship still had them.

The Arkon ship tried the same jinking maneuvers Van used and even tried slowing. But Van had the upper hand and wouldn't give it up. The *Enterprise* flashed time after time with its plasma cannon, which recorded a few hits, but the Arkon continued to elude destruction.

"What the hell?" Van said in frustration and fired the plasma cannon and the old 30mm at the same time. The red tracer rounds coming every five shots from the 30mm tricked the Arkon into believing Van was now firing multiple energy weapons. "Take that, you scaly alien piece of shit!"

Suddenly, the Arkon started trailing liquids, gasses, and small parts. One of those red-hot parts hit the *Enterprise*'s nose, causing the ship to yaw badly and Van to lose sight of the injured enemy.

Van struggled to regain control, but when he did, there was no sign of the enemy. . . until another shock registered on the old ship.

Looking to his left, Van saw the Arkon ship coming at him, plasma weapons firing, albeit slower than before but still scoring hits.

"Warning!" the ship's AI called again. "Shields down to fifteen percent and dropping."

Van goosed the engines as much as he could and pointed the nose of the *Enterprise* down and to the right. Still spitting plasma, the Arkon ship passed over the *Enterprise* and reappeared in the forward view screen as Van pulled the nose up and stopped his turn.

This time Van had the Arkon, and he pressed the plasma cannon trigger. But nothing happened. He tried again. Still nothing.

"Shit!" Van yelled. "Computer, status of plasma cannon."

"No power to the plasma cannon due to battle damage," said the AI.

"Shit, shit," was all Van could say as he maneuvered behind the now slower enemy.

With one last effort, Van pressed the 30mm trigger and kicked the rudders left and right, spraying the old bullets across as wide an arc as he could before the guns stopped firing.

"Weapons out of ammunition," called the AI.

Van slumped in his seat thinking this was it. *How long will the Arkon stay around trying for the last and final shot?* Van thought.

The answer came sooner than expected.

Without warning, the Arkon ship blossomed into a ball of fire and debris and was gone. The *Enterprise*'s view screen went black and all lights went out.

The door to the simulator opened, and Frank poked in his head, smiling. "Not bad for an old guy out of practice and all." He saluted with the metal end of a five-iron golf club he had recently started carrying around in memory of other days in his Air Force past.

Van was sitting back in his seat, soaked with sweat. He turned to Frank and flipped him the bird.

Van cleaned up in his quarters on *New Horizons* after the flight simulator exercise and then looked at Harry as he dried his hands and face on a soft towel.

"Nearly got my ass handed to me, Harry. Not a simulation I expected, but I survived."

Harry said nothing.

A little surprised by Harry's silence, Van continued, "So, my stoic friend, are you looking forward to this coming mission on *New Horizons*?"

"No, Commander," Harry said.

That stopped Van just as he finished with the towel and tossed it into a waiting laundry bin. "What?" he asked.

"I said no, Commander. I will not be going with you on this trip on *New Horizons*."

Harry had never before said no to Van. They may have had a few disagreements, especially in the early days of their relationship when Van had been more of a skeptic, but never just "No."

"That's crazy. We need you. . . I need you."

"Not any longer, Commander. You have learned all I can teach you to this point, and you will have the support of my fellow AI, Jennifer."

Van knew this new AI was impressive and integrated into the ship. In collaboration with Harry, it had chosen the name Jennifer and a female gender for herself. But she wasn't Harry, Van's long-time trusted friend.

Van was frozen in place, stunned at this new behavior of Harry's.

"And what's more important than this coming mission? We still need to find more help in shipbuilding and greater numbers of people. . . or something like people."

"Mr. Carson is more important right now, Commander," argued Harry. "He is responsible for the joint shipbuilding programs and relations between Earth and Zarminia. I can help him to be more efficient, develop new technologies, and, in general, cause our existing alliance to grow faster."

Van didn't have a quick comeback for this. Because, as usual, Harry was right. Dick Carson would need help like Harry's. And the new AI could potentially take Harry's place, though Van had his doubts. It was just hard to get his brain around the idea of Harry not being around. *However,* he thought, *he wasn't around when we chased down the duplicitous Sanal woman, or when we last fought the Arkon.* But the circumstances of those situations couldn't have been helped. This was different.

"I still don't like it!" Van said in a huff.

"Nevertheless, that is the way it must be, Commander."

Realizing there was nothing he could say to change Harry's decision, Van finished dressing and decided to walk through the ship to see for himself how preparations for the mission were coming along and how the crew was shaping up. One of the things he didn't care for in his advanced role as commander was not feeling like part of a ship. When he'd commanded *Aurora,* he'd known it was his, literally, and he'd felt like part of it. As Galactic Force grew, however, he felt more and more like just an administrator. Thank God for his friends, he thought. They were the glue that held him to his role and made it tolerable. Especially and increasingly so with Rose.

As he walked aft, he was reminded how big *New Horizons* actually was. Everything was big. Compared with the narrow passageways of the old *Aurora*, those in *New Horizons* were like the wide hallways of large business buildings on Earth. He decided to go as far aft as engineering and purposely pass through the crew quarters to see for himself how the crew was doing. He did this sort of thing as often as he could as a way of maintaining contact with the crew and, of course, the condition of the ship. He was following an old naval tradition that commanders before him had done for over a hundred years.

As soon as he entered the crew's living area, he was impressed as usual by the sense of pride the crew had in its ship. It was impeccably neat and clean, if perhaps a little colder than he liked it. Someone among the crew was an artist and had recently painted a mural of the ship on a bulkhead midway down the corridor. It was massive, at least fifteen feet long and stretching vertically from the deck plates to nine feet overhead. He stopped and stared at it admiringly.

"Bill Jackson painted that, Commander," said a gravelly voice behind him.

Van turned and saw one of the old crew members from the *Aurora*, Simon Kelly. Kelly was the chief electrician for the ship and had huge responsibilities.

Turning back to admire the painting some more, Van said, "I knew Jackson and was sad to hear he died in that shuttle accident three weeks ago. We'll miss him."

"That we will," came Kelly's response. "It's a shame talent like his had to end."

Van turned back to look at the sturdily built Kelly, whose age was starting to show with wisps of gray in his otherwise unruly shock of dark hair. "It truly is, Simon. Sometimes I wish I had never discovered the Host technology and the threat of the Arkon. Too many have died."

"Not your fault, Commander. It had to be done, and Bill knew that just as we all do."

Van reached out and shook Kelly's hand, saying appreciatively, "Thanks, it helps to hear it."

He continued his walk. From the crew quarters, Van descended to the huge manufacturing bay, which was surprisingly quiet. Catching a passing mechanic in blue coveralls with the name "Ed Connors" embroidered on the chest, Van asked, "Ed, why so quiet down here?"

Caught off guard by being seen and addressed by the commander himself, the blond-haired, spindly young man stopped and stuttered a response. "Ah. . . hey, sir. . . Commander. Quiet, OK, yeah, well, we done all the work we needed, see, and the chief said to go help out the guys above in the flight bays. You know, push stuff around, help fix some things. Like that, you know?"

"I know," Van said with a smile. "How long have you been aboard?"

"Um, three months, sir," said the young man, surprised to be talking with the commander of Galactic Force.

"And how do you like it?"

"Oh, man, this is the best job I ever had. I worked in a machine shop back home in Chicago, and I thought I was good. But I've learned a bunch since I been here. And the people are just great!"

"Glad to hear it, Ed, and thanks for your help. Now you can get along to the flight bay."

"Yes, sir! Wait till I tell the guys I talked with the commander. They won't believe it," Ed said as he hurried off.

Finishing his walk through the relatively quiet manufacturing space, Van reached the bulkhead separating everything from the massive engineering spaces in the aft-most portion of the ship.

He passed the security guard, who opened the hatch for him, and then took an elevator to the upper level, which housed the engineering offices. Before he had to look for him, Van ran smack into a bustling and ruffled Bob Cooper, who had just shot out from a side passageway.

Holding the surprised and confused chief engineer from falling down, Van said, "Oops, sorry about that, Bob. I was just coming to see you."

Regaining his balance and composure, Bob replied, "I didn't expect you here. I was on my way to look at the number three fusion engine."

"Is there a problem?" Van asked, concern narrowing his eyes.

"I don't think so, but some of the engines' performance numbers are varying slightly. I think it needs a small adjustment."

"So, the engine is basically OK?" Van asked, starting to relax.

"Sure, sure. Just making one of those last-minute adjustments," Bob said, now fully recovered from the unexpected collision.

"And engineering overall, how are things?" Van asked.

"Haven't you been getting the reports I've sent? It's all there from *A* to Z."

"I read reports all day, Bob. It's boring. I prefer to get around and see a few things for myself now and then. You know, touch this and that, watch some work being done. I get a better sense of the ship that way."

Bob nodded and smiled. "I know, I'm the same way. I just have a smaller area of responsibility than you."

"How's Elaine doing?" Van asked of the number two engineer, knowing they were very close.

A smile broke out on Bob's face. "Never better, Van. She's down there on the fusion engine now. I don't know how I ever found such a woman. . . I mean, professional engineer."

Van detected a slight blush on Bob's face. "I know what you mean," he said as he looked at his watch. Not much time left to pass by the hospital and then get to the briefing. "Don't let me hold you up from getting to that engine. I have to head back forward."

"See you in the briefing," said the engineer over his shoulder as he ran off.

Watching Dr. Rose Ramos working in her hospital was always a pleasure for Van. Watching Rose at any time was a pleasure.

"Hey," Van said from behind Rose, who was looking over a medical chamber.

Surprised, Rose jumped a little and turned. Seeing Van, she held a hand over her chest and said, "You nearly scared me to death. What are you doing here?"

"Do I need a reason to stop by and see you. . . and the hospital when I can?" Van smiled.

"No, of course not," Rose said as she calmed herself from the surprise and returned his smile. "I'm glad you did."

Van looked around the facility. It was much larger and better equipped than any of his other ships. Impressive, even though he hoped it would see little use in the next few months.

"Everything shipshape here before we depart?" Van asked, only partly meaning the hospital.

"The hospital has never been better. And the staff," she said, gesturing to the many people in the background, "are just tremendous. This is a dream place to work."

Van didn't bother to look at the people she pointed out, just at Rose.

"You're staring again," she said, grinning coyly.

"Am I?"

"Yes." Rose took a step closer to him. "And never stop."

"So, what do you think about taking a shuttle down to the surface tonight for a candlelit dinner? We haven't had much time for just ourselves. And there may not be another chance for a while when we leave on the mission."

Instead of getting closer to Van, she took a step back and turned partially away.

"What's the matter?" he asked, confused at the sudden change in her attitude.

"I don't think I'll go along on this mission," Rose said as she fiddled with a piece of medical equipment.

No, Van thought, *this can't be happening again!* "What is this? A conspiracy?"

Rose stood up from checking the lower part of a medical chamber and looked puzzled and wide-eyed at Van. "What conspiracy?"

"Harry just told me the same thing. Are you staying behind to help Dick as well?"

Looking a little confused, she responded, "No, two months ago I submitted a paper to *Caduceus Research*, the premier medical journal on Earth. I told you that, remember? And they published it!" As soon as these words left her mouth, her confusion vanished and a brilliant smile came alive as she showed her pride and happiness in the achievement. "Now people want me to speak and share my findings all over the place." She was almost dancing as she spoke.

Van was between a rock and a hard place. He could see this was important to Rose. A major step in her medical career. But deep inside, he couldn't think of not having her with him on the mission, or any mission. Still, he tried to take a supportive posture and forced a thin smile in return.

"Rose, that's wonderful!" But Van realized his forced response wasn't enough as he watched her happiness dim and slip from her face as he turned and left the room, all the while trying to think of a way to persuade her to stay.

How did I get myself into this? was the thought running through Dick Carson's head as he sat at his desk in the office provided to him on the orbiting shipyard above Sonara. This was only a day after Harry decided to stay behind to help.

Originally, before Guardian Force, Dick had been the owner of a security firm on Earth that employed some top-notch operational and intelligence people. As the Carson Group, they'd worked under contract with various elements of the US government like the CIA and State Department. Back when Van was first experimenting with the new Host capabilities, Dick had joined with him without realizing how big their relationship would get. Van and Dick were both graduates of the US Naval Academy and had continued as friends ever since. The Carson Group's operational team, led by Brice Johnson and Ross Taylor, had come along as well. Now, they were leading the ground and security forces for Guardian Force.

His best intelligence officer, Barbara Fuller, had also come along, albeit grudgingly. Now Barbara was gone, killed in an attack on the ship she had embarked on and labeled as a traitor for working with Sanal Zafar to undermine Galactic Force and Van Childs. This was a bitter remembrance for him. Barbara had had such great potential and was a friend to everyone for many years. She had been a prominent part of his professional family, and he mourned her passing, especially under the shadowed circumstance.

Now, he was the Guardian Force ambassador to the Earth Federation and to all of Zarminia. If that wasn't enough, he'd also assumed the role of Zarminian minister of production, coordinating technology advances between Earth and Zarminia for shipbuilding. It was this latter job that was causing the greatest headaches and a great deal of concern. In recent months, an increasing number of incidents or accidents had thrown Zarminian production significantly off the planned schedule. He couldn't place his finger on the causes of the problems yet, but he didn't have a good feeling about it. *Thank God Harry agreed to help me come to grips with this,* he thought just before a knock sounded from his door.

"Come in."

When the door opened, it revealed Earth Federation Ambassador James Harris. From Dick's point of view, Harris had proved a staunch ally of Guardian Force and had traveled with the Force on several of its more interesting missions, including the one in which Barbara Fuller had died. Barbara had been serving as Harris's Federation assistant for intelligence at the time. Over a dinner and several glasses of wine, Dick had learned that, aside from being saddened and disappointed about Barbara's death, Harris actually blamed himself for her traitorous actions and ignominious loss. To a point, Dick could sympathize with his ambassador friend because he also should have seen what was happening with Barbara and hadn't. After all, he had known Barbara much longer than Harris. From Dick's perspective, the good news was that Harris was coming out of his sadness and self-doubt, which was good for him and for Guardian Force.

"James, good to see you!" Dick said, rising from his desk and meeting Harris with a firm handshake and pat on the back. "It's a pleasant break in an otherwise fretful day. Have a seat here on the couch. Can I get you something cold to drink? I'm afraid no alcohol here, but we have Coke and Pepsi from Earth and nice cold water as well."

"Water would be nice. I just finished observing some of the assembly operations on one of your ships, and it was getting quite hot."

"It does get hot in a few places as we 'meld and weld,' as they say." Dick shuffled through his small cooler to find the water. While he was looking, he asked after Harris's wife of many years. "What have you heard from Dolores? She took a trip to Chicago, didn't she?"

"Yes, she left a few weeks ago. Wants to see the kids and badger them about having grandchildren. As I think Dee Dee knows, she has missed them since coming here."

"I know the feeling. Our kids are out and about now with lives of their own. Both of them lawyers of all things. I suspect Dee Dee will want to go visit them soon. I haven't been much of a husband since all the shipbuilding activity. But cold water was probably not your sole reason for being here." Dick handed the ambassador a bottle and took a seat in the chair across from Harris.

"No, Dick," Harris said, looking down at his bottle as he rotated it absentmindedly in is hands. Then he looked up and into Dick's eyes. "I have a problem."

"Then join the club," Dick said with an amused look. "We all seem to have more problems than we can ever solve. But things get done anyway. What's the nature of this problem?"

Harris looked down for a moment, his eyebrows pressed tightly together, then looked up at his friend. "It may be more of a dilemma. You see, the Federation wants me to stay here and work with you and the Zarminians to advance and facilitate the shipbuilding programs. Of course, that means going back and forth between here and Earth. It's probably important, but it doesn't excite me." Harris paused as he shifted uncomfortably in his seat on the couch. "To be frank, I don't have the kind of technical skills or interest to do a good job in the role described for me."

"So, James, if I can stop you, what you're really saying is you want to go on the *New Horizons* mission where you can play a role similar to the one that led us to find and work with the Zarminians. Am I right?"

"Am I that obvious?" Harris asked.

"Yes. And may I say you're good at what you do on away missions. I believe Van would welcome your presence. What's more, I don't think he'll be happy to have Harry stay here with me. And his old sidekick Stan Walters will be the deputy commander for Moon Base, Mars Base, and operational missions to Zarminia. I even hear rumors that Dr. Ramos is tempted to stay behind to lecture on some of the medical research she's been doing. Whatever it is, it's receiving great praise on Earth. Given all this, you might be a very friendly face to him on the mission. Would you like me to make the suggestion to him on your behalf?"

Relief showing in his face, Harris relaxed and said, "That would be a great help coming from you, if you don't mind."

"I'll see what I can do. But before you take off, tell me the latest news from Earth and the Federation."

Back on *New Horizons*, Van was in his quarters doing the routine things he hated most: reviewing production data from the various shipyards; assessing and making notes on how to increase the pace of crew training; answering correspondence from the Earth and Zarminian Federations; and, in general, fretting over the fact that they were still behind in their preparations to meet the Arkon. On top of all those important but, to him, mundane things, Van was still unhappy about Harry staying behind even though he was starting to understand the reasons. Dick did have profoundly major tasks facing him, many more than Van had a right to expect. After all, Dick had joined Galactic Force believing he would use his expertise in security, intelligence, and diplomacy to help Van. He was indeed doing all those things but had also taken on the management of an interplanetary shipbuilding effort that had to be the largest industrial effort ever on either of the combined planets. He could only do that with Harry to help him.

More bothersome was the thought of Rose being gone as well. That wasn't as easy to accept. He was still trying to figure out a way to change her mind when another speaker interrupted his thoughts.

"Commander," called out the melodic voice of Jennifer, the ship's AI.

"What is it?" he asked with a certain amount of residual annoyance.

"Mr. Carson is here to see you."

This is a surprise, Van thought. *Dick wasn't scheduled to be here for a while.*

"Send him in, Jennifer."

"Yes, Commander." The cabin door opened to let Dick step in and then closed with a slight hiss behind him.

Van, happy to have a reason to leave the work he was doing, stood and stepped quickly forward to grasp his friend's outstretched hand and offer a seat on his office couch.

"Good morning, Dick. Didn't expect to see you this morning." He took a seat on the couch next to Dick.

"I wanted to be sure to see you before you took off for parts unknown and to thank you for allowing Harry to stay and help, among other things."

"It may surprise you, but I didn't 'allow' Harry to stay; he refused to go."

Surprise flashed across Dick's face. "He refused to go?"

"Yes, very unusual, but realizing what you have on your plate, I could hardly object. . . as if that would have mattered. No, you have a mountain of a task, and Harry can be a tremendous help."

Dick searched Van's eyes and demeanor before asking, "What else is wrong? I've known you too long not to recognize you're unhappy for another reason."

"Am I that transparent?" Van leaned back in his chair. "Rose wants to stay behind."

"So I've heard, and good news for Rose. So, why are you. . . oh, I get it," Dick said with a smile of recognition. "She'll be gone making presentations and getting applauses while you're off on your next mission. Probably going to all sorts of dinners, meeting new people, and, in general, having a good time. Say, that's really terrible. We can't have that."

Dick had forced a smile to Van's face. "OK, Dick, you've made your point."

"I hope so. She has more than earned something like this. I say good for her."

"Yes, she has, thanks for reminding me I'm being selfish. But didn't you say you had some other reasons for coming up here personally?"

"I did. But first I want to be sure you're less depressed than when I came in."

"I'm fine and I appreciate your candor."

"OK. An important part of my being here now has to do with a visit I had from James Harris."

This was unexpected. *Why would Dick be here instead of James?* Van thought. "What about?"

"The Federation wants to keep him here to help with the shipbuilding coordination, but he wants to go on the mission."

"I think he should go. In fact, I thought he would be. This trip promises more new territory to explore and, hopefully, new relationships to create. He would be ideal for the trip."

"I agree. Perhaps you could let the Federation know your thoughts on this. I believe it would help."

"That's easy, but is that the only reason you took a shuttle out here? We could have had this conversation via implants."

"No, there's more," Dick said, shifting uncomfortably in his seat and rubbing his chin.

Van noticed the subtle changes in his friend's demeanor and asked, "Like what?"

"Over the last six months, there have been a number of incidents related to the shipbuilding programs. None of them particularly big in themselves, but cumulatively they've made a difference in meeting our program goals."

"Like what and why haven't I heard until just now?"

"At the time of each incident, it didn't seem worth reporting. But I just had Harry review production history. As I said, each incident has been small, like a fabrication machine going down for a few days, or accidents here and there causing skilled workers to be gone from the job for a while, or processes disrupted. But after his review, Harry suggests there is a trend that is outside the norm even for production in this early stage of development."

Van frowned, squinting in serious thought. "What can I do to help?" he finally said.

"Nothing at the moment. Ross is on top of an investigation. He'll be our security chief here when you're gone, remember?"

"Yes, I remember. Brice had to persuade me to leave him behind to help you. Looks like he was right. So, why make the trip here to tell me?"

"Just a feeling, or perhaps overcautiousness. I wanted you to be aware of what we experienced just in case similar things happen on *New Horizons*. I don't want to run the risk of them escaping your attention like they did mine. What is it they say, 'forewarned is forearmed'? It may be nothing, but too much is at stake for me not to mention it to you. That's why I wanted to chat with you in person."

"Jennifer, have you been listening?" Van asked.

"Yes, Commander. And I have detected no such associated events on *New Horizons*."

"But I expect you are now alerted to watch for any, correct?"

"Yes, Commander."

The time for the launch of the first mission of *New Horizons* was near. Van called all senior officers and ship commanders to the large conference room for the mission briefing. Compared with the briefing room on Mars Base, this one was nearly as big but had no center table and no comfortable chairs and welcoming sideboard with drinks and snacks. This one was theater-like, with tiered seats set in a semicircle around a central podium. Multiple view screens covered the wall behind the podium and were controlled at the podium. The large room was filled to capacity.

Van stood at the podium and waited for the casual conversations to conclude. He noted with pleasure that Ambassador Harris was in the first row. He noted with displeasure that Harry was not there, a week after he declared he was staying behind.

"Thank you for being here on time. As you probably know, this mission promises to be the most extensive and, hopefully, the most important one yet. Despite our Zarminian friends and their capabilities, we still do not have the shipbuilding capability we need to build a force strong enough to meet the estimated strength of the Arkon in the near future. We have done well, that's true. But we need to do better. Take a look at the screen behind me."

The large center screen behind Van snapped into focus, and the lights in the room dimmed. "This is a representative picture of our solar system and the major stars, with suspected habitable planets within twenty light years. A year ago, even six months ago, we didn't have this kind of detail. However, we have been sending drones and courier ships out in all directions to get a clearer picture of our close neighbors. You will see an empty space toward one edge of Orion's Spur and Wolf 359. We were warned by the Host not to travel in that direction, and we won't. It has been marked on all charts as the Forbidden Zone.

"Our drones and courier ships have done a good job of searching the areas associated with Procyon 2, Epsilon Eridani, Sirius 2, and even Tau Ceti. We had high hopes of some sign of life on Tau Ceti e and f, but nothing came of it. In relatively near space, within twenty light years or so, the densest area of stars is in the general direction of Altair. Our investigations of that general area have covered but a fraction of what we know is out there. So, we suspect there is a greater chance of success in that direction. Therefore, I have chosen that direction to take *New Horizons* and our small expeditionary force."

A hand went up near the back of the room and a female voice called out, "Commander, what role will the corvettes play?"

Van recognized Elsa Muller, the talented black captain of one of the attached corvettes, and former captain of the *Aurora*, the ship that had rescued Van when the *Ajax* was disabled chasing Sanal Zafar.

"Good question, Elsa. I plan to make a jump to our targeted star area with all corvettes in their bays or upper docking station. Once we arrive, each ship as well as the courier ships and some combat shuttles will be given either sectors for independent investigation or security assignments for *New Horizons*. The ships assigned to investigations may be sent as far as several light years away searching for other planetary masses that don't appear on our thin charts. Remember, even those charts provided by the Carians and Zarminians become less detailed the farther we go. Essentially, your ships will broaden our search area and increase the chances of a discovery. Assuming nothing is found, we'll retrieve all the ships and shuttles and jump to a new area that will at least be farther than our most forward small-ship investigations. Then we start the same routine over again. That answer your question?"

"Yes, Commander," said the corvette captain, smiling at the response and the recognition.

"Any other questions that aren't answered in the mission plan sent to you?"

Another officer stood. This time Van didn't recognize him. This was becoming more typical with a growing Guardian Force.

"What is it?"

"Do we expect more human civilizations out there?"

Van waited a moment gathering his thoughts, then answered, "Harry says it would be logical, but I'm not betting on it, nor should you or anyone. Mentally, we need to be prepared to meet a race or races who are very different. Remember, we need friends and we hope for steady allies. We can't afford to let any prejudices creep in and turn potential friends away. Personally, I think it's foolish and egotistical to think every sentient life form has to be just like us. At the very least, we need to look back and learn from our own mistakes like this on Earth."

The questioner sat back down, his question answered.

With no more questions coming, Van dismissed his officers and noted Rose wasn't in the short briefing. He knew she'd received a copy of the plan and knew all the basic details. Still, he'd hoped to see her there. While he probably knew why she hadn't attended, he didn't want to come to grips with the truth. He still had mission preparation to do. He had to review the search points he had selected and match them with the navigation charts that had been given to him at the end of the meeting. There were countless other details to check on before launch, but he was having difficulty concentrating as he thought about Rose. Giving in to his emotions, he walked aft and down a level to Medical. He found Rose in her office, pulling files from her desk and placing them in a briefcase.

"You. . . you're really going?" Van asked, beginning to stammer in a way anyone would recognize as being caused by something painful.

Rose looked up from her packing and, seeing the disappointment on Van's face, said with a sigh, "Yes. I need to go. The recognition of my work is important to me, something I've always wanted. And there are many people waiting for me to answer questions and teach them about my findings. It is important to a lot of people and, hopefully, to a lot of lives."

Van couldn't come up with a response. Instead, he looked down and fiddled with things on her desk, feigning interest in each unimportant item.

Finally, he looked up and spoke. "I still wish you wouldn't go. I know your work is important, but so is the mission. We'll need you. . . I'll need you."

Rose's look softened and she stepped forward and hugged him briefly, then stood back holding his hands. "You have a great medical group and this fabulous medical center. It can get along without me for a while. Besides, I'm not leaving forever." Then she gave him the beguiling smile he always loved.

"I guess you're right. But I'll still miss you." He let go of her hands and started pacing, the sign he was upset.

"Oh, stop pouting," she said lightly. "I'll catch a courier ship as soon as I get back and head for *New Horizons*. It will only be a few weeks."

Van knew she was right, sort of. There was no regular courier ship schedule, so it would be longer than a few weeks. But he couldn't change her mind. So, he stood tall and faced her with a sigh of submission. "OK, you're right. Can I walk with you to your shuttle?"

"You bet! Just let me get a few more papers. My bags are already on the shuttle."

It was the best of times, it was the worst of times. Had Arkon Admiral Gulv been aware of Charles Dickens and his *Tale of Two Cities*, he might have laughed. But he wasn't. All he knew was that the Sector 20 force sent to find and destroy some new technology development in an area familiar only to him and his pirate spy, Captain Reeb, had apparently failed. In fact, the force of three capable Arkon ships had never returned. That was the bad news. The good news was the blame for the lost ships fell on the Sector 20 commander, Vice Admiral Agvaald. Agvaald was part of a family that had long been a pain in the ass to Gulv's family, and a simmering feud between the families had been going on for at least two generations. After the disappearance of the Arkon ships, Gulv, as Red Central commander, had sent Agvaald home in disgrace, and in his place promoted kinsman Sub Admiral Daan. This, along with a weak Blue Sector 20 governor, gave Gulv a free hand in Sector 20 with all its forces. It also boosted his and his family's stature in the overall Arkon hierarchy. He really was starting to believe he may have a path to becoming supreme leader. That was traditionally a Blue cast position, but things could change. A Red like himself was not without the ability to lead the empire.

However, he knew he couldn't let this distant upstart group develop into a more viable force. He had to discuss this with now Vice Admiral Daan.

CHAPTER 2

V AN STOOD JUST BEHIND AND to the right of Frank's command chair on the bridge of *New Horizons*. He had his own flag bridge, but he wanted to see how these people worked together after time off and the integration of some new faces. There were also people he knew here like Frank and Rebecca, and, with both Rose and Harry gone, this was a comfort.

"Helm, take us out on the heading Navigation gave us," said the ship's captain, holding his golf club horizontally between two hands like a British riding crop.

"Yes, Captain." The helm officer started to slide the thrust controller forward to signal power to the engines when all the lights blinked off and then on again. The helm officer tried the slider again, but nothing happened. Then he turned in his seat to face a glowering captain. "Sir, I have no thrust control!"

"Try it again," responded the irritated captain.

"I did, sir. There's just no response. At the moment, we're stuck here."

"Jennifer, what's the problem?"

"I'm working on it, Captain," was Jennifer's initial reply. But before Frank could make a sharp retort, she came up again. "The number one helm relay junction sustained a casualty, Captain. Unknown reason."

"But there are at least two backups to that junction. Why aren't they kicking in?" Frank asked, tightly twisting the club shaft in his hands, his knuckles going white.

"Those alternate command lines also suffered casualties, Captain."

"That's impossible. Those redundant lines are separated by distance to avoid helm loss in combat. How could they all fail at the same time?"

"Unknown, Captain. I am investigating."

"How long to get us going?"

"Since parts are available on board, Captain, I estimate it will take nine hours fifteen minutes to repair."

Seeing the bridge team had things under control, Van left the scene with its irate captain to head to his own flag bridge. This was Frank's ship, and he certainly didn't need his commander looking over his shoulder during this inauspicious start of the mission. Van couldn't help but recall Dick Carson's surprise visit to the ship and his subtle warning about failures and problems. Could this be a kink from the *New Horizons'* extensive overhaul or something similar to Dick's problems in the shipyard? Only time would tell.

Dick Carson sat at his desk on the Sonaran orbital shipyard looking at reports on his tablet that reflected a myriad of issues. Just for a moment his mind rejected the problems and shifted to his family. With all that was going on, Dick had encouraged his wife Dee Dee to visit their children, and now grandchildren in Virginia. His kids were doing well in the legal profession they'd settled on, but he missed seeing them and his grandchildren. It seemed impossible he could be a grandfather; time had just flown by. He missed them all and wanted desperately to be with them, but bigger problems kept popping up in their efforts to prepare for the Arkon. He smiled at the picture of his family in his mind but was forced to return to reality and the fact that he wasn't happy. The *New Horizons* mission was three weeks along after its faltering start, and during that time period, ship production incidents had increased. Production was continuing to fall behind schedule in all Zarminian facilities. A schedule that, he knew, was originally less than optimal. That was why *New Horizons* and Van had launched. They needed more production, not less.

His reports described the production problems, but he needed solutions and had asked Commodore Daman, chief of the Zarminian Space Guard, to stop by.

Harry was in the office, but was quiet as usual, standing alone in a corner. Dick knew his friend was actually hard at work processing reports, scanning files, and generally looking out for him. But Harry broke his silence by saying, "Commodore Daman is here, Mr. Carson."

"Oh, good. Let him in."

The controlled office door gave a nearly silent pop and opened. The commodore walked in, and the door closed behind him.

"Commodore, thanks for coming!" Dick said genuinely, motioning for the Space Guard officer to take a seat next to the desk. "Forgive me for staying here at my desk, but I have so little time for pleasure these days."

"Not a problem. As for being here, I have business with some of the Space Guard representatives here anyway," said Daman as he took a seat in front of the desk.

Dick followed suit. "Commodore, as you know, Zarminia continues to fall behind in production in all five major shipyards. Even the new one reaching completion in the space above the colony planet Baylon. We get wrong parts and things we hadn't ordered showing up in supply boxes. Machinery failures are down but now we're faced with a shortage of raw material. That's why I asked you to drop by. The pirates are back and intercepting our cargo ships. Can you update us on our ability to stop them?" By 'us' he included Harry, still silent in the corner.

"I wish I had better news for you, Minister Carson."

"Call me Dick, please."

"Thank you, Dick. We have been successful in retrieving some of the cargo, as you know. But in most cases, by the time we receive the alert that a cargo has been intercepted, the pirates have disappeared without a trace along with the stolen goods. And if they don't steal the ships with their cargo, they destroy them. We have a serious search underway for their base but have found nothing so far. I wish I had better news."

"Yes, I've heard some of that. For your information only, I

have been in contact with Mars Base, and Deputy Commander Stan Walters is sending some ships and combat shuttles to assist you. I hope you don't mind."

Daman touched his throat as he took in the information in silence and appeared to think for a moment or two longer than normal in these kinds of exchanges before continuing. "That will help. As you know, space is a big place, and the more ships the better our ability to cover all the sectors."

"Good, we should see some help in a few days. That, however, brings us back to the parts issues. I've checked our ordering system, and neither Harry nor I can find evidence that orders are at fault. That suggests there are issues in the fulfillment centers and/or with the parts suppliers. I can examine the Zarminian fulfillment centers but not the parts suppliers yet. As a minister, I don't yet know many of the people in the new Federation. That's where I can use some help. Whom do you suggest I contact to make the greatest impact in a short time?"

"I'll have a list of the people I think you should contact before the day is out. I warn you, however, my circle is a small one, being a Space Guard officer. Space Guard is not usually involved with, for lack of a better term, 'ground matters.' I take it Ambassador Harris is not here? Normally, he would be a good person for this task."

"Unfortunately, no. He is on the *New Horizons* mission. Had I known these particular issues would require so much of my time, I would have encouraged him to stay. But it can't be helped now."

"You could ask him to return."

"I could, but I won't. First, it would take too long. Second, I'm not sure he would come. I probably wouldn't."

"Yes, I understand." Daman stood abruptly and reached across the desk to shake Dick's hand. "Unfortunately, I do have to go. Please let me know when to expect your help from Mars Base."

"I will indeed," Dick said as Daman turned and left the office.

Dick sat back down and thought a moment before he turned to Harry. "Was any of that conversation strange to you, Harry?"

"In what way, Mr. Carson?"

"The commodore was a little preoccupied, and when I mentioned help from Mars Base, he seemed, how to say it. . . a bit surprised."

"I did note, Mr. Carson, that he took longer than usual to answer. I also detected his heart rate increase."

Interesting, Dick said to himself, *Daman's new at his job. He's probably nervous trying to juggle all the new pressure and responsibility he's encountering. He never struck me as jittery, but everyone deals with stress differently. Oh well, back to work.*

———

After meeting with several of his most loyal Space Guard officers, Daman returned to Sonara. Before going to his office, however, he took a circuitous route to an old apartment building. Entering from the rear, he paced to a solid-looking door, unlocked it, and went inside, closing the door securely behind him.

The room was sparse, the most prominent feature a chair in front of an old table with an odd-looking box with a microphone in front. Daman sat in the chair and flipped a switch on the box. There was a buzz, and lights flashed and then came on steady. With a blank stare, Daman spoke into a microphone.

"This is Number 1. I say again, this is Number 1."

Nothing but static came from the speaker embedded in the box.

He tried again. "This is Number 1. I say again, this is Number 1."

A moment later the speaker came to life with a crackling voice. Number 1 had to lean forward and turn his ear to it to understand. He recognized the voice as Captain Reeb's, the leader of space pirates and Number 1's recruiter.

"Greetings, Number 1. You have news?"

"I do. You should be aware that Guardian Force is sending ships and combat shuttles to eliminate the loss of cargo ships."

"Interesting. Do you know when they will arrive?"

"No, but it will be soon."

"Very well. We will be alert. Is that all?"

"Yes."

"But remember to finish the task on Earth. Then go about

your business and we will take care of things out here." The voice ended, leaving only static.

Number 1 switched off the communications device, stood, and walked to the door.

Without pausing, he closed the dingy office and followed a different path back to his own Space Guard office. Afterward, all he remembered in the short-term was he had done his duty, and he still had a task on Earth.

The Arkon programming forced on Daman by Reeb after the capture and death of the original Number 1, Minister Ranard, was clever because it allowed the target person to remember only what was necessary when it was necessary.

The next day, Dick Carson and Harry were walking through one of the shipyard construction facilities. This one had a frigate under construction. Normally, this would be an incredibly noisy area complete with welding sparks, melding screeches, and the clang of metal. Today, however, Dick didn't need the normal sound-suppression ear inserts. Work was going on, but at a reduced level.

Stopping to speak with a nearby supervisor, Dick asked, "What's the problem today?"

"Parts from the fabrication machines are delayed. They say it's because of raw-material shortages again." The supervisor shrugged.

Dick shook his head and kept on walking. "Day after day, Harry, the same story. In addition, the list of potential Zarminian contacts Commodore Daman provided hasn't been much help."

"Yes, Mr. Carson."

They both halted in midstride as a loud crack echoed through the big facility behind them. Dick turned just in time to see one side of the big frigate crumble to its side after the underpinning supports gave way.

"This can't go on, Harry. This failure alone will put us back a month!"

"Twenty-five Earth days to be exact, Mr. Carson. I am detecting a strut in the main underpinning that was tampered with, causing the collapse."

"Get Ross Taylor up here now!"

"Yes, Mr. Carson."

Ross was the security lead with Brice Johnson gone; Dick could have contacted him by his internal communications, but he was so upset he just shouted the order to Harry.

It only took Ross a few minutes to arrive, running all the way. When he reached Dick and Harry, Ross could already see the problem.

"This is a big one this time!" Ross exclaimed, staring at the crippled ship.

"No shit! What happened to security?" Dick had lost his normal self-control.

"Spread as well as we can with current staff. Seemed to be OK until now. Have the ships from Mars Base departed yet?"

"No, but they will in a matter of hours."

"Then I'll ask for more security to be sent along with the added ships. We'll need to get more help from the Zarminians also."

Dick realized he was on the verge of being out of control and took several deep breaths. "Take care of it, Ross. Sorry for being terse."

"You should be upset; I would. I'll get right on this." Ross walked quickly away with a finger to his left temple as he communicated his orders. He asked for more than just men.

CHAPTER 3

TWO DAYS LATER ON EARTH, Rose finished up her last presentation on her discoveries. This had been an important trip for her, but she was glad it was over and wanted to go home. In this case, to *New Horizons* and, of course, Van Childs.

She was just making her way through what she expected to be her last series of handshakes and praises when a well-dressed man held a manicured hand up and said with a Sonaran accent, "Wonderful, Dr. Ramos, just wonderful! My name is Garon, and I'm from the Sonaran legation. Might I ask you to join a few of us for just a few minutes before you leave?"

Rose noticed two Space Guardsmen standing a discreet distance away, which buoyed her confidence in the unknown man.

"Sure, what's this about?" she asked as she walked with him to a nearby office.

"Several of our medical people wish to meet you and offer congratulations. It will take very little time."

Rose was satisfied this was the very last thing she had to do before catching a waiting Mars Base shuttle. So, she quickened her pace behind the Sonaran.

Garon opened the door and motioned for Rose to enter. She did, but there were no people inside. She jumped involuntarily when she heard the door shut behind her and turned. There stood Garon and the two Space Guardsmen. She saw the flash of a needle and felt a shock near her left ear and everything went dark.

"What do you mean, she never showed up at the spaceport?" asked a livid Stan Walters, taking over a distressed communications officer's station in the long-range communications room deep inside Mars Base. The spacious room was a recent addition to the base and part of a larger emergency command facility.

"Just that, sir," said the shuttle pilot, a hint of a New York city accent curling his words. "We waited and waited, but she was a no-show."

"Did you look for her?"

"Yes, sir. We combed the convention center and went to her room at the hotel. The room was empty. No baggage or anything."

"How about the local police?"

"We notified them, along with providing her picture and other information. It's being broadcast in all media outlets, but so far, nada."

"OK. Stay there to provide any assistance necessary. Keep me informed at least twice a day and immediately when you learn something new."

"Will do, sir." The young pilot gladly severed the connection.

"Get me Dick Carson on the line!" Stan shouted at the waiting communications officer.

As he waited impatiently for the connection, Stan nervously tapped his fingers on the small desk and worried about how he would tell Van. Over the years, they had become close friends as well as key members of Galactic Force's success. This news would be hard for Van, he knew, and he really didn't want to be the one to tell him. Then there was Danny, Rose's brother. He and Danny had been fellow pilots and drinking buddies long before they'd met Van. He didn't want to leave the news for somebody else to deliver, but there was no choice.

Stan's worried thoughts were broken by the communications officer.

"I have Mr. Carson on the line, sir."

It only took a few moments before he heard Dick Carson's voice. "Stan, what's the problem? The communications folks here are jumping up and down."

"They should be. Rose has gone missing."

The shock kept Dick from saying anything for several moments, then, "What do you mean 'missing'?"

"Just what I said. She failed to get to the shuttle I assigned to her, and a search of her hotel turned up nothing. No bags, no trash, no nothing. My guys also searched the convention center to no avail, and the police are conducting a full-out no-efforts-barred search. Nothing yet."

"What do you need from me?" Dick asked.

"Nothing at the moment. Just wanted you to hear it from me and not the rumor mill."

"Thanks, Stan."

"You going to get a message to Van and Danny?" Stan said, crossing his fingers and hoping Dick would say yes.

Dick thought about this for a few seconds. "No, not yet. Let's see what happens. Besides, there's nothing either of them can do that we can't."

"Roger that. I'll keep you posted," said Stan, gratified to be off the hook. He eased backward into the already uncomfortable communicator's chair and closed the connection. His mind, however, was in turmoil thinking of Van, Rose, and Danny.

Aboard *New Horizons*, Van called a meeting in his quarters with Brice Johnson, Frank Wilson, Rebecca Lewis, and James Harris. Of course, Jennifer was always present.

"Here we are twenty-four days after launch, and we've found nothing," Van said, tapping a stylus on the large table as he looked around at his friends. "Nothing along the way to Ross 154, and a big nothing there. Same for Epsilon Indi and GI 628. Now we're approaching Altair at a little over sixteen light years out with no promise of anything in the area. What do you say, Jennifer?"

"Altair's system cannot be ruled out yet, Commander. We know through the Hubble Telescope a number of years ago there was no supporting evidence for a large Jupiter or brown dwarf-sized object. However, Marcy-Butler calculations suggest the possibility of smaller bodies even in the middle of the habitable zone three point three AUs from the star. We, including the Host, just haven't been able to see anything small, especially with the dust surrounding the star."

"Interesting," Frank muttered, resting his chin on the handle of his club.

"What was that, Frank?" Van asked.

Sitting up straight, Frank responded, "I said 'interesting.' Here we are with this nice big exploration ship, and we have a chance to make some history."

"What do you mean?" asked Ambassador Harris.

"Nobody, including the Host, has been able to see very well inside that cloud of dust. We would be the first. Seems like *New Horizons* was built for this." Clearly, Frank was excited about using his ship in a major exploration, and his abundance of energy did nothing to suggest the contrary.

Van watched everyone at the table nodding their heads as they gave the prospect silent consideration. Then Harris spoke up again.

"I think Frank is right. We've come this far looking for signs of life, and this system is inside the twenty-light-year mark you initially suggested. There's no way we can pass it up."

Everyone around the table, including Van, gave slight nods again.

"OK. Frank, get a crew together and launch a courier ship to Dick's location above Zarminia with all our data collected so far and our plans for Altair. Then, into the cloud we go. Jennifer, we'll need your help in proceeding. Once the courier ship is away, take over the ship and give us the maximum speed you can without hitting something," Van said with increasing confidence. It was a crude command, but he had growing faith in the new AI's capabilities, even though she didn't have Harry's personality.

"Yes, Commander."

Two hours later, everyone could feel the slight vibrations as the big engines spooled up. They were on the way.

CHAPTER 4

R OSE SLOWLY AWOKE. AS HER eyes parted, she focused on the underside of a sagging bunk above her. She closed her eyes and opened them again to make sure she was seeing what she thought she was. It was a bunk all right. But what bunk and where?

Still not wanting to move much, she slowly turned her head to survey the room. It was a small cabin with a double bunk, two chairs, a fold-down desk, and, oddly for a cabin this size, a restroom. . . a "head" in Guardian Force terms.

She started to sit up but quickly let her head fall back down on her pillow. Her head hurt, a lot. It was especially bad on the left side next to her ear. She lifted her left hand to tenderly feel that side and winced as her fingers came into contact with the spot above the implant. Then she remembered the shock to her left side when she'd been abducted.

That is the right term, isn't it? Abducted, kidnapped? she thought. *I sure didn't come here on my own.*

Holding a hand to her head, she swung her feet and legs over the edge of the lower bunk and then took a moment to let the stars fade away. Then she stood and slowly padded to the cabin door and tried it. *Locked from the outside.*

"Hey!" she shouted and winced at her own voice. "Let me out! Who's out there?" But there was no response. She tried banging on the door several more times with the same negative results. Then she slowly shuffled back to the bunk and fell rather than sat back down, taking stock, head drooping.

Somebody kidnapped me but why? It doesn't make any sense. I'm just a doctor. Then it struck her. She wasn't just a doctor anymore.

According to the billing and introductions she received at her speaking appearances, she was not only one of the few doctors from Earth familiar with the advanced Host technology but was apparently the foremost recognized practitioner of aerospace medicine anywhere. In her mind, that alone was probably enough to warrant kidnapping, but the fact that she was also a Galactic Force officer and was in a close relationship with the force commander was, in Earth terms, icing on the cake.

Her head beginning to clear, she tried using her implant to call out or hear something. But there was nothing. Then it dawned on her. *That shock must have disabled my implant. Terrific. No communications and no locator signal. Just my luck!* Then she rolled over and lay back on the bunk, trying to make the pain and her realizations go away.

Reeb was at the place he and Number 1 called "location two." It was newer than the old asteroid base taken from him by Guardian Force. This was the safe spot for him that housed his accumulated fortune. There were buildings housing rare metals and stones, and others that housed expensive equipment as well as decorative items like paintings, statues, and other artwork. This was also a place for his ammunition storage and production and repair facilities for his growing numbers of small attack ships and the *Reaper*. About the size of a frigate, the *Reaper* was similar to the old *Gargon* but larger, faster, and with more powerful lasers as well as rail guns.

More than all that, however, this base had its own bachelors' quarters, bar, gentlemen's club, entertainment center, and community store. This offered his crew plenty of recreation, which he allowed them to indulge in at will. He also turned a blind eye to certain levels of raping and pillaging his men might engage in on raids. From Reeb' point of view, the base was entirely self-contained. He paid his men with credits for the various stores and entertainment centers and set up a voucher system that saved most of their earnings in a viewable savings account that would be distributed when they left the organization. In actuality, however, nobody ever collected from the savings accounts. Either they died in an engagement, or, when they elected to leave, they were given a hail and farewell and then done away with by Reeb's specially selected operatives outside the pirate fold and their purported savings quietly transferred to Reeb's own fortune. Nobody was the wiser.

Reeb ensured that the goods he stole from ships were either maintained in well-sealed enclosures on the base or parceled out as payment for services rendered by outsiders. He seldom used script or credits due to their traceability. Precious metals like gold, however, also substituted for script or credits. That was one reason he intended to demand gold for Dr. Rose Ramos's release.

In that regard, Reeb had just received a coded message from Earth confirming her kidnapping had been successful. Now was the time for the second stage of the plan: getting her to a safe but controlled location. He couldn't stash her on Earth—too dangerous for his men and nearly impossible to successfully hide from the massive search underway. He and Number 1 had agreed a slow and inoffensive cargo ship headed toward Zarminia would be the best way of getting her into Reeb's hands. And that, in fact, was what was happening. Rose was locked away in an officer's cabin in an old but capable freighter making good speed away from Earth.

It was from location two that Reeb sent out a coded message.

Number 1 was about to leave his office to meet with one of his agents who had some urgent information to pass him when he received a message on his tablet. *The draco you ordered cannot be delivered.*

It was the coded message saying Reeb wanted to speak. Quickly, Number 1 reacted in the conditioned fashion, cleared his desk, and left his office for the old apartment building and its locked room. As usual, it took him a while to reach the place as he took careful precautions to ensure he was not followed. Once inside the building, he went to the door marked "Private, No Admittance," unlocked it, entered, and sat in front of the communications device and turned it on. Leaning toward the microphone, he said, "This is Number 1. I say again, this is Number 1."

Captain Reeb sat at a luxurious desk that had been part of a cargo snatched from a ship years ago.

"Greetings, Number 1," boomed Reeb's voice over the speaker. "I have good news. Our flower has been picked and is in transit. I am going to meet the flower and preserve it safely on board my ship. Your job will be to announce the demands for payment, just as we planned."

Number 1 knew the overall plan Reeb had in mind, and that Reeb had sent ransom demands to three entities simultaneously. The first was to the Earth Federation Health Organization (EFHO), the second to the Zarminian Ministry of Medicine (ZMM), and the third to Galactic Force. All three of these organizations had a reason to keep Dr. Ramos safe and have her returned. She was, after all, vastly important to each of them. It was Reeb's opinion that if or when each organization realized that others were also being ordered to pay, they would not dare decline out of fear that if one did, Dr. Ramos would suffer the results. No, they would all pay, Reeb assured him. In his view, the doctor was too important. Number 1 also knew that Reeb's ace in the hole was Galactic Force. They absolutely would not want to see anything happen to her and would press the others to comply. It didn't hurt that the good doctor was also romantically linked to the Galactic Force commander. Number 1 agreed. They would pay, just like all the others had done over time.

Number 1 shut down the transmitter and exited the secret room, locked it, and proceeded to a small park not far away. There he sat on a bench reading something on his tablet. In a few minutes, a tall, thin man with a limp sat down on the same bench and proceeded to massage a painful leg.

Looking over at Number 1, the thin man commented, "Times are tough for us old veterans."

Those were the code words used to initiate conversations between friendly agents.

Number 1 looked up and replied, "Yes, but the war at least is over."

Having given and received the correct code words, the thin man continued to massage his leg while saying, "We have news telling us space reinforcements are coming."

This was not news to Number 1; he had already known that and passed the information to Reeb. But he couldn't discourage his agents.

"Important news. Thank our friends. However, it only means we have to be more attentive in our work. Pass the word to continue the good work, just be wary of strangers. Our efforts are having great success."

The thin man nodded and stood. "Good day to you, sir." He limped away.

CHAPTER 5

T HE NEXT DAY, GUARDIAN FORCE ships arrived off the shipyard floating over Sonara. The squadron was commanded, surprisingly, by Earth Federation Captain Chen Lee, a native of Shenzhen, China, and a friend of Dick's and of Guardian Force from its earliest days. Chen Lee was seconded to Guardian Force from the Earth Federation and given the destroyer *Sutherland*. To Dick's surprise, there was an Earth Federation ship included, the new frigate *Hornet*, commanded by Captain Mia Flores, a second-generation American from Costa Rica and another old friend.

Dick was pleased to see the ships and his friends, but no sooner had the smile formed on his face than it left as a screeching voice called out, "Where can I find Ambassador Harris?"

"Who said that?" called Dick, looking in all directions for the originator of the question. The problem was, he was looking too high. The speaker was short and bald, dressed all in black, and bearing what Dick thought was a perpetual scowl.

"I did!" answered the small, thin man.

"And who are you?"

"I am Envoy McDuff from the Earth Federation. Here are my credentials."

Dick took the raft of papers thrust at him and gave them a cursory look.

"Well, Mr. McDuff, if you will give me a chance to settle these men and women, I'll meet you in my office for a quieter conversation."

"That's Envoy McDuff, and I need to know now. It is most important," he responded with squinted eyes.

Dick was normally a calm and considered man, but this self-important upstart was already trying his patience. "If you must know, the ambassador is not here at present. As I said, I will take all your questions in my office."

"Where is he?" demanded the envoy.

Dick could take no more. "Ross, would you please escort the envoy to my office? I'll be there shortly."

"Yes, sir!" said the imposing man as he glared at the short diplomat. "Please come with me, Mr. Envoy."

The sight of Ross Taylor towering above him stopped the diplomat in his tracks. He had never seen such a big and forbidding man, not up close anyway. He complied meekly.

"Sorry about that, Mr. Carson," Mia said, tilting her head with a soft, apologetic look. "This *chunche,* or thing, came with me aboard *Hornet.* If it makes you feel any better, he was like that all the way from Earth."

"Don't worry, Mia. It takes all kinds. By the way, just call me Dick. Now if you'll all come with me, I'll point you to a place to refresh while I deal with Mister, excuse me, Envoy McDuff."

It was forty-five minutes later when Dick returned to his office and the annoying man waiting. He could have been there sooner, but he didn't want to be.

"Thank you for waiting, Envoy McDuff. How can I help you?"

McDuff was still red-faced, which Dick assumed was probably standard for him.

"Where is Harris?"

"As I mentioned earlier, he is not currently here. Can I help?" Dick knew what was coming. When Harris had left on the *New Horizons* mission, he was technically leaving his diplomatic post without permission. But Dick didn't want to give this little man any satisfaction.

"Where did he go?"

"He went with Commander Childs at the commander's request." Dick knew the ground was thin here despite the Earth Federation recognizing Guardian Force as an independent state. Technically, that made a request by Van a request by a head of state.

"And where did they go?"

"It is a classified Guardian Force mission."

"Don't give me that! Harris is an Earth Federation representative, and any trip or event he embarks upon requires Federation approval. Did he have such approval?"

Dick knew Harris had never asked for such permission. "I don't know. It was and is not my business."

"Can you get a message to Harris?"

"I can try when the opportunity permits."

"When will that be?"

"On this mission, communications are through courier ships. We have none here, so we can only send out a message when one comes in." It wasn't technically true, but it suited Dick. "What message do you want passed along?"

"Tell Mr. Harris he no longer holds the rank of ambassador. Tell him the Federation requires his presence immediately to account for the abandonment of his station and the flagrant violation of regulations. He is to be escorted to Earth by armed guards."

Dick leaned back in his chair for a moment calming himself as he stared at the insolent little man. The he spoke in low and measured tones. "Who will provide the guards. . . and the transportation?"

"You will, and without delay."

What McDuff didn't know was that Dick had been in various positions in the US government as both a diplomat and an intelligence officer. He had seen or had experience with nearly every type of government representative from the very lowest to the highest in over fifty nations. He respected many but was convinced that most were overrated both intellectually and professionally. McDuff was definitely on the lowest level of his tolerance and respect scales. It was also no surprise that upper-level performers like James Harris would be a threat to the careers of others like McDuff. Dick saw nothing but problems surrounding the annoying envoy and wanted to be rid of him as soon as possible.

"I see. Are your bags packed?"

That threw the little man. "What do you mean? They are still on the ship. I will get them after this meeting."

"No, you will not. You will stay here with Mr. Taylor, and your bags will be transferred to a combat shuttle immediately. When the shuttle is ready, you will be escorted to it and wished a bon voyage."

"What do you mean? I'm not going anywhere."

"Yes, you are. You're returning to Earth and as fast as I can make it happen."

A few hours later after Dick had cooled down, the principals, including division heads, Commodore Daman, and Captains Lee and Flores, met in one of the large shipyard planning rooms. It wasn't as luxurious as some conference rooms they had used in the past, but it would do. Just a big table and straight-back chairs in a room usually used to pin plans on the walls and argue about how to make something never designed for a spaceship.

Dick addressed them all straightforwardly. "Before I get to the business we planned, I have the unfortunate duty to announce we and others have received ransom demands from the kidnappers for Rose Ramos's release. To our surprise, they have requested a ransom from three different organizations, counting on all of them to want Rose returned safely. In addition to Galactic Force, demands were also made to the EFHO and the ZMM. We have agreed to coordinate the response. For your information, they are demanding six hundred Earth pounds of gold total from all three organizations. At current prices that is about twelve million US dollars. We are all willing to pay, but Stan and I insisted that Guardian Force attempt to find and retrieve her before the payment deadline. There is always a fear that kidnappers will collect a reward and then kill their prisoner anyway. We want to take that option away. Stan believes he has traced her to an FTL-capable cargo ship that departed Earth shortly after Rose went missing. Based on Earth flight control information, we believe it was the *Navaro*, registered in Synton, one of the five major countries on the planet of Zarminia. So far, however, the registered owners and their location remain a mystery. Most of the registration information Stan discovered was falsified. We know the general direction the ship was headed when it went FTL, but of course, there is no telling from that where she ended up. A description of the *Navaro* as well as Rose's locator frequency have been sent to all our commands and those of our allies. The search continues." The thought that any of Galactic Force's families might be abduction targets, including his own, made Dick shudder for a moment, but he brought himself back under control and continued.

"On a brighter note, Mr. Envoy McDuff has decided to return to Earth, so we need not concern ourselves with him any further."

There was the barest hint of laughter at the mention of McDuff's plight. . . but it ended quickly as each person remembered the more important somber issue of Rose's safety and return home.

When the laughter subsided, Dick continued, "In addition to locating Rose, what we are concerned about today is stopping the pirates from stealing our raw materials. Their activities have played hell with our schedule, and we can't allow it to continue. In addition, the accident and incident rates on the production floors is way out of hand. Tell them, Ross."

The big man, now the senior security officer for Guardian Force on the station, stood and with his deep voice said, "As Dick suggested, we have two problem areas. The first is the swiping of our raw materials by the pirates—"

But before he could continue, the door opened and a tall, ample, bald, and red-bearded man barged through with a broad smile and a greeting for everyone. "Hello, my friends. Tell poor Ootah you didn't forget to ask for Carians' help! Of course you didn't. The message must have got stuck in some kinked wires or something. But we are here now, that is the important thing, yes?"

Everyone chuckled. Of course, they welcomed Ootah and the Carians. A better set of allies could not be imagined.

"Hello, Ootah!" shouted Ross. "Come in, come in. There are plenty of seats for you."

Dick grinned and waved Ootah and a few of his friends to seats next to him.

"As I was saying," continued Ross, "one of our problems is stopping the stealing of raw materials in space that are destined for shipbuilding. Space Guard has provided twenty-five Manaran-class gunboats, which, along with some of our shuttles, have tried hard to intercept and stop the stealing, but until now we were too few in a huge area of space. Guardian Force has brought along more ships and combat shuttles and numerous long-range drones that can be armed to augment the Space Guard. With these forces we could still not cover all the space around Zarminia, but thanks to a few clever people, we don't have to. We will create logistics routes or lanes that will be dedicated to raw material flow and other transport needs. If we can establish a fixed flow pattern, we can concentrate our limited assets to protect them as opposed to having to go all over space at the whim of every cargo captain. Follow the lanes and you get home. Don't follow them and you get captured.

"Drawing from Ootah's experience, we have drafted the proposed lanes and times for material travel and have assigned protection forces, including the Carians, to patrol them. That's what these charts on the walls show. Take a look for yourselves."

The men and women stood and went to the wall to look at the charts. There were shaking heads and lots of questions, but by the end of forty minutes, they had all settled on the plan. All agreed the plan offered the best protection they could provide with the assets they had. It also concentrated the warships, combat shuttles, drones, and Space Guard ships to best advantage. When questions trailed off to nothing, Ross spoke again.

"That addresses the protection of raw material. The second problem is, as Dick calls it, accident and incident rates on the production floors. They are much too high. We propose to eliminate them, or at least drive them down to only a distraction, through multiple ways. Captain Lee brought with him a limited number of human security troopers to help and to manage another asset: our new security robotic force. Many of you may know these robots were developed first by the Host and then enhanced by Harry. Captain Lee's force carried over five hundred of them and brought the plans and capability to create more to share with our Zarminian allies. Harry has promised to help with this and coordinate their activities. You will note they differ from other robots by the yellow stripes on their torsos. They can do almost anything, especially weapons handling. They are very accurate.

"Quick response teams will be composed of human troopers and robots, all geared to present a coordinated assault on a problem or problems. Some might say we have brought the combat zone into the manufacturing areas. . . and they would be right."

"Thanks, Ross," Dick said, standing as Ross sat. "Please tell your people about these new protections and ensure they know all this is as much for them as for production. An injured worker, aside from being unacceptable in itself, is also a nonproductive worker. We need every man, woman, and machine if we are to ultimately survive. Thank you all."

With the meeting finished, Dick saw Commodore Daman heading for the door before he'd even finished thanking him and others for attending. *What's so urgent he has to bolt for the door?* Dick wondered. He quickly forgot his brief impression, however, as several of the attendees approached him with their thanks for his work.

CHAPTER 6

CAPTAIN REEB SLOWED THE *REAPER* as it approached the old but expected cargo ship *Navaro* near one of the many asteroid clusters on the fringes of Zarminian space. He also posted two smaller escorts at a distance to keep a sharp eye out for miners and other potential intruders.

Reeb was the first one through the tube and onto the cargo ship, which looked much more modern on the inside than on the outside. He was met by the ship's captain, a Carian of all things, a nearly perfect cover.

"Greetings, Captain Reeb," said the clean but untidy cargo captain.

"Save the greetings for later. Take me to her." Then he stopped abruptly. "Wait. Her implant was disabled, yes?"

"Yes, sir. It was disabled before she came aboard, and we used the frequency analysis device your men gave us. We've detected no signals since."

"Good. Then let's go."

The two didn't have far to go, given the fact that the ship's quarters were between the tube air lock and the bridge. The cargo captain stopped at a door with a guard and took out a huge key ring. He fumbled for the right key, then inserted it in the door's lock and turned it. There was a snap, and the door partly opened. Reeb gave a perfunctory knock and then entered without waiting for a reply.

At the noise of the lock, Rose stood and waited to see what would happen. She had already eaten, so this was not in the routine she had learned to expect in her time aboard the ship. She was surprised to see somebody very different from the familiar ship's crew walk through the door.

The tall woman and the large man stood for a moment sizing each other up. Rose was a little surprised. From his flamboyant dress, high black boots, and commanding presence, she guessed he might be a pirate, but not a stereotypical one. Instead, this man was handsome. Tall and powerfully built. . . swarthy might describe him, with black hair and eyes.

At five foot nine, Rose was tall, but not as tall as the six-foot-four Reeb. Her hair was jet black and normally rolled up in a bun for work. Now her hair was down around her shoulders and uncombed. She had the same milky light brown skin as her brother Danny, without any of the wrinkles pilots earn when exposed to constant sun while in flight. Her teeth were a brilliant white and usually exposed by a wide, gracious smile. Now in place of an expression of happiness, her lips were pressed tersely together, and her dark eyes flitted around, assessing the man before her.

"Who are you and what do you want from me?" she said, though she believed him to be the pirate Reeb she had heard so much about.

Bowing and sweeping his hand from shoulder to knee, the man said, "I am Captain Reeb of the *Reaper*. At your service."

"The only service I want from you is safe escort to Sonara."

"Yes, I imagine you would. Pining for your commander, are you?"

That threw Rose off balance. Reeb knew more than she'd expected. So, she remained silent and let Reeb do the talking.

"Ah, so it's true. No matter. You will be happy to learn your new quarters aboard the *Reaper* will be nicer than this cramped room. As for what we want, it is gold. A doctor of your high stature and rare skills should be worth a great deal from many."

Rose made an effort to lunge at Reeb, but unseen hands reached out and stopped her.

"A fiery one you are," Reeb said with a grin. Then, turning to his escorts, he said, "Take her aboard the *Reaper* and confine her to her new quarters. We have an appointment just outside the new lanes set up by Guardian Force and the Zarminians."

Later, Rose assessed her new prison. It was larger than the old one. In fact, it bordered on luxurious by comparison. A larger cabin, a single bed replacing the bunk beds of the freighter, a couch and two chairs, a desk, and a larger head complete with shower. One more thing she noted was a view screen acting like a porthole. Most spaceships could not accommodate windows. The hull was usually too thick, and windows put hull integrity at risk. So, ships resorted to view screens, which received camera images from the exterior of the ship. In this case, however, there was nothing much to see.

She took a seat on the couch and leaned back, her eyes closed. *What will happen next?* Then she sat straight up. Her left hand flew to her left ear. The area under her skin itched. *Am I dreaming?* she thought. *Or is something happening to my implant?*

She wasn't dreaming.

CHAPTER 7

NEW *HORIZONS* HAD A FLAG bridge that was different from all the other Guardian Force ships. The principal advantage was to the captain of the ship in not having the commander or other senior persons literally looking over his shoulder. Another advantage of a flag bridge below the main bridge was more practical. If the regular bridge was destroyed, the lower flag bridge could easily take over. This was not the traditional wet-navy set up, but it was designed by the Host with experience in space. Nobody argued about it.

Van sat in his command chair, which looked over an array of consoles mostly unmanned except for the communications station and a battle plot that could project the battle scene, or anything else the commander wanted, on a forward screen. Van could fill all the consoles anytime he wanted, but it wasn't necessary now, especially with Jennifer available.

Presently, the forward screen was set to monitor the external forward cameras as Van watched the ship's progress through the dust cloud.

"Jennifer, is it my eyes or is the debris of this cloud thinning?"

"I am unsure about your eyes, Commander, but the debris is thinning. I project at this rate we should be through the main portion of the cloud in five, four, three, two, one—now."

Van chortled at Jennifer's quirks, which reminded him of Harry. . . then his amusement faded as he was also reminded Harry was not there with him.

Sure enough the various large and small masses surrounding the star thinned to virtually nothing. And the new solar system came into view. Van remembered Altair was a type A main sequence star nearly twice the mass of Earth's sun. A bright star as seen from Earth, it had various names including the Micronesia name *mai-lapa*, meaning "big or old breadfruit." It was fitting somehow.

Right now, however, Van was searching for planetary bodies but seeing none. "Jennifer, can you get a picture of the planets we expect in the habitable zone?"

"I can, Commander, but we are still too far out to get detail. Here is a magnified image."

On the forward view screen, a number of faint lights could be seen. "Jennifer, show me the three planets we are looking for." Immediately, a red box surrounded three objects in the distance. "Pass these to the ship's captain."

"Yes, Commander."

"Frank, are you seeing the three objects on your screen now?"

"Yes. Faint but discernable."

"Then take control from Jennifer and let's be on our way."

"Roger, on the way. Helm," Frank called out, "increase speed and enter FTL as soon as possible on this course. The cloud presents no more danger."

"Yes, Captain, accelerating now," the helm officer responded.

With a flash of FTL light, the scenes on the forward view screens changed. Now, instead of some vague lights, there appeared three planetary bodies. All inside the habitable or Goldilocks zone.

Van couldn't stand being alone on the flag bridge, so he left and took a position standing behind and slightly to the right of Frank's chair on the ship's bridge. Rebecca Lewis looked up and motioned Van to take her seat, but he shook his head and made a sign with his hand for her to sit back down.

There on the screen were the three planets. Van expected one or more of them to look blue like the Earth. But only the most distant had any sort of a blue hue.

"Rebecca, take us into an orbit above the first planet," Frank said, pointing the handle of his club absentmindedly at a spot on the view screen.

"Yes, Captain."

Frank looked behind him at Van. Van nodded.

"And make preparations for launching the corvettes and five of the combat shuttles. Tell Captain Ramos to launch a CAP as soon as possible." CAP was a wet-navy holdover meaning "combat air patrol," fighter protection for the most valuable ship. "Then start assessing this planet."

"Doing it now, Captain," responded Rebecca.

Two days later, Van met with Frank, Rebecca, and Danny in his quarters. The table was big enough for ten people, but he needed just these three.

"OK, Frank. What's the story?"

"Not very good yet, Commander. We assessed the first planet, which Danny named Dan 1."

Van watched as mirthful grins broke out among the group. He saw Danny was exceptionally pleased, and it reminded Van of the early days of Guardian Force when everything was new and exciting and a little more carefree.

Frank continued, "We used all our planet assessment tools, drones, and manned flybys. Absolutely nothing. No water, no color, no signals, and no signs of habitation. So, we moved on to the second planet named Dan 2, and yes, there is a trend here." Frank looked up and smiled before continuing. "Initial assessments show some better results suggesting a modest amount of oxygen and nitrogen in the atmosphere, but not enough to support human life as we know it. There may have been water at some point in the past, but none on the surface now. However, we did find traces of an old and perhaps ancient habitat in one location about halfway up the slope of one of the planetary mountains."

This got Van's attention. He was up to speed on most of the information, but this was new. "Have we sent a team down to look?" he asked.

"Not yet, I wanted to tell you about this first."

"OK, have Brice put together a team to have a look."

"Roger that," replied Frank.

A small group of troopers stepped out of the combat shuttle onto Dan 2.

"Get Margo up here. This is her area," Brice called out.

Using the power of her battle suit, Margo Cranston elbowed her way through the tangle of large men to the front. She was the team's resident archeologist, but she also saw herself as a fierce combat soldier in a small frame.

"I'm here, Brice."

"Great. I want you to lead the way. The site is a hundred feet or so up this slope. I don't want anything disturbed until you see it. . . so you go first."

"Roger, follow me." Margo gave a swooping gesture of her right arm, signaling everyone to move out.

The pace was slow but steady as Margo searched and assessed the rising terrain with both her eyes and the suit's sensors. About five minutes into the climb, they came upon a small plateau, and Margo signaled "stop" with a raised clenched fist.

Everyone watched Margo's helmet sweep slowly from left to right and then back again. The team knew better than to ask questions or even to move. They were disciplined, but they also wanted to avoid Margo's infamous temper when disobeyed. That included Brice.

"This is the place," Margo said over her helmet communicator. "Everyone come up but stay near the edge of the plateau. I'm moving forward."

The thirtyish, blonde archeologist-turned-trooper was fascinated. She immediately thought this could be the find of the century — or longer — in her field. What she saw before her were the ruins of a small village or encampment. Crumbling rock walls scattered their dust over flattened, partially exposed foundations. She marveled that any of this wasn't buried feet below the surface given the probable age of the place. She guessed the winds blowing up and down the mountain kept the remnants relatively clear. Then she noticed something else: small and large craters in the foundations and the surrounding grounds. As she inspected the crumbling walls, she discovered they weren't so much crumbling as exploded. *This was a battleground,* she said to herself. A losing one, in all probability.

"Brice, Jimmy, you can come over here. Have the others establish a security perimeter. Something bad happened here." Behind Brice, Jimmy was second-in-command on this mission.

Brice and Jimmy stood next to Margo near the center of the plateau looking at the remains of the once-inhabited camp as Margo explained what she believed had happened.

"When do you think all this happened?" asked Jimmy, still taking in the destruction and Margo's explanation.

"Hard to say," answered Margo as she knelt and let some of the dust filter through her fingers. "The materials used in the camp's construction defy dating or identification on my sensors. However, there are substantial carbon remains around the blast areas. Preliminary guess is they may be over five hundred or more years old. Could be a thousand years if these building materials are as sturdy as I think they are. It's safe to say, however, that whoever built this was more advanced than we are, that's for sure."

That caught everyone's attention. Brice spoke his thought out loud. "A more advanced civilization here five hundred or a thousand years ago. Amazing."

"Yes, it is," answered Margo, standing and brushing debris dust off her gloved hands. "But perhaps we should be concerned about who or what wiped them out."

"You mean the Arkon?" Brice asked, twisting his neck and cracking it, a sign of nervousness.

"Not likely," she said, with a finger to her chin. "My bet is the losers and the winners here existed long before the Host or the Arkon. And my next bet is that they were more powerful. The concern I mentioned is the possibility that the winners are still around. If they are, let's hope they're friendly."

CHAPTER 8

ABOARD *New Horizons*, Brice and Margo met with Frank and Van in Van's quarters.

"If I understand your initial report, Brice, there was once some sort of life on this planet, but it has been extinct for five hundred to a thousand years. Destroyed by yet another unknown life form," Van concluded.

"That's the short of it. We made another series of sweeps with drones and combat shuttles but found no other ruins except the ones on the mountainside. We concluded the ruins probably were the remnants of an exploratory group or possibly survivors of a wreck. But we found no evidence of any wreckage. Margo?" Brice turned to Margo and nodded for her to take over the briefing.

"Brice is right. We even solicited the help of Jennifer to assist us in locating any other ruins, but there was still nothing. I do have my thoughts, however."

"By all means, let's hear them," Van encouraged her.

"I doubt survivors, exiles, or refugees could have built the structures that existed. They were carefully laid out, and the construction suggests machinery and considerable imported materials. No, this was a planned facility."

"Planned for what?" Van asked.

"Unknown. But my guess is one of two possibilities, or perhaps both. The first possibility is this was the first step in colonization. Any follow-on colonists would've had to have some sort of well-founded base from which to start a new community. The second possibility is the camp or facility was an intelligence or monitoring station of some sort. Either could be the case, but my thought is it was an intelligence or spotting station."

"Why?" Van asked, fascinated by Margo's assessment.

"Clearly, there was some sort of opposition force operating in and around this system. What better form of long-range defense than to have small reporting and sensing stations spread around to warn others of the approach of a hostile force. We did that on Earth with the Defense Early Warning, or DEW, Line from the '60s through the '80s. The allies used a network of coast watchers in the Pacific in World War II. This could be something similar."

Van thought about this and recognized the possibility or problems of this being the case. "It's certainly possible, but why haven't we seen similar facilities on Dan 1 or even elsewhere on Dan 2?"

"Good question. One which I asked myself," said Margo confidently. "My guess is this station could have been the first of an expected large network of stations, but it was destroyed before the larger system could be built."

"Yes, or several other possibilities," Van said with a blank stare that the others recognized as him working a problem. Then, problem solved, he straightened and looked at Frank. "The best way to satisfy our curiosity is to head for Dan 3 and have a close look. Make it happen, Frank."

As *New Horizons* made its way to Dan 3, Frank and Rebecca took a break from their shipboard chores. They sat drinking coffee in the spacious wardroom of the big ship, Frank's now ever-present golf club resting on the table. There were other officers relaxing, but they all knew the captain's and the executive officer's time was not to be interrupted unless there was an emergency.

"That's what was found on Dan 2," Frank said as he finished summarizing the mission results and the brief review in Van's quarters.

Rebecca peered at Frank over her cup, waiting for the steaming brew to cool a little, and said, "So, what's your conclusion?"

"I'm just a ship driver in this case. I leave the archeology and speculation to others."

"Frank Wilson!" Rebecca said a little too loudly as she put her cup down. Then, after looking around to ensure she hadn't drawn too much attention, she continued in a more subdued tone. "You're more than a ship driver and you know it. You wouldn't be here if you weren't. Let's have no more of that!"

This surprised Rebecca almost as much as it surprised Frank.

"Why, Rebecca, I didn't know you cared," said the tall Guardian Force captain with a wry smile.

Rebecca's face reddened as she realized she'd revealed an emotion she should have kept to herself. Her right eye was blinking, some might say winking, as a sign that she was nervous or embarrassed. "That's not what I mean. I mean. . . I mean, you have experience and a good head. I'm interested to know what you think."

Frank saw the nervous tic and the spark she had just loosed and didn't want to get into the exploration of emotions that he was also starting to feel. So, he gave in. "I'm inclined to agree with Margo. All the data I reviewed suggests the facility or station or whatever you want to call it was more than an innocent colonial start. An intelligence-gathering or sensor station seems logical."

"Then you would expect to find something on Dan 3?"

"'Expect' is too strong a word. More like, the odds are high."

Meanwhile, Van was pacing in his cabin. "Jennifer."

"Yes, Commander?"

"What do you think of Miss Cranston's conclusion about the ruins on Dan 2?"

"Miss Cranston's ideas have merit."

"Is there more you want to say?" Van said as he continued to pace. Conversations like this just weren't the same as with Harry. Harry was more personal, more real.

"Yes, Commander. The facility she found could have been an outpost established by an enemy force. It could have been destroyed by defenders when they found it. That would explain why there have been no other traces of such facilities or ruins."

Van stopped pacing and looked at the holographic image of Jennifer that had just emerged. She and Harry had had a number of integrative sessions in which information had been exchanged and their future roles agreed upon. Unlike Harry, however, Jennifer had chosen not to take a physical form but rather to "live" as part of the ship's system and computer core and offer a holographic form when needed. She'd researched Earth cultures and chosen an amalgam of Asian and light-skinned African, with a little Latin American thrown in. Green eyes, long black hair, and an athlete's body rounded out her beautiful appearance.

The vision of Jennifer notwithstanding, a vision of Rose would have pleased him more at this moment. He missed her and he missed Harry. Recovering, Van said, "Then if we find something on Dan 3, it may be from, in this case, the friendlies."

"A good possibility, Commander. Wait." There was a brief pause before Jennifer resumed. "The courier ship has returned from Zarminia."

Van raced from his quarters to the port flight bay as fast as he could. There he found Frank, Rebecca, and Harris waiting ahead of him. News from home was always a time of excitement. Van was excited to see Rose again. To him it had been lifetime of a wait. He missed the way she seemed to have a sixth sense about his thoughts and feelings. . . something he had never experienced before. She could sit with him endlessly, listening to his favorite piano music and enjoying it. Now and then he would find a note in one of his pockets that said something simple like "Have a great day" or "Thinking of you." He had even done that for her after realizing how uplifting such a small amount of expressed feelings could mean. Now she would be here, and they could continue to grow together.

The shuttle ramp lowered with a hiss. Then nothing. "Wait, I see someone," said a voice from the gathered crowd. First came the crew chief with a sealed case, then the copilot, and a few moments later, the pilot.

Van stood on his toes to get the first glimpse of Rose stepping out of the shuttle. But nobody else disembarked. As the pilot approached, Van asked, "Where are the passengers?"

"There weren't any, sir. There was only a sealed case for you. The chief took it to your quarters." Seeing the disappointment on Van's face, the pilot said, "Sorry, sir." Then he started away but stopped and turned. "I almost forgot, Mr. Carson gave me this envelope and told me to give it only to you." He handed Van the envelope and moved on.

Van's excitement crashed in bitter disappointment. He looked around as he opened the envelope. If Dick had sent such a message, it must be personal. It was.

Van,

I wanted to send you this personally because of our friendship and your feelings toward Rose. As of this writing, Rose is overdue from Earth. She did not make the shuttle Stan had ready for her at the end of her last conference. The local and national police on Earth are conducting a search, but so far, no information. She was last seen with a member of the Sonaran delegation, but that member cannot be found either. Stan is doing all he can so far. Her locator beacon has not been detected yet. Have hope. It appears to be kidnapping since we have received ransom requests. I assure you everything is being done that can be done.

Finally, as if that were not enough, a twerp of a man named Envoy McDuff from Earth Federation came looking for James. All I said was James was on an important mission at your request. He wasn't impressed. James's ambassador status has been revoked, and the Federation wants him back as soon as possible. I gave the envoy a boot to the butt and a fast shuttle back to Earth.

The good news is Stan has sent ships, men, and materials (read: robots) to assist us in stopping the stealing of raw material by pirates and to police the manufacturing floors better. By the way, you should know Chen Lee is in command of the new force on Sutherland and brought Mia Flores with a new ship, the Hornet.

Chin up, my friend,
Dick

Van slowly walked away, his head down, unconsciously dropping the note as he walked.

Frank moved forward, picked up the discarded note, and read it. Then he looked up as Van disappeared around a corner.

Frank followed Van to the commander's quarters and reached the door just before it closed behind Van. Holding the door from closing, Frank called out, "Knock, knock," and tapped the end of his golf club on the doorjamb.

"Who is it?" snapped Van.

"It's Frank."

"Go away."

Counter to Van's demand, Frank pushed the door open slowly with his club and carefully stepped inside the comfortable quarters. Van had just taken a seat on his bunk and had his head in his hands. Frank grabbed the nearest chair and pulled it in front of his friend and took a seat, holding out the letter from Dick.

"You dropped this, and I couldn't help but read it. I'm sorry about Rose."

Van said nothing and didn't change position. He wasn't in the mood to talk, especially about Rose and his feelings for her.

Ignoring the silence, Frank continued, "You realize of course, that Stan and Dick will let no stone go unturned until they bring her back. Aside from being the best doctor in space anywhere, she is Galactic Force, and as you once said, we don't leave our people behind. You've built a tremendously capable force that is closer than most families I know. We are all behind you both."

Van stayed immobile initially, letting Frank's words seep into his mind. He knew Frank was right, this was a big family of which Rose was no small part. They wanted her back almost as much as he did. Almost. However, the clouds of pain he felt parted at his friend's honest words. He looked up into Frank's candid eyes and gave a brief smile.

"I know, Frank, and I appreciate your saying so. It's just that this time I've found a woman, a partner, who is not turned off by my quirks and outside demands and who apparently sees something of true value in me. I've managed to screw up all my other relationships in the past, and I was having great hopes with this one with Rose. Losing her would be more than just devastating."

"None of us plan on losing Rose, and you're not the only person who cares about her. . . each in our own way, of course. From a practical point of view, we can't afford the loss of the best aerospace medicine doctor in known space. From an emotional point, we can't afford to lose one of our best friends. . . that includes you also, you know.

"So, sit up, recognize you aren't alone in this, and get on with business. Trust Stan and Dick to act in all our best interests," Frank said, tapping his club on the deck for emphasis.

Van looked up with a smile and a slight tear. "How do I deserve such good friends?"

"By being one yourself," Frank said, leaning forward and giving Van a slap on the shoulder, then departing.

Van thought about what Frank had just said and realized he was right. All that could be done was being done by close friends and a massive organization. They would find her and bring her back. More than that, he could see a picture of Rose in his mind, shaking a finger at him and scolding him to remember he was the commander. He had major obligations that only he could deal with. He should do his job just as others would do theirs. He smiled at the picture, which gave him the energy to get up and face the things in front of him. Rose always gave him that extra ounce of energy he needed.

CHAPTER 9

D ICK HAD BEEN A LITTLE worried at the start of the new antipirate program Chen Lee was leading. The pirates had foiled all initial intercepts by attacking and/or capturing cargo ships at the outermost beginnings of the new travel lanes. Protection forces had not yet reached those areas early on. Subsequently, however, the pirates were less successful attacking ships in the new lanes. The tide was turning. Few of the pirates were destroyed or captured, though. When faced with a defensive force, the pirates often faded away, avoiding combat and capture before an engagement could be started, or avoided Chen Lee's forces altogether. It had turned into a cat-and-mouse game.

Dick met with Ross in the makeshift shipyard briefing room, walls still covered with star charts and other data.

Tracing his finger across the transit lanes and between markers of foiled and successful pirate attacks, Ross came to a conclusion. "They know where our forces are, and they know when they can risk attack."

From a seat at the table, Dick was watching Ross examine the charts. "What makes you say that?"

"This topic has come up before, but there was no data we could grab on to. So, I had Harry help me with an analysis of the pirates' activities and our intercept results since we established the lanes. Sure, we've caught a few of them, but we should be doing much better. Based on a statistical examination of all this," Ross swept his big arm across the mass of charts, "Harry concludes someone is feeding them information."

"Where is Harry, by the way?"

"He's out on the number one manufacturing floor, working with his security robot friends. You have noted incidents are down, haven't you?"

"Yes, I have. But back to your and Harry's suspicion that we have a mole, what do we do about it?"

"We have to smoke out the traitor somehow," Ross said and took a seat across from Dick.

"How?" Dick asked with his arms out in a questioning gesture.

"I'm not sure yet, but I'm thinking on it."

On board *Reaper*, Rose was aware the pirates were destroying or capturing ships. She could see the activity through her view screen porthole. In the last week, however, there had been fewer attacks and successes. What she hadn't seen for a while was the face of Reeb. That was just as well, because each day she was feeling more and more activity around her implant. The nanites were at work, there was no doubt. What she was afraid of was that Reeb or one of the pirate techno nerds would find out before she could use the transmitter. She decided to try the implant the next time the pirates engaged, hopeful there would be a Guardian Force ship close enough to receive the signal.

How could I have guessed, she thought, *that I would one day be in a position like this and wanting to be rescued? By whom. . . my family?*

In an effort to distract herself with better thoughts, she pondered the realization that Guardian Force had indeed become a family for everyone in the Force. For her and her brother, Danny, it was the only close family they had left after the deaths of their parents. Sure, they had a list of cousins, aunts, and uncles as long as her arm, but they had never been close. Then there was Van. Looking back at that first meeting with him in Texas, she was positive that the first embers of a flame had started there. . . for the both of them. Not love at first sight, but a strong pull that even today she had a hard time describing.

When she got to know him better and saw the leadership burdens he had thrust upon him, she marveled that he could keep moving forward at the pace he'd chosen for himself. Then also, at times she believed she saw in his eyes the lingering pain of a serious romance broken in half only to come back to life and be destroyed again with Barbara Fuller's death. Then sprinkle that bad-tasting cake with the bitter realization that his love was not really in love with him, but also that she had taken a traitor's stance against both him and Galactic Force. And yet he persevered where others may have given up. She didn't think anybody saw as much in him and about him as she did. She wondered what her life would have been like without him in it. Then she smiled, realizing that the reality was he was in her life and she in his.

She lay down in her bunk and drifted off to sleep thinking of better things than just her current circumstances.

The draco you ordered cannot be delivered. There was that damned signal flashing again on his tablet, and Daman gave a big sigh as he leaned back in his office chair. Things were getting dicey with the new Guardian Force ships deployed and the new transit lanes in effect. Then there was that AI, Harry, and his robots, which had stifled most of the sabotage efforts his recruits had attempted. All in all, he and Reeb were becoming less and less effective, and he just knew this message from Reeb would be a demand to do better.

Reluctantly, Daman pushed out of his chair, cleaned up his desk, and set off for the apartment building. He was getting tired of this trek.

Once secured in the simple room, Daman sat at the desk, turned on the device, and started the communications routine.

"This is Number 1. I say again, this is Number 1."

Daman had to repeat this only one more time before he got a reply.

"What the hell is happening, Number 1?"

Daman looked puzzled and replied accordingly. "What do you mean?"

"We haven't had a success in days. If things go on like this, we'll become completely ineffective."

"I send you all the information I receive as soon as I receive it. I think it is you who is failing."

Not bothering to respond to the rebuff, Reeb continued, "I'll send you some false information through your own Space Guard information channels. I have contacts. It will make the defenders think we will be striking one place when we actually hit another."

Daman thought about it for a moment, then responded, "That might work once and maybe twice before they catch on to what is happening and pay no attention. Plus, it will open me up to exposure. Then you would get no information."

"Nevertheless, that's what I'm going to do. . . unless you come up with something better. I'll give you two days, and then I'll send it. Reeb out!"

Despite the influence of the Arkon device in front of him and his persistent memory lapses, Daman still struggled with an inner conscience deep inside. Arkon technology could not suppress a person's cultural norms and values completely, just hide them deep in the shadows of a person's mind. In truth, the inner combat of wills never ended but failed to reach surface consciousness. The struggle left him tired and irritable each time he was exposed to the equipment. Arkon technicians might explain this as a yearning in Daman to quit and turn himself in, but he was being overpowered by the Arkon-induced control. He shut down the machine and breathed a sigh of fatigue as he stood and left the room, locking it behind him.

CHAPTER 10

Arkon Red Central Commander, Admiral Gulv, made an unusual but not unprecedented trip to meet with his kinsman at Red Sector 20 headquarters aboard the battle cruiser *Traggva*.

Vice Admiral Daan, Red Sector 20's new commander, met his kinsman in the flight bay of the *Traggva*. "Greetings, Admiral, and welcome to *Traggva*."

"Good to see you, my boy. The new rank suits you, and the ship is a big step from the cruiser *Rygia*, is it not?" said the elderly but fit admiral, his red crest unfurled.

"It is indeed, Admiral, but won't you come with me to my quarters where we may have refreshment and talk?" Daan motioned with a sweeping hand in the direction he wished his commander to go.

Once in Daan's quarters, the ceremonies faded and Gulv spoke plainly from a comfortable cushioned seat.

"This activity in your sector must not be allowed to continue. I know you understand, but I'm not sure you understand why. So, let me explain.

"To date the loss of ships in the sector have been explained as a combination of the hazards of exploring new territory and the failure of the Browns to keep our ships in good order. Also, I have been able to keep this from the attention of the supreme leader and the Home Guard commander. But that cannot last forever. We have to rid ourselves of this vermin and quickly. Therefore, I am authorizing you to take all necessary actions within your level of resources to do away with the problem."

Daan stared at his kinsman and commander as he thought

this through. His crest was mostly folded in a sign of both respect and concern.

"When you say 'all actions within my level of resources,' do you mean there will be no additional resources from you?"

"Yes. I cannot afford to move assets right now that are vital in maintaining control of the empire. We barely have enough ships to meet the current demand. Of course, the Browns are to blame in large part for that. The combination of their poor management and the problems with conscripted labor have our forces at a dangerously low level of operational fitness. Keep this to yourself, by the way. So, you can use anything and everything you have to rid us of this irritation."

"I understand, Admiral. I will handle it," said Daan with a resolute face and tone he'd learned over the year to maintain when talking to superiors.

"One more thing," said Gulv. "For the best impact on the family, I want you to lead the mission."

Daan's crest folded out of sight.

Knowing what was likely going on in Daan's head, Gulv brightened and his crest folded partway out of unusual recognition of his host's obvious worry. "Do not be concerned, Daan. I do have something for you. You will have a contact in that area of space to provide you important intelligence. His name is Reeb."

After a day of uneventful travel, *New Horizons* established an orbit above Dan 3. Planetary analysis started immediately with the assistance of Jennifer. Van remembered what Harry had said about the new consoles on the ship when *New Horizons* had first been discovered. "Through this console and one similar in the manufacturing center, planets, moons, and asteroids can be assessed for material content and structure. It can also assess environmental detail, all without having to conduct a manned investigation." Subsequently, it had been discovered the actual consoles needn't be manned to collect the data if Jennifer was available.

Van was again visiting Frank on the ship's bridge when Jennifer appeared.

"Commander, this planet is different from Dan 2. There are traces of moisture on the surface and water below the surface. There is vegetation in the equatorial regions and an oxygen and nitrogen atmosphere, though the oxygen percentage is below the level required for humans. What is more interesting are the presences of relatively intact cities in multiple locations."

Frank and Van looked at each other as they both took in this amazing news.

"Cities? And life forms?" asked an excited Van, turning back to face the holographic image of Jennifer.

"No life forms, Commander. At least not sentient ones. There are some life forms scattered around, but they are relatively small."

Sentient or not, these were the first real signs of life out here.

The *New Horizons* captain turned to his executive officer and said, "Launch recon drones and alert Brice and his team they will have something interesting to explore."

"Right away, Captain." Rebecca, as always, was on top of things and had already started the investigatory process.

A moment later, Van called out, "Frank, put all our data on our finds and our plans for Dan 3 in a message and get it off in a courier ship to Dick as soon as possible."

"Roger that. I'll take care of it myself." Getting a courier ship off as soon as possible meant getting one back as soon as possible with news of Rose or even with Rose on it.

It only took an hour for the initial planetary assessment to be completed, and it was just as Jennifer had said. A combat shuttle departed the ship headed for one of the larger cities. Aboard was the same team that had investigated the site on Dan 2. Brice again led.

Standing behind the pilot on the shuttle's bridge, Brice watched the view screens just like he would watch out a window. He leaned forward trying to look over the edge of the "window" and take in the amazing sight. Margo was on the opposite side, looking over the copilot's shoulder. They could have done the same thing in the cargo bay, but this seemed better somehow.

Below them appeared a remarkable city with tall spires and rounded domes. There were carefully laid out streets and bridges, which must have spanned rivers or streams at one time. But no activity of any sort. What had happened here?

Brice spotted an open space between several buildings, pointed, and asked the pilot, "Can we land there in the clear area next to the city?"

"No problem, Brice, but you may want to take a seat in the cargo area and strap in." Neither Brice nor Margo hesitated and rushed to their seats aft and strapped in. After all, their seats were closer to the exit ramp, and they badly wanted to get out and see this new place.

Altair, although over 3 AUs away, was bright enough to make the buildings shimmer with color. The battle-suited team stood for a few moments just taking in the majesty of this city, and their minds boiled with questions. Who had built this? Where were they?

Margo broke the reverie. "OK, break time over. Let's head for those buildings on the right, the shorter ones with the domes." As usual in these circumstances, Margo led, with the team following in support in a V formation.

There were remnants of what might have been grass of some sort some time long ago, but nothing green. This city was north of the equatorial zone, where there was at least some green. As they approached the first building, Margo again held up her clenched fist, and everybody stopped and took a knee, weapons up, still vigilant of their surroundings.

Margo moved forward to the nearest building and stopped at its edge. She reached out and reverently touched the surface. Even through her gloved hands she could feel it was solid and very smooth. She was standing next to what by any standard would have been a large street. But there was nothing moving. No signs of vehicles and no people. . . or whatever life form had built this. Then she waved her arm, giving the team clearance to approach.

When Brice stepped next to her, he asked, "What have we got, Margo?"

"A really big abandoned city. My assessment is the building materials are similar to those on Dan 2. Very advanced and very strong. The streets suggest the use of vehicles of some sort, but as you can see, there's no sign of any. What's more obvious and puzzling, there's no sign of damage of any kind. It's as if the people just disappeared."

"How about the age of the place?" Brice asked, prompted by the discovery on Dan 2.

"Hard to say without something like carbon to assess, but my feeling is it's a similar age as the facility on Dan 2. Perhaps older."

That got Brice's attention. "Five hundred to a thousand years and no deterioration? How is that possible?"

"Got me, but what a paper this would make to the Archeological Society back home," Margo said with a small amount of pride and expectation as she scanned the environment around her.

"Can we pin the age down in some way? I don't want to go back and tell Van we only have a guess."

"Carbon would do the trick if we can find some. Have the team spread out and look for something that might have been burned. Meanwhile, I'll work with Jennifer on this. As it stands, it's way beyond my pay grade."

CHAPTER 11

I N THE EVENING, BASED ON the ship's Greenwich Mean Time, the senior team gathered in the *New Horizons'* conference room to receive a briefing for the commander and staff. All ships and away teams had been recalled to the *New Horizons* and their captains or leaders in attendance. Margo, from the surface team, led off.

"It's been an interesting and educational day. Just as you can see on the view screen on the bulkhead behind me, this is a magnificent city built by an advanced race. We searched many of the buildings on and off the main street we started on and had drones surveil much of the rest of the city. Basically, it's the same everywhere we looked. Great city, no people or anything. Other drone searches of other cities revealed the same. Whoever the inhabitants were, they're all gone now, and there are no signs of destruction or combat anywhere."

"How about the age of the city?" Frank asked impatiently.

"I'm getting to that, or rather Jennifer is. Jennifer, care to answer the question?"

"Yes, I will, Miss Cranston. The search team discovered an artisan facility which specialized in metal sculpting and fabrication. I was able to assess some of the remaining products created with heat and other sculpting methods. Those relatively primitive works I estimated at one thousand years old."

The room went silent as each person took in Jennifer's startling announcement. The silence was broken, however, by the blaring sound of alarms and the urgent statement that followed over the 1MC.

"Fire in weapons storage area five. All hands, man your fire stations."

The ship's captain and XO were the first out the doors heading to the bridge. All but one quickly exited the room behind them. Margo remained standing at her presentation spot at the head of the room. She was frozen in place thinking of the implications of the alarm. She was concerned about the fire and the crew, but more worried that this might end her exploration of the planet below and the chance of a major discovery.

———————

Activity on the *New Horizons'* bridge was brisk but controlled. A capability developed by many hours of drilling for these sorts of emergencies. Frank and Rebecca took their seats quickly as Frank started asking questions and giving orders. Van followed the team onto the bridge but stood quietly in front of the observers' seats. This was, after all, Frank's command.

"Status of the fire?" Frank asked of the entire bridge team.

The communications officer replied first. "Engineering reports the fire is not a threat to engine or power systems."

Then came the report Frank wanted most from the weapons officer.

"First responders have confined the fire just to storage area five. Fire boundaries are holding. Automated fire suppression systems are only fifty percent operable. A manned team is now entering the space."

"Jennifer," Frank demanded, "what's wrong with the suppression system?"

"Five of the suppression nozzles have been disconnected from the rest, Captain."

"What? Why?"

"The system was undergoing routine maintenance checks, Captain, and half the system's suppression nozzles were removed for testing. It is a standard practice."

Frank was pissed. He was slapping the iron end of his club in his hand. This was his fault and Rebecca's. One or both of them should have seen the potential problems with leaving only half a system up and available while working on the other half. Especially in a weapons storage area!

"Not anymore, it isn't. XO, make a note to examine fire system maintenance procedures so this doesn't happen again!"

To Frank's relief, as well as everyone's on the bridge, the weapons officer shouted, "Fire is out! No casualties."

There were a few moments of calm in the room before Frank spoke again, pointing at the XO with his finger and not his club.

"Rebecca, take a team to storage area five and start assessing the reason for the fire."

"Yes, Captain," she said as she jumped up from her console and headed out the bridge door. Her right eye was blinking furiously.

Later the same evening, Van invited Frank, Rebecca, and Brice to his cabin after dinner. The cabin was spacious and, by most fleet standards, luxurious. In addition to a large bedroom, a private office and a private bath, the main room contained a ten-person combination dining-and-conference table and comfortable chairs. At the other end of the large room was a sitting area complete with a couch, coffee table, and two comfortable easy chairs. Van gestured for Frank and Rebecca to take a seat on the couch while he took one of the chairs opposite them. Brice took the other chair.

Before speaking, Van reflected on the people in the room. Based on his long experience with the people gathered with him now, he was confident none were capable of such wanton activities. He had also ruled out James Harris based on his dedication to his work and their friendship over many months. However, he had no clue who the saboteur might be. He hoped that sharing his concerns with these trusted people might help them discover who was doing the damage.

"I think we have a saboteur on *New Horizons*."

Rebecca and Frank glanced at each other in surprise. Then both looked back at Van. Brice continued to stare at Van, waiting for him to continue.

Frank spoke first. "A saboteur? I know we've had a few embarrassing issues, but I don't see how you've jumped to such a conclusion."

"If that was all the information I had, I'd agree with you. Unfortunately, I learned something before we started this mission that makes the observation realistic."

"Like what?" asked Rebecca, her brow furrowing.

"Just before we left, Dick Carson paid me a surprise visit. He said Harry had been analyzing accidents and mishaps on all the shipyards and had come to the conclusion they were not random. It appears someone or some group is throwing wrenches into our ship manufacturing. He assured me they were capable of handling the problem, which is why I decided to go ahead with the mission. However, he warned me to be alert for similar things happening on *New Horizons*.

"It's with that knowledge I drew this conclusion, as thin as it might be. We can't afford to ignore Dick's warning."

"What does Jennifer say?" Brice asked.

"I haven't asked her. But before we departed and having both heard Dick's comments, I told her to watch for any patterns that might suggest sabotage. So far, she hasn't said anything. I'm reacting to my own suspicions." What he didn't share was a vague concern that Jennifer might actually have been tampered with even though there had been no abnormalities expressed by Harry. But it was possible. By whom and why, he had no clue. It was also possible that he had not yet developed the level of trust in her he had with Harry, and that left him uncomfortable.

Silence filled the room for a few moments while the possibilities filled everyone's minds.

Van continued, "It's my judgment for now that we assume a saboteur does exist and take what precautions we can. We can't announce it to the crew for fear of scaring off the saboteur. I want to catch him or her and find out where the orders came from. It puts us at risk to some degree, but—"

Van was cut short when the ship shook and the room was bathed in a bright white light.

CHAPTER 12

ROSE HEARD A KNOCK AT her door aboard the *Reaper*. She expected the door to just fly open, but it didn't. There was another knock.

She stood from her seat on her bed and walked to the door. "Who is it?" she asked, then placed her ear near the door to hear the response.

"It is Captain Reeb. May I come in?"

This was new, Rose thought as she took a step back and answered, "What do you want?"

"I would like to invite you to dinner," came his voice. . . but not the harsh demanding voice she had come to expect.

Rose had to think about that. What was he up to? Was this a trick? However, just to break the monotony, she shrugged and said, "Come in."

There was the sound of a key pad beeping, and the door latch clicked open. No old-fashioned keys on the *Reaper*.

Reeb stepped in, but not very far. He was dressed in a three-quarter coat of material that looked like red velvet, and under that, a white dress shirt. He wore black trousers, and instead of the tall pirate boots she might have expected, he wore simple black shoes like those she had seen men wear on Sonara. A significant difference from her clean but washed-out blue ship's coverall. He gave a short, almost imperceptible bow and said, "Good evening, Dr. Ramos. You have been on *Reaper* for a while now, and I haven't had the chance to extend my hospitality. I would like you to have dinner with me if you will step this way." Reeb stepped aside and swept his arm toward the door.

Rose was still a little stunned. This was way out of character with all her treatment so far. But again, the monotony and talking to herself was getting old. Maybe she could find out some things that may eventually be of use to Van and the rest of the force. The simple but clean coverall she wore wasn't a party dress, but it had to do.

"Very well, Captain. Lead the way."

They didn't have to walk far forward to Reeb's guarded cabin, and when he opened the door for her, she stopped.

"Don't worry, Doctor, it is only dinner. I will leave the door open if you like, but my guards have to remain."

Rose was still hesitant, but she had come this far at least out of curiosity as well as for a change of pace. She stepped into the cabin.

The cabin was impressive if not a little gaudy. Reeb's style, if he actually had one, was eclectic, to be kind. Exotic tapestry and strange paintings on the bulkheads, carpets from some faraway and unknown place covered the deck, and a real wooden table and chairs of a brightly polished amber color.

There were two place settings on opposite sides of the narrow table, along with silverware from another unknown place. There were glasses, for wine, she guessed, and finally, napkins made from a rough but artfully woven material.

"Please be seated," Reeb said as he pulled out Rose's chair and seated her.

"This is very unexpected," Rose said. "Not what one usually thinks about aboard a pirate ship."

Reeb's faced tensed at the label of "pirate," but he relaxed as he said, "We think of ourselves as collectors of art and technology. We act as custodians of such things for the benefit of the next generations."

Rose put her hand over her mouth to stifle a laugh and made a coughing noise to cover her involuntary response. "How nice of you," she said, composing herself.

"Yes, we have established quite a collection over time. A few things we sell to handle operational costs, you understand, but the majority is held in safekeeping."

"I see," Rose said, looking around the room for a theme. "Do you have a specialty in what you collect? I mean, are you more into art, or fine jewelry, or something else?"

Reeb also looked around the room, admiring his decorating. "I think we specialize in smaller items of historical worth. As you noted when you looked around, that means art in many forms like the paintings, the carpets, and yes, finely crafted jewelry. On occasion, we discover some larger items like sculptures, but of course, we have weight and space limitations. This is a relatively small ship."

Rose was unsure she could continue this charade, but she pushed on, hoping to gain some valuable insights into this man and his business.

"So, does that mean you look upon me as an historical find that needs saving for the next generations?"

Reeb's smile slipped a little, but he seemed to be prepared. "No, but you do have value."

"Ransom value, you mean," she said, a little more sharply than she'd intended.

"A harsh word you use, ransom. We believe that power and wealth is controlled by a relatively small group of people, and that many of us, like my crew and their families, are being exploited while the rich grow richer. So, we try to balance the scales."

"You mean you steal from the rich and give to the poor?"

"Something like that, yes."

Rose almost laughed in disbelief at this fairy tale. Was Reeb less of an intellect than he appeared to be, or did he think she was so gullible as to believe all this nonsense? No matter, she plunged on.

Conversation stopped for a few moments as a crewman in a blue coat brought in dinner. Rose wasn't sure what it was, but it looked and smelled delicious. Then she continued as they ate.

"And what makes you think I have a high value? I'm just a lowly doctor."

At that, Reeb dropped his utensils on his plate with a sharp bang and held his sides as he gave out a hardy laugh. Slowly, he got himself under control as he forced himself to swallow the piece of meat he had just begun to eat. Then with a big smile, he pointed a finger at Rose and said, "You are funny! Never have I laughed so hard. You almost made me choke on my food!"

Too bad you didn't, thought Rose before she continued. "What's so funny?"

"Think of this," Reeb said wiping tears from his eyes. "What one person in at least two planetary systems knows more about medicine in space? What single person has the most knowledge of advanced medical technology? Then ask yourself what doctor has just been highly honored for her work and received news coverage everywhere. In short, who is the most known medical person in two worlds?" He paused and pointed at her again and said, "You."

Rose chose not to speak at the moment. Early on, she had already considered what Reeb just said.

"That is why people will pay to get you back," Reeb said, back under control.

"But you know efforts will be made to get me back, don't you?"

"Yes, yes. That always happens. But you forget, space is very big."

"Aren't you afraid of Galactic Force?"

"I would be foolish not to respect them. But as I said, space is very big and the number of allied ships is very small by comparison. Excuse me, try some of this wine we recently acquired. It is very good." Reeb poured some of the pale yellow liquid into the glass in front of Rose, and she took a sip.

"It's very good," she said with some surprise. "But back to the ransom, you said something about people, plural, being interested in my welfare. How many?"

"Including Galactic Force, three. The lead medical organizations in both Federations have also been asked to make contributions."

"What kind of contributions?"

"Oh, just some gold. We have simple tastes, but we do need something to trade for food and other supplies."

"You mean supplies for these ships?"

"Yes, of course. But we have other needs as well."

Rose thought she would push this man a little. "Like operating bases?"

Reeb stared for a moment, but thinking there was no harm in answering a simple question, he gave a simple answer. "Yes. We have many mouths to feed, as I said, and responsibilities that need to be fulfilled."

"Are we headed there now? I mean, I'd like to see your home."

"No, we are not headed there at the moment. We have some other business. However, if you would truly like to see what we call home, I might be persuaded to take you there."

Thinking fast, Rose came back with, "Only if it is well protected. I have no desire to be shot up by those trying to rescue me. . . assuming they will try."

"They may well try, but our home is just a small speck in the galaxy. Too small to be easily found."

Thoughts ran through Rose's mind. Reeb's home wasn't a planet or a known moon. It had to be an asteroid or even a space station. Probably an asteroid, given the expertise required to build a space station, and difficulty of doing so. And it was well defended, possibly over a long period of time, since pirate activities had been going on for years. That could spell real danger to Galactic Force.

Not wanting to spook Reeb by asking more about his home, she shifted her questions.

"So, you must have a wide-ranging intelligence network that allows you to know what ships carry and when."

Reeb was enjoying these questions, if only because they were coming from an intelligent and beautiful woman. Not like his dullard crews. He would play the game just for the pleasure of being with such a person. . . and a woman.

"'Wide ranging' may be an overstatement. Well positioned would be a better way of putting it."

"By well positioned, you mean highly placed?"

Reeb hesitated again, but saw no danger in answering. "Yes,

in few cases. We also have valuable people with other skills in a variety of locations."

In the latter case, Rose assumed he was talking about lesser agents. Those who did the dirty work.

Reeb looked at their plates and saw that they had both eaten all their food. "By the looks of it, you enjoyed your dinner."

Looking down, Rose was surprised. She had indeed eaten every last morsel. And it was good. Shaking her head a little and smiling at the realization, she said, "Yes, I guess I did. It was really good."

Reeb beamed. "So glad you liked it. Would you care for more?"

Still looking at her clean plate, she said, "No, thank you. I think my stomach has grown small in the past weeks. I couldn't eat another crumb. But why this dinner? Why take the time with me?"

Reeb frowned a little, then spoke. "Being in space or on our base all the time leaves a great deal to be desired. When the chance occurs, which it seldom does, to talk with an intelligent person, I try to take advantage of it."

"It's that simple? You don't want to fill me with wine and take advantage of me?"

Reeb sat straight up in his chair and stared at Rose. "I'm shocked, Doctor, that you would think of me like that."

Rose saw he was serious and felt just the tiniest amount of sympathy for the man.

"Sorry," she said. "It's the stereotype of pirates that we have."

Reeb pressed a napkin against his lips and stood. "This has been very enjoyable, Doctor, but I have some other work to do. The guards will show you to your quarters." He turned and walked out.

Back in her cabin, Rose thought about the evening. To her surprise, the short evening and dinner had gone better than she'd imagined. The food had been good, even though she wasn't sure what it had been and was afraid to ask. And she'd learned a few things.

There was no doubt Reeb was an opportunist and, yes, a pirate. Yet he was also smarter than Rose would have anticipated. This was no average wine-swilling, loud-mouthed, saber-rattling criminal. He was calculating, alert, inventive, and probably cunning. She guessed that his ambitions were high, and he likely had very specific goals, even though he hadn't mentioned any. And based on the unexpected dinner, she guessed he was lonely, surrounded by intellectually vacant men. The thing that didn't make sense was why he continued to press his piratical actions in the face of a growing opposition that both outgunned and outmanned him. In her opinion, after seeing his small force through her window, he couldn't win, even though, as he'd said, space is very big. Could there be a higher person or force directing his actions? One he couldn't escape? She didn't know for sure, but it was a distinct possibility or even a probability. At least she had some information that might help Galactic Force. . . if she had the chance to tell them.

When the brightness faded and their eyes refocused, the *New Horizons'* senior team jumped into action. Frank and Rebecca ran for the bridge, Brice instituted a tight security alert, and Van sat at the table watching all the activity as a security force formed around him. He decided to take advantage of the ship's AI.

"What just happened, Jennifer?"

"Unclear, Commander. But based on my exterior observations, we are no longer over Dan 3."

That got Van's attention, as well as Brice's, who stood alongside his commander staring at the image on the view screen.

"So, we moved somehow to another planet in the Altair system?"

"No, Commander. There is no sign of Altair or any of the planets and lesser stars. We are in an entirely new system."

"Can't you be more specific?" Van said, staring at Jennifer's holographic image. Brice stared also, wanting to know the answer.

"No, Commander. I can say we are in the Milky Way galaxy, that can be seen. But I cannot determine more yet."

"Any indication of what happened?"

"I can only say there was no malfunction aboard *New Horizons*, Commander. Everything is operating normally. The only explanation available is some outside force or anomaly caused us to move from Dan 3 to this place."

Van had never liked being out of control of the things around him, even in the past when his Navy seniors were giving him orders. Now, however, he was in command and it appeared he had just lost the control he so valued. He hadn't chosen to be here, wherever it was, and he had no idea what he was facing. Despite marveling at whatever had transported them there, he was pissed.

More than just a loss of control, however, all sorts of concerns flashed through his head. Among them was the worry that not knowing where they were would mean not being able to get back home. That would defeat the whole purpose of the mission, to say nothing of all the lives at risk out in the middle of nowhere.

Lastly was the question of whether to launch the other ships from the *New Horizons* or not. If he did and the ship moved again, what would happen to those detached ships and people? On the other hand, what chance did they have of solving the mystery and determining their location if they didn't investigate?

"OK, Brice, let's go to the ship's bridge and see what Frank knows."

Covering the short distance to the bridge, the pair found it abuzz with organized action. Not wanting to interrupt Frank right away, the two visitors watched and listened.

Sitting on the edge of his command chair and using his club to support his forward-leaning posture, Frank was barking orders and asking questions.

"Rebecca, status on engines and life support?"

"Everything checks out perfect."

"How about the corvettes and fighters?"

"Ready to launch."

Frustrated at not finding anything wrong except not being where they were supposed to be, Frank finally sat back in his chair and allowed a big breath out.

"So, where the hell are we?" was his last and most troubling question.

"Save yourself the fretting, Frank," Van said from the rear of the bridge. Everyone turned suddenly toward him, not having seen or heard him enter the bridge.

"Jennifer and I have just been through all that. And the answer is, firmly, we don't know."

Frank slumped in his chair, and, indeed, the air appeared to flow out of the bridge. The crew had been working at a feverish pace to answer all questions, only to find the answer to the biggest one was just a "We don't know."

"So, until we can figure this out," Van said, "the next best thing to do is find out more about the planet down there. Jennifer has started working on it, so treat it just like any new planet we find."

The idea picked people up. Exploration was a routine they knew well. Organized chaos turned into professional execution. But where they were and why were still the questions in the backs of their minds.

Drones, along with high-altitude combat shuttle runs, covered the planet. Like Dan 3, the initial scans were of oxygen and nitrogen levels not breathable by humans. Similarly, there were traces of water both above and below the surface, most being below, and there were uninhabited cities in the northern hemisphere. This was turning out to be a planet amazingly like Dan 3, except for one thing. There were energy readings coming from one of the cities.

Van was pacing in his quarters, a sure sign he was thinking and struggling with something. This time it was mostly about Rose. Here he was, God only knew where, and Rose was missing and a captive. And there wasn't a damned thing he could do about it. He didn't even have Harry to talk to. Jennifer was capable as AIs went, but she hadn't yet grown as Harry had to interact with humans.

To top it all off, he had selected capable officers like Frank and Rebecca, and there was little for him to do at present. At this point all was just routine, except, of course, they didn't know where the hell they were. But he couldn't do anything about that either!

He had to do something or he'd go nuts. Then it hit him, and he turned and went straight to the bridge.

Unlike the last time he appeared on the bridge, all was quiet, or at least at a low hum. Frank was in his chair quietly watching, and Rebecca was giving orders and asking questions from her console.

"Frank," Van called out, surprising Frank and half the people on the bridge again, "call me up a shuttle. I want to see this planet more closely."

Frank turned abruptly in his chair and dropped his golf club to the deck to stare at Van, blurting, "You? Alone? As your captain, I have to advise against it. We have plenty of people doing an assessment. We don't know enough about this place to ensure your safety."

"If I worried about my safety all the time, we wouldn't have this ship or any others. I'd still be an aerospace consulting engineer, and you'd be another retired Air Force pilot living a boring life on the golf course. Give me a little credit." Van was amused as he watched Frank squirm a little. *Not nice,* he thought, *but I should get my way when I want it.*

"Ah, that's true. How about I go with you?" Frank was looking for a compromise.

"But you're the ship's captain; you can't go gallivanting around away from your ship at a time like this." *Tables turned,* Van thought.

Frank was caught in his own trap, but looking over at Rebecca, he said, "OK, but you have to take Rebecca."

Rebecca looked up, a little surprised, but also with a little thrill at the thought of getting away from the demanding ship, which consumed all her time.

"That works for me. Let's go, Rebecca."

She didn't have to be told twice.

CHAPTER 13

H ORNET WAS PATROLLING THE OUTER limits of one of the newly established cargo lanes looking for pirates and had several active contacts dead ahead. Mia Flores, *Hornet*'s commanding officer, was not new to space flight or combat. She had worked as an exchange officer in the early years with the budding Galactic Force, where she'd developed an excellent reputation, which resulted in her being one of the first Earth officers to command an Earth Federation ship after serving as Chen Lee's XO in his first command. That was before the brand-new *Hornet*. Now, she exuded confidence as she sat in her command chair calmly and professionally, watching the contact display screens.

Of the contacts being displayed, one was a known cargo ship carrying raw material on an established lane and emitting the correct recognition signal. The others were unknowns. Just then the cargo ship's signal shifted to emergency. It was being attacked.

Mia could see they were very close to the cargo ship and its attackers, so there was no need to increase speed. In fact, they were going too fast.

With her eyes glued to the forward view screen, Mia called out, "Helm, breaking maneuver. Don't overshoot."

"Yes, Captain," said the young but capable helm officer.

Mia had been drilling him and the rest of the bridge crew hard since they'd left Sol space. Now was the time to see if all their work had paid off.

Reeb was in his command chair enjoying the capture of another ship and its cargo when the sensor operator called out: "Unknown ship closing fast, Captain!"

"What kind of ship?" Reeb asked, pushing forward in his chair.

"Looks like a warship decelerating. Not Guardian Force that I can tell. Might be an Earth Federation ship."

Reeb didn't want to engage any warship at this point. His forces were already spread thin, and the two small ships with him wouldn't do much against an armed opponent.

"Break off the attack. Reverse course and get out of here. NOW!"

Through her small "porthole," Rose saw *Reaper* approaching a cargo ship. As the victim ship got bigger and bigger in her view screen, the *Reaper* made a violent maneuver away from its prey. *Reaper* was running. She had seen this before and surmised it was because the good guys were nearby or on the way. She had vowed to initiate her beacon at the next opportunity and now was the time. She commanded the beacon to broadcast.

"Cargo ship is DIW, Captain. Must have taken a hit to its engines," called the sensor officer. DIW was another holdover from the wet navy that meant "dead in the water." No water there, but the message was the same.

"Roger. Communications, does the cargo ship need immediate attention?"

"Just asked that, ma'am. They're OK, just aren't going anywhere."

"OK, launch a combat shuttle to assist and protect her. Meanwhile, Helm, let's get after those pirates." Mia had no doubt the fleeing ships were pirates. The *Hornet* accelerated after them.

A few minutes into the chase, the communications officer called out, "Captain, I'm getting a strange but weak signal from the big lead ship."

"What's strange about it?" Mia asked.

"My records indicate it's a Guardian Force locator beacon. And it matches the frequency of that Guardian Force doctor, Ramos I think her name is."

Mia turned sharply toward the communications officer. "Are you sure?"

"Yes, ma'am. Our last time in port, all of us communications types were given a special notice from Captain Lee. It described the exact frequency and said if we discover it, call home and stay on the trail."

Mia remembered Chen Lee talking about Rose Ramos's kidnapping and her locator. But until now there hadn't been any luck discovering it. Now, here it was. "*Tuanis!*" Mia shouted excitedly meaning 'awesome' in Costa Rican. "Communications, send an immediate message to Captain Lee and a copy to Mr. Dick Carson on the Sonaran orbiting shipyard. Tell them we detected Dr. Ramos's locator signal and are following. Give our location, course, and speed. Oh, and tell them about the cargo ship. She'll need some help getting home."

"Yes, ma'am."

"Captain, I just lost the locator signal," the sensor operator announced just as Mia was settling in for the chase.

Mia left her command chair and swiftly stepped the short distance to the sensor station.

"Is your equipment working normally?" was her first question.

"Yes, ma'am. It's working just fine. I just ran a diagnostic. But that's not all. We just lost contact with the pirate ship."

Mia stood as the meaning registered. They had failed to capture or track the pirate ship. More importantly, Rose Ramos was gone. *Salado*, tough luck, she thought. Not only was this a tough loss, Mia felt a certain amount of empathy for Rose. They were both Latina women successfully competing in a male-dominated arena in the early months of human space development. They had both come from hardworking middle-class families. They had both become successful and owed much of their growth and success to Galactic Force. . . and its commander. It was a tangled web of commonalities and communities that tugged at her beyond just the mission.

CHAPTER 14

V AN WAS HAPPY HE'D MADE the choice to get off the ship. Here he was, doing something. Maybe not contributing in great detail to planet analysis, but at the moment he had the controls and went where he wanted. Neither he nor Rebecca had been around or on Dan 3. All they'd seen had been on view screens or in videos. This was different. It was great. The pilot in him pushed Van to do a few rolls and take a tour around a mountain just for the fun of it. It reminded him of the time he and a helicopter pilot friend had flown out of Naples, Italy, and up Mount Vesuvius, into the crater, and then back down what looked like the biggest slide in the world. He remembered he'd been surprised there'd been no complaints from the Italians when he'd gotten back to the *America*. It had made it all the sweeter.

Rebecca was enjoying it to. This was a small shuttle that included real windows. Her face was pressed against the crystal-laden glass in fascination. The landscape revealed lots of details, including several beautifully preserved cities. But no sign of life. The cities were amazingly preserved, like new. But abandoned. Like Dan 3, no damage, no signs of combat. It was as if everyone had just left. But where had they gone?

Van wanted to land and do some sightseeing, but Rebecca was having none of it. Privately, Frank had told her "No landing," and she was going to abide by the order even though Van outranked her. . . and everybody else.

Then Rebecca noticed something. "Van, look out there to the south. It looks like a storm of some kind."

Rebecca's statement quickly drew Van's attention to the

horizon. Storms and airplanes and even shuttles just didn't mix. "I see it. Give the ship a call and tell them we're going back. Should be about thirty minutes."

"Roger," she answered as she put her head down to select the right frequency and make the call. She tried, and she tried again. Nothing worked.

Van watched her twisting knobs and pressing buttons, which shouldn't have been necessary just to call the ship. "What's wrong?"

Still working on the transmitter, she didn't look up when she replied. "Don't know. I think we're transmitting, but I get no response. Just a lot of static."

Van looked around at the fast-moving storm coming their way. "Could be the storm is interfering with the radio."

Rebecca didn't respond and kept trying to get something to work.

Then Van noted something more ominous. The *New Horizons'* beacon was gone. It was the beacon all ships used to home in on *New Horizons*. Without a direct link to the ship, finding her, even as big as she was, would be problematic. In situations like this, an old Navy saying about being lost popped into his head: "Climb. Conserve. Communicate." So, he started a climb, using the horizon as a reference. Trouble was, the horizon was starting to get hazy. The storm was kicking up a lot of dust.

Just like a good copilot, Rebecca reached over her head to the emergency control panel and flipped a red cover that protected the emergency beacon from being initiated by accident. Van nodded, and Rebecca threw the switch. They could hear the beacon doing its beep-beep sound, but had no idea if it was being received.

The pair wore lightweight pressurized battle suits with the helmets off. Now, however, both pilots came to the same conclusion at the same time and picked up their helmets and locked them in place. They were now on their own life support.

Van was forced to fly on instruments alone. That was not as much of a challenge as it had been when he had flown for the Navy. In fact, it was normally quite easy. You just followed the path laid out by the computers (there were two, one for backup) on the view screen, and you got where you wanted to go. In this case, though, the computers couldn't find the destination point, *New Horizons*. Something, the storm probably, was preventing it. Without visual or computer contact with the ship, instrument flying could be a lot harder than in those good old days. Up and down, left and right started to lose reference points as you reached space, especially if you had no visual references — like the planet, in this case.

Just then all decisions were taken from him as the starboard engine failed. They were falling, albeit slower than with no engine. And they still couldn't see a foot in front of them.

"Strap in tight, Rebecca. This isn't going to end well, I'm afraid."

"I did that ten minutes ago, thank you very much. If I made these straps any tighter, I'd cut off my blood circulation." She glanced over at Van, who was intent on trying to fly the machine, then back out the forward window, searching in vain for a break in the storm.

But there was no break in the storm, and they were still descending. . . they thought. Mentally, Rebecca was pissed. Not because of the current problem but because she had never told Frank how she really felt about him. Now, she thought, it was probably too late, and her right eye started to twitch.

Then, like a jolt out of the blue, the shuttle hit something and rolled, over and over.

Van was the first to awaken, or rather, to come to. His head hurt, his back hurt. . . as a matter of fact, everything hurt. Surprisingly, he was still strapped in to the pilot's seat. But it wasn't in the shuttle. His eyes slowly focused, and he looked around as much as he could, given the aches and pains and the constraining straps.

Odd, he thought, *no storm*. In fact, there was no evidence of a storm. No dust, no lingering wind, nothing. Just him sitting alone about twenty feet from what remained of the shuttle. Then it hit him — no sign of Rebecca either!

Reason returning to him, Van hit the release button for the safety straps and they fell away. He started to jump from his seat, but the various pains, including his head, slowed him down. When he could stand, he looked back at the nearly destroyed shuttle but still could see no signs of Rebecca. Then as fast as his tormented body would allow, he made his way to the shuttle.

The front of the shuttle was virtually gone, but there, still strapped in her seat, was his copilot. Like Van's, her lightweight suit and helmet were intact. Rebecca herself, however, was slumped forward, held to the seat by the straps.

Kneeling in front of her, he called out through his suit's communications link, "Rebecca, can you hear me?" No response. Then he gave her a gentle shake and again said, louder this time, "Rebecca!" Still nothing.

Not knowing for sure if his suit's transmitter was working, he leaned forward and pressed his helmet to hers. "Rebecca, open your eyes!" he shouted as loudly as he could. He saw her eyes twitch. Then her head moved just slightly. Finally, her blue eyes opened, and she stared at him.

Relief swept through Van. She was alive, but her condition was unknown. When Harry had designed these suits, he'd included a connector that enabled one person to tap into the electronics of another suit. Van pulled the tucked-away cord from the midsection of his suit and plugged it into the open port on Rebecca's. Immediately, he started seeing her vital signs posted on the HUD of his helmet.

Blood pressure good, breathing weak but improving, with all other signs in the normal range. Relieved, Van allowed himself to sit down, or collapse, in front of Rebecca, waiting for her to regain her senses. It only took a minute.

"Van, is that you?" Clearly, like Van initially, she was taking time to return to normal.

"It's me. How do you feel?"

"Like I was hit by a truck," was all she was willing to say.

"Humor! That's a good sign," Van said, trying to boost her morale.

"Easy for you to say. What happened? Where are we?"

"In order, we crashed and we are on the mystery planet's surface. And by the way, the shuttle is a wreck."

Rebecca reached for the back of her head where there was pain, but the helmet blocked her gloved hand. "On the planet, you say? Frank won't like that."

"I'll bet he won't. Neither do I. The good news is, there's no storm."

"Then they can find us," Rebecca said with the first sign of reason.

Seeing Rebecca was OK, Van stood and, with hands on his hips, took a 360-degree look around them. One of the cities was within walking distance and flanked by a small mountain. Some people would call it a rocky hill.

"Since we're here and waiting for rescue, why not see what we can salvage from the shuttle and then take a look at the city? It isn't very far, just past that hill, or mountain, or whatever."

Rebecca released her straps and was happy she hadn't fallen over. Then, with great effort, she struggled from the copilot's seat and stood, a little wobbly, but on her own, and brushed Van's helping hand away. "I'm OK."

The shuttle was not a complete waste. In fact, closer inspection with better eyes and judgment showed the small craft to be mostly intact. . . except for the forward section, the cockpit. After fifteen minutes they had loaded a pack for each of them with rations and basic survival gear. They also took weapons from the arms locker.

Again, Harry helped them. His design included an oxygen-scrubbing system that provided the suit wearers with breathable air for long periods. The two survivors just hoped it would hold out until a rescue could be made. Then, after each checked the suit and pack of the other, they headed for the city.

They were just passing the rocky hill when Van held up a clenched fist, then motioned for Rebecca to move along with him quickly behind a large rock.

"What's wrong?" she asked.

"People."

"What do you mean 'people'?"

"See for yourself." Van moved to his right, giving Rebecca

room to crouch and look over the top of the rock. Then she quickly dropped back behind the rock and looked over at him.

"You're right. People. And they look like humans, but they can't be and breathe this air."

"I agree, but there they are. But did you see what's happening to them?"

Rebecca was usually quick to take in details, but the sight of people thrilled her so much that she'd failed to take in the whole scene. She shook her head.

"Then look again," Van said.

Slowly, Rebecca raised herself just high enough to see over the edge of the big rock. She was at first shocked, then angry as she crouched back down staring at Van.

"They're being herded by two big guys with some sort of sticks."

"I think those sticks are weapons. What else did you see?" Van knew there was more, since it had only taken him a few seconds to see and assess the whole picture quickly, thanks to the Host and Harry.

Rebecca thought for a moment, playing back the sight she had just seen. "The two guys looked like guards with uniforms. They were herding at least a dozen people toward an open enclosure, like a corral. There were two other guards there holding open a gate."

"Very good, Rebecca. What's your conclusion?"

"Hard to say for sure, but the people looked like slaves returning from work to a pen used to house them."

"My initial thought also," Van said, proud of Rebecca's reasoning.

"What do we do? We can't let those people stay slaves!" Rebecca was clearly disgusted by what she'd seen.

"If they *are* slaves. What if they're prisoners paying a debt for some crime? You want to disrupt the legal system on a planet and with people we know nothing about?"

Rebecca was trying to be angry with Van, but she couldn't. He could be right, and reacting too soon could be tragic for all concerned. "Then what do you suggest?"

"Harry always told me to carry some fireflies wherever I went. I always thought he was being a little over the top, but now I think he was, and is, brilliant. I did pay attention, and when you were taking your second look, I launched a few. Let's see what they can find out for us."

The small unseen drones did exactly as Van had hoped. He and Rebecca could see the captors close up. They wore uniforms all right, but they were old and tattered. They weren't even the same from one guard to another. Though neither Van nor Rebecca had seen them from their vantage point, there were two huts wedged between two very large rocks that served as both protection and camouflage. A female, probably also a prisoner or slave, was busy cooking something on an open fire. Beyond that was nothing. But still Van and Rebecca waited as several of the fireflies were commanded to a high-level view of the encampment to ensure no more guards were lurking about. There were no more than they had already seen.

Three of the guards walked to the woman cooking and scooped out food onto a crude plate. Each started eating with their hands, laughing at some indiscernible joke or story. The fourth guard had other things in mind with one of the females in the corral.

The long stick turned out to be a device, which, at the very least, delivered a substantial electrical jolt when applied to something. In this case, to the skin of a young female who had fallen in her attempt to get away from the guard who had entered the corral, closing the gate behind him. The other slaves, for that was what they now appeared to be, huddled in a corner of the corral shaking and crying.

Rebecca was watching the scene unfold on her HUD, which she promptly turned off. "We aren't going to allow all this to continue, are we?"

Van turned off his video as well and looked at Rebecca. "No, I guess we can't. Set your handgun to stun. You head for the guard in the corral, and I'll head for the two huts. On three, OK?"

Rebecca nodded.

"One. . . two. . . three!"

It was supposed to be over in minutes. That was the plan. It started out easily enough. Rebecca disabled the guard in the corral, causing him to release the young female he had in his grasp. She opened the gate and then stopped in her tracks. There was a noise coming from the area of the huts that didn't sound like the guns she and Van carried, in neither stun nor kill mode. There was a problem — she sped off in the direction of the huts.

Van had stunned one guard but then got a surprise. The sticks the others carried weren't just for prodding people with electrical shocks. They also shot red balls of plasma, enough to penetrate his lightweight suit and probably kill him.

After the first and second red balls missed him and hit the large rock next to him, splintering shards all around, Van dropped to the ground and backpedaled to the shelter of the rock.

"Rebecca!" he called over his helmet comms.

"Right behind you."

Van looked over his shoulder, and, sure enough, there was Rebecca, weapon at the ready. "We may have miscalculated," he said as another plasma ball flashed over their heads.

"You think?" said Rebecca with a sober smile, wincing as yet another plasma round hit the rock, again sending fragments in all directions.

"Yeah, I do. And I don't think the stun settings are going to work for us."

"Agreed," was all she said.

"OK, the only way to resolve this is to get them between fires. One of us has to circle around and get behind them. Then we open up together. I'm probably faster so I'll go. Fire a few shots to keep them busy." Van duck-walked backward past Rebecca and then turned and took off at a run.

Rebecca moved forward and fired off the first non-stun shot. She hit one of the huts, causing a large section of it to splinter, and continued to fire a few random shots, waiting for the signal from Van that he was in place.

It only took Van a few minutes to circle the guard's position. He slowed as he reached the edge of the second rock. "OK, Rebecca, I'm in place. On three we fire together."

She replied with a simple, "Roger."

"One. . . two. . . three," he repeated, and they eased around their respective shields and opened fire. But there was no return fire from the guards.

"Did we get them?" asked Rebecca, leaning back behind her rock shield.

Van had already stood and eased around the rock with his weapon in his outstretched hands ready to fire again if needed. There was nobody there. "They're gone."

"What do you mean 'gone'?"

"Just what I said. See for yourself."

Slowly and cautiously, Rebecca stood and looked into the small encampment, where Van was stepping between the huts, weapon poised. But she saw no signs of the guards or the slave woman.

Meeting at the still-smoldering cooking fire, the pair looked around and then at each other.

"Where'd they go?" she asked, lowering her weapon.

"I'm guessing they had enough of someone firing back and they ran. All of them, including the one I stunned. I'm not sure where, but I don't care. How are the slaves?"

"They were fine when I left them. After I disabled the one guard, I heard the shots in your area and came as quick as I could."

"Let's go see," Van said as he holstered his weapon and started off in the direction of the corral on the other side of the camp rocks.

The slaves were gone. The guard, too. Van and Rebecca looked around for some sign of the people who had been huddled in the enclosure, but initially saw nothing. Then a fuzzy head appeared from behind a distant rock.

"Look, peeking out from behind that distant redish rock," Rebecca said as she pointed the direction of the large rock.

Van looked in the direction she was pointing and saw the same head with a frightened face looking back. Instantly, however, the head disappeared followed moments later by the whole group of slaves and even guards running as fast as they could away from the strange helmeted creatures that were Van and Rebecca.

"There they all go," she commented, looking after the fleeing mob as it faded into the distance.

Watching the fleeing group, Van grinned and commented, "When properly motivated, people can run pretty fast. It probably didn't help we look like monsters in these suits. Hopefully they're running to their homes where they'll tell a tale nobody would believe. I don't think the guards will stick with them long, however... if they want to survive."

Rebecca nodded and said, "I did notice one thing about them. Both the slaves and the guard I downed had slits in their throats like gills, which must have allowed them to breathe this planet's air."

Van nodded but said nothing immediately. Then, turning toward the nearby city, he pointed and said, "Shall we?"

The combat-suited pair moved on toward the city.

CHAPTER 15

V AN RECALLED LISTENING TO MARGO Cranston's recordings as
she'd examined the city on Dan 3. "Majestic," "flawless,"
"well designed," and "ageless" were words she'd used to describe
it. The buildings were like new. No sign of deterioration or
damage and perfectly smooth. Wide, empty streets. And like Dan
3, no people. . . at least none to be seen. He and Rebecca knew
there were people around based on their earlier experience with
the slaves. But they either were hiding or had moved to easier
places to defend.

After two hours of checking shops, offices, and stores, they
still came up empty.

"My guess," said Rebecca, "is everything usable was scavenged
and taken away long ago."

"You may be right. It would explain the lack of anything
useful or decorative," Van replied absentmindedly as he looked
around a corner of the nearest building. He remembered Margo
and her team had found an artisan shop off the main street that
had eventually led to material they could use to estimate age.

"Let's try some of these back streets and alleys," Van said,
motioning for Rebecca to follow him.

The street or alley they followed opened up to another big
street running parallel with the one they'd originally started
their search on. Looking to the right, Van saw one large building
standing relatively alone on the street. It looked as though there
had been gardens around it at one time, but now there was only
dirt, some artfully placed stones, and a decorative fence.

"Now there's an interesting place sitting out by itself just asking us to visit." Without waiting for Rebecca to reply, he set off down the short distance to the building.

Standing before the building, they looked up the steep set of stairs leading to tall pillars gracing the front.

"It looks impressive," said Rebecca. "Wonder what all the writing says above the pillars."

"Probably the headquarters of some rich guy. Maybe it's his name at the top," Van joked.

Rebecca chuckled. "Then what are we waiting for? Let's see what's inside."

The suited pair took the steps two at a time and reached the entrance in less than a minute. Van walked to the main doors and gave a push. To his surprise, they opened easily, as if they were counterbalanced.

The inside was more impressive than the outside by far. High vaulted ceilings with glass-like inserts at the top let in perfect light. A smooth floor, probably made of the same material as the outside, gleamed like new, with maybe a little dust.

"Where do you think the huge spiral staircase goes?" Rebecca asked as she strained to see the top of the immense space.

"Don't know. I'm more interested in those big doors to the right of us. They look like vault doors."

Rebecca switched her gaze from the top of the building to the doors Van was pointing to. The doors were indeed huge and had a bronze color, unlike the plain colors of the places they had visited so far. "Is one of them open?"

Van was already walking toward the doors. "Looks like it to me. Let's have a look."

The doors should have screeched or at least creaked, but they didn't. They should also have been nearly impossible to open, but they weren't. Van only had to push softly, and the big doors opened with ease.

"Holy shit!" gasped Rebecca.

If Rebecca hadn't said it, Van would have. Sitting in the center of the floor, surrounded by a crude but apparently sturdy cage, were piles of coins, plates, and other objects, all of which looked very much like gold.

"Is all that what I think it is?" Rebecca asked when her breath returned.

"If you mean gold, I think so."

Van took a few steps forward and grasped the bars of the cage, shook them and then asked, "Looks and feels sturdy, wonder how it opens?"

It took a few minutes to find the crude lock which yielded to one shot from Rebecca's weapon. Van stepped into the barred enclosure and dipped his gloved hand into the pile in front of him and then pulled a cupped fist up. Coins and other small objects fell from his hand and between his fingers as he brought his palm up near his face plate. The sensors in his suit could do a simple spectral analysis, and he commanded it to do so. In seconds the HUD flashed "AU, atomic number 79."

"It's gold, all right. Like a king's ransom."

"Or a pirate's treasure." She giggled. She couldn't help it as she too played with the loose pieces. Then, emptying her hand and looking up at Van, she said, "But why was all this left behind?"

"Good question. Whoever owned it either didn't need it or left here in such a hurry he or she couldn't take it all." Van's voice trailed off as he saw another door in the same room, also partly opened.

"Over there." Van pointed. "Care to guess what's behind door number two?"

"Not me. When I watched that game show, I always got a year's supply of toilet paper for my choice."

"I doubt it will happen here. Let's see."

Like the first doors, though smaller, these doors opened with ease. But there was no light from the ceiling as in the other rooms. Van and Rebecca turned on their helmet lights.

"Wow! I'd say 'holy shit' again, but it would be redundant," said Rebecca, more in control this time.

Stacked in piles smaller than the gold were multicolored crystals. Red ones, green ones, blue ones, and white ones. All colors of the rainbow. They sparkled as the two bright lights swept over them. All surrounded by a barred cage similar to that in the other room.

"Rose would love this!" commented Van. Then he remembered what had happened and went silent.

Rebecca could sense his pain, but it couldn't stop her from blasting open the lock and stepping into the enclosure and digging into the pile of stones as Van had done with the coins.

"If my mother could only see me now," she said, trying to insert some humor into a discussion gone sour. "Can you imagine the wealth and power of these on Earth?"

Not listening, Van shined his light around the room to see if any other surprises jumped out at them. But there was nothing more than the caged enclosure and its many piles of precious stones worth an amount neither he nor Rebecca could guess.

"OK, let's keep on looking," Van said as he turned to leave what he now knew were treasure vaults.

"Wait!" called Rebecca. "You mean we're just going to leave all this here?"

"No use to us. Doesn't make ships get built faster. Doesn't give us personal spending power. . . we couldn't use it. Nice to know it's here in case we ever need it, but we have more important things to do."

"Can't I keep just one? A little diamond perhaps?" Rebecca fluttered her eyelashes and struck an innocent pose.

"No. Now let's go." He just wanted to leave. The thought of Rose had blocked his interest and his patience.

"Party pooper!" Rebecca said softly as she followed.

"What was that?"

"Nothing."

They had been in the treasure-laden building for nearly an hour, though it felt like much less. It was getting darker outside, so Van now wanted to hurry.

"Let's get a move on, Rebecca, and head back to the shuttle before it gets really dark. At least there we can see what's going on around us. Not like here."

Forgetting her dreams of diamonds and gold, Rebecca brightened at a thought. "I'm with you, Commander. We can eat something there. I'm starved."

Neither of them was prepared to see what waited for them outside the building. In a semicircle around them stood dozens of armed men in crude but effective-looking battle armor. Like the guards they'd met earlier, each carried a stick weapon that looked more substantial than the ones the slave guards had used. And standing in the middle at the bottom of the steps was a tall, bulky man clothed in gold-trimmed battle armor and a bright gold helmet. He had no firearm, just a nasty curved blade hanging at his hip. All, the two Guardians noted, had the same slits on their necks.

"Ah Cha!" yelled the prodigious leader, and all the troopers leveled their weapons at Van and Rebecca.

Slowly, Van and Rebecca raised their hands while two guards darted in and took all their weapons and possessions.

"No Cha!" yelled the leader again, and the semicircle of troopers shifted to a full circle around their two captives.

The leader drew his blade and held it in the air as if pointing and yelled, "Do Cha!" and the whole group moved out following him, Van and Rebecca included. They couldn't get away.

CHAPTER 16

B ASED ON THE TIME INDICATOR on Van's HUD, they had been marching for an hour and had left the city behind. Van realized it had been ten hours since the crash, and they were tired and hungry. If needed, they could initiate stimulation injections in their suits to give them some short-duration energy, but neither of them wanted to do that yet. *No telling how long this might go on,* Van thought.

They could not see much of their progress due to all the troopers around them cutting off their vision in every direction. With nothing to focus on, he had time to consider their situation. All he'd wanted to do originally had been to get away from the ship for a while and see this new planet. Perhaps have a little fun with the shuttle. Finding the slaves and the treasures had been interesting but still within his control. Now, however, he wasn't in control. It gnawed at him. They were in real danger at the hands of a totally unknown native leader and his forces. Barring some miraculous change of events, his best hope was that *New Horizons* would pick up their ID signals and come to their rescue. That it hadn't already happened gave him more reasons to be concerned.

He also wondered what would come next. He couldn't see much of anything, being surrounded by his captors. The one thing he was clinging to if help didn't arrive was that the suits he and Rebecca were wearing had not yet been tested by the strangers and would likely prove a problem for them; he hoped. He started to ask other questions of himself, but he stopped thinking when everyone abruptly came to a halt, except he and Rebecca. The lack of warning and their momentum carried Van and his partner forward to crash into the troopers at their front. The angry troopers beat them with their stick-like weapons until the two prisoners withdrew to the center of their prison circle. As Van expected, due to the protection of the suits, the beating didn't hurt, but he wouldn't tell the troopers. The pair just feigned pain as they withdrew. The troopers were satisfied.

Suddenly, the circle around them opened to the side and the leader appeared. He started shouting and gesturing. Van assumed they were supposed to go with him and a few of the guards. And that appeared to be right.

Van also noted some of the words being used around him had started to make sense. His Host-provided translation skills were kicking in. The group came to a stone enclosure with flags draped in front and armed guards standing at the ready. Troopers behind them prodded Van and Rebecca inside. The leader passed them and took his place on an ornate seat in the center of the room. Van and Rebecca were again prodded by troopers to the center, just in front of the leader. Then the troopers took one step back, weapons still leveled on the two prisoners.

The leader studied the two strangers for a few minutes, then made a gesture followed by what Van understood as "Take off heads," meaning take off their helmets.

Van shook his head no.

This angered the leader, and he motioned to two of his troopers to remove the prisoners' helmets. They tried, but they couldn't. They beat on them with their sticks, but still nothing. The helmets were locked from the inside and controlled by their wearers for just this reason. The troopers gave up.

Angry but possibly impressed with the technology, the leader changed his tactics. Van started to understand.

"Who you?" the leader said, pointing a stubby and scarred finger at Van. Looking closer, Van saw that the finger wasn't stubby, it was missing the section of the finger that would normally include a nail.

Van used the thumb of his right hand to point to his chest

and said, "Van." Then he pointed the same thumb to his partner standing next to him and said, "Rebecca."

The leader sat back, shocked these mysterious things spoke his language, even if not so well.

He tried again. "Where you from?"

Van pointed up, this time with his right index finger.

The leader tilted his head as he tried to fathom what the gesture meant. Then it hit him. And in return he pointed up and said, "Sky?"

Van nodded and said, "Yes."

The leader laughed and pointed at the prisoners as he said, "They from sky! Ha-ha." Everyone laughed except Van and Rebecca.

"You lie. No one from sky!" said the now impatient leader, leaning in toward his two prisoners.

Van wanted to get out of this pattern and asked, "Who you?"

Again, the leader was taken aback. Everyone knew who he was. "I am great leader. I am Notar."

"Pleased to meet you, Notar," Van said with a brittle smile.

Shaking off this strange person, Notar asked, "Why you steal from me?"

The question made no sense to Van. While he was trying to think, Rebecca tugged at his suit.

"What's going on? I don't understand a thing."

"This is Notar, the great leader, and he wants to know why we were stealing from him."

"But we didn't steal anything."

"I know that and you know that, but he either doesn't or won't believe us. After all, how could anyone like him pass up all the treasure in that building? No, it just doesn't make sense to him. Unless ..."

"Unless what?" Rebecca asked.

"Unless he was the one who built those cages we broke into. Kinda makes it look like we were breaking into the vault to steal."

"Then tell him to check our packs. He'll find nothing."

Van nodded and turned back to Notar. "We did not steal.

Check our packs." He pointed at the packs at the feet of one of the troopers. "You will find nothing there that does not belong to us."

Notar motioned for the trooper to look in the packs.

The tall trooper didn't so much look into the packs as tear out everything and scatter it around. When he didn't find anything, he held up each pack by the bottom and shook it. Nothing.

"See, I told you. We did not steal."

"You lie! If you not steal, you want to steal. You want to take from Notar."

Van's simple response was, "No."

This made Notar angrier. He pointed at Rebecca. "You tell or she die!"

Shaken, Van glanced over at Rebecca.

Putting two and two together, she asked, "Did he just say he wants to kill me?"

"Well, yes. If I don't tell him what we stole or planned to steal."

"Then tell him. We didn't steal from him or anybody." Her eye started to twitch.

"I know, but he doesn't or can't believe it."

Van was starting to get worried. This conversation had just escalated way beyond where he thought it was going. Most of all, he didn't want to see Rebecca hurt. No, if anybody was going down, it would be him. She was his responsibility. More than that, they were friends. He turned back to face Notar.

"No, I can't let you do that," Van said calmly, his hands clasped behind his back as if at ease.

Notar's grim sneer turned sardonic. "What you mean 'let me'? I take what I want."

"No, you will have to kill me first. And it won't be easy, little man." The last comment on Notar's size was an attempt by Van to cloud the big man's thinking with anger.

The "little man" comment worked and was Notar's last straw. He sprang from his seat with agility not expected from such a big and heavy man. Out came his long, curved blade, and he swung it directly at Van's midsection.

It would have been Van's midsection had he still been standing where he had been a second ago. At long last, his enhanced agility came into use.

Notar looked around, wondering what had happened to his sure kill.

"Hey, over here," came a voice from Notar's left.

"What?" snarled Notar as he refocused on the smaller being. Then he lunged again. And again, Van eluded the bigger man.

After several more tries, Notar threw down his blade and grabbed a stick weapon from a nearby trooper. He fired two quick blasts right at Van's midsection. Couldn't miss.

Van saw the two red balls coming for him and suddenly realized he could only escape getting hit by one of them. He jogged left and closed his eyes, and all the world turned red and orange around him.

Slowly, Van opened one eye and then the other. He looked down at his suit. There was no damage. He wasn't dead. Quickly, he looked up to see what Notar would do next. But Notar was nowhere to be seen. Nor were any of the troopers. He glanced back to see Rebecca sitting on the smooth stone floor looking up at him in apparent amazement. But she wasn't looking at him. She was looking past him. Van turned.

There in the middle of the room was a tall, elderly man with white hair in white robes and sandals. Around his neck, suspended by a golden chain, was a round golden medallion with various symbols in relief. Van thought he looked like a Roman senator.

"Who are you?" was all Van could manage. He was still stunned to be alive.

"You couldn't pronounce my name if I told you. However, in checking the data files on your ship, I have picked a name that I like. You can call me Majel."

Majel. The name rang a bell, but Van couldn't place it.

"How. . . ? What. . . ?" Van stammered. There were just too many questions to get out at once.

"Calm yourself, Commander. You and your friend take a seat

on this couch and I'll explain." There was a couch. It hadn't been there before, but Van and Rebecca took a seat and waited.

The old man took a seat on Notar's former throne. "I brought you here from the place you call Dan 3. That is a planet my people once colonized. It has seen no activity for nearly a thousand of your years. Naturally, I had to see for myself what sort of being could be there.

"My people — let's use another name from your data files and history, the Naskapi — had grown to occupy many planets in our system. We were productive and proud and, I might say, rich in everything we needed. Over time we developed many technologies to help us live better lives and move around our system.

"Our many sources of wealth drew the interest of another race in a nearby system. We will call them the Nokra. The Nokra were a crude people. Crude in culture and intellect, but they embraced new technologies. . . some of which they stole from us. When they felt the time was right, they established outposts in our system like the remnants you found on Dan 2. After studying us, they attacked.

"Now, we were not without protection. We had watched the Nokra grow their fleets and drew the conclusion there could be only one reason: to attack us. So, we also built a mighty fleet as much in secret as we could. But the Nokra did catch us by surprise, and many Naskapi paid the price for our lack of alertness.

"We had never fought such a war before. Yes, we had our internal feuds and battles, but nothing like the Nokra brought to us. It took many of your years for us to learn the skills we needed to perfect our ships and weapons. When we did, we fought with renewed vengeance for our lost people. We fought so hard we lost sight of what we stood for, and we wiped the Nokra from space, from existence.

"Initially, there was great happiness at the victory. In time, however, we began to realize what we had done. In your words, it was genocide. We killed every last Nokra. Eliminated them entirely, men, women, and children, as you call them. The realization was a jolt to our culture, to our core values. We vowed never to let that happen again. We disbanded most of our armed forces and turned our focus to bettering ourselves.

"Eventually, our race reached singularity. We evolved into something better. We left our mortal bodies behind and were free to roam the galaxy, to learn more and enjoy our new form of life."

Majel stopped, waiting to see the reactions of the two humans and hear the questions sure to come up.

Rebecca sat still, eyes on Majel, but said nothing. Her twitch was back with fury. Van, on the other hand, was not so slow.

"I understand your feelings about war. We share them but are forced to defend ourselves. What I'm curious about is where all your people went. There must have been hundreds of millions."

Majel nodded. "Yes, there were and are. We are scattered over this galaxy, which, by any standard, is huge. We have developed the ability to stay connected to one another no matter where we go. It is the same race, just transformed and spread out. We kept our same basic organization. I am, for example, one of the chiefs, or Sachems, of my suborder. Surprisingly, however, this is the first contact with your race. That is why I created the tests you just finished. I and my other Sachems needed to find out what your kind was like."

"We were being tested?" blurted Rebecca.

"Yes, Miss Lewis, and you passed," said Majel with a bow of his head.

Van and Rebecca looked at each other to see if the other was equally surprised at this revelation. Each was.

"Wait just a minute," Van said, holding his hands out in front of him in a gesture meaning *stop*. "Are you suggesting everything that happened to us all day wasn't real and you conjured it up?"

"'Conjured' is such a harsh word suggesting it was difficult. But yes, I devised all of the tests."

"What were we tested for?" Van asked, now on the edge of the couch seat.

"For compassion and the value of life with the slaves. For greed and the desire for power with the gold and jewels. And finally, for friendship and loyalty with the confrontation with Notar. As I said, you passed them all."

"Now what?" was all Van could say.

"If you will permit it, I would like to go to your ship, *New Horizons*. There are people there I would like to meet, including a person named James Harris, a diplomat I believe."

Van could still not get over the extent of knowledge this person, this being, had about them. He knew Majel had access to the *New Horizons'* database, but he didn't know he had also apparently analyzed the crew. Why all this effort on Majel's part? What did he want? Who were these people, really, Majel's story aside? And finally, why wouldn't Majel just go to the ship? He clearly was able without asking for permission.

Filled with such questions, Van finally said, "Before we go any further, Majel, aside from our being a new race to you and piquing your curiosity, why get involved with us? What do you and your people want from the likes of us?"

Majel eyed the Galactic Force commander with knitted brows and a slight nod that, to Van, looked like appreciation.

"Good questions," Majel said at last as a smile spread across his face. "As I mentioned, we don't often come across new races anymore, and we do have a certain amount of curiosity, as you call it. And when we do make an encounter like this one, we apply the same or similar tests. If the tests are failed, we ignore the races and go about our business. As it happens, you are the first in quite some time that has passed all the tests. That makes you exceptional. Also, from what I have been able to learn from your ship's data banks, we have some similarities, not the least of which is an avaricious and dangerous enemy."

"You know about the Arkon?" Van asked with surprise.

"Not directly, no. We have not encountered them yet, but we know a few things based on your data files, and they sound very much like our old adversary. Along with your test results, this has caused us to be, say, *sympathetic* to your problems. We can identify with you and your struggles and would like to help where we can."

"That answers one question, but the other remains. What do

you want from us?" Van asked, still not fully accepting of Majel's apparent offer.

"Nothing," was all Majel said.

Van gave a crooked smile before saying, "Wait a minute, I may be cynical, but in all my experience and even in our history, seldom do people offer such help without an expectation of something in return."

Majel gave a hearty laugh as he looked at the two humans. "We might have said the same thing a long time ago given the same circumstances. However, there is very little we want or need that we don't already have. There is one thing, however, that we no longer have."

Van jumped on that, sure that he had found the real motive. "And what's that?"

"We can't have offspring."

Van and Rebecca looked at each other in utter puzzlement. It wasn't what they had expected.

"I'm not following you, Majel," Van said, rubbing his forehead.

"Do either of you have children?" Majel asked.

Both humans shook their heads.

"Do you have the desire?" Majel continued.

Seeing the apparent reluctance on Rebecca's part to answer as she turned her head away, Van spoke. "I think most of us do, we just find it hard right now with all the problems facing our races."

"Well then, would it surprise you that other beings such as the Naskapi have similar feelings and desires?"

Then it struck Van what Majel was saying, or at least implying.

"You mean you see us as the children you can't have?"

"That may be a bit simplistic, but yes. We are much older than you." Majel stopped for a moment and closed his eyes, then reopened them after accessing the ship's database again. "In your Earth culture you might call it adoption."

Of the many possible motives that Van could have suspected, this one was outside them all. Was the human race up for adoption, so to speak? *Maybe,* Van thought. *We are looking for powerful help and don't have much to offer. Perhaps that's as good a description as there is.*

When he recovered, Van continued his questions. "Do we have a choice?"

Majel didn't laugh this time, but he gave a very wide smile. "Of course. We would like to help you, but if you don't want it, you are free to go."

"Easy for you to say," responded Van. "We haven't a clue how to get back."

"I'll send you back just the way you came if you want. If you don't want to go just yet, I would still like to visit your ship and meet your James Harris."

Van was warming up to this being and was starting to believe him.

"I would take you, but our shuttle crashed and is incapable of flying. In addition, the electrical storm has disrupted our communications and navigation systems. We can't communicate with the ship, much less get to it."

"I think you'll find that your shuttle is in perfect condition, and there is now no problem with communications or a storm. It was all an illusion I created to set you on the path of the tests."

"You mean we can leave whenever we want?" asked an astonished Rebecca.

"Of course," Majel said, toying with his medallion. With a wave of his hand, the trio found themselves standing in front of a perfectly good shuttle.

Still in a semi state of shock, Rebecca had enough presence of mind to quickly enter the shuttle via the extended ramp and went straight for her copilot station, which was in perfect order.

Switching on the communications system, she called the ship. "*New Horizons*, this is *Shuttle One*, how do you read?"

"*Shuttle One*, we read you loud and clear. What happened? We lost you for a few minutes in the storm."

"*New Horizons*, *Shuttle One*, did you say a few minutes?"

"Roger, you've been out of communications for about ten minutes."

"*New Horizons*, wait. Out." Rebecca twisted away from

the copilot's chair and departed the shuttle to where Van and Majel stood.

"Van," she said sternly, interrupting a conversation between the two men, "we do have contact, but the ship says we were only off-line for ten minutes. It was over twelve hours, wasn't it?"

Van nodded and then turned to Majel with a questioning look.

"Oh, that," said Majel "Yes, your adventures here only took a few minutes. The time must have seemed longer to you."

Both humans stood in silence. Any race that could do what Majel just did in ten minutes had to be respected.

Van was the first to respond. "We are beyond impressed, Majel. If you'll step inside the shuttle and take a seat, we'll be glad to take you to *New Horizons*." Majel could probably get there on his own, but he gladly took a seat.

"By the way," Van interjected, "could you teach us that trick of moving from one place to another so fast?"

"At the moment, I would say no. It takes a long time to acquire the skill, and simple training doesn't work," said the older man.

"Had to ask," Van said as he moved forward to take his seat.

CHAPTER 17

When Chen Lee received Mia's message, he was docked at the Sonaran orbital shipyard. A short time later, he went to the planning room that Dick Carson had appropriated. There he found Dick and Ross in conversation in front of one of the space charts.

"Captain Lee, come in. We were just talking about you."

Chen Lee smiled at Dick's words because he knew they meant they had a job for him.

"You got Mia's message, I assume?" Dick asked.

"I did, and it was good news even though she lost the signal."

"Indeed, but how to proceed is the question. What do you think, Ross?" Dick asked.

"I think we have several needs to consider. First, we need to get these pirate activities stopped. And at the same time, we need to get Rose back. Then, at some point we need to find the person leaking information to the pirates."

The other two men in the room stared at Ross for a moment. Dick broke the silence first. "Well said. Do you have an idea that rolls all that up?"

"The first two, yes. But you and Captain Lee will have to fill in the operational blanks in my thinking. As for the informant, I'm not sure yet. I am, after all, just a grunt."

The other two men were amused at Ross's description of himself. They knew his ideas and skills were proven.

"Go on," Chen Lee said.

"First, since we have been unsuccessful at pinning down where they dispose of their stolen goods and where they might celebrate, we need to find a way to attract the pirates to one place. If that works, we need to have a ship or two there to capture or destroy the pirate ships, except one."

"The one that has Rose on board," Dick said as he realized where Ross was going.

"Yes. I believe the chances are good the ship that escaped Mia will show up there, and we can pick up Rose's signal again."

"Then what?" Dick asked.

"There are two possibilities," Ross continued. "The first is overtaking the pirate ship, boarding her, and rescuing Rose. The second is to follow the pirates to where they are going and then effect a rescue."

"Sounds logical. Which of the two choices do you recommend?"

"The first is possible but has significant problems for Rose. To board, even under stealth, we reveal ourselves early to the pirates as soon as we penetrate their hull. That gives them all sorts of time to harm Rose. The second option, I believe, reduces the risks if they go to a base of theirs. Then it becomes a stealthy approach and recon followed by a precision action to first secure Rose, then to take out the pirates. We can bring our firepower to bear and not have such confining quarters as on a ship." Ross stopped a moment, thinking about what he had just said. Then he smiled and clicked his fingers. "That gives me another idea, about the informant I mean. If we can catch the leader alive, we think it's Reeb, we might be able to get the traitor's name from him. Of course, it would take some persuasion." Ross slowly pounded a clenched fist into the palm of the other hand.

"Captain Lee?" Dick asked, turning his attention to the force commander.

"I agree with Ross. We can board the pirate ship and take control, no problem. But we cannot guarantee Rose's safety. As Ross suggested, we would have a better chance of success if they retreat to a base. We may be able to capture Reeb, if he is the leader, as we believe. But how do we get the pirates to gather at a predictable place?"

"I have an idea related to the transit lanes," Dick said. "Before you depart the shipyard, I'll send you a target location, and you and *Hornet* can rendezvous, if that makes sense, and wait for the pirates to take the bait. How you deal with the pirates is your own business. But bring Rose back safely. And," Dick added, "let's not mention anything to anyone except Mia about chasing down the pirate leader and wringing information out of him. Understood?"

The two other men nodded and left to prepare for what they hoped would be an upcoming action.

Sutherland was loaded and underway in less than five hours. *Hornet* already had Federation and Guardian troops on board with their supplies. Chen Lee believed they, plus *Sutherland* and its added force of Ross's team, would be enough to meet any contingency.

"Navigation," called Chen Lee.

"Yes, Captain?" the navigation officer replied. He and all the other Guardian Force officers and crew accepted Chen Lee as captain readily. Not only because of his history with Guardian Force and the commander, but also because he was good at what he did and they respected him.

"Have we received a destination for this mission?"

"Yes, Captain."

"Set a course for the location."

"Already done."

Chen Lee appreciated the efficiency of this crew and wished he was a regular part of this professional force. "Very well. Helm, engage FTL as soon as you are ready. We don't want to keep Dr. Ramos waiting too long."

As the ship prepared to flash into space, the crew could be seen smiling. Like Rose had reflected, they also believed Guardian Force was a family, and they were headed to save one of their own. In Rose's case, most of the crew had a personal connection with her. Not only was she their doctor, but she was also famous on all known habitable planets and in space in general. Her achievements were a source of pride to them.

Dick sat in the big planning room alone, awaiting the routine group for the briefing he had just called. He was thinking over what Ross had said about the traitor before he'd left. Nobody but Chen Lee, Ross, and himself knew about *Hornet*'s fleeting discovery of Rose's locator beacon. As far as anybody knew, *Sutherland* had departed on a routine interdiction mission that, in fact, it had been scheduled to do before Mia's message had been received. For educational and training purposes, Ross had chosen to go along with a few of his men and women on *Sutherland*, leaving Jimmy Fletcher in charge of shipyard security.

The slight squeak of a door told Dick the first people were arriving. He turned in his chair to see Jimmy Fletcher followed by others, including Commodore Daman. A few moments later, Harry and a few Guardian Force members arrived.

Dick stood. "Thanks, everybody, for coming. Please be seated."

It only took a minute for all to sit. Harry, as usual, stood near the table, this time behind Dick. Jimmy walked to the chart wall and stood by.

"As you know, our intercept-to-cargo loss ratio has been improving. However, any loss of material is still a significant impact on production. The transit lanes help greatly, but we underestimated the sheer length of one of the lanes and our ability to patrol its full length." Jimmy used a long pointer to indicate the lane Dick was talking about.

"Therefore, we have no choice but to shorten it. Effective immediately, we are pulling in the start points of lane number one. Jimmy is showing you the effect of that on the main chart on the wall in front. This allows us to distribute our patrols more effectively on the shorter lane." Commodore Daman's hand went up. "Yes, Commodore?"

"If we do that, it will expose incoming cargo ships to increased pirate threats before they can reach the protected lane."

"Good point. However, the truth is we haven't been as effective as we could overall, so the risk seems small, especially way out there. Indeed, the extreme start point places extra stress on our assets and increases time to station and return. We believe drawing in the lane will cause us to be more effective and responsive, not less."

Daman didn't look convinced but sat back in his chair and said nothing more.

The discussion continued, but the main thrust of the event had been made. Many people departed alone or in pairs talking to each other.

As he had done before, Daman left the shipyard for Sonara and cautiously made his way to the old apartment building and the secret room. Seated on the chair in front of the microphone, Daman spoke. "This is Number 1. I say again, this is Number 1."

Daman had to repeat this several more times than usual.

Finally, Reeb answered, but he wasn't happy. "What the hell do you want? I'm busy!"

Daman recoiled in his seat. This was definitely different. "I have good news for you."

Reeb toyed with the idea of cutting the connection. He didn't need this distraction right now. But the idea of good news caused him to pause and see what the news was. "What good news?"

"The longest transient lane has been shortened. The start points have been moved in. There will be no patrols in those areas no longer in the lane."

Reeb only had to think for a few seconds, and a crooked grin made its way across his face. The *Reaper* could easily get there with some smaller ships. "Good, you saved my having to send a message through Space Guard, and you're safe. . . for now. Send me the details on the lane changes."

CHAPTER 18

V ICE ADMIRAL DAAN HAD HOPED he could send Sub Admiral Braak of Red Group 20-2 to command this mission. But Gulv made it clear he had to lead this attack himself. Instead, he would have to leave Braak in charge on the battle cruiser *Traggva*, the Red Sector 20 flagship. The ship was magnificent but in reality hadn't been able to get underway for some time. Those incompetent Browns could never keep it working.

Instead, he would take Braak's 20-2 force of two destroyers, three frigates, and the cruiser *Prydaa*. He would also take the cruiser *Rygia* from his old 20-1 command. The cruisers were also loaded with ground troops eager to fight in any way possible. However, there weren't enough additional ships left in that command to take along after the defeat of Captain Adaar. Those that remained would have to stay with the *Traggva* as protection. *I could take a few of the scout ships*, he thought. *Yes, I have enough that would not be seriously missed.*

Another reason to leave some ships behind was to protect himself politically in case he was accused of abandoning his post with no defense. He was all too aware that this mission was not sanctioned by the supreme leader nor the Blue Sector 20 governor. And two cruisers, two destroyers, three frigates, and a few scout ships should be enough to crush whatever opposition they would find.

Aboard his old flagship *Rygia*, Daan gave the command. "All ships, get underway. Form on *Rygia*." They were off to destroy the vermin that had been plaguing them. . . and subjugate another race for the empire. *The family will be proud,* Daan thought as his red crest rose.

Aboard *Hornet,* Mia Flores received a coded message from Chen Lee directing her to rendezvous with *Sutherland* at a specified location. Mia consulted the charts she had and found the spot.

Why way out there? she thought. But orders were orders, and with them coming from Captain Lee, it meant no diddling around. She sent the coordinates to Navigation.

"Navigation, chart a course to the point I just sent you. Helm, as soon as you get the location, turn us in that direction and proceed in FTL." She knew that in Galactic Force, response time was expected to be quick. The same held for Chen Lee, who maintained his cultural fast paced approach to life and tasks, sometimes known as "Chinese time."

Both officers responded together, "Yes, ma'am!"

Hornet and *Sutherland* rendezvoused half a light year from the former extreme start of Transit Lane 1. Mia shuttled aboard *Sutherland* and met Chen Lee and Ross in the ship's conference room.

She looked around at the room. It was much bigger than hers aboard *Hornet* but otherwise like ones she had seen before on Guardian Force ships like the *Victory.* Big oval table in the middle surrounded by comfortable chaises and large view screens in the front and both sides of the room. She took a seat next to Ross at the foot of the table and across from Chen Lee.

"Good to see you, Mia! It's been a while," Chen Lee said. Neither he nor Ross stood. That was part of the old military culture. Mia was another officer, and they treated her like one.

"Thank you. Good to be among friends again." Mia nodded and smiled at both men.

Getting right to business, Chen Lee pointed to the forward view screen. "As we can see, Dick Carson and Ross developed a plan to trap some pirates, and, we hope, the ship holding Rose. The outer portion of this lane has been shortened in order to invite the pirates to a quick and undefended cargo morsel. However, we will be standing by in stealth waiting for them.

"The object will be to destroy as many of the pirates as possible but allow the largest one to escape. That should be the *Reaper*, captained by the pest Reeb. To make sure it is the right ship before doing away with most of them, we need to look for Rose's locator and pinpoint the ship she is on. Ross thinks, as I do, it will be the *Reaper*.

"Hopefully, he will head for someplace safe like his home base, and we can follow. If all goes well, we retrieve Rose and capture Reeb and the base. We care less about keeping the base intact than we do about saving Rose and capturing Reeb, of course. There are a lot of questions we want to ask him."

Mia took all this in and nodded as she stared at the view screen. It made sense to her, and it gave her a chance to redeem herself for letting Rose get away from her before. Then she turned her attention to Chen Lee and said, "I'm in. When do we leave?"

"Ross has a package for you to take to your combat team that also contains some instructions for you."

Ross slid the sealed package to Mia. "As soon as you're ready, we'll get going."

Mia didn't have to be told any more. She stood, nodded, and left the room. The plan was underway.

It took the better part of a day before anything stirred in the spot of space the two stealthy warships were watching. Unfortunately, it wasn't pirates. Transit plans and identification codes confirmed it was the cargo ship *Pella* headed for Sonaran space and the orbital shipyard there. It made a relatively quick passage through the area now thought to be unprotected and into lane one with its cargo of raw materials.

Next came the cargo ship *Ratina* carrying dry goods and household materials in its inventory. This was starting to look like a failed plan.

Hornet picked up the anomaly first. Was it a radio transmission of some sort, like two ships talking with each other? The ship's communications officer pressed her headset closer to her ears to hear more clearly. Mia noticed the change in the woman's posture as she involuntarily bent forward, wishing she could get closer to the sound's origins.

"What is it, Helen?" she asked the communications officer.

"Not sure, ma'am. I thought I heard ship-to-ship chatter, but now it's gone." Then she looked sideways at nothing in particular and said, "Wait."

After a few more seconds, the communications officer relaxed just a little. "It is ship chatter, and it sounds like ships coordinating their positions. At least three or four maybe. But there's more." The young woman looked up at her captain, this time with a happy look of success. "I have Dr. Ramos's locator beacon."

"*Tuanis!*" called out Mia, clapping her hands together. Everyone knew what that meant by now.

———

Mia transmitted those details to *Sutherland* via laser link, and both ships listened and watched carefully for the emergence of the pirate force they were sure had now arrived in the area. It didn't take long. On the passive detection screens and like shimmering ghosts, five ships slowly appeared out of the blackness of space, four small and one relatively larger, then stopped. Like spiders, they waited for their prey.

"Which ship has the doctor's signal?" Mia asked.

"The bigger one in the middle, ma'am," said the sensor operator confidently.

Mia passed the information to *Sutherland* and Chen Lee via laser comms.

Chen Lee and his *Sutherland* crew made the same observation and reached the same conclusion as Mia and the *Hornet*.

Chen Lee personally took the laser comms microphone and said to Mia, "We'll come out of stealth and fire at the same time. *Hornet* will take the two small ships to the left of *Reaper*, and *Sutherland* will take the two on the right. With any luck, we'll put the fear of God into Reeb and he'll flee for home. Stay sharp, we may have to follow inside FTL, not an easy thing to do. Ready?"

Mia immediately responded, "Ready."

"Then on the count of three, we dump stealth and open fire. One. . . two. . . three!" Both ships appeared in space at the same time and opened fire on their assigned targets. All four small ships yielded to the larger weapons of the warships and were either destroyed or severely damaged and weren't going anywhere. Not so with *Reaper*. From a standstill, it pivoted to a new heading and shot away from the ambush. Shifting back to stealth, the warships followed.

A few hours into the chase, Chen Lee came up on laser comms to Mia. "His course has remained the same this whole time."

"Yes, steady as a rock," agreed Mia. "When we started the chase, however, we launched a stealthy drone to look ahead of his course, but so far, there's nothing there but empty space."

"The drone is still out there?" Chen Lee asked, an idea forming in his head.

"Yes, why?"

"He may be traveling this way to confuse or elude any potential followers. What if we had the drone transmit a short signal or, better yet, drop its stealth mode for an instant? Faced with a potential Guardian Force ship in front of him, he may decide to go where there's more protection."

"You mean like a base or other ships?" replied Mia as she started to see what Chen Lee was thinking.

"Yes. We can outrun him anytime we want. But as Ross pointed out to me, the risk to Rose is too great at this point to try to board. So, why not use him?"

"That makes sense. I'll make it happen." She ended the laser connection and called out, "Sensors!" the generic name used for sensor operators.

"Yes, ma'am?"

"Turn the drone's stealth mode off for a few seconds and then back on."

"Captain Reeb!" shouted a crewman on the bridge of the *Reaper*.

"What?" was all the gruff pirate would say.

"I just had a brief scan of a ship ahead of us. It was there and then it was gone."

"What kind of ship?" asked Reeb as he quickly stepped to the sensor station.

"Hard to say what type it was, but it had the characteristics of some of the Guardian Force ships we've seen before."

Reeb's attention was piqued. *Guardian Force out here? Ahead of us?* he thought as concern raced through his mind. He stood silent for a moment behind the sensor operator. Then he made up his mind.

"Helm, change course, head for location two. We'll find help there. When we get closer, alert our defenses and send our ID signal."

"Yes, sir."

Rose noted the *Reaper's* change of course and apparent change in speed as the engines rumbled more than before. She looked out her view screen porthole, but there was only black space. She wondered if she should try to communicate with someone. It would mean problems for her if she was detected, but she had learned a few things that others might need to know. Maybe a quick broadcast in the blind with a message hoping it would get through, then stop. So, she began.

"Guardian Force, this is Rose Ramos broadcasting in the blind with the following information. I am safe, for now. Being held by Captain Reeb. He has a secret base, probably on an asteroid. Well defended and self-sufficient. Has a major accomplice placed high in the Zarminian government, plus other lesser agents in various places. Suspect he is controlled by another person, location unknown. Will not transmit again, out."

Seeing the change in their quarry's course and speed, Mia clapped her hands together and laughed out loud, "Ha, it worked!" The chase she had fumbled before was on again, and this time with *Sutherland* and all its power.

"Captain!" called out the communications officer. "I have a message from Dr. Ramos."

Mia stopped her small celebration and looked sharply at the officer. "What?"

"We just had a short message from Dr. Ramos, in the blind."

"What did she say?" Mia asked, rotating her finger in rapid circles indicating she wanted him to hurry up.

The communications officer hit the replay button on his view screen, and the message played back for all to hear.

Not a second after hearing the message, Mia called out an order. "Get me a secure comms with *Sutherland*, now!"

CHAPTER 19

NEW HORIZONS REMAINED IN ORBIT over the planet for which they now had a name, Vespasian, thanks to their guest. It was not a name Majel drew from the ship's database; it was the real name.

Over the last several days, Van and his senior staff had learned much about the Naskapi and about Majel. And although there was an obvious bond forming between James Harris and the Naskapi Sachem, Van felt there was something like that developing between himself and the alien as well.

Harris was hosting Van and Majel in his cabin. The cabin had several comfortable chairs, and they sat facing each other. "Would you say, Commander, that your kind seeks peace and not war?"

Van glanced at Harris, remembering discussions like this the two of them had had over time. "I would say," Van said thoughtfully, "it is the general feeling of humans both on Earth and Zarminia. However, the ambassador and I agree that we have not yet reached the level of smooth coexistence the Naskapi apparently have. It has only been a few years since we united into one Federation, and even that has experienced growing pains. And the motivation for the formation of the Federation was more out of fear of the Arkon than the betterment of our civilization. Is that not like your culture and its fear of the Nokra?"

"Yes and no. Before the Nokra began to show a hostile nature toward us, we had already merged our various clans, as you might call them. Fighting the Nokra drew us closer."

"But these clans or suborders of yours have not gone away," observed Van, leaning forward in his chair. "You yourself said they are still part of your larger society, and you are the leader of one of them."

Majel smiled and said, "I think your phrase is 'touché,' Commander. Yes, we still have suborders, but the distinction now is mostly administrative. I am more like a magistrate and a representative of my order than a leader."

Van leaned back in his chair, satisfied he had made a meaningful discovery. Humans and the Naskapi were more alike than it had initially appeared. The Naskapi just had nearly a thousand years head start.

Later, Van, Frank, and Rebecca were gathered in Van's quarters reviewing the mission status.

"What more can we do here?" asked Rebecca as she tapped a stylus on Van's table. "Through Majel we now know, or at least suspect, there are no sentient life forms that can help us for over five hundred light years. And if you ask me, we don't have the time or resources to make that kind of trip unless Majel could just zap us there and back. But he said he couldn't—or wouldn't—if there's a difference."

Frank nodded. "She has a point, Van. What's holding us here?"

"Nothing. . . now," Van said, standing. "I just wanted to get a better understanding of Majel and his people. Thanks to James, we know a lot more, and I think we can trust him."

"So, we can get out of here?" Frank asked.

"I think so, as long as you know where we are. Do you?" Van said with a sly grin, then took Frank off the hook he had just set. "I don't know the answer either. Do you, Jennifer?"

The ever-present AI answered immediately. "No, Commander."

"I didn't think so. The only choice is to ask Majel's help again to at least get back to Altair. He was willing to do it before. I'm going to see him now in James's quarters. I'll let you know what I find out."

Van reached James's quarters in just a few minutes, knocked, and entered.

"Pardon the interruption, gentlemen, but I believe it's time for *New Horizons* to move on. However, since we don't know where we are, we need your help, Majel. Can you send us back to the Altair system?"

"If it were up to me, Commander, we could leave now. But it isn't," said Majel, slowly shaking his head.

"Why not? You were willing to do it before. I thought you were all-powerful and could do almost anything," Van responded, looking first at Majel and then at Harris. Harris just shrugged his shoulders, indicating he knew no more than Van.

"At the time, I could have and would have. Since then, however, the council has decided to deliberate," Majel said simply.

"The council? What council?" This was a new revelation to Van, and to Harris also.

"Ah, I failed to talk about that. I am sorry. You see, for important issues like this one, contact with a new race in this case, the Sachems often appoint a council to deliberate or arbitrate significant decisions or issues. A council was just appointed and is in session now."

Van asked the obvious question. "How long will it take?"

"I don't know. It has been several hundred of your years since the last council was appointed. That one lasted about a month, using your calendar."

"A month!" cried Van, starting to pace. "We have to stay here a month?"

"It could be longer. Or, it could be shorter," said Majel calmly.

Van couldn't speak. He paced faster, anger and frustration seething from every pore. Then he stopped, looked at the elderly Naskapi, and took a deep breath.

"Majel, you need to know something about us, this new class of life forms you just met. Generally, we want to be trusting and expect the same from others. We value truth, integrity, dependability, and, most of all, our sense of freedom and independence. We can be very good friends to those who keep these values in mind or serious enemies to those who don't. You say the Naskapi share the same views. However, you have violated them twice now under the cover of testing and the agency of an unknown, unseen council." Van started his pacing again but kept his eyes focused on Majel, pointing the occasional index finger at the older man when emphasis was required. "You stripped us of our freedom and toyed with the truth. Humans have gone to war for less, willing to die for these simple but ingrained precepts. Until now we have given you the benefit of the doubt, but you are trying our, and especially my, patience." Van stopped, waiting for his message to sink in.

Majel leaned backward in his chair as if being blown back by the force of Van's rhetoric and passion. Harris was speechless.

Recovering, Majel responded, "My sincere regrets, Commander. It has been a long time since we have met and dealt with another civilization. Obviously, we failed to remember the common courtesies that accompany contact with a new race. We also apologize for compromising your freedom and not knowing its value to you. Having said that, I hope you can understand that we also want to ensure that before we engage with another race, we want similar assurances. I hope you see our actions as a different but well-meant methodology."

Van's energy-filled anger was dissipating, him having said what he wanted to say and, hopefully, making his point. Majel's apology went a long way toward calming him down as well.

"I accept your apology and your own need for assurances. Now, if you don't mind, Ambassador Harris and I have some business to attend to." He motioned for Harris to follow him out of the room. When he thought he was far enough away from Majel, he stopped and looked at Harris. "I'm really pissed."

Harris smiled and said jokingly, "I never would have guessed."

Van ignored the comment. "I was starting to have some confidence in Majel, but this last thing about the council has me seeing things differently. Until now, I've refrained from calling this whole thing pure abduction, but that's what it is, don't you think?"

His friend absently turned and resumed walking, his hands

clasped behind him and his head lowered in thought. Van followed silently.

"I don't think I would go that far," Harris said. "Like you, I had built up some confidence and trust in Majel, then, as you say, *this* happened. On the one hand, I could say that holding us here is immoral and seemingly against what Majel says his people stand for. On the other hand, based on all our talks, I still have a feeling that he is OK, that he means us no harm, and this is likely a cultural difference in addition to being a first-contact scenario."

"That was my impression until this latest revelation," Van said, slowly shaking his head and calming down.

"However, what can we do about it?" said Harris, looking up at Van.

"That's the problem. We aren't in control, and even the slim options are bad ones."

"What options?" Harris asked. "I don't see any, not with Majel's capabilities."

"I know. My first thought was to just assume the reverse course that brought us here and go. Unfortunately, we don't know what that course was; even Jennifer doesn't know. We could try to capture Majel and try wringing out the truth, but I doubt we could get our hands on him before he'd disappear and reappear someplace else. We could even try to lure him to the surface and leave him there and try escaping. But again, we don't know what direction to go, and even if we did, he'd just blink us back here or some other place. I just can't see any workable alternative at the moment. Can you?"

"Not one," Harris said. "However, I still think that his intent and that of his council is to do no harm and eventually send us on our way."

Walking with his head down, Van said all he could: "I hope you're right."

CHAPTER 20

R EEB FINALLY REACHED SAFETY AT location two and disembarked *Reaper*. The facility was newer than the old asteroid base he'd lost to Guardian Force in the past, and cleaner. This was the safe spot that housed his accumulated fortune, which now also included the fortune of the previous Number 1, Ranard. In the better part of the last year, he had increased the base defense systems and created a new headquarters, which included living quarters, a command-and-communications center, and an underground bunker. He was heading for the command-and-communications center. His prisoner was taken to the living quarters and placed under armed guard in a guest room on the top level.

"What do our sensors show out there?" Reeb asked no one in particular as he strode boldly into the room, removing his helmet and gloves.

"Nothing on any sensors, Captain," said a man seated at equipment on his right.

Reeb turned to him and glowered. "And if something does show up, I don't care how small or vague, you will speak up, or there'll be a new sensor operator at your seat in the blink of an eye."

The small man gulped and could barely get out a response. "Yes, Captain."

The suggestion of a Galactic Force ship earlier was still worrying him more than the two ships that had attacked his force. At least he appeared to have outrun those two. More annoying, his plans to collect the various ransoms for Dr. Ramos had to be placed on hold temporarily, at least until after these immediate threats to his operations from the allied forces were resolved or eliminated. While Galactic Force was undoubtedly doing its normal duty of patrolling space, he now thought that they would likely do so with increased vigor knowing Dr. Ramos was at risk. He felt stupid for thinking that Galactic Force would react like any other fool from which he had demanded and extracted ransom in the past. But he still held out hope that the ransom for Rose might yet be paid.

Reeb fell more than sat into the center's command chair, one he had stolen from a cargo ship. Now that he was relatively safe on his own well-defended asteroid base, he could think. His initial feeling was to wait and do nothing. Keep a low profile for a while, hoping he had made a clean escape. On the other hand, that was a little too much suspense for him. Instead, he dispatched several of his smaller ships to patrol approaches to the base. He also had an emergency escape plan he began to review if it was needed.

What Reeb wasn't aware of was the effect of his Arkon programming. It was working against his internal desire to depart this sector completely and, perhaps, come back much later when things had calmed down. Or, maybe never.

The *Sutherland* and *Hornet* slowed and stopped. Their chase had come to rest on a large asteroid ahead of them. Chen Lee noted that Rose's signal was still steady and called for Ross to meet him in his quarters. He also asked the communications officer to patch in Mia Flores via short-range laser communications.

Chen Lee and Ross sat a small table with a speaker module in the center.

"Can you hear me, Mia?" Chen Lee asked.

"Loud and clear Captain."

"We were glad to hear Rose's message and that she is safe, relatively speaking. She risked a great deal in making that transmission. I don't think she realized she and her captors were so close to the asteroid base she told us about. But the idea of a highly placed agent on Zarminia has to get back to Dick. I launched a communications drone to him with the message."

"Good!" Mia said.

"Ross Taylor is here with me to discuss what he plans to do. Ross, go ahead."

"Thank you. First, we need to recon the base to see what we're facing. Then we need to locate Rose before we do an assault."

"How do we do that?" Chen Lee asked.

"I go down in a combat shuttle in stealth mode and look around. I'll take a few guys with me, but the main assault force will stay behind on *Sutherland* and *Hornet* until we know more. If I can get Rose out on my own, I'll do it. Then it will be up to you whether to just blow the place up or try to take prisoners."

Chen Lee realized that this asteroid base could be an asset to Guardian Force, and therefore, he wanted as much of it intact as possible.

"I'd rather not blow the place up if I can avoid it," Chen Lee responded. "And it would be important to capture their leader, Reeb, and get a look at his records and data logs."

"I understand and expected that's what you'd want. In any case, the recon comes first, then Rose, and then anything else."

"I agree. Mia, any comments?" Chen Lee asked.

"Not really. Our troopers are ready to go when called. All weapons and shuttles are up and ready. Just give us the call when you want us to play."

Chen Lee liked Mia's attitude. As long as he had known her, she had always been ready for a challenge and quick to respond. Out of habit and even though Mia could not see him, he tapped two fingers on his table, a Chinese way of saying thank you. He gave Ross a nod, and the big man pushed up out of his seat with ease and disappeared ahead of a closing cabin door.

As Chen Lee watched from *Sutherland*, the launch and flight down to the asteroid base was uneventful. The stealth gear on the shuttle was working as expected. To begin, they did a high-level recon just to map out the base and its facilities. After that, a slow

low-level recon looked for energy emissions, weapons, and of course, Rose's locator beacon.

The team spotted numerous weapons positions, as well as a few small craft and the *Reaper*. However, to Chen Lee and others, one building stood out from the rest. First, it was newer than all the others. Second, it had a variety of antennas sprouting from its roof. Third, there were more energy emissions coming from it than any other building. And fourth, Rose's locator beacon was coming from it.

Rose was lying back on the cot that served as a bed in this bare-bones room when she heard something familiar. She sat up and, by force of habit, pressed her finger behind her left ear.

"Rose, this is Ross. How do you hear?"

Could it be true, could Ross actually be nearby?

"Ross? I can't believe it. I've been waiting a lifetime to hear from somebody!" She lowered her hand from her ear and wiped away the tears that had started flowing.

"It's me and I have friends. First of all, how are you? Are you free to walk around?"

Still wiping away tears, Rose managed to say, "I'm fine. I'm fine. I'm also free to walk around, but I'm locked in a room at the top of the building I'm in."

"What about the others? Is there a Captain Reeb around someplace?"

Finally getting control of her emotions, Rose thought for a moment, then said, "Yes, Reeb is here. Most of the people in this building are in a command post one floor down. I saw it when they brought me in from his ship, the *Reaper*."

"Good. Where are you on the top floor?"

Rose walked over to a window and looked out at the asteroid base. "I'm not sure of my exact location, but I can see the *Reaper* from where I'm standing and what looks like a fuel dump just past it."

"OK, just a minute," said Ross as he looked over the map

they'd made and then the central building. He had her position in a second! She was in a corner room on the top level.

"Rose, I know where you are. Walk to the center of the room and stand by."

Rose didn't have to be told twice. She nearly leaped from her position in front of the window and stood firmly in place, waiting for what she was sure to be transport from this horrid room to the safety of Ross and the shuttle she surmised he was in.

However, no sooner had she taken her place than there was a rattle at the lock and the door flew open.

"Come with me!" a gruff little man in ill-fitting clothes demanded.

But Rose stood frozen in place, hoping the transport would hurry up.

"What's the matter, you gone deaf? I said come with me. The captain wants to see you."

Still, Rose did not move. *Hurry up, Ross,* was ringing over and over in her head.

The pirate messenger had enough of waiting, and he stepped forward, grabbed the prisoner, and dragged her out of the room.

In the combat shuttle, Ross waited to see Rose appear. When she didn't, he checked with his sensor operator. "What happened?"

"We lost the lock, Ross. She isn't in the same place."

"You still have her locator signal?"

"Yes, but the transporter can't get a lock. She must be lower in the building."

The small pirate led Rose down the stairs to the operations center and a waiting Reeb.

"You're a doctor and I need your skills," he said, staring at the woman.

Rose stood up straight. "What for?"

"What's wrong with this man?" Reeb pointed to a young pirate doubled over in pain on the floor next to a console.

Rose said nothing, but her training kicked in as she rushed to the young man's side.

Carefully helping him to roll to one side, she asked, "Where do you hurt?"

With a struggle, the man pointed to a spot on his right side at belt level. Rose placed her hand there and pressed. The man screamed in pain and threw up.

The others in the room recoiled at the involuntary reaction and the smell.

Equally disgusted but holding in a reaction suggesting weakness, Reeb asked, "Well?"

"He has appendicitis and needs an operation *now*," Rose said.

"You can do that here?"

"No, I need an operating room, a hospital. Where is yours?"

Reeb thought for a moment. "The medical facility is located on the other side of the base. I can't send him there yet. Can't you do anything to help here?"

Looking at the suffering young man again, Rose said, "Unfortunately, no. I don't have the equipment or the medicine here I need."

A faint trace of regret seemed to pass across Reeb's face as he raised his pistol and fired a red charge into the shaking man. "Now he doesn't need any help. Take her back to her room and clean this mess up."

Rose was still on the floor next to the dead man, recoiling from the shot and the man who had delivered it, a hand involuntarily raised in a fruitless gesture of protection if Reeb fired at her, too. She had started to think Reeb had more humanity in him after the dinner aboard the *Reaper*. Apparently, she'd been wrong on that count. The same small pirate grabbed her outstretched hand and jerked her to her feet, then hauled her off to the upper floor and her prison room.

"Got her!" yelped the sensor technician. "Got a lock."

"Then get her up here pronto," Ross said sharply.

The short pirate who had just pushed Rose into the room was dazzled by a bright light behind him as he started back through the doorway. He turned to look, but there was nothing. Not even the prisoner. He regained his wits, turned, and ran toward the operations center.

Moments later, he burst into the command center, shouting something Reeb couldn't understand.

"What is it, man?" Reeb shouted back as he gave a solid backhand to the now tumbling and nearly incoherent man.

Pulling himself off the floor and shaking his head to clear the stars, the man could only say, "She's gone!"

"What do you mean 'she's gone'?" Reeb shouted again, grabbing the man by his pullover shirtfront and lifting him off the ground.

With flailing feet and gasping for air, the man croaked, "She was there. . . and then there was a bright light. . . and then she wasn't there."

Reeb dropped him to the floor and went directly to the sensor station.

"What's out there?" he demanded.

The operator, looking first at the shaking man on the floor and then at Reeb, replied, "Nothing, sir!"

"Impossible! Sound the base alert. We have intruders!" Reeb looked around the room, hoping, perhaps, somebody had an answer for what had just happened.

From the stealthy shuttle drawing away from the pirate base, Rose looked at the nearest view screen and blinked as red lights started to flash everywhere.

"Surprise is gone now," Ross said absently.

Rose couldn't respond as she clung to the big black man and wouldn't let go.

Ross held her tight as he softly said, "That's OK, baby girl, you're safe now and in the first step to going home. Just a little while." Then, thinking of the message Rose had sent, he added a few words. "You know, that was a brave thing you did sending that message. Chen Lee got it off to Dick as soon as possible." He felt Rose squeeze him just a little harder in response.

By the time the shuttle arrived inside *Sutherland's* flight bay and pressure was equalized, Rose had regained her composure. "Thank you, Ross. I'll never forget this."

"Well, there's more than just me involved," the big man said as the shuttle ramp lowered.

Rose saw Chen Lee standing there waiting to greet her. She'd never felt more like such an integral part of Guardian Force before. It was a big family, all right.

Chen Lee, Ross, and Rose sat at the circular table in Lee's quarters. Once again Mia was tuned in by laser communications. Chen Lee opened.

"For your information, Mia, Rose is safe and sound and with us here."

Unseen by those on the *Sutherland,* the five-foot-four Mia was bouncing up and down on her toes, her shiny, black, shoulder-length hair bouncing in rhythm. But they could hear as the *Hornet* team cheered in the background.

After a moment, Chen Lee continued, "She has given us all the information she has on the central building where Reeb operates. She didn't see it all, but it's the best we have. When Ross went in to retrieve Rose, he loosed a number of fireflies, and it shouldn't take long to get a really good picture for the assault team.

"When Ross is satisfied, he will give the order to launch from both ships and will coordinate the attack. There are two things we want to do. The first is capture Reeb himself. We need to interrogate him. Second, and I mean second, save the base for future use if we can."

Finally, Chen Lee said, "Any questions? No? Then take your guidance from Ross, and good luck. Rose, may I see you after this?"

Rose nodded.

The message Chen Lee passed to Rose was from Dick Carson. "Got your important message, especially about an agent in high places. Am shocked. Narrows our search tremendously, however. Get here quick. Holding a courier ship for you."

Chen Lee knew the courier ship *Vega* was waiting to whisk her to *New Horizons*. He tapped Rose on her shoulder and said, "We have a combat shuttle ready in the flight bay. You had best take it before the assault starts."

To his surprise, however, a calmer Rose turned to him and said, "I'm not going anywhere while Reeb is still free. Tell Dick he can hold the courier ship till I get there."

———————

Captain Lee leaned toward the main view screen on the bridge of the *Sutherland*. From his command chair, he nodded as it became apparent to him what had to happen next. Ross was next to him when he spoke.

"Ross, before I send you or anybody down there again, I want to eliminate all the weapons you mapped out. Between *Hornet* and *Sutherland*, we can do that pretty quickly and eliminate the obvious threats to our ships and our shuttles. Then it will be your turn. What will you do?"

Ross was ready, having given this a great deal of thought when doing the recons.

"The most valuable target is the same building we got Rose from. She saw Reeb there and what they were doing. Based on her description, it's their command-and-control center and probably has all their historical data, assuming the pirates kept any. Plus, Reeb is there. After your ships get done with the fire mission, our force will surround the building and enter from two places. The first group will transport to Rose's room and hold. The second group will make a forced entry from the main air lock. If we're quick, which we are, we'll catch most of them between the two forces, and it should be over quickly."

"Should be and reality are not always the same," replied Chen Lee. "Is there a backup plan?"

"Not really. This will be a manpower-intensive mission. The plan is to overwhelm them."

"And if Reeb isn't in the building?"

Ross nodded and gave the only possible answer. "Then we have to go looking for him. That could take some time."

"Yes," Chen Lee said, massaging his chin as he thought about Ross's simple plan. "Very well. You're the expert here; we'll do as you say. Is there anything else we can do from here?"

Ross nodded. "You can disable or destroy all the ships you can see on the base. That way Reeb and others can't escape. . . unless, of course, there are a few ships we can't see."

"In that case, we'll destroy any building we think could hide and launch an escape ship, providing there is no activity at the target. We want to minimize harming any prisoner labor, should there be any," Chen Lee said. "Get on with your preparations. I'll coordinate our plans with *Hornet* as well as the bombardment." Ross left the bridge, and Chen Lee got on the laser comms to Mia Flores aboard *Hornet*.

Reeb was fidgeting in his command chair when the first plasma and laser shots struck his defenses and several of the base buildings. There was nothing he could do, but he yelled at people anyway.

"Return fire, you fools!" he screamed as he pounded the arms of his chair. "Hit those ships before they kill us all!"

"But we have no targets, sir," said a nervous weapons operator. "They fire and then they disappear."

"Then fire where you think they are! Anything is better than just sitting here."

The crews tried, and the defense guns and missiles fired multiple shots with no results. Then, one by one, all defenses fell silent under the barrage from space.

Reeb's next impulse was to get to the *Reaper*. In fact, he was donning his pressure suit helmet and gloves while making for the center door when he heard a shout from one of the console operators.

"*Reaper* has been hit! So have the other ships, sir." Taking their cue from Reeb, the rest of the crew who didn't already have pressure suits on started donning them.

If losing the *Reaper* wasn't bad enough, there was a dull blast from the front of the building, and pressure in the command room started dropping. With most of the pirates occupied with survival on their own, Reeb headed down the stairs toward the bunker, along with a few hand-chosen people he normally kept close.

CHAPTER 21

A S DISORGANIZED AS THEY WERE initially, the remaining pirates quickly reverted to their defensive and offensive ways, and Ross found himself in a real fight. Close-quarters combat meant, among other things, there was lots of cover for both sides. More importantly, after the initial surprise, advantage can easily fall to the occupants. Then there was the room-by-room clearing of a relatively intact building in which defenders and aggressors are often intermixed. The fight raged on for the better part of a half hour until resistance ceased. Not because the pirates gave up, but because those who remained were all dead. But the elusive Reeb was nowhere to be seen.

Looking around, Ross saw a stairway leading to a lower level. Silently, Ross pointed to the stairs and gave hand signals to a few men to follow him. They slowly made their way down the stairs, shifting their weapons back and forth while loosening some fireflies. But they saw nobody. A few steps from the bottom of the stairs was a large sealed hatch. Ross tried to manually open it, but no luck. This was no time for finesse, so he had Robby Calhoun wire the door with explosives and took cover. When everyone was alerted, Ross nodded to Robby, and the door blew free of its hinges and clattered to the floor as the explosive detonated with a subdued *harrumph*.

Like the well-trained team they were, they made an orderly entry, with each person calling "Clear" when he or she had their sector under control. Again, however, there was nobody there.

Robby broke team silence. "What the hell, Ross? Where'd they go?"

Ross was just as puzzled. "Beats the shit out of me. They didn't go up and they didn't go outside. We would have seen them. They had to come down here." Then it hit him. "Start looking for a hidden door or something. Be sure to check outside this room also."

Everyone started searching their sectors for some sign of a hidden exit. After half an hour of frustrated searching, however, they all came to the same conclusion. Robby gave it form.

"There ain't one."

Ross nodded in agreement. But that just wasn't possible. He sat down on the edge of a console and braced the butt of his shoulder weapon in the console's center. There was a click, and one of the wall-mounted consoles slowly motored away from the wall, hinged at one side. Inadvertently, Ross has tripped a console switch, which opened the door into a dark passageway.

Following Robby's helmet light into the passageway, Ross couldn't see an end, or anything at all.

"Get some more people down here, Robby. We have to follow this to wherever it leads, and no telling how many pirates are at the other end."

When his team had grown to a level acceptable to him, Ross took the lead into the tunnel. Fortunately, the tunnel was high enough that despite his great size and height, he didn't have to bend over. Again, they released fireflies as the team switched their helmets to night vision and proceeded.

The *Sutherland* technicians had converted Ross's surface map to a form that could be projected onto the team's HUDs. In this way, they could get a general picture of their route compared to the surface buildings and other landmarks topside. It quickly became apparent they were on their way to one of the larger buildings on the base. For reference sake, the technicians had also given a numeric label to each building or landmark. They were headed for number sixty-seven.

Ross made a call to the *Sutherland* and Chen Lee.

"Looks like we're headed for location sixty-seven. Anything to report on that building?"

There was silence before Chen Lee came up on the frequency.

"Yes. That's a building we hit with plasma fire, suspecting it could be a location for potential escape vessels. Don't expect much when you get there."

"Roger. But we have to have a look. We think Reeb went there."

"Good luck. We'll be standing by." Gone was the old "over and out" of past communications protocols. Guardian Force just no longer had a use for it in an age of nearly perfect communications.

Ross halted and held up a clenched fist as they came to another hatch. This one opened with relative ease. But nobody stepped through it. They knew better. Instead, the fireflies, which had gathered at the hatch, were now freed to explore whatever awaited them beyond.

Reeb was pissed beyond belief. His "secret" escape shuttle and its building were collapsed in a central heap of mangled, charred matter. There weren't even walls to the building left!

He threw down a piece of what he thought was a remnant of a shuttle thruster and cursed using some strange Zarminian oaths. His four companions just looked up and away, not wanting to focus Reeb's wrath on them. So intense was his rage, he failed to notice the dozen suited men surround his small party. Then, out of a corner of an eye, he glimpsed a weapon fall to the ground. When he looked up, his four guards had raised their arms and hands in the universal signal of surrender. With a dozen rifles leveled at him, he knew it was over.

One of the suited figures, the largest one, stepped forward and said, "Captain Reeb, I presume. Been looking forward to meeting you."

Cleaning up the rest of the base was relatively easy. Most of the buildings and facilities were occupied by slave laborers who were happy to be freed from this place. The relatively few guards gave up with only a token fight when they heard their captain had been captured.

Guardian Force had acquired another base.

Chen Lee and Mia shuttled down to the captured pirate base where Ross met them. "This is it," Ross said, arms out, turning in a circle. "Pirate HQ. You can see it's more sophisticated than you might expect, but the real place of interest is down below. Follow me." He motioned with a wave of his hand and led them to the lowest level of the complex, pointing out how the tunnel had been hidden behind a console.

"We would have missed this tunnel if I hadn't accidently flipped a switch. . ." Ross stopped. Chen Lee had walked across the room and was studying something. "What is it, Captain Lee?" He and Mia crossed the floor to where Chen Lee was bent down looking at a piece of electronics gear.

"This piece of equipment looks like communications gear. See the microphone?" Chen Lee stood and pointed.

The other two both nodded as they looked at the big electronics box, then back at Chen Lee.

"But it is different than all the other pieces of equipment in the room," Chen Lee continued. "Plus, it has strange writing on it."

This time Mia and Ross bent low to look at the writing above the dials and across the top, then stood and nodded in agreement.

"What does it mean?" Mia asked, looking over at Chen Lee.

"I have no idea," he answered, "but I have the feeling that whatever it is, we shouldn't mess with it until somebody smarter than us has a look."

"You mean Harry?" asked Ross.

"Yes."

CHAPTER 22

J UST AS VAN WAS GETTING over his anger at the revelation of the debate of the Naskapi council, klaxons started going off and general quarters was called.

"General quarters, general quarters. Man your battle stations. This is not a drill!"

Van immediately abandoned his thoughts on the council and rushed to the ship's bridge to join Frank at the captain's chair. "What's happening?"

Frank, his ubiquitous club stowed away, turned to Van and said, "We have unknown ships approaching. We made a call but got no response. Two of the corvettes were already on patrol and have formed up on us as protection. The third corvette is suddenly grounded in her flight bay, problem unknown. Finally, Danny is launching fighters as a CAP. *New Horizons* is underway and picking up speed."

A quick and succinct report. Van liked it. He also remembered that Danny had given up command of a ship to become the carrier air group commander (CAG) even though there was no such job. . . until he persuaded Frank to create one. Small, fast ships were Danny's love, and Van's heart was there also.

Snapping out of his reverie, Van focused on the current problem. *Who or what are these guys? Where did they come from?* he asked himself.

Satisfied Frank and his team were on the ball, Van patted Frank's shoulder and retreated to the flag bridge, which was fully manned during general quarters.

Van took his command chair and called the ship's AI.

"Jennifer, what can you tell me?"

"There are seven ships approaching, Commander. Two are destroyer size, one possible cruiser, and the rest are small escorts. They are braking now. My sensors detect they have shields up, and there are energy build-ups in all ships."

"Frank knows all this as well?"

"Yes, Commander. He heard what I just said to you."

"Good, make another call to them. Tell them we are friendly explorers. Use your translation capabilities and transmit in all known languages."

"Yes, Commander."

Van waited a minute, then asked, "Any response, Jennifer?"

"No, Commander."

Then Van tapped into Frank's implant. "Frank, keep your distance if you can, see if we can outrun them. I'd rather avoid a fight."

"You bet," answered Frank.

That's all Van needed to hear. "Jennifer, get Majel up here right away."

"Yes, Commander."

Ten minutes later Majel was escorted onto the flag bridge by James Harris and Brice Johnson. Van noted the security men outside the bridge entrance.

Without leaving his chair, Van looked over at Majel. "What is this? Do you know who these people are?"

"I am as surprised as you, Commander. I don't recognize the ships."

"What can you do about it? Use your advanced skills and persuade them to halt and at least talk."

"I have tried to contact them to no avail. As for my advanced powers, as you call them, what would you have me do?"

"If they won't talk, get rid of them. Just running from them is incredibly dangerous out here in the unknown."

"I am sorry, Commander. I cannot take aggressive actions. It would be against our beliefs."

"Then blink us out of here!"

"I cannot do that either, Commander. Not as long as the council is in session. I haven't the power."

"Terrific," Van commented in disgust as he turned to focus on the view screens around him and the various reports from the bridge crew.

Two hours had passed, and the engagement had turned into a chase of the *New Horizons'* force. They dared not go into FTL unless absolutely necessary. They knew absolutely nothing about the space they were in.

Then a sensor operator called out, "Unknowns have increased speed and are closing, Commander."

"Our speed?" Van asked.

"Short of FTL, we are going as fast as we can," the helm officer answered.

For this ship, that was about 0.2c. The corvettes and the fighters could go faster, but they had to stay with the relatively lumbering *New Horizons.*

"Enemy ships firing, Commander!" shouted an anxious sensor operator.

Van was about to call Frank to take evasive actions, but Frank had already done so.

Several green plasma balls raced through the position *New Horizons* would have occupied had Frank not maneuvered. But Van knew it wouldn't last. The firing continued, and *New Horizons* and her corvette escorts started firing back. The CAP remained overhead in anticipation of an enemy fighter or small-craft threat. . . which suddenly appeared. The four smaller enemy craft began closing on *New Horizons.* Two were hit by fire from his ships and slowed with obvious damage. But two continued on, closing rapidly on *New Horizons.* That was the signal for the CAP to go into action.

Unknown to Van and Frank until now, Danny Ramos was in the

lead of the four Guardian Force attacking fighters, and everyone recognized his voice.

"Alfa flight, this is Alfa One. Alfa Three and Four, take the bogey on the right. Alfa Two and I will take the one on the left. Don't miss!"

The enemy's two remaining small craft, each about the size of a gunboat, flew on undeterred by the oncoming fighters. They opened fire on the fighters but could not initially grasp the fighters' tactics.

Both pairs of fighters successfully made a pass firing plasma shots at their respective targets. Danny scored the first hit.

"Way to go, One!" shouted one of the pilots.

"Don't watch me, concentrate on your own targets!" the pilot yelled, a rebuke none of the pilots had time to dwell on.

"Alpha Three is hit!" called his wingman, Alfa Four. Then there was a red-orange blossom in the darkness of space marking the death of Alfa Three.

"Shift to missiles," Danny called out just before his first missile streaked out to its target. Another red-orange blossom emerged where Danny's target had been.

"Two, this is One, let's go help Four." But no sooner had Danny's words left his mouth than there was another fiery bloom in a fighter battle. It struck him in the heart. More than that, it pissed him off.

The two remaining fighters rolled in unison onto the path of the last enemy small craft. As if of one mind, both pilots released a missile at the same time. They watched as the crystalline vapor trail of each missile successfully penetrated the small ship's defenses and struck home in a fiery ball of debris.

"Take that, you bastard!" Most people thought that was Danny, but weren't exactly sure. It didn't matter. The two fighters rejoined the CAP as *New Horizons* flew on.

Undeterred by the loss of their small escorts, the three remaining enemy ships continued the pursuit, each firing bright green bursts of plasma, which were absorbed by the shields of the three Guardian Force ships.

One of the corvettes, Van thought it might be the one commanded by Elsa Muller, started falling behind. He heard Frank make repeated calls to the corvette, but there was no answer. *New Horizons* stepped up her firing, hoping to attract fire away from the corvette, but it was no use. Nearly all the enemy's firepower shifted to the now obviously crippled corvette. Then it happened. Van watched as the brave ship started trailing gasses and pieces of hull, small ones at first, then larger ones until the ship came apart completely. There was no fireball. No red-orange blossom. Just a scattering of parts and, Van knew, bodies.

Next, the two destroyer-sized ships began to speed up, one concentrating fire on the remaining corvette and the other on *New Horizons*. Van watched as Frank made an effort to shield the smaller ship by attempting to move *New Horizons* between the destroyer and the corvette. But the corvette commander wouldn't have it. The closer *New Horizons* tried to get, the farther the corvette moved away, until Frank gave up in admiration.

As if on signal, the flight bays of both Guardian Force ships opened and released additional fighters and combat shuttles, all of which sped off to attack the two destroyers. The enemy ships tried maneuvering, but the swarm of smaller ships with their stings started having an effect. The lead destroyer took a hit from *New Horizons*, and then a dozen more from the fighters and shuttles. It started falling behind. It only took two more shots from *New Horizons* to start it tumbling out of control into space. But the second destroyer came on.

Now it was *New Horizons'* turn. The remaining destroyer began concentrating most of its fire on the big fleeing ship. Then the cruiser took aim. Her fireballs were white, not green, and huge.

"*New Horizons'* shields are down to thirty percent, Commander," called a concerned flag bridge console operator. Van knew they were getting low, but the action in space had diverted his attention. Frank undoubtedly knew, but he was a fighter and willing to slug things out.

"Frank!" called Van over his implant. "We can't continue this."

"I agree, but what else can we do?"

"Bring more of *New Horizons'* firepower to bear. We have to use her broadsides."

"But that'll slow us down and give the enemy a bigger target as we turn. Besides, we're going too fast. At this speed we'd never be able to make a turn and present a broadside."

"Not going to turn. If we slam on the brakes, we'll get both ships to pass us or at least draw even."

It was an old fighter-pilot trick. When the bad guy was on your butt, pull back the throttle, and maybe hit the speed brakes, and with any luck the bad guy would go screaming past and into your forward guns. This wouldn't be quite as dramatic. All they needed to do was get the enemy ships to react late and come within the dozens of weapons not capable of firing to the rear.

Van knew Frank was smiling. After all, Frank was an ex-Air Force fighter pilot and knew the trick. Van had even used it in a recent simulator flight, which now felt like ages ago.

"Just make sure our corvette friend knows what you're about to do," was all Van had to say.

It took a few minutes for the corvette captain to believe what Frank and the *New Horizons* were about to do. But he agreed there wasn't much left for them to do. It was better than nothing. So, he crept ahead of the bigger ship, which would take longer to slow than his relatively small one. When in position, he gave the "ready" to Frank.

Frank had alerted engineering about what was going to happen. Essentially, the main engines would be cut for only a few seconds while the helm operator hit his forward thrusters. If both were done just right, they would slow the big ship enough to cause the pursing ships to pull alongside or pass them by. Either was acceptable. It didn't hurt that Frank had been lucky enough to get both Bob Cooper and Elaine Parker assigned as the chief engineers. This was an old and experienced team.

Firing from the remaining two enemy ships continued. The corvette was receiving less as it pulled farther away.

"Commander, shields down to twenty percent and falling." This time the sensor operator was definitely worried.

"Very well," Van said calmly from his chair, but he was thinking, *Come on, Frank, anytime!*

The big ship shuddered a little and, in some parts of the interior, went deathly quiet as it slowed. But only for a few fleeting seconds, then everything returned to normal, if combat was normal. If the gamble worked, they should be exchanging major fire soon.

It was impossible to say what went through the minds of the two enemy ship commanders as they began rapidly overtaking their prey, but what had been a winning chase turned into a life-and-death broadside battle in seconds.

New Horizons opened fire first with all guns and missiles on both sides that could be brought to bear: one side at the destroyer and the other at the cruiser.

The destroyer was the first to go. Overpowered by the larger ship on one side and the corvette slightly ahead on the other, it shed gasses, liquids, and parts until there was nothing left but small pieces of glowing debris. But the cruiser was a different story.

Van breathed a sigh of relief as the plan appeared to be working. But soon it was apparent that *New Horizons* might be overpowered. Then, over the flag bridge speakers, he heard, "Tally ho!" A voice he instantly recognized as belonging to Danny Ramos.

After the attack on the first destroyer, Danny had gathered the ragtag combination of fighters and combat shuttles and called in to Frank. For some reason Frank had told him to hold off in safety until called, which he had done. Then he'd seen the maneuver, which he'd also recognized as an old fighter-pilot trick. It had been amazing to watch, until Frank had called out to Danny, "Alfa flight, cleared in hot."

Laser shots, plasma blasts, and missiles sprang from Danny's small harrying craft. A few of his ships were hit and destroyed by the Arkon cruiser defensive fire, but the diminutive surprise force was having an effect. Slowly, the cruiser's fire power began to dwindle as turrets and missile launchers were hit by Danny's force. And the cruiser started to slow. Then all fire from the enemy ship stopped.

"Cease fire!" commanded Van. Then there was a slight flash.

Van looked around him. He wasn't on the flag bridge. He was standing in the center of James Harris's cabin with only James and Majel present. Both were seated.

Then it hit him. "You did it again!" he said, pointing at Majel with more than just a little irritation. "You tested us a fourth time. Didn't my speech teach you anything about us?"

Majel sat calmly in his chair, a smile on his face, and the tips of his fingers touching. "Believe me, your speech had a significant impact on me and the council. But I didn't implement the test. The council did, and it was set in motion before you spoke. They wanted one last assessment of your capabilities and your values."

Harris, who had also just figured it out, asked, "Did we pass?"

"Yes. We find your tenacity, skill, loyalty, and compassion for the enemy to be very commendable."

Van stood with his hands on his hips, glaring at Majel. All he could say was, "Can we go now?"

Majel nodded.

CHAPTER 23

BACK ON *SUTHERLAND*, ROSS AND his team had been interrogating Reeb for hours with very little success. Reeb had no problem admitting to being a pirate. After all, everybody knew it. But with regard to the identity of his informant, Reeb was silent. He neither could nor would shed any light on the strange equipment they'd found at the base command center.

"I've reached the limit of my capabilities, Captain Lee," said Ross. "No matter what we try, Reeb resists what we really want to know. Either that, or he actually doesn't know, which I find hard to believe."

Sitting across from Ross at the meeting table in his quarters, Chen Lee nodded as Ross spoke. Rose sat attentively, listening.

"I certainly can't add anything to this mystery. What do you think, Harry?" Chen Lee asked. Harry had just arrived aboard *Sutherland* at Chen Lee's request.

"I don't have an answer yet, Captain. I will need to see the equipment you found to know more. When can I do that?"

"Right now if it will get us answers."

"I'm going with you, Ross," Rose said.

"I don't think —" Ross started to say, but she cut him off.

"I do think," she said sharply. "You forget I have a big stake in this whole affair, and I'm a doctor. You may need me."

Ross looked over at Chen Lee, who paused a moment before nodding his approval.

Chen Lee had Ross, Rose, and Harry shuttled to the asteroid surface and to the pirate command center. Robby greeted them at the entrance to the lower-level control room. He and several other

Guardian Force troopers had been left behind to guard the room and its mystery equipment.

As soon as Harry saw the device, he said, "It is Arkon equipment."

The simple statement stopped everyone in their tracks. Arkon equipment here? How could that be?

Ross was the first to recover from the shock. "What kind? What's it for?"

"Unknown, Mr. Taylor. But the writing on the face is Arkon. It is a good thing Captain Lee made sure it was not turned on, especially if it is what I think it is."

"Like what?" Rose asked.

"I need to examine it more closely to provide an answer. I recommend all of you leave this room and close the hatch behind you. Do not come in until I say you can."

Trusting Harry knew what he was talking about, they did as he said. When everyone had left and the hatch was closed, Harry switched on the Arkon communications device.

Standing outside the room, the Guardian Force men and women either stood against a wall or took a seat on the floor. This was likely to take some time. Ross, on the other hand, fidgeted and walked around. In less than five minutes, however, the hatch opened and Harry announced, "It is an Arkon communications system. But there is more to it. Could you have Mr. Reeb brought down here?"

Thirty minutes later, several guards from *Sutherland* descended the command center steps with a restrained Reeb in tow.

"Please bring him in, Mr. Taylor, then go back out and close the hatch again," Harry said.

Ross did as he was told, and after closing the hatch behind him, resumed his walking and fidgeting. He couldn't imagine what was going on inside.

A tall but definitely overweight man named Barth in bulging brown shipyard coveralls was busy pouring a caustic liquid on one of the main power-feed lines to a fabrication machine on the

Sonaran shipyard while his partner, a short, lean, similarly dressed man named Grub stood watch. If Barth could cut this power line, it would take days if not a week to replace it.

Both were former thugs who a now deceased traitor named Blatock had recruited from the colony of Manara over a year ago. The two had been prisoners and had left the colony with a group of men who had tried and failed to overthrow the Sonaran government. Most had been killed or captured, but these two, like cockroaches, had survived. Reeb knew of them and others and had provided their names to Number 1. These were Number 1's agents in the disruption of Zarminian shipbuilding.

"Stop and get over here. Company coming!" called out Grub in as low a voice as he could without giving himself and Barth away.

Barth sealed the container he was using and tiptoed to Grub's concealed position behind a relay box, then crouched next to his partner. "Who is it?" he whispered.

"One of those damned yellow robots!"

"That's the third one today," noted Barth. "And the day isn't half over."

"I know. A lot of the other guys have bugged out. Too much security. Maybe we should do the same."

Grub wasn't known to be very bright, but Barth thought, *We may need to.*

This time it took nearly twenty minutes before Harry opened the hatch and peered out. "Everyone can come in now."

When all had gathered in the room, Harry pointed to the Arkon device. "That is a specially designed Arkon transceiver. It has significant range and probably has repeaters between here and the Arkon system."

"You mean it can be used to communicate with the Arkon?" a shocked Ross asked.

"Yes, Mr. Taylor, and others. But there is more. When I turned on the machine, I detected several short-range frequencies. Based on Host records, I deduced they were meant to affect neurons in the brain. That being the case, I further deduced Mr. Reeb and perhaps others have already had their brain structure altered through its use. It would account for your interrogations not being successful.

"To test the theory, I reversed the polarity of the related frequencies and exposed Mr. Reeb to them. It worked. You may ask him any question now."

Ross looked over at Reeb, who had taken a seat in front of one of the consoles and was just staring at Ross with slowly blinking eyes.

Remembering Rose's speculation about Reeb working for somebody else, Ross asked, "Whom do you work for?" The answer was unexpected.

"I work for Admiral Gulv, commander of Arkon Red Central Command."

"Yes, I was right," Rose said, giving a fist pump of satisfaction.

Ross looked up at Rose and then Harry to see if the AI was as shocked as he was, but Harry was as stoic as ever. Then he asked the next most important question: "Who has been feeding you information on our operations?"

"Number 1."

"Who is Number 1?"

Reeb was about to answer, then his partially opened mouth closed. He stiffened, his eyes went wide, then he rolled out of his chair onto the floor, unconscious. Rose rushed to the still pirate and kneeled to examine his eyes using a small light she carried.

"The pupil contracts, so his brain is working but he's in a coma. Let's get him to sick bay and then to a better facility," she said as she stood and motioned for some of Ross's men to carry the limp man out.

CHAPTER 24

HAVING SUPERVISED THE TRANSFER OF Reeb from the *Sutherland* to the Sonaran station medical facility and watching *Sutherland* return to space, Rose thought she could finally head for *New Horizons*.

"Dick," she called over her implant, "is the *Vega* still here?"

"Yes, it is. I held it for you as you requested."

"Good. I can't see anything more I can do with Reeb that the current medical staff can't do. So, I guess I'm ready to leave. Will Harry be going along with me? I know Van would like him there."

"The ship is ready when you are. However, I still need Harry here to help with this damned sabotage stuff and perhaps with work on the Arkon communications system. You have been a great help, but I think it's time for you to leave. I suspect you have work waiting for you aboard *New Horizons* and. . . Van will be worried."

That was all Rose had to hear, and she wasted no time getting to the courier ship.

She knew these sleek little ships were fast, but it surprised her they weren't roomier on the inside. If she recalled her last private jet flight, it was much like sitting inside an older Cessna Citation. Nice but cramped. Even she couldn't stand up fully when moving about the cabin. But she wasn't about to complain.

She dozed off in her comfortable chair. Actually, she fell fast asleep, the ordeals she had been through taking a toll on her energy.

She awoke to a shake by one of the female crew members.

"Ma'am. Wake up, ma'am."

Rose slowly opened her eyes and brushed a lock of her hair from her face.

Then she went stiff and grabbed the arms of her chair. "What's wrong?" She flashed back to her time with the pirates, her mind not yet fully disengaged and healed from the ordeal.

"Nothing, ma'am. We'll be at our destination in a few hours. I thought you might want the time to freshen up."

"We're there already?"

"Not quite, we still have a ways to go, but our navigation track in our database will carry us through the Altair dust cloud with no problems. Then it will just be a short flight to *New Horizons*."

But *New Horizons* wasn't there.

The captain of the courier ship gave them twenty-four hours to wait for signs of *New Horizons*. After that, they would have to leave, not having fuel and supplies to stay longer. That time was up too soon.

"I'm sorry, ma'am," said the ship's captain, "we can't stay any longer. We have to return to Zarminia while we still can."

Rose had been pacing in nervous anticipation mixed with disappointment. "Can't we stay just a little longer? They have to be here soon; I feel it."

The captain knew his passenger was being torn apart, but he had no choice.

"I'm afraid not. I am sorry. Engineering, fire up the engines and get ready to leave."

Rose hoped that before they could get underway, *New Horizons* would miraculously appear, but the vessel didn't.

"All systems up and ready, Captain," the executive officer called out a few minutes later.

"Very well. Helm, take the reverse course we used getting here and let's go."

Rose could feel the engines vibrate as power increased and moved the ship from its floating position in space toward the high speed these ships were known for.

In the same way they'd departed the space around Dan 3, they arrived back. Just a flash and it was over.

"Dan 3 below, Captain," the *New Horizons'* bridge sensor operator reported.

"Very well," Frank said, his golf club back in his lap. "Go active on all sensors."

A moment later, the sensor operator said, "All clear except in quadrant two, Captain."

"On the view screen!" Frank commanded, leaning forward in his chair. "What am I looking at?"

"A small contact exiting the system, sir."

"What kind of contact?" Frank asked, a little annoyed at having to ask the question.

The sensor operator was slow to report as he examined his readings more closely.

"Well?" Frank said, turning to stare at the busy operator.

"It's a courier ship, sir, one of ours."

"Communications, can you get ahold of that ship?" Frank asked as he turned in his seat to face the communications officer.

"Yes, sir, she's the *Vega*. And she has Dr. Ramos on board."

"Then get her back here!" Frank said, slapping the soft end of his club in his hand. He meant Rose, though the communications officer thought he meant the *Vega*, but it didn't really matter.

After the port-side flight bay of *New Horizons* had repressurized, a small crowd gathered outside the *Vega*. This time Van stood in the front row.

The forward door of the sleek ship opened and a ramp extended. The first thing Van saw was Rose as she walked into the doorway and searched the crowd. Then she saw him, and her familiar smile broke out. She waved frantically as she hurried down the ramp.

Casting command protocols aside and giving up on maintaining the not-so-secret nature of their relationship, both people were swallowed in each other's embrace, tears rolling down Rose's cheeks. Van didn't want to let her go, but he had to back away a little just to look at her. She was every bit the woman he had grown to love.

Did I say that or think that? Van thought and then answered himself, *Yes.* He then reached out for Rose again as they turned to walk toward the crowd.

Until that moment, neither person had realized the crowd was clapping and cheering. The couple flushed a little. As they approached, Rose observed Frank, Rebecca, and James Harris in company with an older man she didn't know. But her eyes quickly flashed back to Frank and Rebecca, both waving. She saw, to her surprise, Frank's arm around Rebecca and vice versa. Then the crowd closed around them with multiple welcomes and expressions of goodwill.

When Van and Rose reached his cabin, they embraced hard and long. Looking into Rose's eyes, Van was the first to speak.

"I was so afraid I'd lost you. I never want to feel like that again. It made me realize how important you are to me." He paused for a moment, fighting his penchant for stammering at the admission of emotions, and then said, "I love you." The pause he knew was the realization that he was about to take a step he had thought would never happen again after Barbara. It was a relief to be able to say it without reservation.

Tears fell from Rose's eyes as she hugged Van even harder. "And I love you," she said, sniffling and trying to wipe the tears from her face with a free hand.

Van saw the tears and took a step back still holding her hands. "What's the matter? Did I say something wrong?"

Rose smiled. "No, silly, you said everything right. I realized on the pirate ship that I wanted a place with you and hoped I could help you in everything you do. Your burden is bigger than any man should face, especially alone, and I'm here for you."

"No, Rose, we're here for each other," Van said. They embraced again as both time and place melted into a tangle of released feelings.

In the morning, there was a gentle, muffled tapping at the cabin door. There was a pause, and then the tapping continued, this time just a little harder. Before a third knock, Van went to the door and opened it. There stood Frank, holding his club and getting ready to tap again.

"Frank, come in," Van said with a big smile. "Rose and I were just getting ready for breakfast."

"You mean lunch?" Frank asked with a wry smile as he stepped into the large cabin. Rose was seated at the small conference table enjoying tea.

Van blushed a little and said, "Lunch, of course. Care to join us?"

"No, not this time. I just came by to ask what your plans are. Do we depart for Zarminia right away?"

Van hadn't given that much thought in the past few hours. The time with Rose had been much more important.

Still standing and now scratching his head, Van looked at Frank and smiled. "I'm in no hurry, and I know James wants all the undisturbed time he can get with Majel. Have we learned all we can about Dan 3?"

"I was just going to mention that Margo Cranston has been bugging me to go back down there to play archeologist. Keeps mumbling about some sort of paper she wants to write."

"We can do that. It can't hurt to know more about this place and the Naskapi beyond what Majel wants to tell us. Give her a few days, but tell her to be quick."

"I'll do it," Frank said, starting to leave, then he stopped and turned back to Van. "Oh, Rebecca asked if, when you and Rose are ready, you might have dinner with us in my quarters this evening."

Van gave a knowing smile for the couple's growing relationship but let Frank off the hook and said, "We'd be glad to. See you then."

Barth and Grub, still in their brown, sloppy shipyard clothes were on their lunch break in the cafeteria. They were arguing.

"I'm telling you, Grub, this is getting too risky. Those damned yellow robots are everywhere. And five other guys have quit. Pretty soon we'll be the only two left."

"But we can be more careful," said Grub. "Besides, I like

getting paid for a real job. Even if we stopped getting money from Number 1, we can still make a living here."

"But you won't like it when somebody snitches on us and we're still here caught like rats in a trap. As for being careful, we've already been forced to cut our work for Number 1 by more than half. All because security keeps getting stronger. We can't get more careful!" Barth emphasized the last words by rapping a pointed finger on the lunch table.

Grub couldn't argue. Both men fell into silence as they finished their lunch.

The Arkon force led by Vice Admiral Daan came out of FTL near the place the destroyer *Chimaa* under the late Captain Adaar had first reported contact with an unknown force using ancient but dangerous Host technology.

On the bridge of the cruiser *Rygia*, with his red crest unfurled, Daan ordered, "Go active on short – and long-range search. I want to know about anything that moves." The Arkon were never known for being cautious. Other species would probably have used passive sensors first.

"Yes, Admiral," was all the sensor officer could or would say, and he busied himself commanding the sensors to do exactly as told.

A few minutes later: "Nothing on any sensors, Admiral," reported the sensor operator.

On the off chance any potential targets may be playing dead, Daan decided to wait. "Cease active scans. Go passive. All ships resume stealth mode."

Daan was relieved. In the few battles he had been part of, all the enemy combatants had been known, and all had been inferior. It was like swatting flies. Now, however, little was known about these upstarts. More importantly, the Arkon had lost ships and didn't know why or how. Daan was not comfortable, and his red crest slowly furled backwards.

After her logical and a little emotional argument, Jan St. Clair received permission from Stan Walters to conduct combat training of four new corvettes and their crews. Aboard the cruiser *Reliant*, Jan was in her element doing just what she wanted this trip. It fit with her hard-driving nature as an ex-Navy F-18 fighter pilot. She had been working the four corvettes hard, and they were starting to show improvement. In an effort to streamline small-ship production, both the Earth and Zarminian Federations had turned to assigning numbers to frigate-sized and smaller ships. The two Earth Federation ships, for example, were called EFC 705 and 707, EFC meaning "Earth Federation corvette." The Zarminians had elected to use the same system. Their two corvettes were ZFC 101 and 102. But for practicality, only the numbers were used between ships.

"All ships," called Jan over the tactical frequency, "reverse the roles of aggressors and defenders, 705 and 707 will attack, and 101 and 102 will defend. Take your positions and commence when ready."

Jan was surprised the Zarminian ships were showing better scores than their Earth counterparts, but both sets of ships were doing well overall. However, her thoughts were interrupted by the sensor operator.

"Contact! Unknown contacts emerging from FTL."

Jan's heart fluttered for just a second. Nobody was supposed to be out here. *Must be some misguided or lost merchant ship,* she thought, or she hoped. "What location?" she asked.

"From the direction of the Forbidden Zone, ma'am."

To all forces in both Federations, including Guardian Force, the Forbidden Zone was the area placed off limits by the Host. Something coming from that quadrant could only mean bad news.

"All ships, CANEX. I say again, CANEX and form up on *Reliant,*" called Jan on the tactical frequency, CANEX being the abbreviation for "cancel exercise."

Jan's small force was in no position to fight a real battle, and she knew it. The corvettes were getting better at their job but still had a long way to go. Plus, the corvettes were loaded with training rounds and had only a few live rounds locked away in their storage areas. Nobody wanted a ship sending live fire to a training opponent.

Reliant was fully armed, but in any emergency, Jan's job was to defend her smaller charges and get away as soon as possible. Those were her orders from Stan. That is, if the intruders were not friendly.

"Sensors, what do we know?"

"Looks like warships, Captain. Sensor readings correspond to the Arkon files. Two large ships and several smaller ones."

This is it. They're here, Jan thought as she rubbed the palms of her hands together rapidly in anticipation. It was a quirk she had when excited. She was excited about combat, but knew she couldn't do much with these ships. Then she took action.

"Sensors, shields up on all ships. Navigation, set a course for Point Foxtrot. Communications, inform the corvettes and launch a stealth drone to Point Bravo with our details." Point Foxtrot was a prearranged location to which ships would flee in an emergency. It was away from both Earth and the Zarminian space and roughly opposite the Forbidden Zone. The decision did not sit well with her Naval Academy training of not giving up, but her orders were to save valuable ships. Plus, she knew that going there was the best insurance against any enemy being led to either home system. This was the first time it had ever been used. Point Bravo was another planned point for ships to send communications drones and still avoid a direct path to Sol. In the latter case, Jan was sending a message to Stan Walters that an Arkon force was on the move.

Unfortunately, the four small training ships were slow to react. They did their best, but they were still too green and caught off guard.

Aboard the *Rygia*, Daan, with red crest high, was savoring the obvious surprise he had given the unknown force of five ships.

"Sensor operator, who or what are they?" Daan demanded from his command chair as he strained to see his prey on the forward view screen.

"Unknown enemy, sir, but the designs are old, very old. Our database suggests as much as two hundred-year-old Galactic Host technology."

Daan looked over at a sensor operator, who was still manipulating the database to prove to himself the information was in error. But it wasn't.

"Host technology? It can't be. They are long dead. Are you sure?" Daan asked.

"Yes, sir. I've checked the data three times. It is old Host technology."

Daan eased back in his chair a little and refocused on the view screen. He spoke in a whisper to himself, "This will be easy." His red crest was now on full display. "Weapons, fire at will!"

"Yes, Captain!" replied the weapons officer, his red crest also rising with excitement.

———

As red balls of plasma started passing through the loose formation, Jan shouted, "Communications, get those corvettes moving out ahead of us now! Weapons, we'll shield them from behind until we can go FTL. Fire when you have a target."

Reliant opened fire with plasma cannons and prepared to fire defensive missiles.

Perhaps unnerved by the instant combat or through lack of judgment, two of the corvettes, EFC 705 and ZFC 102, collided. With their defensive shields and engines off-line, they rapidly fell behind the other three fleeing ships.

"Weapons, put as many defensive missiles as possible around those two ships!" Jan knew it was unlikely to help, but she had to try. And for the sake of the other two corvettes, she didn't dare fall back to engage the enemy. She was outnumbered and outgunned. Besides, she was following a protocol already established by Stan.

She had to save as many ships as possible. They were too valuable. And she didn't want Stan to be disappointed in her.

Daan laughed out loud as he watched the collision.

"Not only old, but unskilled. Destroy those two damaged ships and continue after the others," was all he needed to say.

The crew eagerly did what he commanded. Plasma balls made the two crippled corvettes glow before they exploded and disappeared.

"This will be easier than I thought," Daan said to himself. "It will bring great favor on the family. . . and me." He eased back into his chair, stroking the bridge of his nose with one long, scaled finger while anticipating the destruction of the other three ships. But the target ships disappeared.

"Sensors, what just happened?" shouted Daan as he once again strained in his chair to stare at the cowering officer.

"Enemy ships have entered FTL, Admiral."

Daan's crest retreated as he absorbed the news that his quarry had escaped. *So, they have FTL. No matter,* he thought. *We will see them again and defeat them. We always do.*

To the bridge crew, Daan announced, "We will continue on the last course reported by Captain Adaar and the *Chimaa*. We will meet these weaklings again and destroy them." His confidence grew, as did his crest.

Jan winced as the two corvettes disappeared in a bright glow. It must have had an impact on the remaining two ships also. They quickly took the positions their commander demanded, and all advanced to FTL.

When the small force eventually came out of FTL, Jan saw they were at Point Foxtrot. . . nearly five light years away from *Reliant's* last position and away from any simple route to Earth or Zarminia. It was a lonely point in space.

Jan wasted no time calling the two remaining corvettes into shuttle distance of *Reliant* and started passing live munitions, mostly missiles, to the smaller ships. In addition, each of the two corvettes broke into their locked storage and began replacing training ammunition. Finally, technicians set about changing the training power settings on lasers and plasma weapons to war-shot levels.

At least if the Arkon find us, we can defend ourselves better, Jan thought. *But how willing am I to take these two ill-prepared ships into combat?*

CHAPTER 25

S TAN WAS PACING IN HIS office. He had seen Van do the same many times and laughed at the habit. Yet here he was doing it, and with good reason.

A comms drone had appeared at Point Bravo and transmitted Jan's urgent message. The Arkon had appeared. He heard nothing after that and feared all ships were lost. But there was nothing he could do about it right now. The thought that immediately went through his mind was, *How many ships that can fight do we have?*

He knew the number was small, and with *New Horizons* gone, there were fewer in Zarminian space. Stan reviewed the overall offensive capability of the allied force. The five Zarminian shipyards were starting to produce warships, but only a few had made it to Earth or Mars Base for crew integration and training. Jan St. Clair had been working up four of them when she'd encountered the Arkon. The few ships that remained were parked in orbit near the Zarminian shipyards awaiting crews and training. The other shipyards controlled by the Earth Federation and Guardian Force weren't much better off. Only the destroyer *Sutherland* and the frigate *Hornet* plus added combat shuttles were in the Zarminian space, along with twenty-five Manaran gunboats and the small Space Guard ships. The gunboats had been retrofitted with a plasma cannon each, but the Space Guard ships had lasers only. Of course, there was the *Gargon* belonging to the Carians, but she wasn't much more capable than an older corvette. Altogether, a questionable force to face the Arkon in any strength. He might be able to spare a corvette, like *Condor II*, and maybe the old frigate

Ajax. But Earth had to be a major priority for defense and ship allocation. *Where is New Horizons?* Stan thought.

"How is Margo doing?" Van asked from his seat across from Frank as the two men drank their coffee in Frank's quarters.

"As she says, 'happiness is finding the truth beneath the dirt.' Whatever that means. But I can't get her to take a break."

"Sounds like dedication," Van said just before taking a sip of coffee.

"Or obsession. How is James coming with Majel?"

"Oddly enough, their conversations keep getting shorter and shorter, James says. He thinks Majel is getting bored."

"That at least makes two of us. The crews of all ships have done about all the periodic maintenance they know how to do. Even Danny is getting bored with CAP assignments and shuttle runs."

Van nodded. "I know what you mean. Rose has also been asking when we're going back." He studied his coffee cup before continuing, "Let's give Margo a little more time. After all, it isn't every day we find a mystery planet like this."

Feeling confident that there were no more pirates to fight for now, Chen Lee ordered *Sutherland* and a few of the smaller ships back to Zarminia while *Hornet* and the remainder of the former lane patrols continued keeping a watchful eye for other intruders. The Arkon were always a potential threat.

Dick Carson stood at the foot of the exit ramp as Chen Lee descended into the Sonaran shipyard maintenance bay followed by Ross Taylor.

Shaking his friends' hands, Dick said, "Welcome back! You guys did a great job. I wish we had time to chat and get your whole story, but we'll have to do it later." Dick's face turned serious. "Right now, we need to talk. Let's go to my office."

Chen Lee and Ross glanced at each other, shrugged, and followed their friend.

Once seated at Dick's oval conference table, Chen Lee spoke up. "What's this all about, Dick?"

Not knowing a better way to say it, he took the direct approach. "Stan sent us a message saying the Arkon have been seen, and they attacked *Reliant* and her training group."

The attention of the two visitors sharpened.

Ross thought first of his friend. "Is Jan OK?"

"Sorry, Ross, we don't know. Stan hasn't heard anything since the drone report off Point Bravo."

Ever pragmatic and logical, Chen Lee asked, "What was the force size?"

"Unfortunately," replied Dick, "we don't know much about that either. All *Reliant* passed along was two large ships and several smaller ones."

Chen Lee took it all in for a moment. "Where were they?"

"Jan picked a training area outside the Sol system. She planned to go no farther than Harris Station." Harris Station was the first non-Sol system base for Guardian Force that had been captured from pirates with the aid of the Carians.

"And we think she headed to Point Foxtrot afterward?" Chen Lee asked, still thinking about the potential issues.

"It's the protocol for such an encounter. Jan's a good officer. If she survived, that's where she would go."

"Yes, she is good. How many ships in her group?"

"*Reliant* and four corvettes under training."

"That's not so good. Those corvettes probably had only training ammunition and couldn't defend themselves."

The three men sat in thought for a minute before Chen Lee broke the silence. "We're in big trouble. If the Arkon come here in the size we think, we don't have a big enough force to defend the five shipyards and Zarminia. Did Stan say he would send reinforcements?"

"All he can spare from Earth defense is *Condor II* and *Ajax*," replied Dick.

"A corvette and a frigate," Chen Lee said, slowly shaking his head. "That's not much, Dick. Even with *Gargon* and the gunboats, we would be hard-pressed to defend all our vital positions. It only leaves us with one choice."

Dick sat up straight and asked, "What?"

"We have to find them and fight them before they can get here and spread out."

CHAPTER 26

DAAN MADE A SHORT ATTEMPT to follow the fleeing unknown ships, but gave up. Space was just too big to be running around blindly. Instead, he consulted his records and decided to once again follow the last known track of the late Captain Adaar before he'd disappeared. In addition, from his commander and kinsman Gulv, he did have an approximate location of the operating area used by the adventurer Reeb. Gulv had extracted the location from Reeb when he'd first been captured.

The Arkon admiral showed a toothy grin, and his crest flared. If the opposition he found there was anything like what he had recently seen, this would be over quickly.

The reinforcements, such as they were, arrived and rendezvoused with *Sutherland*'s force. That made one destroyer, two frigates, one corvette, the *Gargon*, and half a dozen combat shuttles brought in from the pirate patrols. Commodore Daman had not been as generous or cooperative with his ships as Chen Lee had hoped and expected. The Space Force commander was holding all the gunboats and other ships back as protection for the shipyards. While this may have been logical to some on the planet, Chen Lee knew it was a bad strategy and wondered what compelled the Zarminian officer to be so unreasonable. But he didn't have time to dwell on it. There were more pressing things to think about. . . like where were the Arkon?

Aboard *Sutherland*, Chen Lee hosted an all-captains meeting in the conference room. To his surprise he saw Ootah sitting at the table.

"Ootah, what are you doing here?"

"I captain the *Gargon* in this fight," said the jolly bald man with the red beard.

"I thought you gave that command to your son?"

"I did, but this is too important. I make him my number one. Good team!"

"Glad to have you here!" said Chen Lee, tapping two fingers on the table and receiving a nod from Ootah. Then he addressed the entire group.

"By now everyone knows why we are here. The Arkon have been sighted and attacked the *Reliant* and a small training force. We don't know the fate of those ships yet, though we do hope they survived.

"The last time the Arkon were in the same area, they turned up here and I expect they will again. We," and he gestured to the assembled captains, "are the only force standing between Zarminia and destruction. We cannot expect any more help."

The assembled captains whispered comments and nodded to the captains nearest them.

Chen Lee continued, "Currently, as was done the last time the Arkon showed up, we have drones and, thanks to the Carians, small ships patrolling the outer limits of this system. With luck we will get some advanced warning of the enemy location. Then it will be up to us. Frequency tables, formations I might use in addition to our latest intelligence on the Arkon, have been sent to you. Are there any questions?"

Ootah's hand went up.

"Yes, Ootah?"

"Where is Commander Childs and *New Horizons*?"

"The last position we had was in the Altair system. A courier ship was recently sent there and would have returned if the *New Horizons* was not where she was supposed to be. The ship, the *Vega*, has not yet returned. I choose to take that as confirming *New Horizons'* latest location."

Chen Lee saw Mia Flores make a gesture. "Yes, Mia?"

"Can we get a message to the commander to tell him of the Arkon? We could use the help."

"True enough. Unfortunately, the *Vega* was the last courier ship available to us. We have to wait for its or another's return. Anything else? No? Then return to your ships, and good luck!" It was "Chinese time" again as Chen Lee pushed to get started quickly.

Commodore Daman was uneasy as he sat in contemplation tapping a stylus on his desktop. Many of his agents had quit due to the increased security in the shipyards, especially the security robots. He also knew some people would question his denial of ships to Captain Lee, even though he had presented a good reason in protecting the orbiting shipyards. Finally, there was the lack of any contact with Reeb. He had tried several times to call from his secret location, but with no results. Things were getting complicated, and he was having trouble staying focused. He thought several times about giving himself up, but when he tried, he couldn't do it.

CHAPTER 27

WHEN LEE LEFT REEB IN Dick's custody before departing to defend the planet. Dick still had work to do, and, with Harry's help, things were running more smoothly. Reeb was in a secure cell with medical attention and was still essentially comatose. When not commanding his robots, Harry studied the Arkon communications equipment retrieved from Reeb's base and its abilities to affect human neurons in the brain.

Considering Reeb had been captured by Galactic Force, a nation state in its own right, there was no significant objection on the part of the Zarminian Federation for Dick to control access to the prisoner as long as information was shared with the Federation through Commodore Daman. What might happen to Reeb down the road would be based on his future actions and negotiations between Galactic Force and the Federation. There were plenty of people on Zarminia who wanted Reeb's head. But so far, reason and cooperation were prevailing.

Today, Dick and Harry were in the planning room that Dick had appropriated. There was no reason to be there rather than his office, but Dick liked the openness of the room and the informality it fostered. He reclined back in his chair with his feet on the table in front of him. Harry stood next to him. The AI never seemed to sit.

"Anything new on Reeb or his equipment, Harry?"

"Not on Captain Reeb, Mr. Carson. He is still not conscious. I did locate the communications equipment to a separate room, which I control. While there, I received a communication from Number 1, but I did not answer."

Harry's last statement grabbed Dick's attention, and he took his feet off the table as he turned in his chair to look at Harry. "You heard from Number 1?"

"I did, Mr. Carson. But the contact was short, and I had no way of tracing the signal then."

"But you do now?"

"Yes, Mr. Carson. I constructed a simple device that I linked into the shipyard receivers and transmitters, along with the same on the next closest orbiting shipyard. With such an arrangement and knowing the transmission frequency, I can triangulate the next transmission with a great deal of accuracy."

Dick beamed satisfaction. He wanted Number 1, and he believed his capture would put an end to the sabotage going on in all the shipyards. Rose's information that Number 1 was a highly placed person in the Zarminian government had been a great help in narrowing the field of possible candidates. But there were still a gracious plenty of people to survey. If they could use Harry's triangulation system, that would narrow the gap even further.

Daman was being pressed by circumstance to take bolder moves. With a decreasing number of agents in place in the shipyards and given the effectiveness of the robots at improving security, he had to try something bolder. Despite the looming Arkon threat, Daman had arranged to meet with the same thin, limping agent he'd met before when he'd needed to send orders to the shipyards. With the man sitting on the bench again, Daman was tempted to not exchange the code words, but his programming forbade it.

The thin agent was reading a book and, without looking up, said, "Times are tough for us old veterans."

Daman replied, "Yes, but the war at least is over."

Nodding at receiving the right response, the agent said, "What do you want?"

Daman's reply was short. "I need one of those robots."

"You mean here, in Lowondia?" said the agent with a look of surprise.

"Yes, I mean here, and I will give you an address not too far from here for delivery."

The agent shook his head. "Impossible. We only have a few people left, and they're not too bright. Oh, they're good for breaking things all right, but to capture a robot and then transport it here? No way."

Daman thought about that and agreed transport might be too much to expect. "OK, then capture one and deliver it to a point I determine on the Sonaran shipyard, and I'll arrange transport."

The agent nodded. "That might work. But no guarantees and the price will be high. These guys don't work for nothing."

"Don't worry about the cost. Just get me a robot."

It was almost logical that Barth and Grub would get the job of capturing a robot. They were one of the last teamed pairs of agents now on a shipyard.

"I don't like it!" Grub said, stamping his foot.

"I don't much like it either, but the pay is more than we've made in total so far. With it, we can leave this place and have a good time dirt side," said Barth, trying to be convincing.

"What's he need one of those things for anyway?" asked Grub.

"Don't know and don't care. Just get one, get paid, and get out."

"But what about those Arkon? Shouldn't we worry about them?" Grub and all the crews in the orbital shipyards knew about the Arkon possibly showing up. They were somewhat pacified by the knowledge that a fleet was out looking for them, and, of course, there were the gunboats guarding the stations.

"We don't have to worry about those guys right now. Besides, the sooner we complete the job, the sooner we can leave this place with enough money to live well. Just one more job."

That made sense to Grub, and he nodded his consent.

For two not-so-bright crooks, they managed to come up with an interesting way to capture a robot. In the fabrication area, Barth found a sheet of woven wire mesh that would just stretch flat across one of the narrow passageways in the fabrication room.

Robots often traversed the entire area around each fabricator as part of their programming. It was easy to tap into a fabricator's power source and run a heavy gauge shielded electrical line from the fabricator to the wire mesh through a simple switch. All Grub and Barth had to do was wait for a robot to walk over the wire mesh and throw the switch. The electrical charge would short out the robot's electrical system and essentially kill it. They hoped.

Having set their trap, the two robot thieves waited for their robotic prey. The opportunity wasn't long in coming. A yellow-striped robot walked around a corner of the fabricator the two men were hiding next to. However, just as Grub was about to throw the switch, Barth grabbed his hand.

"No," the larger man whispered as a human rounded the corner right behind the robot. "We don't want a witness or a body. Let's wait for one alone."

They waited and they waited. Grub was getting impatient, and his knees were starting to hurt as he knelt next to the switch.

"Maybe there aren't any more this shift," said Grub in low tones as he shifted and rubbed his knees.

"Don't be stupid. There are always more than one or two in a circuit around the area. Just wait."

Grub wasn't happy and complained, "My knees hurt."

"Just suck it up. Remember what we're getting paid," Barth said, more than just a little annoyed at his partner.

Finally, another robot rounded the corner, this time alone. As soon as it walked across the wire mesh, Grub threw the switch.

There was arcing and sparking and a sizzling noise before Grub opened the switch and cut off the power. The smell of ozone was strong.

As quick as their sore knees would allow, the two men jumped up from their hiding place and took the few short steps to their prize. Each man grabbed a robot arm and pulled, attempting to drag the robot out of sight. But the robot hulk wouldn't budge. They pulled harder, and the metal mass moved only a few inches. They had underestimated the robot's weight, which was a little over three hundred pounds.

"Now what do we do?" whined Grub.

Barth wasn't immediately sure. With one hand on his forehead and the other on his knee, all he could say was, "Quiet and let me think!" Then it hit him.

"Didn't I see a handcart near the entrance door when we came in?"

"I don't know," Grub mumbled.

"Well, go look and be quick about it," commanded Barth.

Two minutes later, Grub came back. "There's one there all right."

It was all Barth could do to keep from punching the little man. "Then go get it and bring it here." Off went Grub, this time to get the cart.

When Grub finally returned, both men used all their energy to roll the heavy robot onto the cart. Sweat was rolling down their foreheads by the time they were done.

"Now what?" asked the perpetually curious Grub.

"Now we take it to the loading dock and cover it with the tarp we left there just like we were instructed."

"What if somebody sees us?"

Barth wondered if Grub ever ran out of questions. "We say this one malfunctioned and we're taking it to the repair station."

"Oh."

"Now, let's clean up this mesh and wire and get out of here."

Only hours later, the inert robot was delivered via a Space Guard shuttle to a warehouse just outside Lowondia, Sonara's capital. Daman, not in uniform, was there to receive it, and had brought with him some loyal technicians. Loyal in the sense they were paid handsomely from funds left in Lowondia by Reeb.

"Here it is, gentlemen," Daman said to the men surrounding the robot. "What I need from you is to figure out how to defeat these machines as easily and quickly as possible."

CHAPTER 28

T HE SEARCH DRONES AND THE Carian ships spotted the Arkon, and the news was not good.

The *Sutherland*'s intelligence officer stood before the collected captains once again in the *Sutherland*'s conference room. Behind him was the large view screen showing information as the officer spoke.

"I'm afraid, Captains, that there is no really good news to tell you. The Arkon force is stronger than we guessed. The location is as depicted in this screen." Everyone could see a red dot appear about five hundred million miles from the allied formation. "Next, we have drawn a representation of their formation, as you can now see behind me. The formation consists of one cruiser in the lead, followed in line by a frigate, two destroyers, and another cruiser. There are two additional frigates, one each on the flanks of the destroyers. And if that were not enough, there are five small craft, we estimate, which are likely armed scout ships arranged in a star pattern around the main force. Twelve ships in all. The only good news is, we know, because they are currently not proceeding in stealth mode, they are either extremely arrogant or just plain stupid."

Immediately, the room turned into a buzz of sound as the captains exchanged their views with their colleagues. When the noise calmed down, Captain Lee took the podium.

"Seven capital ships, gentlemen, to our four. Their scout ships may be a wash against our combat shuttles and fighters. However, they have two cruisers against our heaviest ship, the *Sutherland*, a destroyer. I welcome ideas."

One hand went up, Mia Flores's. "Our stealth drones are now able to accept small-yield nuclear warheads thanks to the grim work done on torpedoes by the Earth Federation traitor Zafar. My estimate is we could launch at least a dozen from this range programmed to attack the capital ships. They could attack the Arkon from twelve different directions."

"Interesting idea, Mia," said the captain of the *Ajax*, "but if the Arkon aren't in stealth mode now, they would surely shift to it after or even during an attack. Then how would we track them?"

"Good question, Captain," replied Mia with a smile, knowing she had the answer. "However, our experience suggests their feeling of superiority will drive them in on the same course, and they'll appear again closer in. Before and during the attack, we can relocate most of our search craft and long-range drones along their course and wait for them to show themselves. A few drones need to stay behind to do BDA." BDA has long stood for "battle damage assessment."

Lots of nodding heads and whispered sounds of agreement came from the room.

"Then what?" the *Ajax* captain asked.

"Then we engage," answered Chen Lee. "We will adopt the plan Mia has described and then position ourselves down course of the Arkon. For the moment, let's plan to have a portion of our combat forces on each side of their course at a point and in formations I will send to you after you return to your ships. Meanwhile, I would like all drone-equipped ships to replace current recon mission tips with the nuclear devices Mia mentioned. I want to be able to fire in four hours. That should cut down the range for the drones."

Exactly at the four-hour point, twelve nuclear-tipped drones leaped from their host ships and accelerated in stealth mode toward the unsuspecting and closing Arkon.

Confident of a victory, Daan proudly flew his ships along the course he'd created to take him to the location Gulv had specified. He didn't see the need for FTL at this point, because, he reasoned, he didn't want to bypass any enemy ships that might attack from his rear. Though, he did have the cruiser *Prydaa* in that position just in case.

Boldness was always a trait of Red and Blue Arkon and the admiral, with his red crest high, flew on at .02c in the active search mode. Shields were up, however, which was just good practice.

Suddenly, the sensor operator shouted, "Admiral, we are under attack!"

Daan was confused. They couldn't be under attack, there was nothing out there. Sensors proved it.

"Where and by what enemy?" was Daan's first response.

"Unknown enemy, Admiral, but there have been four nuclear detonations in and around the center of the formation. It looks like both the outboard frigates have been either destroyed or severely damaged. Wait, *Prydaa* has taken a hit. Damage unknown."

This is impossible, thought Daan just as the forward view screen went white and the *Rygia* shook violently.

"Nuclear burst amidships, Admiral, starboard side. Damage unknown, shields at seventy percent," the sensor officer cried.

When it was over, there had been ten nuclear strikes on the formation. The two outboard frigates were gone. The aft-most destroyer was severely damaged but could still make speed. Both cruisers had been hit but suffered little damage. Unfortunately, a number of *Rygia's* stealth transducers were off-line, causing her to lose stealth coverage on her starboard side amidships. The Browns were slowly working on repairs, to the extent they could.

After receiving all reports, Daan gave his orders.

"Communications to all ships. Shift to stealth mode. Maintain course and speed."

A moment later the communications officer responded, "Done, Admiral."

Daan just grunted a reply as he eased back into his command chair, red crest folded.

The time it took for transmissions to travel the expanse of space was painfully slow, even with the transmitting drones headed home and closing the distance. Nine hours later, the first BDA reports came back.

Chen Lee was on the bridge in his command chair when the communications officer gave a big hoot.

"Captain, we hit them hard! Ten drones made it, two malfunctioned. Two frigates gone and a destroyer damaged. Both cruisers seem OK overall, but it looks like the lead cruiser has a stealth problem. She is visible on her starboard side."

Chen Lee took this all in. A good strike all right, but the remaining force was still a big one. Two cruisers, one and a half destroyers, and a frigate remained, plus the five scout ships.

No, Chen Lee thought, *still not good news.*

CHAPTER 29

D AMAN WAS BACK IN HIS office reading a report his hired technicians had just provided. He knew the first shots had taken place in the developing space battle. But it was long-range for now. He still had time.

As he finished the report, he laid the tablet slowly onto his desk and sat back in contemplation. His technicians had discovered the robots had a fatal flaw. The machines communicated on a frequency higher than the human hearing threshold, 25 kHz. Disrupt or block that frequency and the robot network would become ineffective. All that would have to be done would be to transmit the same frequency 180 degrees out of phase, and the control signal would be eliminated for as long as the out-of-phase signal was transmitted. The robots would temporarily be reduced to so many pieces of metal junk. *Simple,* thought Daman. And he knew how he could transmit the signal on all five orbital shipyards. He ordered five small transmitters, which could be made in just hours. Meanwhile, the forensics on the stolen robot would continue.

But there was another issue hanging over his head. Reeb, he'd just found out, was alive and in custody on the Sonaran shipyard. True, he wasn't conscious. . . yet. But what would happen when he awoke?

"Something will have to be done about that," Daman whispered to himself as he stared out the window of his office.

Chen Lee started receiving reports on the Arkon movement more frequently as the distance between the forces diminished. Now that he knew the enemy was dead set on maintaining course, he could use another weapon not yet tried in battle. Mines. A few had been loaded aboard *Sutherland* before it had left Mars Base. The idea was for him to arrange some tests for the new stealthy weapons. They were supposed to be able to detect a nearby ship and maneuver a short distance to detonate near or on the target. This would be a good test.

"Weapons, how many of those test mines do we have on board?"

"Twenty, Captain."

Not many, Chen Lee thought, *especially for this force.*

He called up a space chart on the forward view screen and projected the Arkon course on it. Then he used the controls on his chair arm to circle an area where he thought the mines could best be placed.

"Weapons and Navigation, I want to go to the location I circled on the view screen. Then we lay our mines in a circular pattern and return to our waiting position."

In just a few short minutes, *Sutherland* was on her way to lay mines for the first time in any known space engagement.

Daan was unhappy. His proud force had been hit without the ability to strike back. That was, to him, a devastating blow. *A cowardly attack,* he thought. But rather than make him cautious, he was filled with sufficient rage to keep the ship going as if nothing had happened. *I'll show these upstarts, these peasants!* His red crest unfurled and shook with his anger.

Suddenly, *Rygia* shook as lights went out and then back on.

"What happened!" Daan demanded of anyone within the distance of his voice.

"An explosion, Admiral, this time on the port side. Shields are holding."

"Source?" demanded the alarmed Arkon admiral.

"Unknown, Admiral. But we now have a hit on the forward frigate and on the lead destroyer."

"Damage?"

"Unknown at this point, Admiral."

As quickly as the attack had occurred, it was gone, and damage reports came in.

"First three ships in the formation were hit, sir," said the communications officer, holding one hand to the side of his head to press the earpiece more tightly to his ear. "Limited damage. Shields holding. We believe they were stealth mines."

The news let Daan ease back in his chair as he lowered his head to massage his temples. *Mines,* he thought. *What will they do next? This was supposed to be easy.*

By now the BDA reports came in more quickly to *Sutherland* as the two forces drew closer together.

"Only three hits, Captain. No discernable damage," said the communications officer with a note of dejection in his voice.

"Thank you, make a record of the engagement," Chen Lee said, tapping two fingers on his command chair arm. It was all he could say. *Three hits out of twenty,* he thought. *Not a very good first use.*

Daan watched as his force rapidly approached the coordinates Gulv had given him.

"Helm, begin deceleration. I don't want to overshoot our planned location."

"Yes, Admiral. I have passed the word to all ships."

"Good," was all Daan wanted to say.

"They're decelerating, Captain!" called out the sensor operator.

"What? Why?" Chen Lee blurted out in surprise.

"Unknown, Captain, but at this rate they will be at a crawl in about an hour."

"Navigation, where is the point the Arkon are expected to complete their deceleration?"

The nav officer busily made his calculation and then spoke. "I estimate the spot on the view screen now, Captain."

Chen Lee turned and looked up at the screen and gasped shallowly. "Are you sure?"

"As sure as my math and the computer can tell, Captain."

The spot, Chen Lee observed, was well short of any weapons range of Zarminia. The enemy would detect the planet, if they hadn't already, but it would still take time to get there at their slower speed. This was a good thing for Chen Lee and his forces. They were still undetected, and when the enemy reached their final speed, Chen Lee would be on top of them. It hadn't been planned this way, but it was a welcomed advantage.

Chen Lee had already divided his force to his advantage. *Hornet*, *Ajax*, and four combat shuttles were positioned on the far side of the enemy path, while *Sutherland*, *Condor II*, *Gargon*, and two combat shuttles were on the near side. They would catch the enemy in the middle like a classic Western ambush. Luck was with them.

Back in the warehouse on the outskirts of Lowondia, just hours after he'd ordered them, Daman admired the five transmitters prepared by his technicians and ready to be distributed to his remaining agents on each orbital shipyard. They were to connect them unobtrusively to the public address systems and turn them and the address system on at a fixed time, all shipyards together for maximum results. While the public address systems were on, the robots would be frozen in place and the agents free to wreak any mayhem they could until the public address systems were used by someone else. Then the transmitters and address systems would have to be reset. Each time the robots were disabled, the agents could maximize their work with substantially reduced risk. Simplicity itself.

Daman reminded himself this might be his last chance of

interrupting ship production and was silently hoping that after this the Arkon would solve the problem for him by eliminating the shipyards completely. That would be ideal since he had run out of ideas.

CHAPTER 30

V AN WAS GETTING A STRANGE feeling. He got them now and then and had learned to pay attention to them. His gut was telling him to go home. No clear reason, it was just time, regardless of Margo's work or his personal time with Rose. He knew the crews of all the ships were bored anyway.

"Frank," Van called over his implant, "I know Margo would be happy to be here forever, but I want to get underway as soon as possible."

"But Margo has been on the surface for only a short time and has a bunch of work planned. I told her to expect two days. What's changed?"

"It's hard to explain, Frank. Get everyone up here ASAP. I want to get underway in five hours."

Frank knew better than to second-guess his commander. Everyone knew Van wasn't exactly like anyone else. Besides, he was the commander and could do what he damned well pleased.

"I'm on it. We'll be ready to go in five hours."

"Thanks, Frank."

Rose could only hear Van's half of the conversation. But it was enough to get the gist of it.

"We're leaving in five hours? What's the sudden rush?" she asked from the couch in Van's quarters.

Standing behind one of the easy chairs, both hands on its back, Van replied, "Can't explain it, but something is telling me to get home. Margo can do her thing later."

"What about Majel? Do we leave him here or take him with us?"

"I don't know, but I'd like him to come along and see firsthand what we are all about. I think he can help us if he has a mind to."

Rose stood and walked toward the exit door. "Then let's go see."

As was the case most often, Majel was in James Harris's quarters exchanging questions and answers about nearly everything. Van, with Rose, knocked on the cabin door and heard James say, "Enter."

When the important couple entered, James stood, as did Majel. The old man was learning about Earth customs fast.

"What a pleasure to see you both," Harris said. "My humble quarters are nothing like yours, but grab whatever chair or bucket you can find and have a seat. Majel and I were just discussing Earth history."

Rose let Van take the only remaining chair next to Majel and she sat on the edge of Harris's bunk.

"Thanks, James. I came here to chat with Majel for a moment. I just gave Frank orders to get underway for Zarminia in five hours. Before you ask, just call it one of my feelings. But I need to know what you want to do, Majel. Will you stay behind, or would you like to come with us?"

Majel rose from his seat with an air of excitement. "I would very much like to come along with you. I want to see much of what the ambassador has been telling me."

"Based on the last message delivered from the *Vega*," Harris noted, "I'm no longer an ambassador, Majel. In fact, when I get back to Zarminia, I'll probably be arrested and taken back to Earth."

"Yes, you did mention the possibility. But I don't think it will happen. You see, I like working with you and would be very sad if any other ambassador was sent to replace you."

Harris assumed an amused grin as he visualized the clamor that would cause in the Earth Federation's foreign ministry.

"In fact," Majel went on, "I would feel most comfortable if you were an ambassador from Galactic Force. I understand that is possible, is it not, Commander?"

Van was smiling at this cagey old man. In just a few words, he had stated he would only deal with Harris, and Harris needed to be a Galactic Force ambassador. And Van knew Dick would love it. He could shed some of his duties on to James. This could work.

"It'll work for me and Galactic Force if James accepts."

"I'll do it!" said Harris with enthusiasm he had not shown in a long time.

Majel nodded his agreement also. "Then there remains only one more practical thing to ask, Commander."

"What's that, Majel?" Van asked.

"Do you want to go to Zarminia the slow way or the fast way?"

As Chen Lee and his ships were learning, large-scale space combat could be incredibly slow. The time it took for the initial stages of a battle to be completed was necessarily long due to the great distances ships, weapons, and communications had to travel. But time was about to compress. The Arkon deceleration was about complete, and Chen Lee wanted to take advantage of any surprise he could obtain in the final Arkon speed transition.

The lead Arkon cruiser and the damaged destroyer, both with the damaged stealth gear, were the first to be seen on the allied force view screens. Chen Lee expected the Arkon force to drop stealth very soon and anticipated the same formation as seen in the last BDA. Based on what he expected to see, he assigned targets for each friendly attack force. All that remained was the signal to engage. As soon as the Arkon came out of stealth, Chen Lee gave the order.

"All ships, attack!"

Chen Lee's ships emerged from stealth, raised shields, and commenced firing. Those ships with fighters launched a CAP for each of the two friendly formations. So far, nobody had seen Arkon fighters in any action, but Chen Lee didn't want to take chances. For now, however, the fighters would park in two fixed spots above the battle. One group over the forward allied team and one group over the rear-most team. They watched for fighters or other targets they could intercept when called but, for now, stayed away from the main fight.

Initially, Daan was confused. Until now on this mission, there had been no sighting of enemy ships. This time they suddenly appeared all around him. He had himself just emerged from as much stealth as he could generate, considering the *Rygia*'s one destroyer's damaged stealth systems. The Browns, as was typical, couldn't repair either set of systems.

Surprise was on the side of the attackers at first. One gunboat on each side of Daan's formation went down quickly. Then the damaged destroyer started taking hits as the clever enemy focused on wounded prey. Overall, however, Arkon shields were holding, and Daan was ready to strike back. First, *Rygia* and then the other Arkon ships opened fire. The fight was on. In Daan's mind, it wouldn't take long. All the Reds' crests were up and shaking on the bridge.

Sutherland recoiled as the first plasma rounds from the lead cruiser hit. Sparks flew from overhead, and a small fire broke out in an unmanned console. It was quickly put out, but the pounding was relentless. In seconds, *Sutherland*'s formation had flown past the lead elements of the Arkon force and began turning back for another pass. *Hornet* and her ships had done the same from the opposite side as they targeted the rear half of the enemy formation. Chen Lee's plan was to attack the forward and rear half of the Arkon formation at the same time so not all the Arkon weapons could be focused on any one element of the small allied force.

On the second pass, Mia in *Hornet* and her other ships focused on the damaged Arkon destroyer. Her initial pass showed the destroyer with more damage than the BDA suggested, and she wanted to take advantage of that. But the fire from the trailing cruiser (later Mia learned it was the *Prydaa*) demanded more defensive and offensive attention than she'd initially expected. As a result, she did little added damage to the crippled destroyer while her ships took brutal hits from multiple Arkon ships. Next time she would focus on the cruiser and come in from its rear where the other Arkon ships could not provide as much cover. She was learning.

Chen Lee and his combined force were finding a routine, sweeping in one group aft and one group forward again and again. The fighters stayed out of the battle of the elephants. *But how long can that last?* Chen Lee thought. The answer was, not long at all.

Unexpectedly, the Arkon broke formation and divided into two groups just as Chen Lee had done at the start. The forward group, Group A, consisted of the lead cruiser, the frigate, the undamaged destroyer, and one of the remaining scout ships. The aft group, Group B, split off with the trailing cruiser, the damaged but fighting destroyer, and two scout ships. What had been a harassing attack by allied forces changed into two separate close engagements. The old pilots in the ships would call them "two fur balls" bringing up the image of multiple dogs fighting in groups.

This sort of fighting was new to both Mia Flores and the *Hornet* group, as well as to the *Sutherland* group. It wasn't straightforward and organized. Mia, like Chen Lee, knew it would be all over if the fight turned into a chase scenario, especially with the Arkon as the chasers. So, the key to the battle was maintaining tight turns after each combat pass and making repeated head-on attacks. "Tight turns" might have been a loose term given the high speed of engagements. But allied turns had to be as tight or tighter than the Arkons'.

Mia watched closely what happened in the first pass at Arkon Group B.

"Weapons, what have you noticed about our Arkon group that's different than the group fighting *Sutherland*?"

"Well, ma'am, every time we pass the formation, we get hit

by both Arkon ships. The cruiser is still protecting the damaged destroyer by placing it in her wake and parking the two scout ships behind her. That makes the destroyer nearly impossible for us to hit, and we take it in the butt from the destroyer and the scout ships on every pass."

"Exactly. So, how can we take out or disable the destroyer without exposing ourselves to the cruiser broadsides?"

The question made the weapons officer think. Then it dawned on him, and he smiled as he looked at his captain. "We break off the four combat shuttles to attack the destroyer!"

"Very good," Mia said with a smile of her own and a nod toward the weapons officer. "But if the shuttles attacked the destroyer alone, I don't think it would work. Even disabled, the destroyer has a big sting. On the other hand, if we timed both our groups to attack at the same time, the combat shuttles could attack when the destroyer is focusing largely on our pass."

The weapons officer slowly nodded as he pictured the attack in his head. Then he nodded faster as he clearly saw the picture Mia was suggesting. "It might work, Captain! But can we call in the CAP to help with the scout ships?"

Mia was surprised she hadn't seen the opportunity to use the CAP against the smaller scout ships. "Good call! Let's make it happen. Work with the comms officer to pass the word to the shuttles and the six CAP fighters. Have them break away now and stand off until we begin our pass. Let them decide exactly how they'll do it and how they want to deal with the enemy scout ships as long as we're coordinated."

"Will do, ma'am!" said the excited officer as he turned to his communications companion and went into a huddle.

While Chen Lee was maneuvering for advantage with Arkon Group A, he kept an eye on what Mia was doing with her group. He watched her break off the combat shuttles and merge them with the CAP and wondered what she was up to.

Mia made what she hoped would be her last head-on pass at Group B. She hoped the Arkon commander of Group B would think the small craft had been told to stand off and keep out of the larger fight. In some respects, that was what it looked like. Except, the group of combat shuttles and fighters were maneuvering behind and to the left of the cruiser and destroyer lineup. The plan, she could tell, was for the group of small craft to attack from the enemy port quarter as she made her pass overhead. The timing had to be perfect.

Hornet and *Ajax* came roaring in at the Arkon and opened fire. The two larger Arkon ships took up the same firing routine as before and did not see the group of small craft start their run simultaneously.

The first victim to fall to the small allied force was one of the Arkon scout ships aft and to port of the destroyer. The scout ship captain was also fixed on what he thought was the main fight up forward and didn't see the real danger until too late. The combat shuttles and fighters flew past the debris of the scout ship and opened fire with missiles and plasma rounds on the crippled destroyer.

Caught unaware by the small enemy force attacking his port side, the captain of the Arkon destroyer wasted precious seconds trying to train port-side weapons from the two larger ships to this small band of gnats. The allied group of small craft were having an impact. The destroyer's already weakened shields dropped completely. Gun after gun on the destroyer went silent. But the larger ship's missiles could still be brought to bear on that side. Out shot the first Arkon destroyer missile volley, and almost immediately two of the combat shuttles' shields were overwhelmed. They exploded. In return, the fighters released their missiles, which were aimed at the damaged areas of the now looming destroyer, several penetrating into the holes already in the bigger ship's hull. Gasses began streaming from already damaged areas, and pieces of hull were floating away. Then it was over, the small craft maneuvering to keep away from the destroyer's starboard guns. Another combat shuttle was hit and tumbled off into the distance, while two of the fighters met a similar end. Only one combat shuttle and four fighters remained. The destroyer was still there and fighting.

CHAPTER 31

C HEN LEE COULDN'T FOLLOW MIA'S last attack. He had his own problems. Like Mia, he didn't want his Arkon group to fall in behind him in a chase. Instead, he kept maneuvering and finally his group of smaller ships was in position for a forward-quarter attack. Not quite head on, but close. Chen Lee in *Sutherland* took the lead position, with *Gargon* slightly to the left and aft, and *Condor II* to the right and aft. The two combat shuttles were tucked in behind the three larger ships for protection and to provide extra firepower when the allied ships flew past the Arkon. Chen Lee's CAP stayed above the fray for the moment.

"Stand by with Mk-2s," Chen Lee called to the weapons and communications officers. Mk-2s were long-range, antiship missiles carried on Guardian Force ships but not the *Gargon*.

"Fire!"

"Sixteen missiles away from us and *Condor II*," responded the weapons officer, followed quickly by, "Contact! Twenty missiles inbound from the Arkon, Captain."

"Time to impact for both sets?"

"One and a half minutes for ours, two minutes for theirs, Captain."

"Point defense fire now!" commanded the harried captain.

Lasers and plasma fire from all allied ships reached out for the incoming missiles.

"Only two hits on the Arkon cruiser and one on a destroyer, Captain," the sensor operator yelled in excitement. "The rest were hit by point defense."

"Never mind that! What about incoming?" Chen Lee barked.

"Four missiles down. Now six more. The rest are going to hit!" *Sutherland* shuddered as missile hits registered.

"Four hits, Captain. Shields down to seventy percent."

"*Condor II* and *Gargon* both hit! *Gargon* is falling back," the sensor operator reported.

Come on, Ootah, get away! Chen Lee thought anxiously of the brave Carian ship captain. "Engage with lasers and plasma weapons now!" he ordered as the Arkon formation closed rapidly.

Hits were scored by both sides as the two opposing groups passed each other and began their long turns back.

"Damage reports on all ships!" Chen Lee demanded.

"Numerous plasma hits on *Sutherland* and shields now at sixty percent. *Condor II* has been hit harder. One plasma cannon out and one missile launcher gone. Her shields are at fifty percent. *Gargon* is still falling back. No reports from her."

"What reports from *Hornet*'s group?" Chen Lee was worried about the weaker allied force and hadn't heard anything since before Sutherland's last attack.

"Checking, Captain."

Mia Flores had attacked an additional time, and the results weren't good. As she led the two remaining ships in a turn to attack again, Mia asked for a status.

"Sensors, what's the count and damage?"

"We got their last remaining scout ship, Captain, but the cruiser and the damaged destroyer are still operating after multiple missile hits from both our ships. I estimate the cruiser's shields at seventy percent and the destroyer's at thirty percent.

"We lost our remaining combat shuttle to enemy missiles, and both the *Hornet* and *Ajax* have been hit hard multiple times. Both our ship's shields are down to fifty percent or less, and both ships lost several plasma cannons and at least one missile launcher each."

"*Que torta!*" Mia said out loud meaning 'this is awful' in Costa Rican slang, not good news. She was forced to make a decision she didn't like.

"Communications, call down the remaining CAP and have them attack the destroyer on our next pass." It was probably a suicide mission, but the destroyer had to be taken out. Then she could focus solely on the cruiser, perhaps at longer range.

The communications officer stared at her captain for a moment, then turned to her station and said, "Yes, Captain."

Mia and her diminishing force were once again lined up for another attack. The four remaining CAP fighters left their high perch and headed down to attack the destroyer.

As in the last engagement, both sides opened with long-range but uneven missile barrages.

"Eight missiles away, Captain," the *Hornet*'s weapons officer reported.

"How many from *Ajax*?"

"Eight missiles from both our ships, Captain."

Mia slumped in her chair. Eight was half what the combined ships should have fired.

"Very well. What about inbound?"

"Sixteen inbound," was all the weapons officer could or would say.

"Time to enemy missile impact?"

"Two minutes, Captain."

"Point defense," Mia commanded as she waited for the hell she knew was coming to break loose.

But all the point defense the two allied ships could muster could not keep at least half of the enemy missiles from hitting.

Hornet rocked and the bridge lights went out. Emergency lights came on, and the latest damage was horribly visible.

The sensor officer was thrown from his seat and lay motionless on the deck. His station was sparking and smoking. The communications officer was wiping blood from her forehead while trying to keep things together.

Mia was stunned but still able to react. "Communications, take over from sensors."

"Yes, ma'am," called out the communications officer as she reconfigured her console to do both her job and the sensor's job.

Both ships continued to fire all remaining weapons as they flew past the enemy formation.

"Damage reports," Mia commanded when the pass was complete, leaning forward in her chair, her back screaming in pain.

"*Ajax* is out of action and tumbling. All four fighters gone. We took multiple hits, and shields down to thirty percent."

"The Arkon destroyer. What happened to the destroyer?" Mia was hoping the sacrifice of the fighters had been worth it.

There was a pause as the combination communications-and-sensor operator took an inventory.

"The destroyer is gone, Captain. And the cruiser has changed course toward the other Arkon group."

Poor Chen Lee, Mia thought as she realized the two cruisers were merging to face the remainder of the *Sutherland*'s group in one last battle.

With the little information reaching him, Daman suspected the battle in space wasn't favoring the allied forces. Something within him tried to surface and show some remorse, but it didn't happen.

He had quickly and successfully had his new transmitters delivered and installed to each of the five main shipyards. He looked over at the time piece on his desk as the seconds ticked away to the exact minute they were planned to initiate their signals.

In his office on the Sonaran shipyard, Dick saw Harry jerk for just a second. That seldom happened.

"What is it, Harry?"

"The security robots have gone off-line, Mr. Carson."

"Off-line? What does that mean?"

"It means, Mr. Carson, that all the robots have stopped and are not functioning."

"On this shipyard?"

"No, Mr. Carson, on all shipyards."

It took a minute for Dick to absorb this.

"How could it happen—and why?"

"Uncertain, Mr. Carson. But this has never happened before."
Then Harry abruptly stopped for a few seconds.

Dick noticed the pause and was about to ask Harry what was
going on when his AI friend spoke again.

"There are reports of incidents on all shipyards, Mr. Carson.
Several fabrication machines have been disabled and one corvette
under construction has been damaged. Similar reports continue to
come in."

"How is this possible?" Dick said as much to himself as
to Harry.

"Unknown, Mr. Carson."

CHAPTER 32

A S SUDDENLY AS THEY DISAPPEARED from Dan 3, they reappeared over Zarminia and, more specifically, over Sonara.

Van was again behind Frank on the *New Horizons* bridge, marveling at what Majel had just done, when the communications operator called out.

"Captain, I'm getting really strange broadcasts from some of our ships."

"What do you mean 'strange'?" Frank asked, looking up with irritation.

"Sounds like a battle, sir, but the clarity is not good."

His irritation turned to keen interest. "Who's fighting?"

"I'm getting transmissions from *Sutherland*, *Hornet*, *Condor II*, and other calls I think are from a few fighters. Plus a lot of other transmissions I can't understand."

"Sensors, what do you have?"

"Something is going on about five hundred thousand miles out, Captain, but I can't separate the good guys from the bad guys at this distance. There are numerous energy spikes consistent with weapons discharges."

"Jennifer, what's going on?"

The holographic image of Jennifer instantly appeared. "I detect both human and Arkon communications, Captain. The energy emissions are a mixture of both human and Arkon technologies. I conclude there is a significant battle going on with the Arkon."

"General quarters!" the captain called out. Immediately the now programmed call went out over the 1MC. "General quarters, general quarters. All hands, man your battle stations."

Frank looked behind him to ask Van a question, but the commander was gone. Frank stowed his golf club in the new custom-made holder at the side of his chair. This meant he saw trouble ahead.

Van took his seat on the flag bridge, which was now fully manned. He barely noticed James Harris and Majel enter and strap in to the observer chairs.

"Frank," Van called through his implant, "contact *Sutherland* or *Hornet* and find out what's happening. Meanwhile, launch the corvettes and turn the whole group to *Sutherland*'s position and move out."

"We just tried calling *Sutherland* and *Hornet*, but no response. Two corvettes, *Kirk* and *Decatur* are launching from the flight bays, but the external corvette, *Valley Forge* can't break her moorings. Elsa Muller has tried everything to get her ship free," was all Frank had to say. It was enough.

"Time to repair?" Van asked.

"No estimate yet. She's stuck fast."

"Communications, get me Dick Carson on the Sonaran shipyard."

"Right away, Commander." Two minutes later: "Mr. Carson is on the line, Commander."

"Switch him to overhead and patch this to Captain Wilson."

"Done, sir."

"Dick, this is Van. Any idea what's going on here?"

"Van! What a godsend! The Arkon have attacked. Chen Lee is in command of our forces, which have split into two groups. Chen Lee in *Sutherland* has one group, and Mia Flores in *Hornet* has the other. From what I can tell, they are outnumbered and against at least two Arkon cruisers."

Van strained to hear Dick with static building on the radio. "Did you say two Arkon cruisers?"

"Yes."

"Where's the Space Guard? With Chen Lee?"

"No. Commodore Daman kept all Space Guard ships here to protect the shipyards."

"Did I understand ALL Space Guard ships are here and not with Chen Lee?"

"That. . . correct." Dick's voice was now starting to break up.

What is the man thinking? thought Van about Daman. "OK, Dick, we're on our way to help."

"Roger. . . luck."

"You get all that, Frank?" Van called through his implant.

"Every unbelievable word."

On Chen Lee's last loop to turn back on Arkon Group A, *Hornet* joined with *Sutherland* and *Condor II*. The frigate and the corvette were in bad shape and their shields failing. *Sutherland* was not much better. Chen Lee could circle the Arkon, but he couldn't run.

"Captain," called *Sutherland*'s sensor operator, "the cruiser from Group B has rejoined with the other Arkon. But now all that remain are the two cruisers, a destroyer, and a frigate."

"Good to know we now face only two cruisers, a destroyer, and a frigate. It makes all the difference." Chen Lee's sarcastic comment was not lost on the rest of the bridge crew. "Communications, did you get a message off to Space Guard asking for reinforcements?"

"Yes, Captain. But there's been no response."

What is Daman doing? Chen Lee asked himself. *Those gunboats will mean nothing if this force gets past us.*

Chen Lee gave up on any communications secrecy and called his two accompanying ships directly.

"*Hornet* and *Condor*, this is *Sutherland* actual. I am going to tighten our turn to close the range for a few minutes. On my command, fire every Mk-2 missile you can before turning outbound again to the wider circle." Both ships acknowledged receipt of the message.

"Helm, come left twenty degrees," Chen Lee ordered.

"Left twenty degrees, Captain."

When he estimated the turn was tightened sufficiently, Chen

Lee called out, "Fire!" A pathetic salvo of fifteen missiles shot out as Chen Lee ordered his ships to widen the range again.

Twenty minutes later, the sensor operator called, "Two hits on each cruiser and one on the frigate. No appreciable damage, Captain."

"There was a chance we could have been lucky. But not today I guess," mumbled Chen Lee.

"What, Captain?" asked the communications officer.

"Nothing."

Chen Lee knew he couldn't keep this up forever, so he shrugged and took a gamble, hoping luck would be with his three suffering ships. "Communications, alert *Hornet* and *Condor* we're attacking and to follow *Sutherland*." He didn't wait for a response.

"Helm, hard left. Head for the lead cruiser."

"Hard left it is, Captain."

It's done. For better or worse here we go, thought the *Sutherland*'s commander as he steeled himself for what was about to happen.

"New contact!" the sensor operator called out in alarm.

A pain went through Chen Lee's chest as he sagged in his chair.

Then the excited officer relaxed just a little. "It's *New Horizons!*"

CHAPTER 33

V AN WATCHED THE VIEW SCREENS as the *New Horizons'* ships exited FTL. They were close. The forward view screens showed blue and red dots representing the allied and the Arkon forces respectively. The blue dots were closing on the red. *Sutherland* was turning in to the larger Arkon force.

"Frank!" called Van over his implant. "Tell *Sutherland* to break off and fall in behind us. Get a status report."

Van could see the representations of *Sutherland*'s force break away from their attack run and maneuver toward *New Horizons*.

"Thank God we caught Chen Lee in time. *Sutherland* and her two ships couldn't have survived alone," Van said to nobody in particular.

"Arkon force changing course, Commander," called the sensor operator. "Looks like they're headed toward us."

Van knew Frank and Danny Ramos had put together a force of twenty-four fighters and four combat shuttles. Danny took command of one of the shuttles to assume command and control of the light force. The remaining CAP, which had been covering *Sutherland*, had returned to their parent ship for a change of crews and reloading. The plan was to launch them again with fresh crews to join with Danny.

New Horizons' firepower was greater than any of the Guardian Force ships engaged so far, but Van knew it would be touch and go against two cruisers.

"You may attack when ready, Frank. But save the fighters and shuttles for the destroyer and the frigate. Work with Chen Lee on how best to use his ships. They are tired and shot up."

"Roger that. Danny had the same thought about the two smaller Arkon ships."

Rose entered the flag bridge just as she heard Danny's name. Quietly, she eased next to Van and asked, "What is Danny doing?"

"He's taking command of all the fighters and the shuttles. His targets are the destroyer and the frigate."

"Isn't that really dangerous?" Rose asked, pulling nervously at a strand of her hair.

"Yes, it is. This whole thing is dangerous to the extreme." Then, trying to buoy her spirits a little, Van smiled and said, "You'd better take a seat in the back and strap in. It's going to get bumpy."

Daan was a little shaken when the sensor operator called out, "New contacts!"

"What ships?" the admiral asked, his crest folding.

"Not Arkon, Admiral. Two are old Host corvettes. The larger one is not in our databases," called out the sensor operator.

"What do you mean? A ship that big not in our databases? Impossible."

"Nevertheless, Admiral, the ship is an unknown class. It is not a cruiser or battle cruiser that we can tell. But it is the size of a battle cruiser. Certain emissions mirror Host technology. The previous enemy ships are joining with this new force, and as many as twenty to thirty fighter types are emerging as well."

Daan was still driven by the expectation that the Arkon could beat anything thrown against them. They were, after all, on the edge of defeating the previous force and would have done it quickly if not for this interloper.

"We'll defeat this rabble in short order and then attack the orbiting stations and then the planet surface. Nothing and nobody will survive." Red crests appeared all over the bridge.

To meet this big ship, cruiser *Rygia* led and was followed by the cruiser *Prydaa*, then by the one destroyer and a frigate. To maximize firepower forward, Daan ordered his trailing ships to step one level above the ship before it so each could fire forward over the one in front. Sort of an echelon up. It was a proud Arkon force.

"You see that formation, Frank?" Van asked incredulously over his implant.

"I see it. We're not doing it, though. That guy has to be nuts. If we miss one ship in that formation, we can probably hit another. Not like shooting fish in a barrel, but close. I'm keeping our two corvettes to port and starboard and slightly aft. The rest I'm protecting directly behind. They can get their shots in as we pass."

"Good man. What happens after this attack pass? This ship is great in a lot of ways, but she's slow to turn and slow in general compared with the other ships."

"I was thinking of going to FTL and then coming back."

"We might have to do that, but it would still take a long time to reengage. The Arkon may think we ran away and then go after the planet right away. There has to be another way of keeping their attention on us." Van felt a tap on his shoulder and turned in his chair to see Majel standing there.

"Excuse me, Commander. I couldn't help but hear your conversation with the captain. I might be able to help."

"You heard us over our implant communications?" Van asked in wonder.

"Yes, Commander, it wasn't difficult."

Remembering this was Majel, Van recovered. "What can you do?"

"I cannot destroy your enemy, it would be against our values. However, I might be able to distract them when you complete your attack."

Van just stared at Majel wondering what he would do and slowly spoke over his implant. "Frank, did you by any chance hear Majel?"

"Yes, I did. How would he do that?"

"I don't know, but any help he can provide will be welcome.

Continue the attack. Don't go to FTL, and commence your turn to reattack."

"Roger that. Weapons, *New Horizons* and the two corvettes will engage with missiles when in range," Frank said. "Let our trailing friends know what we're doing, but let them fire as we pass."

"Yes, Captain," said the energized weapons officer. This was a new and exciting adventure for him. He had never seen real combat, only the artificial test Majel and the Naskapi council had arranged.

Daan watched with confidence and a raised red crest as the allied force sped down on him. He was the first to act.

"Aim for the large target. Fire with missiles now!" Forty missiles jumped from their launchers and headed for the *New Horizons*.

"Many contacts, Admiral. Enemy missiles inbound. I count thirty. Estimate impact in five mets."

"All ships, activate point defense."

"Yes, Admiral."

Daan and his force were close enough now to the enemy to see the blossoms of missiles being intercepted or hitting their target.

"Thirty missiles intercepted, Admiral. Five were hits on the lead ship. No detectable damage. However, five missed the lead ship and hit one of the escorting corvettes." The sensor operator turned with a raised crest. "No trace of that ship. It was. . ."

The sensor operator was interrupted as the incoming enemy missiles began to be intercepted or score hits. *Rygia* shook with multiple hits as lights dimmed but stayed on.

"No damage, Admiral. Shields at sixty percent. *Prydaa* reports two hits, shields holding at seventy percent. The destroyer and the frigate both took hits. The frigate's shields are down to sixty percent."

Daan had no idea *New Horizons* was designed with an emphasis on self-defense. It wasn't really an offensive combat ship.

"How can that be? We fired more missiles at one ship but scored fewer hits," Daan demanded, his red crest up in anger.

"Unknown, Admiral," was all the weapons officer dared to say. His crest was folded out of sight.

Then the two combatants were swiftly passing through cannon and laser range. At the same time, an unexpected attack came from the starboard side of the Arkon formation.

Rygia and its consorts again took multiple hits while scoring few on the opponent.

"Fighters attacking the destroyer and frigate, Admiral," yelled the sensor operator.

Daan kicked himself, figuratively, for forgetting about the fighters and combat shuttles. "Damage?"

"Both ships took hits and damage, Admiral. They are maintaining speed and formation, but their shields are down to forty percent."

"How many fighters did we kill?"

"Initial assessment is six fighters destroyed or out of action, Admiral."

Daan gave out a grudging, "Good." Getting back to the overall engagement, Daan thought there was something strange about the attack. Then it hit him. "Sensors, is that large ship slow by our standards?"

It took the sensor operator a few moments of review. The he responded, "Yes, Admiral."

"So we can turn inside her, take up a chase, and fire whenever we want with little danger?"

The sensor operator looked over at the navigation officer and joined in a brief conversation. Then the sensor operator turned and said, "Yes, Admiral. We can do that."

Daan smiled to himself in satisfaction. The enemy was now his for the asking. His red crest came up again.

Then the sensor operator broke his admiral's reverie. "Multiple new contacts dead ahead. I count five, no, six ships."

"Who are they?" asked an upset Daan.

"Unknown, Admiral. Nothing matches in our database."

"Size and types?" Daan demanded.

"Unknown types. Sizes vary between corvettes and destroyer equivalents."

"Time of arrival or weapons range?"

"They are coming on fast, Admiral, perhaps as soon as ten mets."

This is not good, Daan thought. The balance of forces had just changed dramatically. He had several choices, but in order not to be caught between both sets of opponents, he decided to divide his forces to meet each set of challengers. He and *Rygia,* along with the frigate, would pursue the slow original opponent. *Prydaa* and the destroyer would meet the new force. When *Rygia* dispatched her opponent, it would rejoin *Prydaa* to finish off the newcomers.

"Yes!" Daan exclaimed out loud and then gave the order.

CHAPTER 34

FRANK AND VAN WERE BOTH lamenting the loss of the corvette *Decatur*. However, both nearly jumped out of their respective command chairs when they heard about the new contacts. Help had just arrived. But who were they?

"Majel, is this your distraction?" Van asked over the implant he now knew Majel could use and Frank could listen on.

"Yes, Commander."

"What kind of ships are these?" Frank chimed in, a big smile on his face, though neither Van nor Majel could see it.

"They are not ships, Captain. They are illusions," said Majel smoothly.

"What?" Van and Frank asked at the same time and both equally shocked.

"The ships you see are illusions I have made. To your enemy, they appear as real ships with energy readings, communications, and every other fingerprint of real warships."

Van was the first of the two men to recover. "Can they fire weapons of any sort?"

"No, Commander. Only simulated fire."

"Then what good are they?" Van asked, throwing his hands in the air in frustration.

"Look for yourself. The enemy has already broken into two smaller forces, making one more vulnerable than the two combined."

Van pulled his hands down and looked at the forward view screen. It was true. One cruiser and the accompanying destroyer were now chasing the artificial ships. But the other group was maneuvering to get behind *New Horizons*.

"You hearing and seeing this, Frank?" Van asked.

"Every word. Fortunately, the Arkon delay caused by the fake ships allowed us to turn back on our reduced enemy group. We're heading for an attack as we speak."

Van relaxed in his chair. He looked over at the smiling Majel. "How long can we fool them?"

"It depends. If they are happy to chase the illusions, then it could be quite some time. If your enemy realizes what they are chasing isn't real or not worth their energy, it will take them little time to rejoin their friends."

That wasn't good enough for Van. "Jennifer, do you have an estimate on how long we can fool the Arkon?"

"Not exactly, Commander. However, if the illusions can carry their pursuers far enough away, the time to reengage will increase. Given their current speed and location, we have at a minimum another thirty minutes before they can reengage our forces."

"Got that, Frank?" Van asked.

"We have at least thirty minutes to stop or severely disable the group we're heading for. Not much time given our speed and turn rate. Maybe only two attacks," responded Frank.

"Then make the most of it and hope the bad guys are fooled as long as possible."

"I'm contacting Danny right now to coordinate. Cross your fingers," ended Frank.

Cross my fingers, Van thought. *Who would ever have guessed I'd be doing just that in combat?*

Frank and Danny did a quick revamp of the previous plan they'd devised for Danny's force. With fewer enemy ships, it should be easier for Danny to at least flank the damaged but viable frigate.

———

Daan saw the same ships as before, less one corvette, bearing down on him. He did not, however, fail to remember the fighters and warned the frigate captain.

This time Daan made a last-minute course change to starboard to allow his missiles to include the destroyer and any other ship becoming a target. Both sides fired their missile barrage. After firing, Daan turned back to his original course, making a smaller target of his ships. Even the Arkon could learn a few things.

The Arkon missiles were into space just before the allied force fired, so Daan was able to get reports of his results before having hits on his ships.

"Missile hits on the large lead ship, the destroyer, the frigate, and the two corvettes. One corvette destroyed, the other is falling behind, out of the fight."

Daan gave a toothy grin, and his crest rose at least halfway up. Then it was his turn.

"Multiple hits on us and the frigate, Admiral. As you expected, enemy fighters are maneuvering to strike the frigate, but she is prepared."

"Good. Tell our rearmost guns to fire on the fighters when in range."

"Yes, Admiral."

In no time, the two formations were past each other and starting to maneuver to their individual advantages. This time, there was more advantage on the Arkon side being able to turn inside the larger enemy ship and begin a chase. However, the supporting Arkon frigate was DIW and falling behind. The *Rygia* continued alone but was closing fast.

"What's the bill, Frank?" called Van.

"*New Horizons* took several hits but is combat ready. *Sutherland* took a hit, and shields are at thirty percent. Same for *Hornet* but her shields are at twenty percent. *Condor II* was destroyed. *Kirk* is out of action and falling behind with no communications."

Van allowed that to sink in when Frank continued.

"The fighter and shuttle force took a beating. This time the Arkon were ready and waiting. Only eight fighters and one combat shuttle survived."

"Which shuttle?" Van asked, then held his breath for the answer.

"Danny's shuttle."

Van relaxed. In addition to Danny being an old friend, Van wanted no part of having to give Rose bad news about her brother. "Good to hear. Were the fighters successful?"

"That's more good news. The frigate is disabled and showing no energy readings. She's out of the fight."

"What about the cruiser? Is she following?" Van suspected she would be.

"Yes, and we can't out-turn her. We're being chased."

Van leaned back in his chair, slumped at the shoulders. "Do the best you can, Frank. At least the other Arkon group hasn't given up the chase of the fake ships." Van stared at the forward view screen. Then he had an idea.

"Wait, Frank. With just the cruiser, this may be the time to risk *Sutherland* and *Hornet*. They can out-turn the cruiser and attack multiple times. And with them out of the way, our rear firing weapons can be more effective."

"True, but if we lose those ships, we'll be red meat for the other group when they get tired of chasing phantoms."

"I know, but it's better than getting picked off one by one in a chase."

Frank thought about it for a moment and then nodded. "You may be right. I'll make it happen."

CHAPTER 35

THE CAPTAIN OF THE PRYDAA was an old and senior captain named Skaal. He had no significant family ties but was reasonably good at what he did. As good as or better than any Red officer. But he was getting irritated and losing patience chasing these fast ships. As soon as it looked as if he was gaining, they moved ahead. He briefly tried turning inside them, but failed. He fired a few missiles at them, but they ran out of fuel before getting close to their targets. He also thought of sacrificing the faster destroyer in a rear attack. But that made little sense.

So, he continued the chase. It did not fail to register on him, however, that he was getting farther away from the other battle with each passing met.

From his safe perch high above and aft of the Arkon cruiser, Danny watched what was unveiling. Frank gave him a warning, but watching it happen was surreal. The *Sutherland* and the *Hornet* peeled away and accelerated out of range of the cruiser. *New Horizons* was then allowed to open up with a missile barrage to the rear. Not all her launchers would face aft, so only eight missiles roared into space at the trailing cruiser. The cruiser did the same since both ships were now in range.

Free to maneuver and do what he thought best, Chen Lee circled back behind the cruiser, waiting for the missile barrage to cease. It didn't take long. The cruiser took several hits, but *New Horizons* took more. At this rate, Chen Lee knew, the cruiser would start taking *New Horizons* apart from the rear. He made his decision.

"Mia," Chen Lee called out, "we have to attack the cruiser now before *New Horizons* fails. Form up on my starboard side and we'll attack. Missiles first, then everything we have to stop that Arkon."

Mia solemnly nodded in her chair and replied, "*Hornet* is with you." Both ships aimed for the cruiser and accelerated.

Sutherland and *Hornet* were able to get off six Mk-2 missiles between the two of them. They were now out of long-range missiles and reloaded their remaining launchers with the short-range Mk-1s. *New Horizons* continued to fire plasma weapons at the cruiser and a few short-range missiles. They had hits, but the cruiser kept closing, and the Arkon plasma hits were taking their toll on the *New Horizons'* shields.

"Four missile hits on the cruiser, Captain," called the *Sutherland*'s sensor operator. Then he called out, "Contacts! Ten missiles inbound."

Chen Lee wasn't sure either of his ships could take so many hits and survive. "Point defense!" he ordered, then: "Engineering, engines to a hundred and ten percent—we need more power to the shields." There was no answer, but Chen Lee could feel the engine vibrations increase.

Sutherland rocked as at least three missiles hit. Two struck *Hornet*. But the pair of warships continued, opening up with plasma and short-range missiles. Shields on both ships were near the zero point.

New Horizons was taking hits, and her shields were falling. She was, however, scoring plasma hits on the cruiser, which had ceased closing and was maintaining distance.

Danny was in agony. His friends were being killed, and he could do nothing. As he watched, the *Hornet* flared in a white cloud of gasses and rolled right and aft, out of the action.

Sutherland and *New Horizons* continued to battle the irrepressible

Arkon cruiser until *Sutherland* fell back trailing gasses, with smoke roiling through holes in her hull.

Danny couldn't take any more.

"All fighters form on me. I'll take lead. We're attacking."

The small band of fighters and the lone combat shuttle closed on the cruiser fast, all weapons firing. Defensive fire flamed from the cruiser as first one fighter exploded and then another and another.

Danny was fixed on the cruiser's bridge. His eyes didn't blink and his lips were drawn back in a snarl exposing his white teeth.

He was close now and alone. All the fighters were either destroyed or damaged. It was just him. The big cruiser filled his view screen and he yelled, "Rose!" as he hit the shuttle's FTL button.

"Holy shit, what happened?" Frank yelled as he saw the blossom of fire and parts where the cruiser had once been.

Van knew. A tear rolled from his eye as he explained to Frank, "Danny went to FTL and right through the cruiser, shredding it to bits."

There was silence all around. Nobody had seen anything like it.

Quickly, Van turned around and saw Rose bent over in her seat, head in her hands, sobbing. She'd heard everything.

Van wanted to rush to Rose's side to hold her and console her. But he couldn't. Not with another Arkon force out there.

CHAPTER 36

F ROM THE BRIDGE OF THE *Prydaa*, Captain Staal watched the *Rygia* and his admiral die. Now there was only the *Prydaa* and her accompanying destroyer.

"How can this be happening?" shouted Staal to no one in particular.

Nobody on the bridge wanted to answer, and they didn't have to.

"Helm, bring us about and get a course from Navigation to intercept the large ship. She's alone now and we should be able to make a quick kill."

"Yes, Captain. But what about those ships we are chasing?" It was a logical question.

"Forget them for now. I don't think they have the belly to fight anyway. If we need to, we can deal with them after we deal with the other trash."

"Yes, Captain, coming about now."

Van absorbed the ugly fact that *New Horizons* was now alone, weakened, and waiting for the other Arkon cruiser and destroyer to swoop in and finish them off.

"Jennifer, how much time do we have before the other cruiser attacks?"

"Forty minutes, Commander."

"You get that, Frank?" Van asked over his implant.

"I got it. We are making repairs including some damaged weapons. However, a number of our shield transducers are out, and we can't effect repairs in that amount of time."

"How about the topside corvette? Any luck breaking it free?"

"No, it's frozen in place. It can and has fired a few weapons, but that's all."

"How about fighters?"

"We can launch about a dozen, but that would be it. There are no more."

"Combat shuttles?" Van asked, going down a list of possibilities.

"We have one up and ready. Two took damage in the flight bay when some equipment was jarred loose from Arkon hits and fell on them."

"Your overall combat assessment?" Van finally asked.

"Propulsion is undamaged, as amazing as it seems. Seventy-five percent of our defenses are up and ready, but we lost more than thirty percent of our offensive capability, which wasn't great to begin with. We're supposed to be an exploration ship, not a battleship."

Grim news, Van thought. "OK, Frank. Do your best. I'm going to talk with Rose."

"Better you than me," was all Frank could say.

"You mean somebody stole a robot, analyzed it, and figured out the network control frequency?" Dick asked, or maybe yelled, standing as close to Harry's face as he could get.

Harry was unperturbed at Dick's closeness and apparent anger. "Yes, Mr. Carson. Robot number 467 was reported missing and has not been found. From my analysis of the transmitters found in the public address systems of all five shipyards, I deduce that 467 was used to determine the operating frequency. Then it was relatively easy to construct the transmitters and place them where they could be most effective."

Dick wheeled around and paced back to his desk, and then back toward Harry. This time not quite as close but with sweeping arm gestures as he spoke. "Do we know where this robot. . . 457 is now?"

"It is 467, Mr. Carson, and no, we do not."

Dick caught himself getting too excited, took a deep breath, and stopped waving his arms. "How many times were these transmitters used?"

"Just twice, Mr. Carson, before I located the one on this shipyard and had the other shipyards searched."

"And they're all gone now?"

"Yes, Mr. Carson."

Dick nodded with a little satisfaction and returned to his desk and sat in his chair with a huff, arms folded, still looking at Harry. "What has the damage been?"

"Two corvettes and one frigate damaged, Mr. Carson. Three fabrication machines temporarily put out of action, and twenty-five workers injured and off the job."

Dick had picked up a tablet stylus and was fidgeting with it when he threw it down on his desk. "Outrageous! And all while our ships are out there fighting a losing battle."

"Yes, Mr. Carson."

Sometimes Dick wished he could be as stoic and emotionless as Harry. But that probably wouldn't have been good in the long run.

"So, all the robots, except one, are back on the job?"

"Yes, Mr. Carson."

"At least there's some good news in all this. Anything else?"

"Captain Reeb has still not regained consciousness, Mr. Carson. Do you still want to continue to hold him here?"

"I can't think of a better place, even with our security hiccups. We'll keep him here for the time being."

Van found Rose in her cabin. She was curled up on her bunk, still crying. Van gently sat down next to her and stroked her hair.

"Danny was a fine and brave man. You should be proud of him."

No response from the sobbing doctor.

Van's old tendency for emotional stammering around Rose was contained by knowing what he wanted to say. "When I look back at my combat in the Navy, I realize those were the most intense moments of my life. Things seemed to happen in slow motion; seconds were like minutes as I saw every detail roll past me like a movie. In combat, every other thought is squeezed from your mind, and all that exists is that extended moment and your purpose. In those moments, I don't ever remember being afraid or regretting anything. I was where I was supposed to be, doing what I was good at.

"I can tell you that in those last moments, Danny felt the same way. He was on a high that you just can't describe to most people, and in those moments, you see everything with perfect clarity. He wasn't thinking about dying or sacrifice. He was smiling and soaking up the adrenalin rush of being exactly where he was supposed to be. I guarantee he had on his biggest and best grin as he pressed that FTL button."

Van could see a slight change in Rose's tenseness as she shifted from a curled-up ball and straightened her legs.

"We'll miss him, but those of us who live that life have to respect and admire his dedication, ability, and most of all, strength of purpose. He was really good at what he did, and he loved every minute of it, including the last one."

Rose turned her head toward Van and gave a brief smile as she said, "Thank you."

Van smiled back and rolled softly onto the bunk and held her tight.

Frank was standing on a scaffold inside the *New Horizons'* pressure hull and just below the *Valley Forge*. He was a hands-on guy who used to like nothing better than tearing down old cars and rebuilding them. This time, he was frantically looking for ways to free the corvette from her frozen moorings. As a last resort he had pressure-suited workers with torches attempting to burn through the mooring clamps.

Staring up at an open control box, Frank asked the ship's AI a question. "Jennifer, are you sure there's no way to get the clamps to automatically or manually release?"

"I have tried all pathways within *New Horizons'* systems to cause the clamps to open, Captain, but none work."

Frank slowly shook his head in frustration, then climbed down from the scaffold and started toward the bridge. "How long before the remaining Arkon force is in range?"

"Twenty minutes, Captain."

Frank quickened his step and gave Jennifer an order. "If the workers can't cut through the clamps in ten minutes, have them stop and get back inside. We have to be prepared to fight again."

"Yes, Captain."

Ten minutes after he left the scaffolding, Frank reached the bridge and took his command seat, club still in its holder. "Rebecca, as soon as the exterior workers are back inside, go to general quarters."

"The last one just entered the air lock, Captain, and the external hatch is closed," answered Rebecca as she pressed the button for the now automated warning and klaxon.

"General Quarters, general quarters. All hands, man your battle stations."

CHAPTER 37

SKAAL WATCHED THE SLOW ENEMY ship get larger as the distance closed. It was trying to evade, but it was useless— *Prydaa* had the advantage. In a bold attempt to increase his force's immediately useful forward firepower, he ordered his trailing destroyer to assume a position abeam the cruiser, to starboard.

"Time to missile range?" the captain called out.

"One met, Captain," answered the weapons officer. Again, all red crests were up, anticipating the final kill.

"Where is the force we were chasing?"

"Astern and slightly to starboard, Captain. They are over twenty mets away and closing."

Skaal nodded his crested head in silent reply. Plenty of time to do away with the force in front and then turn and attack the other one. *Tight, but easy,* he thought as his mental clock ticked at the completion of the met.

"Fire!" sounded Skaal, his crest now shaking with anticipation of a swift victory. Thirty missiles streamed away toward the *New Horizons.*

Aboard *New Horizons*, sensor operators on both bridges reported at the same time: "Contacts! Thirty missiles inbound."

Van, having returned to his bridge, could only watch while Frank fought the ship.

"Time to impact?" called out Frank.

"Three minutes, Captain."

"Fire all available missiles!" Frank ordered, not realizing he was shouting.

"Eight missiles away, Captain," the weapons officer replied.

"Roger, point defense!"

New Horizons' defensive systems blazed away at her reduced rate of fire.

"Five missiles down. Nine down. Fifteen down. Twenty down, Captain, but ten will hit!" cried the weapons officer.

This time the *New Horizons* shook more than ever before. Lights went out all over the ship, replaced by dimmer red and white emergency lights. Fragments of material fell from the bridge's overhead, and crew members rocked in their seats. One crew member screamed as a metal retaining bar fell on her shoulder.

"What about our missiles!" cried Frank.

"Three hits on the destroyer, Captain. None on the cruiser."

"Fire again!"

This time only four missiles left their launchers.

"All Mk-2s expended, Captain," said the weapon's officer, afraid to look up at his captain.

"Incoming!" cried out the sensor operator. "Fifteen missiles inbound. Time to impact, two minutes."

A little over a minute later: "Two hits on the destroyer. She's slowing. No hits on the cruiser. We downed eight of the Arkon missiles, but the rest will hit!"

"Point defense!" Frank ordered, though it was probably not necessary. Everyone was in the defensive mode now.

Again, *New Horizons* shuddered. This time the lights went out again but didn't come back on. The bridge view screens went out, and the only light was from four consoles still working. The air reeked of smoke and ozone.

"Damage report!" Frank yelled out as loudly as he could.

"Fifty percent power loss throughout the ship, Captain. Shields down to fifteen percent, and we're venting gas and liquids from the lower starboard flight bay."

"Weapons?" Frank asked.

"Less than half our defensive weapons, less missiles, aft are available. Forward weapons about the same."

"The destroyer has fallen out of range, Captain, but the cruiser is still coming on strong," the sensor operator added.

Skaal was grinning and his whole body quivered while his brilliant red crest flashed. This is what every Arkon lived for: the final kill of a worthy foe. But his joy was interrupted.

"New contact, Captain!" the sensor called out as his crest fell back a little.

"What? Where?" was all Skaal could say.

"Dead ahead, Captain. One ship. A big one. Estimate a battle cruiser with Host characteristics."

"Impossible. Nothing like that has been seen for over two hundred cycles."

"Nevertheless, Captain, it is there and coming on fast."

"Break off the attack. Helm, right ninety and up twenty, prepare to go to FTL."

"Coming right and up, Captain. FTL in five mets."

Just then, the new ship fired a huge ball of green plasma headed straight for *Prydaa*.

"Launch the communication drone, NOW!"

"Drone away, Captain." Then the *Prydaa* was struck with a force Skaal could not remember feeling or seeing. The lights went out but were replaced by emergency lighting.

"Damage report?" the Arkon captain shouted, his crest retreating.

"Shields down to twenty percent. Forty percent power loss through the ship. Plasma weapons off-line, but missiles available."

"Weapons, lock on to the new target and fire all available missiles, now! Navigation, set course for Emergency Point 4. Helm, head for Point 4 and engage FTL as soon as available."

There were no replies, just frantic action until the weapons officer reported, "Fifteen missiles away, Captain."

Skaal hoped it would be enough to distract the new contact, at least long enough for the *Prydaa* to escape.

The big ship started picking up speed and turning to the new course when another huge plasma ball rushed toward them.

Van was sitting in his darkened flag bridge, his face reflecting the glow of consoles.

"What's going on, Frank? We're nearly blind as bats here!"

"We're not much better off, but our sensor operator reports a new contact. A big one, and it opened fire on the Arkon cruiser, which has broken off the fight. I think they were running away, but now they're gone."

"You mean they went FTL?" Van asked in alarm.

"No, I mean they're gone. A second blast from the mystery ship destroyed them."

Van sat back quickly in his seat and stiffened as he took in this incredible news.

"Jennifer, what's going on?"

"The Host are here, Commander."

CHAPTER 38

D AMAN WAS WORRIED. HIS LAST effort to scuttle ship production had worked for a short while, but ultimately ended when the transmitters were discovered. And to his disappointment, the forensics on the stolen robot had not produced another idea. All he could think of now was to save himself. And that meant ensuring Reeb didn't give him up. He wasn't concerned about the agent on the *New Horizons*; she had no idea who he was. Reeb, on the other hand, was a different matter.

He could find a way to kill Reeb, but his programming wouldn't let him. There was just one other choice left. He had to free Reeb and get him away from Zarminia.

Space around the two large ships was filled with debris and crippled ships, but none interfered with the small shuttle that had departed the newcomer en route to *New Horizons*.

Recovered enough to stand, Rose took ahold of Van's hand as they and an entourage of others waited for the shuttle ramp to drop and its occupants to emerge. Behind Van and Rose were Frank, Rebecca, James Harris, and Majel.

Noticeable tension mixed with excitement in the group as a tall gray-uniformed man bent through the shuttle opening and strode down the ramp. He was alone.

The silver-haired officer strode up to Van and gave a brief bow. "Greetings, Commander. I am Admiral Barton Namath of the Galactic Host."

The buzz of tempered conversations came to an abrupt end.

Grinning, Van took a half step forward and shook the admiral's hand. "You're the one who gave us *New Horizons*, correct?" he said as he released the admiral's hand.

"Yes, I am, along with an old cruiser I think you now call *Reliant*."

"So, it's true. You have been watching us."

"All of us have, Commander."

"All of you? How many of you are there. . . the Host that is?"

"Altogether, approaching a million now. Not bad, considering we were down to fifteen thousand after the Arkon defeat." Namath smiled and looked around at the group with obvious pride.

Van's grin fell to not quite a frown as he thought about this last statement from the Host admiral. *Growth to a million population in two hundred years. That doesn't seem like much.*

"I can see you're doing some math, Commander. Perhaps you think we should have a larger population by now, and perhaps we should. But if you are trying to compare our growth with your growth in the United States, think again. In 1776, you had a population of just over two and a half million. So, in a comparable period of time, of course you would have grown to much more than a million, especially with immigration. Try comparing us to your Boston. That city also had only fifteen thousand or so in 1776. Today, the Boston population is just under six hundred thousand. So, we haven't done too badly."

Van smiled for two reasons. First, the admiral was right; and second, Van was amazed at the Host familiarity with Earth.

"You're right, Admiral, but let's move to a quieter place where we can talk."

Once they'd arrived at Van's quarters, Van invited Namath to take a seat next to him and across from Rose at the head of the table. Those closest to Van on *New Horizons*, including Majel, took other seats.

The admiral, who had been introduced to Majel, couldn't keep his eyes from wandering to the Naskapi man as Van spoke.

"The first order of business, Admiral, is to thank you for saving *New Horizons* and all aboard. The second is to say the same for the

Zarminians, whom you will meet later if you have the time. The one cruiser alone could have wiped out all the orbiting shipyards, as well as done considerable damage to the planet surface.

"While remaining grateful, we are, however, a little surprised to see you and your ship here. You must have been close by."

Namath nodded and looked around at the people at the table. "As you already knew, we have been watching you all. I must say you have exceeded all our expectations. You have done in a few years what we expected to take twenty or more Earth years.

"We also did not expect the Arkon to show themselves as soon as they did. That original scout ship, in fact, was drawn to Earth by the work of a traitor our ancestors had on board as they were building and supplying the depot sites on Earth over a hundred years ago. Our ancestors knew nothing about him at the time." Namath stopped for a few moments and looked around the room letting his statement sink in. "Our apologies for the failure."

The admiral stopped and looked at each person at the table and gave each a brief nod of recognition of his ancestor's failure. "However, there is nothing to be done about it now except increase our alertness and preparation."

Before the admiral could continue, Van interrupted. "Excuse me, Admiral, I understand increased alertness, but you said increased preparation. What does that mean?"

"It means we, the Host, will have to take a more proactive role. We hoped watching and guiding would be enough. However, this loss of Arkon forces cannot go unnoticed. Whoever is commanding their forces may have been hiding his failures so far, but it is unlikely he can continue."

"His name is Gulv," Van said.

Namath had been looking around the table as he spoke, but his head snapped back to Van. "What did you say?"

"I said his name is Admiral Gulv. He commands Arkon forces and is a Red."

"How do you know?" the admiral asked in amazement, staring intently at Van.

"In the last transmission from the Sonaran shipyard below us and before we joined the fight, I had a brief burst transmission from Harry—that's the name we gave to your AI Caretaker. He filled me in on a few things that happened while we were away."

Now the whole room had Van's attention. This was new to them also.

"This guy Gulv had, actually has, a spy in this area of space named Reeb. We don't know all about Reeb yet because he's currently unconscious on the shipyard as a prisoner. We do know Reeb was equipped with at least two Arkon devices that he used to both communicate with and alter the minds of his agents. We captured one of the devices but, so far, haven't located the other one being used by his principal agent."

Namath was riveted by the disclosure and only said, "Who is this principal agent?"

"We only know he is referred to as Number 1. We know he is the second of his kind and highly placed in the Federation, but we don't know who he is yet."

Namath's mind was in turmoil. This was all news to him also, and the thought of an Arkon agent being captured and alive had huge potential. Then he brought himself under control.

"This is important news, Commander. I would like to bring along several of my medical team and pay a visit to this Reeb."

Van glanced over at Rose, who gave him a brief nod.

"That can be arranged. But he is our prisoner and of extraordinary interest to the Zarminians."

"Yes, I understand, and we will not attempt to take him. We may be able to awaken him and learn what he knows."

"We can arrange it. But my impression was you had more you wanted to tell us."

"I do. But this news must be followed up immediately. Then we can talk again."

CHAPTER 39

D ICK SAT TRANSFIXED AT HIS desk. *New Horizons* had moved closer to the Sonaran shipyard and well within range of his Host implant technology. He and Van were talking.

"So, those are the details of the fight and our rescue by Admiral Namath and his ship. It's called *Triton*, by the way."

"I can't tell you how relieved we all were when we knew you and all aboard *New Horizons* had survived. I am sorry to hear about Danny, however. Such a fine man, carefree and full of life. How has Rose taken it?"

"As you would expect, it has hit her hard. He was the last of her immediate family and they were close. She's still not one hundred percent, but she's coming to grips with his death."

"I understand. By the way, *Gargon*, *Sutherland*, *Kirk*, and *Hornet* are under tow. Ootah is in fine form and demanded we take him home to Carian Station, where, he says, they can do better work than 'all those dirt people.'"

Van laughed as he pictured the red-bearded Carian railing against a tow away from his home.

"Chen Lee and Mia are OK, but their crews suffered significant casualties," Dick continued. "There are even a few Arkon ships out there without power. We sent a few Space Guard ships out to corral them until we can get tows to them. Like the last Arkon ship we captured, there are virtually no command officers left alive. Just a bunch of Browns, as they call themselves."

"Good work, Dick. Any change in Reeb?"

"No, still unconscious."

"How about the problems in the shipyards?"

"None. Aside from the normal snafus, we're back on track. We are behind schedule, however."

"Good to hear things are under control again. Anything on Number 1 yet?"

"Not a thing."

"OK, we plan to take our last combat shuttle down to you in a few hours. We'll have Admiral Namath and some of his medical staff with us. They may be able to revive Reeb, and we can get to the bottom of all this mayhem.

"We are also bringing along a new friend whose name is Majel. We met him on our journey, and I think you'll find him interesting. By the way, you'll be glad to know Majel wants James Harris as his constant link between Majel's people and us. He insists, however, that James be the Galactic Force ambassador since he was fired by the Earth Federation. It lets you off the ambassador hook!"

"That's a relief! I've too many hats as it is. I'll arrange quarters for all of your guests. See you later."

Dick leaned back in his chair, reviewing in his mind all that had happened over the last month or so. He shuddered at the thought that he and everyone he knew here had just escaped destruction. He was glad Dee Dee wasn't here during all this. He was afraid for her and the possibility that she might perish in a violent attack way out here, far from Earth. She would have been better off on Earth with the kids. . . maybe. Earth was at risk also, just not as dramatically.

He wondered if he would have been better off never having gotten involved with Van and Galactic Force. Then he might have had a more normal life with his family. On reflection, however, he realized his life had never been normal, even in the last few years in Washington D.C. No, he would do it all over again, he decided. With few exceptions, the people of Galactic Force had become his larger family; even Dee Dee said as much about him. Recently, she'd told him she used to be concerned about all his world travels on Earth and the effects on the family. Now, in retrospect, she saw that their family had become stronger, not weaker because of all their experiences. Today, she was excited to be involved in even a small part of the new adventures affecting everyone. Out here, she said she felt like she was on the front lines compared with her friends back on Earth. While he was afraid for her, she wasn't afraid at all. *Get a grip,* Dick thought as he returned to business.

Daman knew Van Childs had returned to Zarminian space and was due aboard the shipyard in a few hours. He had to move now.

He and four of his most loyal Space Guard officers presented themselves to the guard of the shipyard brig.

"I am Commodore Daman, and I have orders to take custody of the pirate prisoner for trial below," he said as he presented an official-looking document to the guard.

"But the prisoner is unconscious," said the perplexed guard, looking up from the document.

"Yes, we know and have brought a litter for transport." Daman pointed behind him.

"I'll have to check with the chief of security first." The guard reached for a communicator. But not fast enough. The shock of a stun gun fired from one of the Space Guard officers caused him to slump at his desk.

"Hurry, we don't have much time," said Daman as he took the pass card from the guard and opened the door to the cells.

Harry jerked and then spoke. "Mr. Carson, the shipyard brig doors have opened. It is not part of the schedule."

Dick had been making final preparations for Van's return and looked sharply up from his desk. "Opened out of schedule, you say?"

"Yes, Mr. Carson. There were no openings scheduled for the next hour. And the chief of security knows nothing about it."

Dick jumped from behind his desk and sprinted for the door. "Sound the alarm, Harry. Lock down everything and get a security force there now! Nobody leaves this shipyard."

Daman heard the alarm as his men rolled Reeb onto the litter. "Quickly, we haven't any more time." The five men pushed the litter forward and moved as fast as they could, hoping not to attract attention.

Numerous guards flashed past the small group but, seeing the commodore, kept on going. It wasn't until Dick and Harry rounded a nearby corner that Daman knew he was in trouble. Still, he remained calm as his group came to a halt.

Dick and Harry stopped in front of Daman. "What are you doing, Commodore?" Dick asked, looking first at the Space Guard officer and then at Reeb on the litter.

"We are transporting the prisoner to Lowondia for treatment and interrogation. These are my orders," Daman said, handing Dick the same orders he had shown the guard.

Dick looked up from the document. "Sorry, Commodore, but I can't allow that. He's a Guardian Force prisoner and not in a state for travel." Then it dawned on him. "You're the highly placed spy. You're Number 1," Dick said, frozen with the sudden realization.

Daman gave a subtle signal to his guards, and they raised their weapons.

"Nonsense, Dick. This is a Zarminian facility and this man is a traitor to his country. We have not only the authority but also the obligation to take him into custody. Please step aside."

"Like hell I will," Dick said just as he was struck by a bolt from one of the guards' stun weapons and fell to the deck.

Harry was also hit, several times. To the guards' amazement, however, Dick's companion was not fazed.

Harry said calmly, "Please put down your weapons, Commodore, and return with me to the brig."

"We will not." The guards fired again.

Harry had no choice but to react, and a bolt of jagged blue light jumped from the AI, knocking each man to the deck, stunned and unable to move.

Dick opened his eyes to the blank white ceiling of the shipyard dispensary. Two indistinct faces loomed over him. When his eyes focused, he saw the smiles of Van and Rose.

"Welcome back, Mr. Hero," Van said.

Dick was confused still. "Mr. Hero?"

"Yes," Rose said, clutching her hands in front of her face, barely concealing her delight as she bobbed excitedly on the balls of her feet. "You captured Number 1!"

The words didn't immediately register. Then he remembered his conclusion. "Commodore Daman."

"Yes," Van said. "When he came to, he confessed. He even revealed his agent on *New Horizons*, who was posing as a cook. Harry is with him now, using the Arkon machine to try to reverse the power it and another one like it had over him.

"Now if you can get your lazy butt up," Van said with a cheeky grin, "we can go meet some new people."

"Not today," Dick said, holding one hand over his eyes and forehead. "My brain still isn't working. Go away and I'll see you all tomorrow."

The next day, Van and others gathered in the makeshift room Dick and his aides had been using to plan for and stop the piracy and sabotage. Zarminian Foreign Minister Gortah had been invited but was not in attendance due to a long-planned Federation meeting on trade.

"On the one hand," Dick opened, "I want to apologize, in a way, for the surroundings. It isn't the type of conference room you are used to, but we have grown to like it, and it's served us well recently. But I'm not the leader of this session. That would be the commander." Dick motioned for Van to take over while he took a seat between James Harris and Majel.

"Thanks, Dick. Before we address a wider audience, I wanted you all to meet our first actual contact with the Galactic Host, Admiral Barton Namath." The admiral raised his hand in a slow wave just for a moment. Van continued, "He and the *Triton* saved many of us from destruction. I doubt we would be seeing him at all had it not been for the large and unexpected visit of the Arkon. More importantly, his medical team was able to awaken Reeb and extracted some significant information. Admiral, would you like to tell the group?" Van took a seat and Namath stood.

"Thank you, Commander. If some of you didn't know, Reeb has been the first Arkon agent we have discovered alive. After the Caretaker, I'm sorry, after Harry was able to reverse the effects of the Arkon mind-control technology, we were able to use our technology to revive Reeb to consciousness and learned several things. First, Reeb and the main Arkon commander, Admiral Gulv, have actually met."

This caused a buzz around the room.

Namath let the buzz continue for a few moments while he stood tall and glanced around the room until all eyes were back on him. "Reeb was captured by Gulv a number of years ago. But rather than dispose of the rogue as a pirate, Gulv exposed him to a mind-control device like the ones you captured. I think there are two now, am I correct?"

"Yes, Admiral," responded Dick. "Once Daman confessed, he led us to the second machine."

"Yes, of course. As I was saying, Gulv used one of these devices to alter Reeb's mind and turned him into an agent working for them. Reeb then recruited others, including your Commodore Daman. Reeb was tasked to report to Gulv any advances in technology, especially space technology, which might be a threat to the Arkon. In addition, it was Reeb's task to interfere with such developments by any means possible."

Namath observed Chen Lee trying to get his attention. "Yes, what is it?"

"Admiral, I'm Captain Lee of the *Southerland*, I have two questions. First, why would Gulv have an agent in Zarminia? Why not just send in some ships and take over? Second, to maintain contact with the Arkon, wherever they are, how could Reeb's signal get to this Arkon admiral?"

"Good questions, Captain. As to the first, we aren't sure why the Arkon didn't just, as you say, take over. My guess is their empire may be hard-pressed at the moment to take over another world. Perhaps they have a shortage of ships and ground forces, or both. To answer your second question, the solution was, and is, one or more relay stations between Zarminian space and Gulv's headquarters."

Again, the room was filled with the whispers of people commenting to their neighbors.

Then the admiral continued, "It is the discovery of these relay stations that might be the greatest find. To our knowledge, Gulv is not aware Reeb has been compromised. In a trade for his life, in fact, Reeb has agreed to work with us in sending messages to and receiving them from the Arkon."

"Excuse me, Admiral, when you said 'work with us,' you did mean all of us, yes?" Van asked.

Namath offered a mirthless smile and nodded at Van. "Of course. This is information we all can share and use to our mutual advantage. A great find." Namath, still standing, looked pointedly at Van. "This brings me to another topic, Commander. It is sensitive, and I am wondering if you would rather have a smaller group to discuss it?"

Van looked around the room, seeing nobody he didn't trust with his life. "This group is fine, Admiral. What do you have on your mind?"

Namath nodded and continued, "Very well. Everyone will agree the Arkon have shown themselves much earlier and in greater force than we expected. And despite your combined amazing efforts to prepare, Earth and Zarminian forces are still woefully short of having the kinds and numbers of ships and forces to meet the Arkon in force at this point."

Heads nodded around the table.

"Therefore, we propose taking a more active role in assisting you to grow."

"I have two questions, Admiral," Van said. "First, why now? Why have you waited till now to be more engaged? And second, what does 'a more active role' mean? You mentioned something like that before when you used the word 'proactive.'"

"Good questions both," replied the admiral. "To answer your first question, we thought we had more time until the Arkon showed an interest in Earth and potential neighbors. However, they have appeared much sooner than we would have liked, and you have already paid a price. That alone warranted our getting involved now.

"The answer to your second question is related to the first. Now that we've realized our expected time buffer between you and the first Arkon contact has nearly collapsed, we believe we can bring in our people and some of our support resources to help build ships and forces faster, train crews, and provide advice to the respective governments on both the importance of increased production and the threat they face."

Van thought about it for a minute. He agreed that the combined forces of Earth, Zarminia, and Galactic Force were behind the power curve in preparations to meet the Arkon. That's why he and his allies had been out looking for help. And here was some of the help. Then he spoke.

"What you say has both truth and some merit. However, it's been our thinking that in addition to being more efficient ourselves, we would need at least one or more new allies with added capacity to meet the accelerated Arkon threat. That capacity would be in addition to whatever the Host, you, already had. Are you suggesting your readiness is near the point of being able to take on the Arkon, and we," Van gestured around the room with one hand, "would provide the remainder, the tipping point as it were?"

"An interesting point of view, Commander," Namath said, "and I wish it were so. The truth is that if the Arkon came out in force right now, we would all be ill prepared to meet them and survive. We, the Host, are getting close, but are not yet there. That is why, for example, I left you the *New Horizons*. We saw what you did in allying with the Zarminians and hoped you would find yet another civilization to join with. From what you have told us, we know a little about your discovery of the Naskapi. But given their vow of nonaggression, I am unaware of any immediate support they can provide, which suggests discovering the Naskapi has not significantly changed the imbalance of power in the near term.

"Therefore, given the current state of affairs in which we find ourselves, what we hope to do is accelerate preparations on all fronts, which forces us to take a more proactive role."

"I see," Van said, hearing that word "proactive" again without a definition. "I wonder if we could adjourn for a while so I can meet with my staff and friends."

"By all means, Commander. I need to get back to my ship in the meantime. Your AI, Harry, can get a message to me when you would like me to return."

CHAPTER 40

AN HOUR LATER, VAN CALLED his closest confidants to meet him in his quarters aboard *New Horizons*. It was time to talk about what the admiral had said and what direction to go next. Majel was not in this group, but Harry was.

From the head of his table, Van took a drink of water from a glass next to him and looked up. "To quote somebody, we live in interesting times," he said, swirling the water in his glass. "I can't tell you how surprised I was to see a Host officer here, especially now. I had given up on seeing any of them for a long time. But I guess what he said is true. Our timeline has been accelerated. For those of you who might not know, when Harry and I first started on this adventure, we thought we had about a hundred years to get ready. Now, it would seem, we have very little time at all. I'm interested to hear what you think about what Namath said."

Nobody jumped to be the first to speak. Finally, however, it was James Harris who broke the ice.

"I have mixed feelings. On the one hand, what he said made sense. Failing to find additional capacity and help elsewhere, we have to find ways of being more efficient and productive. It may be the Host can help. On the other hand, in my experience people and organizations that say they want to help often have something else in mind."

"Like what?" Brice Johnson asked.

"Like some sort of payment. In traditional Earth foreign relations, it has usually meant money, or what passed for money. . . gold, land, trade concessions, and so forth. Or something like the controlling interest. I think the Host are aware of that, but by comparison, we don't have much wealth or concessions to offer. After all, what would they do with it, since they appear self-sufficient?

"To me it seems more likely they would want a controlling stake in how things are done, how resources are allocated, and who should do what."

People around the table took it all in. Some just looked down at the table in thought. Some nodded slowly while looking at Harris.

"You mean give up our identity and hand over control to them?" Brice asked again with an expression of incredulity as he began twisting his neck.

"Maybe not our identity. Not all of it. Earth people would still be Earth people and Zarminians would still be Zarminians. They might, however, be marching to somebody else's drum," Harris replied.

"I don't like it!" Brice said as he leaned back in his chair.

"I think James is right," Dick said, looking around the table. "I've had some similar experiences in my work on Earth, and what he says makes sense. The questions are, what and how much are we willing to give up for their help. . . and maybe survival?"

Then Rose spoke. "All of you have more experience than I do in these matters. But why do we have to give things up altogether? Isn't there some middle ground?"

"Like what?" Van asked, having a similar thought.

"For example, are we done looking for help elsewhere? Couldn't we make some partial deal with the Host, but still have a modicum of self-control and freedom to act?"

There were nods all around.

"How do we know the Host have the sort of capabilities they imply?" Frank asked, surprising everyone. "I mean, we all have a sense that they do, but nobody has ever seen any of their existing capabilities other than the big ship in orbit here and what they've given us. Seems to me we are making a lot of assumptions. Who's to say they're much better off than we are?"

Van's eyes sparkled and he pointed an approving finger at the ship's captain. "Great point, Frank. We've been in awe of them for so long we may have started to think they are omnipotent, or close to it compared with us. I'm thinking it's time for a road trip."

"You mean, Commander Childs, you want to see proof of our capabilities? Haven't we done enough with this ship and everything else we've given you?" asked an indignant Namath speaking over a ship to ship communications channel in his quarters aboard *Triton*.

"I wouldn't put it quite like that, Admiral," said Van sitting in his flag bridge aboard *New Horizons*. "After all, if my friends and I have interpreted your statements correctly, we'll be giving up some amount of our self-determination and control if we go along with what you've outlined. We have a great many people we are responsible to and for, and we would like some added confidence that what we choose to support is in their best interests. Add to that our relationships and responsibilities with Zarminia and Earth."

Namath eyes narrowed as he thought about what Van had just said. Then he relaxed. "I see your point, Commander. Very well, you will be able to see many of our capabilities, but for security purposes, there will be limitations."

"Like what?" Van asked.

"I will take you and three others to one of our production-and-development centers. The AI, however, must stay behind."

"Why?" Van asked, surprised.

"That generation of AI is without the safeguards we subsequently learned to program into our automated assistants. It would be difficult to control, and, therefore, a security risk we are not willing to take."

"Does your offer to go to the production-and-development center extend to the Zarminians?" Van asked, thinking the Zarminians might like to be involved.

"Not now, Commander. Perhaps some other time. In my view, you and your group will appreciate and understand what you see better than the Zarminians at this point, resulting in fewer questions and less time expended on this effort."

Van wasn't exactly happy about this, but it wasn't under his control. So, he thought about whom he could take. James Harris could not go since he was Majel's closest contact. And Van didn't want Majel on this trip. Not until Van knew more about what was going on with the Host. However, he felt an engineer would be helpful, so he picked Bob Cooper. Brice would go as a security expert, and Rose as their medical expert.

"OK. I have the people in mind. When do we leave?" Van asked.

"We can leave as soon as you have collected your team. It will take us about twenty-two hours since we will have to make three jumps."

"Why three jumps?" Van asked.

"We can't go in a straight line on any but the last jump. We have to avoid a few objects in space."

Van and his three companions were ready in just a few hours and boarded the Host shuttle in *New Horizons'* port flight bay.

This was a VIP shuttle, Van concluded. Perhaps the admiral's. The interior bulkheads and the overhead were covered in a pale but attractive fabric. All the seats were plush and comfortable. And there were windows on this shuttle. Everyone shifted to the port-side windows as they approached the *Triton*.

"Wow, what a ship," Bob said with professional admiration. "I'd love to see what makes her tick."

Van too was impressed. The *Triton*'s size was similar to *New Horizons*, but this was a ship of war, an offensive powerhouse. It bristled with weapons emplacements, communications antennas, and domes. Its engine-thrust nozzles were bigger than *New Horizons'*, suggesting more power and speed. Van could appreciate the difference in power and capability between this ship and Guardian Force's largest line ship, *Reliant*.

As they closed the distance, everyone had a chance to appreciate another battle cruiser feature: big flight bays. *Triton* only had two compared with *New Horizons'* three, but these were huge. The comparatively tiny shuttle entered the bay on the starboard side and settled to the deck. Van expected to see some monstrous pressure doors close, sealing off the bay from space. But there was no movement. That was probably why he jumped when the shuttle's ramp went down with a hiss.

"Don't worry, Commander," said a Host officer waiting at the foot of the ramp upon seeing Van's concern. "There is a force field in place to seal the bay. It's safe to exit."

After Van's group collected at the foot of the ramp, still looking nervously at the picture of space and no bay doors, the officer spoke again.

"I am Captain Raynaldus. *Triton* is my ship and serves as the flagship for Admiral Namath. The admiral is busy at the moment but asked me to greet you. Come with me to the admiral's quarters. Your bags will be taken to your quarters."

As the group trailed the *Triton*'s captain, Brice was impressed with the security guards on both sides. They weren't at ceremonial attention. They were poised and ready for trouble. He was especially interested in the combat rifles they carried. He didn't recognize them, and they looked very dangerous.

"Come in, come in," the admiral said in greeting as he strode from behind his desk. "Please have a seat over here."

His quarters, at least what could be seen, were impressive. A big desk at the forward end, a conference table in the middle, and a large sitting area at the aft end. It was obvious the admiral wanted them seated at the table as he took a position at its head and sat.

"How was your trip up?" Namath asked.

"Smooth and uneventful," Van said.

"Good! The pilots on my shuttle are the best. I'm always impressed with their skills. Refreshments?"

Van shook his head and spoke for the group. "We're fine, Admiral, and looking forward to the trip. Where exactly are we headed?"

"The location is classified, as you might imagine. But as I

mentioned before, it is one of our production-and-development centers. We have several in various locations. In this case we used a large asteroid we found long ago. We were immediately impressed with its unique formation. It had a honeycomb interior. We could see the potential and set about reconstructing it to meet our needs. Fortunately, it has a sturdy crust and can resist any weapons we know of."

"How large is it?" Bob asked.

"Fortunately, I have an answer. We wondered ourselves how to compare it to other asteroids. It is approximately the size of what you call 19 Fortuna, 225 kilometers in diameter or about 140 of Earth's miles."

"That is big," Bob said softly as he pictured the asteroid in his head.

"Does it have a name?" Rose asked.

"We liked the name Fortuna, so that is what we call it."

CHAPTER 41

R<small>EEB AND THE</small> A<small>RKON TRANSCEIVER</small> were relocated from the shipyard brig to a newly refurbished holding cell near Dick's office. Harry had modified the Arkon equipment to eliminate its mind-altering capability, and it had been temporarily placed in the room between Dick's office and Reeb's place of confinement, the idea being that if the Arkon called, Dick, Harry, and Reeb would be close by to answer. While they waited for a call, however, things went on as usual until Harry spoke.

"Mr. Carson, I would like to go to *New Horizons.*"

Dick looked up from his desk at the AI, who had been less busy and quieter now that the attempts to sabotage shipbuilding had been brought under control. "What for?"

"I have been analyzing the battle just completed, Mr. Carson, and discovered some anomalies I cannot explain."

"Like what?" Dick said, putting down his tablet in order to focus on Harry.

"It is too early to speculate, Mr. Carson. But I need access to the *New Horizons* and to Jennifer."

"I thought you and Jennifer could communicate from here?"

"True, Mr. Carson, but when I say Jennifer, I mean the ship's computer system."

Dick knew better than to ask too many questions of Harry; he never wasted his or anybody's time on frivolous activity.

"OK, Harry, I'll arrange a shuttle and contact Captain Wilson about your plans."

"I would appreciate it if you would not contact Captain Wilson yet, Mr. Carson, and just allow me to go aboard the next supply shuttle, which is scheduled to leave in twenty minutes."

It was a very different kind of request from any Dick could remember Harry making. But again, he and many others had learned to trust this AI.

Still looking puzzled, Dick said, "Very well. But don't go too long without letting Captain Wilson or his XO know what you're doing."

"Thank you, Mr. Carson," Harry said as he turned and left the room for the supply shuttle flight bay.

Once on board *New Horizons*, Harry wasted no time heading for the ship's computer core. As a precaution and before launching in the shuttle, he'd shut down all his active sensors and communications links. He didn't want to alert Jennifer to his presence.

Reaching the hatch to the core, the guard acknowledged Harry's authority to enter, and he went inside.

To most people this space would look like a maze of wires, blinking lights, and fans. But to Harry it was like a picture of order and logic. He quickly went to the section of the core he needed to access. With just a few quick motions of his mechanical hands on a few switches, the lights on the panel in front of him went out. Then he opened the interior and removed several circuit boards and placed them in a small bag he carried with him.

Satisfied he had done what he wanted, he proceeded to a location far from the original panel and did the same with a different control panel. He had just disconnected Jennifer's primary and secondary control panels. The ship's AI was off-line.

Frank Wilson was in his quarters and was about to step into his shower when he heard a knock at his door. He stopped and wrapped his robe around him and asked, "Jennifer, who is that?" But there was no response. He asked twice more, but still no response came.

Shrugging, Frank went to the cabin door and opened it. He was more than a little surprised to see Harry standing there.

"What the devil?" was Frank's first response. He'd had no idea Harry was aboard, and he should have. "How and when did you get here?"

"My apologies, Captain. I came aboard forty minutes ago. I did not announce my coming or arrival for good reason. If I may come in, I will explain."

Frank opened the door wide, motioning for Harry to enter, and asked, "What's this all about?" He closed the door behind the AI.

"I must tell you, Captain, I have shut down Jennifer."

If Frank was surprised to see Harry, he was shocked at what he'd just heard. Forced to take a seat in his sitting area, he asked, "You did what?"

"I shut down Jennifer."

"I heard that, but why?" he asked, mystified.

"I needed to access the ship's communications logs, Captain, and I could not do it with Jennifer active."

Frank lay his head back on the chair as he tried and tried to come to grips with what Harry was saying. "Lord knows we all respect and trust you, Harry, but you have me stumped."

"I am sorry, Captain. While on the shipyard, I detected some unaccounted for high-frequency transmissions from this ship during the battle. I wanted to locate the source of those transmissions and determine what they meant."

"We were all communicating like crazy in the fight," Frank commented. "It was a mess, I'll agree, but we tried to keep things to a minimum."

"Our communications are not at issue, Captain. There was something else going on."

Triton had an observatory lounge, not with a big window, but with a huge view screen connected to a series of exterior cameras, which afforded people in the lounge the picturesque panorama of space all while sitting in the comfort of a big living room. At this moment the Galactic Force team was seated and talking while the kaleidoscope of colors created by a space jump flew across the screen.

"This is so exciting!" said Rose as she watched the view screen.

"Colorful at least," Brice said, not paying much attention to the color show. "But does all this seem too easy?"

Van looked away from the color streams at Brice. "What do you mean?"

"I mean, that Namath guy gave in to this trip awfully easy. I, on the other hand, would have been more resistant to taking anybody to a secret base."

"That's because you're paranoid. It's part of your job," Van said and chuckled.

"Maybe not," Rose said. "I agree with Brice. I expected more resistance or even to have had him say flat out no."

"But why would you think that?" Bob asked. "We asked for some confirmation of his capabilities, and he said OK. What's wrong?"

"Nothing," Rose said. "It's just that his capitulation was so fast."

"I think you're all overthinking this," Van said. "We asked for something and we got it. Let's take advantage of it."

Van listened to the conversation of his friends for a few minutes then said, "Rose and Brice may be right. Maybe we can test things a little while we're en route and learn something. I'm sure Bob would like to see the engineering section. Rose has to be dying to see medical, and Brice to learn more about the small arms he saw. And I want to see the control center and flight bays. I'll ask Raynaldus to give us each a tour."

After the first jump was completed and the *Triton* had settled on the course to the second jump point, Raynaldus approved Van's request, with the understanding some areas would be off limits and they would each have an escort. The escort turned out to be an officer from each section visited and an armed guard.

Van was escorted by Raynaldus himself. And he was proud of his ship.

"As you saw, command centers are all alike, Commander. Ours

isn't much different from yours aboard *New Horizons*. Just a few more weapons systems. However, when we see the flight bay, I think you'll appreciate it. You were a pilot yourself, weren't you?"

"Yes, a long time ago. I get to play with a shuttle now and then, but I'm afraid my flying days are rapidly disappearing."

"It happens to us all, I'm afraid. I rarely get the shuttle opportunity you mentioned. But when I do, all the old feelings come back. For a short while, I'm a young altern again with no other business than flying."

Van smiled at the captain. He was much more personable than the admiral, and likeable. "I guess we pilots all have the same memories," Van commented. "But here we are on a great ship like this one. I can tell you're proud of her."

"It shows, does it? Yes, I am proud. Not many men get the opportunity to command a battle cruiser."

"There are few of them, I take it?" Van asked, thinking he had discovered something.

He did not fail to note that Raynaldus didn't answer. Instead, the captain said, "Here we are. The air lock to Flight Bay 1."

As the captain had predicted, Van was impressed. He thought the *New Horizons'* flight bays were huge, but this one made them seem small. Van could swear it could hold two corvettes.

"Wow!" was all he could immediately say as he looked around. The first things he focused on were all the smaller craft, including the largest of them. "What are those bigger birds in the rear of the bay?"

"Those are a new class of combat shuttle. Their troop capacity is twice as great as a standard combat shuttle. Like the others, they are FTL capable. Their armament is somewhat greater also."

"I'm impressed, Captain. Could I see inside one?"

"I'm afraid not. The security level on these is much higher than the other craft in the bay. However, let's walk this way to the force field."

Van was still a little apprehensive about approaching the open bay doors, but he forced himself to overcome his concerns.

The pair of pilots stopped about five feet from the opening, and Van could feel a slight tingling over his body.

"This is as close as it's safe to get. You can probably already feel some of the effects of the field."

"Indeed I do," Van said in both reverence and respect for the technology. "Why didn't *New Horizons* have these same types of shields?"

"Honestly, I don't know. It may have something to do with available power. We have more than *New Horizons*, I know."

The two men spent another half hour enjoying each other's company, telling flight stories, and admiring the huge bay.

As the third and last jump began, Van and his team found themselves gathered back in the observation lounge.

"Did everyone have a good time?" Van asked half in jest, knowing they actually had had individual missions. There were nods from everyone. "Who wants to speak first?"

"I do," Rose said, hardly able to constrain her excitement.

Van offered an upturned palm, signaling her to start.

"Every time I see new Host technology, I'm impressed. While it's true this ship and *New Horizons* have similar equipment, *Triton*'s medical facility is at least twice as large as ours. Most of the extra space is devoted to bigger wards and several more surgical centers. A few pieces of equipment I didn't recognize were there, but one thing was clear: they are geared up for many more casualties than any of our ships."

"Probably because *Triton* is a true warship, not an expeditionary ship like *New Horizons*," Brice commented.

"That could be true. I suppose there could be more casualties on this sort of ship, but it still seemed like a lot of extra capability."

"Brice, what did you see?" Van asked.

"Not as much as I would have liked. I did get to see and feel the assault rifles we see with every guard. They are energy weapons capable of both laser and plasma fire. No stun capability, which is interesting. Their power sources have more capacity than ours, but how much more, I don't know. The combat-armored suits I saw were at least a generation newer than ours and made of more-advanced material. I suspect they can absorb or deflect more power. I asked for details, but wasn't given any.

"I also saw some large doors on both ends of the armory I visited, but was told they were off limits. Based on the size of the doors, whatever is in those rooms is big. But that's all I was able to see."

"Bob, what about you?"

"As you might expect, the engineering spaces are much larger than ours on *New Horizons*. Beautiful spaces, and Elaine is going to be incredibly jealous she didn't get to come!"

"What else?" Van asked, getting Bob back on track.

"Well, not a lot of difference between *Triton* and *New Horizons* except for several sealed-off spaces."

"Let me guess," Brice said sarcastically. "Off limits for security reasons."

"Yes," Bob said, not recognizing Brice's comment for what it was. "But there was something more."

"What?" Van said impatiently.

"There were security guards everywhere. We don't have anything like that on *New Horizons* except at general quarters."

"Come to think of it," added Rose, "there were security guards outside medical also. Not inside though."

Van commented, "Interesting, I noticed armed guards all over the flight bay, especially around the large combat shuttles. Putting together all your observations, I would say this ship, at the very least, is in a heightened security level hardly warranted by the presence of the four of us."

"So, what do you think it means?" Rose asked.

"I don't know. Still thinking about it."

CHAPTER 42

ADMIRAL GULV WAS UPSET. HE hadn't heard from his kinsman Daan since his departure on a punishment mission. In addition, Red Sector 20 continued to be undermanned while Daan was away. Gulv wasn't sure how long he could keep the information from the supreme leader and his staff, even at the slow pace of information flow in the Arkon empire. He had hoped Daan would be back with news of victory, thus increasing Gulv and Daan's family power.

Gulv had taken the extraordinary step of asking Sub Admiral Braak for news, Braak being the acting Red Sector 20 commander. But there was nothing. The last thing he could think of or wanted to do was to contact the pirate Reeb through his special communications.

Dick had an orange light installed on his office wall that would silently flash when the Arkon communications equipment was activated. It started flashing just as he was wrapping up his day and getting ready to leave his office. He dropped everything and ran the short distance to the room next door. A security guard already had Reeb in tow for just this eventuality. By prior agreement, Dick and Reeb had arranged that if the Arkon called and asked about the attack, they would call it an Arkon victory, informing him that the majority of allied fighting ships were destroyed, the shipyards were left in flames, and there was significant destruction on the surface. They would admit to a few Arkon losses, but would say the main force was intact and had moved out of the system.

The transceiver crackled and Reeb recognized Gulv. "Reeb, this is Gulv, come in," was the simple call. The same call had been used before, albeit infrequently.

Reeb sat in a chair facing the microphone and steadily said, "This is Reeb. I read you loud and clear, Admiral."

"Reeb, what is going on there? I sent forces to take action against the Zarminians. Have you seen them?"

"They were here, Admiral, a force led by two cruisers, some destroyers, and a few smaller ships. They attacked four days ago and wiped out the allied space forces here, in addition to the orbiting shipyards. Before leaving, they also bombarded the surface of all five countries, hitting tech and manufacturing centers. It has brought this planet to its knees. I am unable to estimate when they will be able to rebuild."

If Reeb and Dick had been able to see Gulv, they would have seen a fully raised red crest shivering with excitement.

"Excellent news, Reeb. Excellent news indeed. Where are Admiral Daan and his forces now, and can I talk to them?"

"The Arkon force departed after, I suspect, hitting all their planned targets. I did not hear from Admiral Daan, and I don't know where he went."

Gulv took the news in somberly. There had been no plan to go anywhere else, but if Daan found an opportunity, then all the better for the family.

"Very well. This is all good news. Your cover is still good?"

"Yes, Admiral."

"Then keep it that way and contact me if Daan comes back or other forces show themselves."

Reeb was about to say something like "Roger, out," but the line had already gone dead.

"Good job, Reeb," Dick said. "If they think the mission was complete, they won't send any more forces this way."

"True, but if they don't hear from Daan soon, they will start to get suspicious."

"We'll dream up something if and when that happens. But for now, we have some time to repair things and get back to a better combat position."

Leaving Reeb and his guard behind, Dick went down several levels to the secure communications center to call Stan Walters at Mars Base. Mars Base and Zarminia were linked by a series of relay buoys Harry had designed and put in place when they'd first made friends with the Carians and then the Zarminians. It was a private Guardian Force connection. Dick called for and connected with Stan.

"Dick, how are you way out there after surviving the Arkon?" Stan asked.

"OK, under the circumstances, but I can't say the same for the Arkon. We were lucky."

"I guess you were. By the way, *Reliant* and one of our supply ships is en route to you now. In addition to normal supplies, I rounded up two squadrons of fighters and crews along with a number of combat shuttles for replacements. Nobody asked, but I thought it the right thing to do."

"Frank will love it. Right now he's a sitting target, as he puts it. But I have bigger news. Van and *New Horizons* were saved at the last minute by, get this, a real live Host battle cruiser commanded by an admiral named Barton Namath."

"You're kidding!"

"No, it blew up an Arkon cruiser at the last minute. Scary stuff. By the way, how is Jan St. Clair?"

"She and the *Reliant* and two corvettes survived and followed orders to beat feet to Point Foxtrot. When she finally contacted me, I told her to come home. They barely had enough war shots to keep away a few gunboats if they met any. She was pissed though. Wanted into the big fight. But I told her no. We would have had our hands full if the Arkon had taken a path for Earth. Sorry we couldn't send you more help."

"That's OK, we understand the priorities."

"What's Van doing now?"

"Interesting you should ask. He persuaded the Host admiral to take him and three others to see one of their manufacturing-and-supply facilities."

"Why? Was he just curious?"

"No, it goes beyond curiosity. As I understand it, the admiral thinks the Host need to play a greater role in getting humans ready for the Arkon. They were quick to mention the fact that the timeline is getting shorter for a major confrontation, and I'm inclined to believe him based on this last attack. Van, however, is reluctant to hand over some or all of the reins to a greater or lesser extent until he can see what the Host have to offer."

"Interesting. Did the Host say anything about approaching the Earth Federation?"

"Not that I'm aware of. Van had the impression that if he could be convinced the Host could do what they say, he and Galactic Force would support the Host proposal when Earth is approached. Same with the Zarminians."

"Then you might want to keep an eye out in your area for another Host ship. A Host cruiser passed here yesterday headed for Earth with a Federation corvette in escort. I learned there was a Federation envoy aboard the cruiser named McDuff."

Dick nearly knocked over the receiver as he lowered his head to the table in front of him and slowly bumped it a few times on the table surface. "Not McDuff!" he cried. He had hoped that he had seen the last of the annoying little man. Even the hint of McDuff re-inserting himself into Guardian Force business was more than just annoying.

When he recovered, he sat back up and continued, "One last thing. When we captured the pirate Reeb, we also recovered two Arkon communications devices. One is set up next to my office on the shipyard.

"Today we intercepted a call from an Arkon admiral called Gulv. He talked to Reeb in my presence. As we'd planned for such an event, Reeb told the admiral the Arkon were successful in their mission and then left to go elsewhere. That should keep them quiet for a while, but eventually they'll get curious again. I don't know how long we can keep this Arkon disaster secret from them. Just wanted you to know."

Stan absorbed this and then commented, "Good to know. At least we have some breathing room."

"Yes, we do," Dick responded. "Reeb also said the Arkon are slow to react to almost anything, so that means more time. But eventually, and probably sooner than any of us want, they'll be back."

"Thanks for the information, Dick. Have Frank call me when he gets a chance and I'll see what more he needs. We have to get *New Horizons* back to fighting shape as soon as possible. My regards to Van and Rose when you see them next, and to Dee Dee."

"Will do, Stan." The call was ended.

CHAPTER 43

EXACTLY TWENTY-TWO HOURS AFTER DEPARTING Zarminian space, *Triton* exited jump, and the pinpoints of light from distant stars appeared. No more flashing colors. Van and his team had gotten a few hours' sleep in the quarters provided and had a meal in the officer's ward room. Now they were back in the observation lounge, intently watching the big view screen.

"I don't see any big asteroid," Brice said with disappointment.

Van nodded and said, "We probably won't for a while. *Triton* wouldn't exit jump right next to the thing, too dangerous. It's probably in front of us and outside the camera view of this screen."

The first thing they did see was not the asteroid but rather a ship pulling alongside *Triton* in formation.

"That looks like one of our corvettes," Brice commented as they watched the smaller ship settle into its position.

"Yes, it does," Van said, also watching intently. "Looks like an escort. Interesting it still looks so much like ours. You would have thought there would be a whole new and different class by now."

"Those Agora-class corvettes like the old *Aurora* are pretty stout," Bob said. "Once we started building new ones, I think they're pretty reliable. Why change what works?"

"Some truth to that, Bob, but *Aurora* was two hundred years old when we got her. You'd think there would be a lot of changes by now," Van said as they continued to watch the smaller ship.

"I'm guessing there are a lot of internal changes, and probably weapons systems changes as well. Maybe we'll get a chance to see," Bob replied.

"Don't bet on it. We've seen precious little detail so far," Brice said sarcastically as the edge of a huge asteroid began to creep into the picture on the view screen.

"Welcome to Fortuna."

All heads turned to the voice behind them and saw Namath standing there. No one had heard him enter.

"As far as the corvette is concerned, your observation is correct. Externally, it is quite similar to the traditional corvettes of our past. We kept the basic design in order to maintain a high production rate. This one named *Ditona* is about ten of your years old and is part of revision twenty of the series."

"Will we be able to see inside this one?" Brice asked, thinking he knew the answer.

"Unfortunately, no. *Ditona* is scheduled to depart on a mission very shortly and will not be available for a visit," Namath said.

Brice folded his arms and tilted his head at his friends as if to say, *I told you so.*

"Now, if you will all come with me to the flight bay, we will shuttle into Fortuna. *Triton* will stay in orbit."

The shuttle's view screen was keyed to a forward camera. As the small craft got closer to the asteroid, the "weathered" appearance became clearer and clearer. Craters from ancient impacts pockmarked the surface. Ridges from some ancient upheaval, perhaps at formation, took on the appearance of mountains. Then it became apparent they were headed for a particular crater.

As the crater vista widened and began appearing in the side windows, an opening formed in the center.

"This is Fortuna's small-craft entrance. We have several others for our larger ships located in strategic places around the asteroid," said the admiral as part of a narration. "We will continue through this entrance for about twenty of your miles, making course changes as we go along. The path is not straight for security reasons."

Sure enough, the shuttle occupants observed several nearly

90-degree turns, until finally the small corridor opened to a large cavern, every bit as large as the *Triton's* flight bays.

"Here we are in Transport Bay 2. As soon as we touch down, we will be able to exit the shuttle. I have arranged for another short tour for you before we meet again in my office. That should be in about four of your hours."

When the admiral stopped talking, there was a gentle bump as the shuttle came to rest. Almost immediately, the ramp hissed down, revealing another Host officer and an honor guard.

"Atten-shun!" called out the officer, and the guards took a rigid stance with weapons held firmly in front of them as a salute.

The admiral exited and gave a brief salute as he quickly disappeared through a nearby door.

"Dis-missed!" the officer called out, and the guards snapped their rifles smartly to a carry position and most marched off. Four remained, watching the visitors carefully.

"Welcome to Fortuna," said the officer to the visitors. "My name is Senior Altern Bourdain. I will be your guide for the next few hours. Before we start, however, please follow me to the visitors lounge where we have some refreshments and you can relax a little. Your bags will be transferred to your quarters."

Bourdain showed the visitors to the lounge and then stepped out, promising to be back soon. Once seated in the comfortable visitor's lounge and after freshening up, Bob was the first to speak.

"They don't waste any time, do they? Guests arrive, blow their respective noses, and start the tour."

Van chuckled at Bob's spoken thought. "No, they don't. But this isn't exactly a social call. Remember, Namath wasn't very excited about our coming to begin with. I imagine he wants us out of his hair as soon as possible."

Rose was about to say something but stopped when Bourdain returned.

"Everyone feeling better? If so, we can start. We will be traveling by cart and when necessary by train as we go along. There is a lot to see, so please step outside and take a seat in the cart."

The Guardian Force team did as requested and found a comfortable cart, larger than a golf cart and apparently powered by an internal power source, like a battery. The difference between this cart and others the group had seen elsewhere on Earth or one of their bases was the complete silence of the drive system.

After everyone was seated, the senior altern put the cart in motion and began the tour.

"This bay you landed in and we are leaving is for craft up to the size of combat shuttles and is used mainly as a reception area and for small-craft maintenance. You can see multiple small craft on our right, including mining craft, in various stages of routine maintenance or repair. Ahead is a short tunnel leading to our first maintenance-and-construction bay for capital ships."

"You said your first maintenance-and-construction bay, how many are there total?" Van asked.

"Presently, there are ten with two more under construction, sir. Five on this side of Fortuna and five on the other side. For security reasons, they are not connected," said a proud Bourdain.

"Why not?" Rose asked.

"If we were to be attacked or if there were some major catastrophe like a major fire on one side, the other would remain up and operating, ma'am."

"Makes sense," Rose said with an approving tilt of her head just as the cart finished its passage into the next bay.

"Wow!" said Bob. "This is amazing. How many ships can fit in here?"

"That depends," Bourdain said, "on the ship type and size, sir. Currently, as you can see, there are three destroyers and a cruiser undergoing maintenance or modification here in Bay 1."

"But no new construction," Brice observed.

"Correct, sir. Not in this bay, but when we enter Bay 2, you will see some of our newest in the construction process."

"I don't see a lot of people in this bay, why not?" Van asked, looking around the huge facility.

"Most of the people are on the inside of these ships working on command systems, propulsion, and other supporting systems," said Bourdain.

"Could we stop and have a look inside?" Van asked with one eyebrow raised in expectation of a negative answer.

"No, I'm sorry, Commander. I've been given a tight schedule to get you around and then to the admiral."

Van and Brice shared another quick glance.

The next tube between bays appeared before them and then disappeared as they made a quick passage in their quiet cart. This time, to everyone's surprise, the cart stopped midway through the bay, which was similar in size to the previous one.

"Please feel free to get out and stretch your legs. We can walk for a short distance, but for safety reasons, please stay on this side of the yellow lines. You can see three ships under construction here, two frigates and a destroyer. They are hard to recognize at this stage, but the destroyer is on the extreme right."

The visitors looked over the scene intensely. Van noted to himself that much of what they could see was like their own construction facilities on Mars Base and on the Zarminian shipyards. The big difference was the buzz of activity and the speed of progress. They could see the ships developing. Then they saw why.

"What is that?" exclaimed Bob, pointing to a semi-human-looking object emerging from behind a newly raised bulkhead.

"Construction robots," said Bourdain as if it should be obvious. "They do all the heavy lifting, melding, wiring, and so forth."

"They work autonomously?" Bob asked, now fixated on the huge machines moving smoothly up and down the production line.

"Yes and no. They can be programmed to do a great deal of work on their own, but periodically they are forced to divert their work while quality checks are completed by the human workers. At other times they may be directly controlled when one type of work interfaces with another. Like when electrical and communications lines run between sensitive compartments."

All Bob could say was, "Amazing. But where do all the parts come from?"

"Next door is a fabrication center. There is one for every two construction bays. If you look to the rear of this bay, you can see automated carts traveling a small roadway bringing in the parts and returning for more. This center also serves the small craft bay and the maintenance bay.

"If I can anticipate your next question, raw materials for the fabrication center come from another bay above, which our mining ships keep full."

The group stood fascinated as several compartments were completed and the robots moved to the next ones. Their attention was eventually broken by their guide.

"If you will step back into the cart, we can move two bays down. We will pass through the fabrication area, but there isn't much to see there."

"Wait a minute!" Bob said urgently.

Bourdain stopped the cart and looked around at the engineer. "Yes, sir?"

"How do you get these ships in and out of here? I mean, there's plenty of room to build them, of course. But I don't see how you get them out. . . or in, as the case may be."

"Good catch. I failed to point out the doors built into the rear walls of each bay. The doors open on to a single receiving bay that attaches to a transport tube leading to the surface. There is just one tube, which services all the manufacturing bays in this location. Does that answer your question, sir?"

"Yes, I guess. Any chance of seeing the bay and the tube?"

"I'm afraid not, sir. Not on this visit at least." The driver turned forward again and continued on his planned route.

They did pass through the fabrication bay, and it was as huge as the former bays. To Van, the fabrication machines looked like the ones at Mars Base and elsewhere, but bigger and noisier.

As they sped through the center, Bob leaned over to whisper into Van's ear. "He's wrong about nothing to see here."

"What?" demanded Van. "I can't hear you."

Putting more energy into his voice, Bob repeated, "He's wrong about nothing to see here."

"Why?" Van asked as he leaned in to hear Bob better.

"These fabrication machines are bigger, but they're also different. From what I can see, the controls are different and they must be powered by something bigger than our systems. Something really big."

Van nodded, but he couldn't continue the discussion when the cart entered another tunnel into the next bay. This time it was Van's turn to say: "Wow."

Van saw that the majority of this bay was taken up by two immense ships, smaller than *New Horizons*, but bigger than the cruiser *Reliant*. He noted that there were defensive weapons similar to *New Horizons* and one flight bay, which was open. And he could see straight through it. *Massive and open to both sides,* he thought. As he watched, construction robots were going in and out of the various hatches.

The cart stopped and Bourdain took the time to turn and explain what they were seeing.

"These are our two newest cargo and transport ships. They have both been out for flight trials and are now being revised to fix a few things that didn't work right the first time and to add a few capabilities."

Van gazed with amazement, especially when trying unsuccessfully to measure them against the Guardian Force cargo ships *Griffin* and *Orion*. . . or even the modestly larger *Bayfield* under construction at Mars Base. He estimated these ships to be at least twice as large as those.

"Why such large ships?" Van asked.

"The specs were given to us by the Host Regents, I'm told. As a total population, we are getting large enough now that we need larger ships to transfer people and cargo back and forth among our various locations."

Van nodded in understanding. At least, he thought he understood. There was something about these two ships that bothered him, though he couldn't put his finger on it.

"Now we're off to our next stop," said the smiling guide as he faced front and goosed the cart forward.

But the next area wasn't a huge bay. Instead, it looked like a small train station. Turning to look at his charges, Bourdain explained what was next.

"This is one of our transportation centers. It moves people about from one bay to another or to other parts of Fortuna. If you will leave the cart, we have a train waiting for us."

Their guide led the visitors a short distance to a capsule that looked like a long bullet, and gestured for them to enter and take a seat. When everyone was seated, the doors closed automatically and the tram began to move.

"This particular route will take us to one of the living areas for those of us who work here. I live in this one with my family. Interestingly, it was one of the first areas to be developed after the initial excavation of the core."

"How long ago was that?" Van asked.

"You know, I'm not sure. I've never been asked before. My family and I have lived here for about two of your Earth years. It was here before me, that's all I know. I just started these tours about a week ago."

The trip took about twenty minutes, and there was no way of guessing how deep into the asteroid they were headed. Then the train began to slow.

"Here we are in Area 1. Once we pass through security, we will be able to view the city from a mezzanine."

"How deep are we into Fortuna?" Bob asked.

"Like so many aspects of Fortuna, to nonresidents it is classified. But it is deep enough to afford substantial protection to the residents from any intruders."

As they exited the train, Bourdain directed them to a security checkpoint overseen by armed guards. After they were scanned for weapons or dangerous substances, they were allowed to proceed through a huge set of thick double doors.

"As I'm sure you can appreciate, we protect those who work and live here. Hence the screening and these blast doors and air locks. If you will move to the right, you will see the mezzanine, and from there you can see where we live. Recently, at the request of the residents, we stopped taking visitors from the home world and other Host facilities into the city. They didn't want to feel like displays and didn't like the intrusion on their daily lives."

The vista before them was impressive yet familiar. This was a larger version of the park and living area on Mars Base. Much larger.

"It's beautiful," Rose said as she admired the beauty of the place.

Van agreed. He saw that, like on Mars Base, the parks were filled with kids playing along with one or more of their parents. He saw apartment buildings as high as three or four stories with narrow roads winding between and among them. Based on the gentle yellow-white light, Van guessed it was daytime in Area 1.

"How many people live here?" Rose asked.

"Area 1 is the smallest city, with about fifteen thousand residents."

"How many cities are there?" Bob asked.

"Five at present and we're building another one."

"So that means about one hundred thousand residents total?" Bob asked again, ever the man with numbers on his mind.

"More or less," Bourdain replied.

"Where do they receive medical treatment?" Rose inquired, her medical profession getting the best of her.

"There are aid stations scattered about each city, modeled after the medical centers on our ships."

Rose wanted to ask more questions, but a look from Van kept her from it.

Bourdain looked at a digital clock on the wall behind the group. "I'm sorry, but our time is running out and we have to go. The admiral will be waiting after you have a chance to refresh yourselves."

Bourdain took the group back to the same visitor's lounge they had used earlier and excused himself. "Relax for a while and then

I'll be back to take you to the admiral." As before, when their guide left, they could see the armed guards stationed outside the doors.

Van and the others chose something cold to drink from the refreshment bar and sat on a comfortable couch that circled a coffee table.

Van put his feet up on the table and leaned back, letting energy flow back into him. "What a whirlwind tour," he said, taking a drink of what tasted like apple juice.

"You can say that again," Rose said, also leaning back in her seat. "In retrospect, I'm glad you stopped me from asking medical questions; we'd still be out there."

Van smiled. "I wasn't sure you saw my look."

"I'm learning," Rose said with a slight blush of pride as she realized she was recognizing more intimate details about Van every day.

"So, what does everybody think?" Van asked. "Bob, I know you have something on your mind."

"It was an impressive, though quick, trip. I would like to have spent some time in one of their ship's engineering spaces. But, failing that, I have to agree that their overall manufacturing and construction processes are more efficient than ours. . . and bigger," Bob started.

"Linking the fabrication and raw material bays with the various construction and repair facilities is brilliant. So too are those construction robots. They had to be over ten feet tall and able to lift and carry huge weight. No comparison to our robots. In addition, I saw not all the robots were configured the same. Some wore packs for melding, others had packs with spools of wire and torches, and I couldn't tell what the others had on them. Clearly, they are modular, able to be shifted from one role to another easily."

Brice interrupted. "Pardon my military nature, but could they be equipped with weapons modules?"

"I don't see why not," answered Bob. "But who'd want something so big running around a ship?"

"I didn't say anything about a ship, Bob."

Bob didn't get it and continued, "Then there were those fabrication machines. To the unpracticed eye, they may have looked like bigger versions of our fabricators. However, the controls were different, and I can't guess how they work. More importantly, the power required for just the one bay of fabricators has to be huge. Much more than all our bays in Mars Base together. I'd like to know, where does the power come from, and what does it look like?"

There were nods all around when Brice spoke up.

"I recognized, as I'm sure all of you did, a lot of armed guards everywhere. Just like on the *Triton*, but more of them. Seems like more than they should need, but more importantly, where do they all live and eat? I suppose many of the more senior people with families live in the cities, but how about all the younger types, the bachelors, if you will? I didn't see any barracks or armories either.

"Then, I ask you, Van, what did you think of the weapons on the ships we saw? I'm no expert, but they did look bigger than our biggest ones even on the smaller ships. And there were a few I didn't recognize at all."

Van reflected for a moment. "You're right, Brice. I did notice larger, different, and more numerous weapons on the capital ships. I even noticed a few on the escort ship we watched when we got here, the corvette *Ditona*."

Then Rose gave a discreet but audible, "Ahem."

"Something on your mind, Rose?" Van asked.

"I thought you'd never ask, and yes. For a population of over one hundred thousand, a few small medical centers in each city hardly seems adequate to handle the more serious medical cases. In addition, if there are more troops around like Brice suggests, where do they get treated? We're missing a few things or, at least, haven't been shown them."

Van thought about all that, then said, "So let me summarize. The Host here are clearly better at construction and manufacturing than we are. They have access to and knowledge of power generation exceeding ours significantly. That's a good thing.

"However, generally speaking, they have bigger ships than

we do, with unidentified armament. There's a large presence of armed troops and probably more in facilities that we haven't seen. There are bigger and better combat shuttles to carry more troops than ours and, what's more, at least two cargo and transport ships that dwarf anything we have. The cherry on top is the admiral not really wanting to show us any of this. What does that sound like?"

Bob and Rose just shrugged their shoulders. It was Brice who suddenly grinned.

"They have a large, and probably growing, assault capability."

"Bingo!" Van said, pointing at Brice. "But why?"

Just then Bourdain entered. "The admiral will see you now."

Admiral Namath rose from his seat at the long table in his quarters, leaving a tablet on the table in front of him. "Ah, you're back and right on time. I trust you had an interesting few hours and a little rest?"

"Was it only a few hours?" Rose asked. "It felt like a whole day; there was so much to see, and all that travel!"

Everyone took a seat at the admiral's gesture, with him last.

Folding his hands in front of him, he looked at the group. "I hope this tour has given you a greater appreciation of our capabilities, especially in the manufacturing and construction fields. I wanted to be sure you saw how we do things and, I hope, how efficiently. Having done so, I trust you can see how we can be of significant assistance in advancing your preparation for meeting the Arkon now that the timeline has been shortened."

Van took a moment to gather his thoughts before speaking. "Based on what we saw, there is little doubt your systems, processes, and power sources could considerably increase our production and preparation. Casual observation tells me that you may even be able to advance our weapons technology. However, while I may have influence within the two human Federations, I'm only a part of any decision process. My team and I are willing to share what we have seen with our allies, but any decisions will have to be mutual ones. I'm sure you understand."

The admiral didn't smile. "I'm sure you underestimate your position and influence within the human alliance, Commander. May I assume you can offer your support to our proposal?"

Again, Van was slow to respond as he thought about what James Harris had taught him about negotiations and diplomacy.

"To a certain extent, yes. However, what you suggested back in Zarminian space brings up an additional question."

"And that is?" asked the admiral, showing a slight loss in patience.

"A wiser man than I suggested that to be successful in the help you described, you would need or want a certain level of control in how things are done, how resources are allocated, and so forth. Is that true?"

Van thought he saw the admiral's posture change from relaxed to a little more rigid.

"That would likely be the case, Commander. But only to the extent it is required for an efficient effort. I'm sure you understand."

Van now had his hands pressed together with the tips of his fingers resting on his lips. He nodded slowly. Then he spoke. "I understand. Would it be possible to get a closer inspection of some of the weapons on your ships? I believe that would help us in our discussion at home."

The admiral eased back in his chair, giving the appearance of consideration. "I think you have seen what you need to see for the present, Commander. Host security protocols are very strict, as you might imagine. However, once we can agree on moving forward, you will see and have access to many more advanced systems, including weapons.

"Now, I'm sure you are tired after this eventful day. Senior Altern Bourdain will show you to your quarters and arrange to have you sample some of our fine cooking here on Fortuna. The *Triton* will return you to Zarminia tomorrow."

"Will you be returning with us, Admiral?" Rose asked.

"Unfortunately, no. Not this time." The admiral stood and offered his hand to each of the visitors. "Have a good evening and a safe trip back home."

As if by magic, the door opened and Bourdain appeared.

CHAPTER 44

THE *TRITON* AND VAN'S GROUP had been gone for over a day, which was enough time for Harry to do what he needed. He went to Frank Wilson's cabin aboard *New Horizons* and knocked.

Frank looked up from his desk and was about to ask Jennifer who was there when he remembered she was off-line. "Enter," the captain called out.

Harry stepped in, closing the door behind him.

Frank stopped what he was doing and twisted in his chair to give his full attention to Harry. "Are you finished?"

"Yes, Captain, and I am afraid my suspicions were correct."

"Care to share, Harry?"

"Yes, Captain, Jennifer was in communications with the Host prior to the battle."

"What?" Frank asked in amazement.

"I said—"

But Frank interrupted. "I know what you said, Harry. I'm just stunned. Tell me more. Link Dick in on this as well."

"Yes, Captain. It is done. Prior to the battle, my attention was diverted by problems on the shipyards. Once those were resolved, I detected several burst transmissions I could not identify. I could tell they came from *New Horizons*. They were in a form familiar to me, and I suspected Jennifer.

"The only way I could discover the meaning and detail was to board *New Horizons* and place Jennifer off-line. I then scanned all the transmissions in the computer core storage until I found them. After that, it was easy to translate."

"And?" pushed Frank.

"Jennifer was communicating with the *Triton* before the *Triton* appeared and the battle began. I also found other transmission before *New Horizons* departed on its mission."

This time it was an equally amazed Dick Carson who chimed in. "What was exchanged?"

"In months past, it was information about the progress of Galactic Force and the allies, Mr. Carson. Production rates, resources available, number of shipyards, and the state of relations among the allies. Most recently, some of it was position information about *Triton*, but most of it was related to the first appearance of the Arkon and a narration of the subsequent battle."

"So, the Host were following our progress closely for a while, and it increased before and during the battle?" Frank asked.

"Correct, Captain."

"Harry," Dick asked. "Do I draw from this that the Host could have intervened earlier and not at the last minute?"

"Based on the information I found, Mr. Carson, that is a possibility."

Dick was about to ask another question when he received a message on his tablet. He read it quickly and then said, "I just got a note from the Ops Center. *Reliant* and her cargo ship have just entered the system, which means you'll be busy, Frank. I suggest leaving Jennifer off-line for now and having Harry return here while I, and probably James Harris, can look more deeply into this."

"Works for me," Frank said approvingly. "I've never been much of a fan of mysteries. And you're right. We'll have our hands full here with the supplies and repairs."

The Galactic Force team was seated again on the couch in the *Triton*'s observation lounge watching the light show on the big view screen.

Bob broke the silence. "That was the biggest bum's rush I think I ever saw or was a part of."

"If you mean we got kicked out in a hurry, I think you're right," agreed Rose.

Van looked as if he were watching the light show, but he was, in fact, deep in thought. "What did you say, Bob?"

"I said, that's the fastest I've ever been kicked out of anyplace."

"Yes," Van said, not yet fully engaged.

"What are you thinking about, Van?" Rose asked, seeing they only had part of his attention.

"Oh, I'm sorry. I was thinking the same thing. Only. . ."

Rose gave him a slight elbow jab to his side. "Only what?"

"Only there's much more going on here than we know."

"Like what?" Brice asked, his curiosity rising.

"I'm not sure. And I just don't like it."

"So, we won't be recommending the Host's help?" Bob asked, a little disappointed. He was eager to jump into all the Host technology and capability he had seen.

"I didn't say that. The question is, as we mentioned before, at what price? And there is Namath himself."

"You don't trust him either?" Rose asked with some satisfaction.

"No, I don't. But I should and that's the problem. He and the Host have given us a tremendous head start in preparing for the Arkon and in our development in general. Put aside the original technology left behind by the Host in the past and just think of *New Horizons* herself. A recent gift I don't think even Bob and Elaine fully understand yet."

"True enough," agreed Bob.

"So why don't I trust him?" mused Van.

"Because he's a creep," Rose said, folding her arms over her chest.

"Or is it the growing assault force that's being developed?" Brice asked.

"I'm sure that's part of it, especially the 'why' part," confirmed Van. "However, did you notice he never mentioned the Host Regents like Bourdain did once? Then there's his specific interest in the Federation governments."

"All good questions," agreed Brice, straining to relieve a ghost irritation in his neck. "How about another one? Why are they taking us back on this huge ship without the admiral? We could have been put aboard a corvette or a frigate just as easily."

After a moment of no responses, Rose said, as though it was the obvious thing to say, "Let's ask Captain Raynaldus."

"*Triton* is going back to Zarminian space to take parts and supplies to the *Kara*, along with a pouch for Ambassador Tafaris. It was the first ship headed that way with the storage capacity *Ditona* didn't have," said the *Triton's* captain simply.

"Wait, wait, wait." Van held up his hands in confusion. "Back up a minute. What is the *Kara*, who is Tafaris, and what are they, along with *Ditona*, doing in Zarminian space?"

Raynaldus was more than just a little surprised at the questions. "You mean the admiral didn't say anything about them?"

"No, the admiral didn't say anything about them," Van said as his face reddened and anger started to build.

Raynaldus shifted in his seat on the lounge couch and looked around in vain for some help. "I don't know what to say, Commander."

"How about an explanation now that the cat has been let out of the bag?"

Cats and bags didn't make any sense to the *Triton's* captain, but he got the drift. "*Kara* is one of our cruisers. *Ditona* is the corvette you saw when you arrived at Fortuna. She was scheduled, I believe, to join *Kara* as an escort. Ambassador Tafaris is a mystery to us all, but he has been aboard *Kara* for at least one of your weeks, as far as I know. *Kara* was with us until just before we encountered your battle with the Arkon. She broke off and headed in a different direction. I thought she was headed to investigate a disturbance we previously detected en route to Zarminia. Her orders came directly from the admiral."

Every one of Van's team was confused, and it looked like Raynaldus was also.

"OK, part of that makes sense," Van said. "About the *Kara*

and the *Ditona* anyway. But what does the ambassador have to do with anything?"

Raynaldus' face was growing pale. He was beyond uncomfortable. "I can't tell you. I mean, I don't know the ambassador's mission. That is the truth."

"I believe you, and I appreciate your willingness to talk with us. I think the admiral keeps more than just us in the dark. You said the ambassador was a mystery. What did you mean?" Van said.

"Just that. We know nothing about him. There is a powerful family with his name in our culture, but that's about as far as it goes. As are most ambassadors I guess, he is secretive and not very personable. Likes keeping to himself. That's my total knowledge."

"So, you've met him?" Rose asked.

"Only to greet him from a shuttle and take him to the admiral's quarters," answered the nervous captain, who was himself starting to see the path of the questions, which also interested him.

"So, he went back and forth between the *Kara* and the *Triton*?" continued Van.

"Several times. The last time, just before the *Kara* broke off."

Van observed that the *Triton*'s captain was becoming more than just a little uneasy. His eyes were flitting back and forth between his guests as Van watched. *I can't let this man stop talking now, just as information is starting to flow.* Van decided to, at least temporarily, change the subject and the mood.

"Tell us about your family, Captain. Do they live on Fortuna?" Van asked.

The captain came more alive at the question. "No, not yet. *Triton* has only been stationed on Fortuna for a few months. None of the families have joined us yet."

"You must miss them, yes?" Rose added.

"Indeed we do. We expected them to be with us right away, but we are told that they may not arrive until the new city is completed."

"A disappointment, I'm sure," Van commented.

"Yes," said the captain. "And —"

"Captain to the bridge," came a report over the ship's address system.

"Excuse me," said the relieved Host captain as he exited the observation lounge.

All faces then turned to Van.

"Don't look at me. I'm as confused as you are. Hopefully, it will become clear when we get home."

CHAPTER 45

A FTER *Triton* ENTERED ZARMINIAN SPACE and approached *New Horizons*, Van called Dick on his implant.

"Thank God you're back," Dick said.

"Why, what's the problem?" asked Van, concerned.

"Whatever you do, come here to the shipyard first. Don't go to *New Horizons* yet. Frank will be here. And don't bring that Host admiral or any other officer with you."

"What's the mystery?" Van asked, now also curious.

"We'll talk when you get here. I'll send a shuttle for you and the team." The link ended.

Rose was with Van in his quarters on *Triton* and heard the brief conversation over her implant. Fortunately, Harry had long ago changed the frequency of the implants to ensure Guardian Force security. Now it should have the advantage of keeping the Host out of the Guardian loop.

"What was that all about?"

"I have no idea, but Dick was more upset than I've heard him in a long time. We'll do as he says."

Van and his team said their good-byes to Raynaldus and took the Guardian Force shuttle down to the Sonaran shipyard. Harry was there alone to greet them, which was unusual.

"Hi, Harry!" said Rose, glad to see his familiar face.

"Greetings to you, Dr. Ramos, Commander. Mr. Carson asked me to greet all of you and invite you to the shipyard planning office as soon as possible."

"What's this all about?" Van asked as they struggled to keep up with Harry's pace.

Looking over his shoulder, the AI responded, "Mr. Carson asked me not to say until we are in a more protected environment, Commander."

The group shared confused looks but reached the office in record time. Passing a pair of security guards not normally there, the group swept through the doors and found Dick and others gathered at the long worktable.

"OK, Dick. Here we are. What's so important?" Van asked.

"Our Host admiral may not be exactly what we think he is," Dick said as he motioned everyone to a seat.

That got their attention.

"Explain!" was all Van said while seating himself, his eyes solidly on Dick.

"Harry has discovered Jennifer has been in communication with the admiral for some time. Both before and after your mission in *New Horizons*. Not during. Harry shut her down before investigating her. She remains off-line."

It couldn't have gotten quieter in the room. Even the outside construction noise seemed to fade after what Dick had said.

Seeing Van was at a loss for words, Dick continued, "What's more, it may be that the admiral could have intervened in the Arkon battle before he did." He let that sink in. "We can't say for sure he did delay his actions, but the possibility is there. And one more thing, maybe two. I had a communication from Stan saying he observed a Host cruiser passing Mars Base headed toward Earth with an Earth Federation ship in escort. Subsequently, Stan discovered that our weasel friend Envoy McDuff was on the Earth Federation ship."

Van immediately thought of Majel and James Harris. If Namath was in communication with Jennifer, he knew a lot about Majel. The admiral couldn't ask more about the strange man without compromising his link with Jennifer. Van didn't want the Host engaged with Majel until he knew more about what was going on.

"Where are James and Majel?"

Dick smiled for the first time. "Fortunately, James has been taking Majel around on a sightseeing tour. They visited some folks on Zarminia, stopped by Carian Station to meet Ootah, and then proceeded to Mars Base, where they are now. James had no desire to go to Earth under his present persona non grata status. I told Stan to keep them there for a while."

"That's a relief," Van said, easing out of his rigid posture in his chair.

"A small one," Dick said. "Just before you got here, Stan alerted us that the same cruiser and Earth Federation ship, along with an unknown Host corvette, were headed back out of the system. Possibly toward us."

Then things started clicking for Van.

"The cruiser is the *Kara*, the Host corvette is the *Ditona*, and one of them is carrying a Host ambassador named Tafaris." All but Van's team were surprised.

"How on Earth do you know that?" Dick asked.

"It's a long story, Dick. But this is what happened. . ."

When Van finished the story of his group's trip to Fortuna and the conversations with the *Triton*'s captain, the room its quietness as everyone absorbed what they had just heard.

Shifting into his old ambassadorial mode, Dick looked at Van and spoke. "Interesting and alarming all in one. I do have a recommendation. Assuming this Host ambassador is on his way here, I suggest listening to what he has to say before we jump to any conclusions. Further, I suggest we not conduct the visit on *New Horizons*. Instead, let's do it in my office. Just you, me, Tafaris and, regrettably, McDuff."

Van nodded, saying, "Sounds right."

Everyone else in the room, though curious, didn't really want to be in the office for the meeting. Especially not with McDuff.

The next day, the three expected ships arrived. The Earth Federation ship turned out to be the *Diligent*, Chen Lee's old ship. As previously arranged, Dick had a shuttle ferry Tafaris and McDuff to the shipyard and then an escort bring them to his regular office. Harry was in the room next door. Van and Dick waited for the Host ambassador to introduce himself, but McDuff beat him to it.

"May I present Ambassador Tafaris of the Galactic Host."

"Thank you, Envoy McDuff," Dick said before greeting the ambassador.

"That's Ambassador McDuff. I am Harris's replacement."

Van and Dick glanced at each other, and Dick continued, ignoring McDuff. "Ambassador Tafaris, a great pleasure to meet you. This," he pointed to Van, "is Commander Childs of Guardian Force, and I am Dick Carson, the acting ambassador while ours is away."

Van bowed his head slightly but remained silent, watching McDuff squirm and try to figure out the meaning of what Dick had just said.

"My pleasure, Commander and Mr. Ambassador. May we sit? I have had a long journey."

"Of course," Dick said, gesturing to the comfortable chairs. Tafaris's chair groaned a little under his weight.

When everyone was settled, Dick resumed, "As you might imagine, to see a second senior Host representative in about a week is quite remarkable. We just recently met with Admiral Namath, who did us a great service."

"I am aware, and that, in part, is why I am here. On behalf of the Host, I am here to continue the discussion started by the admiral following your visit to Fortuna."

"You are well informed, Ambassador," Dick said, glancing at Van.

"Yes, but I did receive a diplomatic pouch, I think you call them, from the *Triton* before I was brought here. The admiral gave me the basic details of the commander's visit." Turning to address Van, the ambassador said, "Were you suitably impressed, Commander?"

"We were impressed indeed. Fortuna is quite the model of efficiency and production,"

replied Van briefly.

"Yes, it is. As you may have guessed, I am here to open discussions with the allies, as you call them, but would like to know if we have your endorsement."

"Yes, I can see," Van said, looking at McDuff, "you've already started without us."

"Just a formality, Commander," said Tafaris, seeing Van's glance toward McDuff. "I wanted to get better informed about Earth while you were away, and Ambassador McDuff was quite helpful."

McDuff assumed a look of pride at the praise, but stopped when he watched the glare of disapproval grow on Van's face.

"Ambassador McDuff is well known to us," Dick said and let it go at that.

"If we have your endorsement, Commander, I would like to start discussions with the Zarminians as soon as possible."

"What's the hurry, Ambassador?" Van asked.

The Host official looked puzzled at Van's question and then twitched and looked around. Both Van and Dick saw it. McDuff was totally unaware.

Returning his gaze to Van, the Host ambassador continued, "Time is important, Commander. The sooner we can start, the sooner we can be prepared. As the admiral said, the Arkon timeline has been shortened."

"Yes, so he told us," Van said, wanting to know how Tafaris knew that. "But there are details to work out, wouldn't you agree?"

"What details?" asked Tafaris.

Surprised, Dick interjected. "We are talking about getting two different cultures and one intermediary, Guardian Force, to come to an agreement as to how this shift in production and your involvement will be implemented. How —"

But McDuff interrupted. "The Earth Federation will be for this, gentlemen. I've already told the Arkon ambassador. The Host clearly have the advanced knowledge and capability to push things forward so we can all survive. All that remains is to get the Zarminians to see what's best for everyone."

Annoyed at the interruption, Dick took a deep breath and

then spoke. "You mean to say, Mr. McDuff, that Earth has already agreed to whatever the ambassador has proposed?"

"That's Ambassador McDuff, I'll remind you. And the answer is not yet, but they will after I brief them on what I've learned from the Host on the trip to Earth and back here."

"I see," Van added, "and the Earth Federation would be much more inclined to say yes if the Zarminians do. Correct?"

"Of course. So, what's the problem?" McDuff asked.

"There are many," Van noted. "But let me ask, did the Earth Federation promote you to ambassador based on a recommendation from Ambassador Tafaris here?"

"Yes, why?" asked the puzzled man.

"Never mind," Van said, turning his attention back to the Host official.

"I'm afraid, Ambassador Tafaris, you may have been given a false sense of reality. I can assure you the Zarminian Federation will require details of the expectations you have and then will negotiate a final agreement."

"But why?" asked the ambassador. "The mutual rewards are plain, and not to join together would mean the destruction of all."

"I don't think the underlying logic is at fault," noted Van, remembering the speech he had given to Majel a while ago. "However, the cultural natures of both Earth and Zarminian are heavily steeped in fierce independence and the demand for freedom. To give some or all of that away will be difficult or nearly impossible, even facing the Arkon threat. As I told a friend not long ago, we have gone to war willing to die rather than see our freedom infringed upon."

The Host ambassador twitched again suddenly and stood. "I must leave and think about this. We can reconvene tomorrow on *New Horizons*."

Everyone, including McDuff, was thrown off by this sudden decision on the part of the Host guest.

Dick recovered and said, "*New Horizons* is not available at present. It is undergoing significant repairs. We can meet here again."

"I think *New Horizons* would be better," replied the Host ambassador with a stern look.

"Why?" Van asked.

The ambassador paused for a moment. "It is a shorter trip by shuttle. The sooner we get started, the sooner we can finish."

"I'm sorry, Ambassador, but until *New Horizons* completes repairs, the ship's captain has requested no visitors," Van said. Frank hadn't said that, but it was the best excuse Van could come up with that made sense. "We can meet here again tomorrow morning."

"Very well, I would like transportation to *Kara* now, if you please."

"We'll take you where you want to go, Ambassador. Just not *New Horizons*," Dick said.

After the ambassador departed and McDuff went back to *Diligent*, Van, Dick, and Harry met back at Dick's office.

"What the hell was that?" Van asked, flopping into one of the soft office chairs.

"Beats me," replied Dick, doing the same. "One moment he was rational and a bit pretentious, and then he just changed into another person."

"Not a person, Mr. Carson," Harry said from a corner of the room.

Both men turned in their chairs to look at Harry.

"What?" Van asked first.

"The ambassador is not a person, Commander."

"OK," Van said slowly. "What do you mean?"

"The ambassador is not human, Commander, he is an AI."

"That can't be," exclaimed Dick. "He looked as human as any of us. More human than you. No offense, of course."

"No offense taken, Mr. Carson. This AI's appearance is much more advanced than my creation. A great deal of work went into his design. It also has better interpersonal programming than I originally had."

"Yet you could tell," Van said with admiration.

"Not at first, Commander. I was also fooled. But twice in your conversations, I emitted a single short sensor burst to assess the ambassador. It only took those two sensor bursts for me to receive the feedback confirming he is an AI."

"The twitching!" Dick nearly shouted. "I've seen you do that now and again, Harry."

"I did not see the twitching, Mr. Carson, but that would be consistent with the AI reaction to my sensor bursts."

Calming down from the extraordinary discovery, Van asked, "So what now? Just because the ambassador is an AI, does that mean something bad is going on?"

"Not necessarily," Dick said while thinking. "To the Host, AIs had and probably continue to have an important role in their society. Look at Harry, for example, and even Jennifer. No, I don't think we can attribute anything nefarious yet to this discovery. How about you, Harry?"

"You are right, Mr. Carson, about the historic and current role of AIs in Host culture. However, keep in mind, AIs are not completely autonomous. Even I respond to programming. Therefore, AIs will rely on the logic and desires of the people who program them."

"Could that be Admiral Namath and his technicians?" Van asked with suspicion.

"It could be, Commander. But it could also be anybody within the Host system with the ability to program."

"So, what now?" Dick asked.

"We continue with the talks tomorrow and see what happens," Van said. Then, with a smile, he added, "And let's not tell McDuff yet."

Both men laughed heartily.

In *Kara*'s flight bay, Tafaris paused a moment after departing the shuttle to ask a question of the ship's captain. "Has the special equipment been transferred from the *Triton* to *Ditona*?"

"Yes, Ambassador," said the captain. "And *Ditona*'s captain reports it has been installed. Also, *Kara* has received its needed supplies, and both *Triton* and *Ditona* are free to depart orbit based on the orders you provided from the admiral."

"Good. Send them off now," said Tafaris as he turned and started walking away. "I will be in my cabin."

The ship's captain watched the gruff man walk away, shrugged his shoulders, and then proceeded to carry out his orders.

From the bridge of *New Horizons*, Frank watched the *Triton* and *Ditona* depart Zarminian orbit. But they didn't exit the system.

"Sensors, what's happening with those two Host ships?" Frank asked, tapping his club handle in the palm of his free hand.

"Nothing at the moment, Captain. Once they reached a position near the edge of the system, they just stopped. There were two burst transmissions from the corvette after they stopped, but we can't read them."

Frank looked over at the navigation officer and said, "If I'm right, those two ships parked exactly between a course for the Forbidden Zone and a course for the Sol system. Correct?"

"Yes, sir," said the officer.

"Keep me informed of any changes," Frank said as he eased out of his chair and left the bridge.

"Yes, Captain," answered both officers.

CHAPTER 46

V AN AND ROSE WERE STILL on the Sonaran shipyard in the commander's quarters. It was morning and the two were having breakfast before Van had to leave for a meeting with the Zarminian president.

"What do you make of the two ships leaving and stopping where they are now?" Rose asked before taking a sip of her coffee.

"Your guess is as good as mine. I haven't figured out this whole thing with the Host. I am, however, starting to worry."

"About what?" Rose asked, putting her coffee cup down and focusing her attention on Van.

Van was still holding his cup in both hands, but not drinking.

"About what's going on with the Host and Admiral Namath being so demanding, for one thing. For another, I'm worried about how Majel might see Namath and the Host."

"I can understand the first thing, but not the second," Rose said.

"Majel and his people have a great deal to offer us," responded Van. "I'm hoping we can persuade him and his people to help us, but what if Namath has something going on that might reflect negatively on us all? We could all lose out before we have a chance to see the full potential of what Majel can offer and persuade him to help."

Between bites of toast, Rose added, "What you really mean is you're uncomfortable not being in control of all this. True?"

Van put his cup down, folded his hands in front of him on the table, looked at Rose, and smiled. "Am I that transparent?"

"To me you are," she said with a sparkle in her eyes.

Van looked at Rose for a moment as he realized how much

insight she had into him. Then he realized he was staring and resumed the conversation.

"In this case, you're right. With James and Majel at Mars Base I can't talk with our new friend. And I can't leave right now or call James back."

"Is it wise," Rose asked, "to have Majel on Mars Base? I mean, he seems trustworthy, but he's still an outsider."

Van shrugged. "He is an outsider, that's true. But I think Stan knows where he can and can't go and will remind Majel of it. In the end, however, all we can do is trust Majel to respect our privacy. We really can't do much about it since he can go wherever he wants. Anyway, they need to stay where they are for the moment until the Host leave."

"To where?"

"Ideally, back to Fortuna. Then we can do pretty much what we want."

"Then," Rose said, rubbing her hands together to get rid of the toast crumbs, "maybe you need to find a way to make them go home, at least for a while."

Van suddenly leaned over and kissed her.

"What was that for?" Rose asked with a grin.

"You may have just solved my problem. Have to go to Dick's office. See you later," Van said as he disappeared through the door to his quarters, leaving a puzzled Rose behind.

The door to Dick's office flew open as Van entered, surprising even Harry. "I've got it!" he said.

Dick looked up from his desk and, with a smile, said, "Is it contagious?"

"What? Oh, no. I mean, I think I have a way to get us free of the Host, for a short while at least."

"That would be nice. Care to share?"

"We give Tafaris what he wants."

"Which is?" Dick asked, still not completely following.

"We tell him the Galactic Force is willing to endorse the Host's suggestions, but we want to talk with the two Federations alone first. Tell him it will take ten Earth days in our estimation.

With nothing to do for ten days and to get further direction from Namath, they'll go home and then return in ten days or so."

Dick bridged his hands together in front of him while he thought. "That might work. But why ten days?"

"An arbitrary choice. I just want some uninterrupted and unobserved time to think. And I need to go to Mars Base for a number of reasons, not the least of which is Majel. We can't leave him with James indefinitely."

Dick nodded. "Makes sense, assuming Tafaris will go."

"I think he'll have to. I'm betting that he'll need to consult with Namath before acting on my offer."

"It's worth a try."

Two hours later the negotiating group met again in Dick's quarters and had taken the same comfortable chairs. Harry was next door, as he'd been the previous day. Dick opened.

"Thank you for being here on time, gentleman. While you were gone, we had some discussion of our own, and Commander Childs would like to share the results. Van."

"Thanks. As Dick said, we did have a considerable discussion last night. Our conclusion is Guardian Force would be happy to recommend accepting the Hosts' help."

McDuff sported a toothy grin, thinking he had won with his comments from the previous day. Tafaris showed no emotion.

"There is one caveat, however," Van continued. "Guardian Force wants to be the sole leader of the negotiations between the Earth and Zarminian Federations. And we'll need at least ten Earth days to be ready."

"Wait just a minute!" interrupted McDuff. "I represent the Earth Federation. If any talking is to be done with the Earth, it will be through me."

Van expected this and looked at McDuff with a nod of recognition. "Understood," he said and turned back to addressing the whole group, especially Tafaris.

Tafaris blinked and said, "May I think on this, Commander?"

"Certainly," Van said. "Take all the time you need. We'll understand if you have to return to Fortuna for consultations."

"That won't be necessary. I have some papers here in my briefcase I want to consult. May I have an office and some privacy for a few hours?"

Dick and Van looked at each other in surprise and fear their plan was unraveling.

"I have one we use for shipyard design," Dick said. "It isn't pretty but we can make it secure for you."

Tafaris stood. "Good. Please take me there now."

Dick called to one of the guards to escort Tafaris to the workroom.

"Now that the ambassador is gone," said McDuff, sitting back in his chair with an air of confidence, "I'm sure there are talks we must have."

"I'm sure there are, McDuff," Dick said, not waiting for the small man's predictable correction to his title. "But not just yet. One of our security guards will escort you to the VIP lounge where you can rest and refresh yourself while Tafaris prepares his response."

"But—" McDuff tried to complain, but he was whisked out the door before he could continue.

"We have a VIP lounge?" Van asked.

"No. It's the workers' break room. But there won't be anybody there for a while. I doubt McDuff will notice the difference."

"You're bad!" Van said with a smile, then took on a more solemn face. "But it doesn't look like Tafaris took the bait. What do you think?"

"I agree. He must be better programmed than we thought."

"He is not," Harry said as he entered the room.

"What do you mean?" Van said, still seated in his chair.

"The AI Tafaris is communicating with someone far away, Commander."

"How do you know?" Dick asked as he took his seat again.

"I am detecting the same type of communications bursts from him I detected from *New Horizons* during the Arkon battle, Mr. Carson. And he is receiving the same types of bursts in return."

"So, whom is he communicating with?" Van asked.

"Ultimately, that is unknown, Commander. What I do know is that the Host corvette *Ditona* is acting as a relay station."

"But it took us over twenty hours to get to Fortuna in FTL. That's a long way away. How could a corvette bridge such a great distance?" Van asked with confusion.

"Correction, Commander. It took you three jumps to get to Fortuna. And you didn't go in a straight line. You could just as easily have gone on a jump out, then a jump in return, and then another jump out in a different direction, which took twenty-two hours to complete. Or, they could have dropped communications buoys along their path coming here. In either case, quick communications could be made with the right equipment on board."

Dick and Van suddenly realized they had been duped or, at the very least, outsmarted. Round one was going Tafaris' way.

"So, what do we do now?" Dick asked.

Van held up his hand, indicating he was in thought. Then he spoke. "Tell me, Dick, in your old days as a diplomat, what would you have done or said if one of the negotiators had a large military force looking over the shoulders of the other negotiators?"

"That's easy. I'd make it clear that intimidation wasn't allowed and all forces would have to clear the area." Then a grin of collusion crept over Dick's face. "You mean. . ."

"Yes. We can't have armed forces being around to intimidate the discussions. We clear out our ships, and the Host clears out theirs. It's the only right way to do this. *New Horizons* will have to leave, as will *Diligent*, but all the other ships the alliance has in this space are in shipyards and can't move under their own power. Correct?"

"Pretty much. *Sutherland* could possibly be brought out if needed. Maybe *Hornet* also. But they wouldn't be at full strength."

"So, all we have here is *New Horizons*, which we can move to Mars Base. Everything else would have to leave. Meaning the three Host ships."

"You think they'll buy it?" Dick asked.

"Don't know unless we try. But there is one bad thing about this."

Dick thought for a minute and then hit the arm of his chair in annoyance. "McDuff has to stay!"

Van just nodded.

It was just over two hours later that the escort brought back Ambassador Tafaris, and McDuff was retrieved from the "VIP" lounge.

When everyone had taken a seat, Dick asked, "What have you determined, Ambassador?"

"We agree."

Tafaris made no sign of pleasure or any emotion, but McDuff slapped the arm of his chair and said, "Yes!"

"Good," Van said. "When can we expect you and your ships to leave?"

"You are talking to me?" asked Tafaris.

"Yes," was all Van wanted to say. He was enjoying the theater.

"I do not understand," said the ambassador with a blank stare.

"It is traditional in Earth and now Zarminian diplomacy that all military forces will clear the area while negotiations are underway. In this way, no side feels intimidated. We will be sending *New Horizons* away, and I expect Ambassador McDuff will ask *Diligent* to depart. He, of course, will stay."

McDuff was about to object until Van added the last part. Then the little man relaxed, realizing he was still in the game, and nodded in agreement. "Of course."

Now the ball was in the nonhuman ambassador's court.

Tafaris surprised everyone by saying, "Agreed. How long will you require?"

"Ten Earth days should do it," answered Dick, seeing Van was still in disbelief.

The ambassador stood. "If you will give me transportation to *Kara*, we will be on our way. I will be back in ten Earth days."

Later, when Tafaris was gone and McDuff was retrieving his

things from *Diligent*, Dick and Van again sat in their respective chairs in Dick's office.

"Van, I never expected such a thing to happen. Especially so quickly. So, now you have your time, what's next?"

"First," Van said, having thought this out, "you get your diplomatic butt down to the surface and brief our friends on what we're doing. Who knows, this whole thing may work out, and it wouldn't be bad if we had some coordinated thoughts."

"What about McDuff?" Dick asked.

"Brief them about him, too. Tell them we're sorry to plague them with him, but it can't be helped for now. Make him feel part of the whole thing. Make him the meeting secretary or something to keep him busy and out of your hair."

"That can be arranged. What about you?"

"I'll go with Frank in *New Horizons* to Mars Base. That will give me a chance to see how we're doing there and to talk with James and Majel."

CHAPTER 47

NEW *HORIZONS* WAS TOO BIG to fit into any of the current Mars Base receiving bays and assumed geocentric orbit above the base. Shuttles started flying back and forth immediately, hauling parts and workers to and from the big ship.

Stan Walters greeted Van and Rose in one of the reception bays, but the pair declined any conversation until they got some rest. They both went straight to Van's private quarters.

Rose immediately fell on the large, soft bed with a big sigh. "Finally, home again. It seems like we've been gone forever."

Van fell to the bed beside her, joining Rose in relaxing and letting months of stress flow out.

Staring up at the solid ceiling, not the thin skin of a ship, Van said, "Want to have some fun?"

He turned his head to Rose. Then he smiled. Rose was fast asleep.

The couple woke up late but refreshed. Rose was first out the door, wanting to see her medical facility and friends. Van was not far behind, heading for the deputy commander's office.

Stan stood from a couch littered with design drawings and supply reports as Van walked in. "I'd say good morning, but I think good afternoon would work better," Stan said, taking a few steps toward Van and shaking his friend's hand.

"Yes, and don't make fun," Van said. "It's good to be home."

"As it should be. Does this mean I can give up this job and get back to commanding a ship?"

"No, you're not that lucky," Van responded, moving a few papers aside as he took a seat on the littered couch. Smiling, he asked, "You always keep such a messy office?"

"Only when the commander makes such a fuss about production," Stan said as he took a seat across from Van on a well-worn chair.

The opening banter stopped as both realized this was their first meeting since Danny's death. Stan spoke first.

"How has Rose taken Danny's loss?"

Van took a second to respond as he remembered their mutual friend. "I don't think people ever get over something like that, especially a brother or sister. They learn to live with it, and Rose is doing that."

"I think I know how she feels. Danny was nearly a brother to me. We spent so much time flying and living together before Galactic Force. We were like right and left hands." Stan was a little misty-eyed.

"I think I know what you mean. Remember, you and Danny were our first recruits outside the Carson Group."

"I remember that first meeting, getting shot down by a Chinese missile on the Moon, no less. Then finding out space and our opportunities were really big just when we thought it was all over. Danny could hardly control himself. It was something, he said at the time, he'd been waiting for all his life. And he got to do it."

Van nodded as pictures of an excited Danny ran through his head like a movie. "How many people can say that in their lives?"

"Not many, that's for sure. I guess if he had to go out, he did it with a flourish doing something he loved." Stan went silent for a moment, remembering his friend. Then he shook his head and came back to reality. "What was it you wanted before I got distracted?"

"How are we doing with ship builds?"

"Oh yeah, not bad considering the Zarminian yards have just come up to capacity in their five existing sites. Earth's orbital shipyard is now up and running, and Moon and Mars Bases are running as fast as they can.

"We have a new cruiser we named *Nelson*, which has just

completed flight testing and has a full crew. Our frigate *Lancaster* is midway through construction, and the destroyer *Kidd* is nearly done and bound for the Earth Federation. We also have one new corvette, *Bedford*, completing flight testing and another, *Speedwell*, about to complete construction. Our new cargo ship, *Bayfield*, is out of construction but awaiting a crew and testing."

"What about the Federations?"

"Earth Federation has one frigate under construction, no name yet, and another operational one called the *Richmond*. The Zarminians have two corvettes and a frigate out of the yards and awaiting testing and crews, with more under construction. That's quite a lot. Don't you think?" asked Stan.

"Under normal circumstances, you'd be right. But times aren't normal, especially after the licking we just took from the Arkon. We lost some good ships and people in the fight, and *Sutherland* and *Hornet* are still in the repair yards and will be for a few weeks. The people are much harder to replace."

Stan nodded. "You're right. But we have expanded the space training center in Australia, and the rate of graduations in all flight capacities is increasing. Dick may have told you, but we are also working with the Zarminians to set up a training center there as well. There are plenty of volunteers, but they all need to be trained and it takes time."

"You're right. You and Dick have done an amazing job. I just wish I had foreseen this personnel need when I first launched the building campaign. I just didn't understand the time it takes to create crews. But it is what it is. Now I have some different news."

Van then launched into the intervention of the Host and subsequent meetings, especially with Admiral Namath and Ambassador Tafaris. He concluded with the subterfuge he and Dick had used to buy some time for everyone to consider the Hosts' offer.

That was a lot for Stan to take in. But after a few moments of thought, he responded, "So, the Host have offered to help us increase production and assist with training and other things. On the surface, that's great. But I see your point about handing over total control to them. I don't like it either. What do you have on your mind?"

Van was ready for this question. "First, I want us to put together two battle groups. One with the *Reliant* as the core command ship, and the other using *Nelson* in the equivalent role. Second, I want two destroyers in each battle group, along with as many frigates and corvettes as we can spare from training roles that we can man. You know all the ships best, so you can pick them. Use whatever Federation ships you can get to augment the two groups.

"Now here's the part you'll like, sort of. Hand over as many duties as you can to Phil Loomis and take command of, let's call it Strike Force One, with *Nelson* at center. I'll take *Reliant* and command of Strike Force Two."

Stan was now sitting upright with a grin of excitement. "That's more like it. But I see you get Jan St. Clair on *Reliant*."

"Yes. If I'm right, we may need her expertise a little more than you if things go badly. Besides, I'll be on *New Horizons* most of the time."

"What do you mean 'if things go badly'?" asked Stan.

"The last time we were meeting with Namath and Tafaris with their Host ships around, he had the advantage. The next time, in six days, I want to be better prepared — if not the advantaged one — if he gets more aggressive."

"You think they'll fight?" Stan asked in alarm.

"I don't know. I do know they were being intimidating. Maybe we can equalize the playing field in this next visit. Now, where can I see James and Majel?"

"Ah, you can't," said Stan apprehensively. "They both went to Earth."

"What?" Van said, standing up and clenching his fists.

"Now calm yourself, Van," Stan said, motioning for him to sit back down. "I told them to stay here until you arrived. But Majel had other ideas."

"So, you gave them a ship and sent them on their merry way. Just like that?" Van was flushed with anger.

"The good news is no. I refused to provide a ship," said Stan with a certain amount of satisfaction.

Digesting Stan's statement, Van suppressed his rising outrage. But he was puzzled. Then the light dawned, and he relaxed a little.

"So, Majel just up and vanished in a flash of light, taking James with him?"

Now it was Stan's turn to be surprised. "Yes, how did you know?"

"I've seen that trick before."

CHAPTER 48

J AMES HARRIS WAS TRYING TO keep his balance and not doing a very good job. He solved the problem by putting a hand on Majel's shoulder as the scenery passed below them. They were cruising above the Earth at about a thousand feet as nearly as Harris could determine. His feet felt as if he were standing on a solid surface, but he couldn't see one. Further adding to his discomfort was the realization that below them was water, which sparkled as the rising sun reflected off the waves. He could hear things, but they were a jumble of radio and TV programs, along with confused phone conversations and other things he didn't immediately recognize.

"So, what are we doing?" Harris asked, still holding tight to Majel.

"I'm examining your world," Majel said simply.

"OK. But when we talked before coming to Earth, I thought we would visit a few places and maybe talk to some people I know."

"We will do those things, but first I want to see more on my own. Especially the places you and the commander are from. I believe the commander is from here." Majel pointed down as the water gave way to a narrow peninsula, a bay and a blue bridge connecting to the mainland. "You call it San Diego, I believe."

Harris had to think about it for a moment. He had visited the city a few times in the past and enjoyed its moderate temperatures and relaxing atmosphere. It was the sweeping blue bridge that gave it away.

"If that's the Coronado Bay Bridge, this is San Diego all right. But won't people get a little excited seeing us up here like this?"

"They can't see us," was all Majel would say as the pair hovered over the city for a number of minutes.

"What are you doing?" Harris asked.

"Listening and watching. I'm learning a great deal about this country and the people who live in it." Then as quickly as they had arrived, they departed and stopped again.

Harris had fallen to his knees with this abrupt change but used Majel's arm to right himself. There was no wind, and it was nice and warm, especially as they cruised slowly by a snow-covered city he recognized immediately as Chicago, his hometown. Once again, he could hear radio, TV voices, music passing at a high rate of speed, and the beeping and buzzing noises he thought were data transfer sounds.

"I believe you are from the place below," said Majel. "Chicago, you call it."

"That's the place all right. Dolores, my wife, is here visiting friends, but the children are grown and away."

"Shouldn't we visit her?"

"I don't think so. I mean, I'd like seeing my wife, but the shock of just showing up and my inability to explain you may be too much."

"I see. But won't you have the same problem with the other people you want me to see?"

"Not as much. Plus, I still want to keep knowledge of my presence here to a minimum. If I saw Dolores, it would be all over town and the news before you could blink. And it would be hard to leave her quickly. Sorry."

"I think I understand. Where do you think we should go next?"

"Have you heard of Geneva?"

Namath was in his quarters on Fortuna seated at the head of his long table. He was leaning forward with his elbows balanced on the table while he held a stylus between his fingers, absentmindedly tapping it on the table's smooth surface. He was not alone. Tafaris was seated close by at the same table. The admiral stopped his tapping and looked over at the AI.

"So, you think the Earth and Zarminian governments are considering my proposal?"

"Yes, Admiral. They gave every indication of having serious discussions in the ten-day period they requested."

"And all their capable military forces left the area?"

"Yes, Admiral. The spy satellite we left behind confirms the *New Horizons* and *Diligent* left the area and have not returned."

"Good. We need those production facilities and manpower, along with our operational control of them if my plan is to work. We don't have enough ships yet to overpower the Regents and its forces and take offensive action against the Arkon. We can't just sit and wait for the Arkon, as the Regents seems to be doing." Namath shifted his thinking back to his immediate problem. "You are sure the ships you saw on your trip to Earth and Zarminia are still not a match for us?"

"The allied forces are growing, Admiral, but even with Galactic Force, we still have the advantage if we were to bring all our power to bear."

"Yes, that is my assessment also," said Namath thoughtfully. "Let us hope they see the advantage of what we offer and we don't have to use force. If dealt with and managed in the right way, they could be great assets to us as we grow in strength."

Aboard *Triton*, Captain Raynaldus was walking about his great ship. He found it refreshing to get away from the bridge and command center and visit with his crew. He was a people person, after all. But today there was another reason to walk. He could think better when walking around, and some things were troubling him. Today's ambling was taking him slowly to the engineering spaces where his longest and best friend was the engineering officer.

"Good morning, Captain," said a passing young petty officer.

"Good morning, it is indeed, Petty Officer Jardin," Raynaldus said as the two nodded at each other in the long passageway.

Raynaldus prided himself in knowing the names of as many of the eight hundred men and women aboard the giant ship as he could. It was a tall order, but he was good with names.

A few feet away, the captain stopped to talk with another of the crew, this time a young officer. "What's going on here, Maris?"

The young altern, busy at a gun emplacement with his team, looked up and grinned but continued working. "Doing periodic maintenance on this plasma cannon power cable, Captain."

"Who is teaching whom?" Raynaldus asked.

"Actually, sir, they are teaching me."

"Good," the proud captain answered. "Keep it up."

Finally reaching the guarded hatch leading to main engineering, he watched the guard snap to attention.

"Good morning, sir. The chief engineer is waiting for you inside." Relaxing from his posture of ridged respect, the guard opened the heavy hatch and motioned for the captain to enter, then closed the hatch as Raynaldus passed through.

"Greetings, Captain!" called out a short, round, and jovial man coming forward while cleaning his hands with a blue rag. "I'd shake your hand, but I don't think you'd like the grease."

"No problem, Jason. Remember, I've had my hands filled with grease and grime in my time."

"That's the truth. Just like when we were both alterns together years ago."

Raynaldus smiled in reflection. "And good years they were too. Can we go to your office for some privacy?"

"Of course. It's this way, you remember," the engineer said as he turned and headed to his office one compartment away. "Should I worry about having a private meeting with the captain? I mean, is there something wrong?"

"No. This is a meeting between old friends."

The chief engineer's office was quite different from the captain's quarters-and-office combination. This space was cramped and filled with books, manuals, and paper schematics. The engineer pulled a pile of papers from a chair, dropped them to the deck, and motioned for the captain to take a seat.

"Still not embracing technology, I see," Raynaldus commented, gesturing at all the books and papers scattered around the small office.

"Technology has its place. But I do some of my best work when I have the original products to help me."

Raynaldus laughed softly at this comment. . . one Jason had been making for all the years they had known each other.

"So, what is it that brings you all the way down here to chat with a friend?" the engineer asked.

"I'm not quite sure, and that's the problem. You know, of course, we have been here for several months now, and I keep getting questions from the crew about when their families are coming. Mine too. All I get from the admiral is 'it will happen soon.' That doesn't go down well with the crew. But there's more. Have you ever seen so much security in one place before?" the captain asked.

"Now that you mention it, no I haven't. Especially on Fortuna."

"Yes, but have you asked yourself why?"

"Not really. Unlike you bridge types, I have plenty of things to keep me busy."

Raynaldus was amused at the familiar jab of "you bridge types." There was always a certain amount of good-humored jesting back and forth between the "real" workers like the engineers and the "we got it easy" types on the bridge and other command positions.

"I know you do, Jason, and I appreciate it. But nonetheless, security is much higher everywhere than seems necessary. In addition, I and the other ship captains are kept at arm's length from the admiral and his few confidants. As flag captain, I assumed I, at least, would be more informed about what we were doing, where we were going, and why. Take for example our latest visitors. I know where they are from and a little about who they are. But why they made their visit wasn't completely clear. What's more, I was reminded by the admiral that I should tell them the minimum I could get away with and given a list of things and places they would not be granted access to or information about. The other captains and I are wondering why we decided to get involved with these races when all along we have been staying in the background. To our knowledge there has been no change in the views of the Regents."

"But we are not all kept in the loop about Regents' affairs," responded Jason.

"True enough," Raynaldus agreed, "but several of the captains have family and political ties back home, and they haven't heard anything that would cause us to move out and make contact before we knew of a positive threat. And there's another thing."

"Don't keep me in suspense, Captain, what is it?" asked the engineer, fully focused on the conversation.

"When we were traveling in company with *Kara* and before we entered the battle against the Arkon recently, the admiral did something I still don't understand."

"What?"

"Before entering Zarminian space, we detected a disturbance a ways from our course. The admiral ignored it and kept going. Later, the *Kara* broke off and headed to Earth."

"You mean the Earth from our history books?" asked a wide-eyed engineer.

"The very same. I think the admiral and others have been watching Earth and its system for some time. But back to the disturbance. I later reviewed our digital sensor history. It now seems plain to me that the disturbance was combat between two opposing forces."

Now the engineer was on the edge of his seat. "What forces?"

"The Arkon for one. The other force was using Host technology, and we identified an old Host cruiser the admiral gave to Galactic Force anonymously some time ago."

"You mean there was a fight between the Arkon and a Host-friendly force and we didn't intervene?"

"That's exactly what I mean," said Raynaldus.

"Why would the admiral do that?"

"I'm not sure," said the captain, leaning back in his chair and thinking for a few moments. "It makes me wonder about something else."

"If there is more of the same, you're really making me uneasy," said Jason.

"And rightly so." The captain nodded. "While I was reviewing the sensor logs, I also took a look at the communications logs. There were a number of incoming and outgoing messages in a code none of us can break. It was clear, however, that the incoming communications were from the Zarminian system."

"Doesn't sound alarming to me."

"On the face of it, no. However, the volume and time span of incoming communications before we intervened in the Arkon and allied battle were substantial."

"I'm not following; what are you suggesting?" asked the engineer.

"That the admiral could have intervened earlier and may have delayed his intervention until the last minute."

"But why would he do that?"

"I don't know for certain," Raynaldus said.

"But you have an idea, don't you? I've known you for too long. Spit it out."

Raynaldus looked his friend in the eyes and leaned forward in his seat. "The only reason I can think of is the admiral wanted to save the defending force in the most dramatic way possible."

"Why?"

"To gain their undying thanks and admiration as fast and as fully as possible. But before you ask me why again, I haven't got a clue."

"But what does your gut tell you?" asked the captain's friend.

"I'm not sure. I just have a bad feeling and can't say more. Now, here is what I need to hear from you. If I have to take some action on my own that may appear strange to others, will you support me?"

"You know I will. We've spent too many years together for me to second-guess you."

CHAPTER 49

NINE OF THE TEN DAYS had passed, and the discussions between the allies had not progressed any appreciable amount. Much of the lack of progress was probably due to the dysfunctional and arbitrary nature of Ambassador McDuff.

Seated in the comfortable living area in the home of Zarminian Foreign Minister Gortah, Dick Carson and Carian Ambassador Vaca discussed events with Gortah. Harry was there but standing silently a few feet away from the three men.

"I cannot abide that man McDuff. Just when we are on the point of agreement, he steps in and makes a mess of things," Gortah commented, taking a sip of Zarminian wine.

"He's good at it, I'll agree," Dick said. "But placing him aside, how willing are the Zarminians and," he looked at Vaca, "the Carians, and to what extent, to give up some degree of autonomy and control to get the Host's assistance in production?"

The other two men in the room did not answer immediately. Then Vaca broke the silence. "Speaking for my people, I would have to say we aren't willing to give up much. We concede the Host are better at manufacturing, and their grasp of technology is substantially better. But what use is all such help if we lose our sense of freedom, of being in charge of our dreams?"

"Exactly," said Gortah. "The Carians and Zarminians have descended from the same people and we have many of the same values. I can't see our people voluntarily giving up what they believe is their cultural core. . . their freedom and independence. Not even for survival."

Dick nodded, knowing the people of Earth felt the same way,

even if their governments didn't always see things the same way. As for Guardian Force, Dick had no doubts that it would be a cold day in hell before Van Childs would give up total control of Galactic Force to anybody.

"You realize," Dick said, "we are assuming what Ambassador Harris suggested about the Host price for help would be more control of our lives is true. It may be a bad assumption."

"I do not think so, Dick," said Gortah. "I think he was right."

Vaca nodded.

Playing the devil's advocate, Dick spurred them again. "But shouldn't we expect to give up some control if our survival is at stake?"

Vaca spoke for the group. "If we give up some now, when will it stop? Do we give up a little more for some wonderful new technology next cycle? And a little more for new medicine? Soon there would be no freedom left. I think we have to agree to be partners. . . they provide the new technology, we provide the additional labor, shipyards, and material. If they have better processes and controls, we can assess them and implement them on our own, or not."

Dick smiled at Vaca's summary. "Then, McDuff aside, we seem to be in agreement. It should also occur to the both of you that the forces and beliefs shared among the three of us constitute the majority opinion and force of the allied powers. Further, I believe Earth can be persuaded to agree with us despite all the efforts of McDuff to the contrary."

"So, what are you suggesting?" asked Vaca.

"When the Host show up tomorrow, we agree to accept their help, to be partners, as Vaca said, but not to relinquish our autonomy or overall control of our production and resource allocations. We welcome their suggestions and council but, in the end, we retain ultimate authority over and for our respective people."

The two other men thought about this for a moment, then nodded their agreement.

"But what about McDuff?" asked Vaca.

"Leave him to me," Dick said with a wink and a smile.

On the morning of the tenth day, Galactic Force Strike Force Two appeared over Zarminia in escort of *New Horizons*. Almost immediately, the remaining strike force with Jan St. Clair in command aboard *Reliant* broke away from *New Horizons* and took a position several thousand miles away, as directed by Van.

An hour later, *Triton*, *Kara*, and *Ditona* appeared and entered orbit around the planet. If Admiral Namath was aware of the *Reliant* and her ships at a distance, he didn't seem to care.

"Captain Raynaldus, I'll be shifting my flag to *Kara* for the duration of our visit," Namath said. Seeing the question forming on Raynaldus' lips, he added, "The ambassador and I can function better that way."

"Yes, Admiral. I understand," was all Raynaldus was expected or required to say.

"Call my shuttle right away. I'll stop by *Kara* to drop off a few things and to pick up the ambassador and continue to Zarminia."

Raynaldus nodded and excused himself from the admiral's quarters to make the arrangements.

Aboard *New Horizons*, Van was making similar arrangements to go to the surface himself.

"You want me to go with you?" Rose asked as she watched Van straighten his gray uniform with the single gold sunburst on the high collar.

"Normally, I'd love for you to be there. But I don't expect it to be a very pleasant meeting. Dick has let me know by implant what they have resolved to say and do. Namath won't like it. Besides, I have something else planned."

That brought a lift in Rose's spirits as she coyly asked, "And what would that be?"

Reacting to Rose's coy response, he chuckled. "Not what you think. I asked Frank to invite the *Triton*'s captain to dinner this evening aboard *New Horizons*."

"Hardly a thing a girl could get excited about," was all Rose would say as she looked off at an imaginary vista.

"Now, don't get huffy. There's method in what I'm doing."

"Like what?"

"Like trying to see what information we can get from Raynaldus. I'm still convinced there is something strange going on, and he may have an answer."

"Will Rebecca be there also?"

"That's the plan. As I understand it, Raynaldus and his crew have been forced to leave their families behind for several months now. I'll be curious how he'll react to you two women at dinner."

"So, we're just so much fluff in your plan?" Rose asked, a little miffed.

"No. I expect all of you to watch and evaluate our guest. I'm guessing you and Rebecca will have different insights than Frank and I will."

"OK, you're out of trouble for now," Rose simpered and hugged Van as he readied to depart.

The same afternoon, all the major players gathered in the luxurious presidential conference room at the headquarters of the Zarminian Federation in Lowondia. For this session a large round table was installed to seat the various representatives, including Namath, Tafaris, Carson, Vaca, Gortah, McDuff, and Van Childs. Harry was present, but stood silently in a corner. Dick Carson called the meeting to order.

"Gentlemen, thank you for being here on time. You have all had a chance to meet, so we will dispense with the introductions and get right to the meat of the matter, so to speak. Our debate here has been spirited in the absence of our Host friends and Galactic Force. We carefully considered all of what the Host have offered and are most appreciative of its generous nature."

Admiral Namath allowed an air of success to creep over his face as he anticipated the good news to follow.

Dick continued, "We recognize our serious need for

manufacturing help and technical expertise, which the Host can provide, and we welcome their support."

Namath's smile was getting broader.

"However, the majority of the allies are concerned about the extent of our autonomy over resource allocation and supervision of this massive proposed project."

Namath's expression soured. But before he could say anything, McDuff jumped up.

"Wait just a minute!" the man unceremoniously interjected. "That is not what the Earth Federation and I agreed to."

"No, it isn't, McDuff. Unfortunately for you, I sent a courier ship to Earth early in our discussions, with a message saying you have been an obstruction to our conversations. A message that was subsequently endorsed by the other representatives here. Just prior to our meeting, I received a reply. You have been relieved of your duties and recalled."

"But you can't do that. There is no one here to take my place as Earth's representative."

Dick nodded at Harry. "That has been solved temporarily by the reinstatement of Ambassador Harris as Earth's representative."

Harry opened the door, and Ambassador Harris entered followed by two guards.

"The two gentlemen escorting the new ambassador have your things ready and will escort you to an awaiting shuttle to take you home."

"But, but, but. . ." sputtered McDuff as the two guards led him out of the room.

Dick resumed. "For our Host representatives, Ambassador Harris has been on a mission to Earth and has just returned. He has a long association with the Zarminians, as well as Earth's involvement in advancing allied needs. I'm sure he will meet all your standards."

Namath was stunned at this sudden change in the diplomatic landscape. So much so he had no immediate response. Tafaris remained stoic.

"Now, if we can return to the subject of allied autonomy,

perhaps, Admiral, you can expand on what you had in mind." Dick took his seat and yielded the floor to the Host representatives.

Slowly, Namath stood and took in the new set of representatives as his mettle returned to him.

"Neither I nor the Host wish to assume control of your allied nations or assume the duties of governmental control. However, we believe that to maximize production in time to meet the ultimate meeting with the Arkon, we should be free to manage the gathering and allocation of required resources. It also means selecting locations for optimal manufacturing centers that meet the best logistical support system and overall control of the manufacturing and assembly process."

That did not meet with overwhelming approval, and discussion continued until late in the afternoon, at which point the meeting was adjourned until the following day.

"So, what happened?" Rose asked as they prepared for the captain's dinner aboard *New Horizons*.

But Van didn't immediately respond—he was too stunned by Rose and her new dress. Van was radiant in admiration. Every time Rose shed her uniform for more feminine attire, her beauty impressed him anew. Not that she wasn't a good-looking woman in uniform. It was just that she so seldom got all dressed up, and Van was caught speechless every time.

"Cat got your tongue?" Rose asked after his silence. "By the way, you're staring."

Struggling to regain his composure, he finally blurted out, "You're beautiful."

"Thanks! You might do well getting some nice civilian clothes also. Don't you ever run out of uniforms?"

"No. Harry keeps me supplied."

"That was a rhetorical question. Next time we go to the surface, remind me to take you shopping. Now, how about my original question?"

Van shook his head and refocused. "Aside from getting rid

of that pest McDuff, not much. Tafaris was silent all through the afternoon with Namath doing the speaking. Not a surprise there. However, Namath is still seeking more control than the allies are willing to give. Some concessions were made by the allies, but they, I mean we, still insisted in maintaining overall control."

"And Namath doesn't like that," Rose commented.

"No, he doesn't, which makes this whole thing more interesting, or puzzling, depending on how you look at it. From my point of view, we have offered him wide latitude, but it doesn't seem to be enough."

"Interesting," Rose said in earnest. "Now, however, let's go before the dinner gets cold."

When Van and Rose arrived in Frank's quarters, he and Rebecca were deep in friendly conversation with Raynaldus.

"Ah, welcome, you two," Frank said, standing. "We were just getting to know Basil here." He gestured to Raynaldus, who also stood.

"Basil?" Van asked with a grin.

"I'm sorry, Commander, but you and I never got around to exchanging names informally," replied the *Triton's* captain.

"True enough. I'm Van and this is Rose."

Raynaldus' face lit up at seeing Rose and Rebecca, who was almost equally as lovely when dressed up. The combined presence of two such lovely women was having the impression Van was looking for.

"Delighted to meet you, Rose," said the Host captain, giving a slight bow.

"The honor is mine, Basil," Rose said with her biggest smile.

"Well then," Frank said, rubbing his hands together. "Dinner is ready and I've taken the liberty of serving some wine I got when last on Earth. It comes from Napa Valley. I think you'll like it." They did, even into the second bottle.

As the dishes were cleared by the captain's steward, Raynaldus surprised everyone by broaching the subject of the discussions taking place on the planet below. They were more surprised by the question itself.

"So, how are your discussions with the admiral and the ambassador? The admiral doesn't share much."

Van recovered quickly and explained what was going on. This was the opening to find out more about the admiral and his mission that he'd hoped would occur. Van summarized the meetings. To his credit, Raynaldus didn't display any outward reaction until Van was done.

"Interesting," Raynaldus said. "I knew the admiral and the Regents wanted more manufacturing capability. I assumed it was all part of a coordinated effort. However, what you just told me is strange."

Frank took this as a cue to ask a few questions. "We know so little about the Host. What can you tell us about the Host Regents, where you come from, and what your people are like?"

Raynaldus was a little surprised his hosts knew so little, but could see no security risks in answering.

"The Regents is our governing body comprising twelve men and women and led by the First Regent. Since there are only about a million of us at present, the government doesn't have to be larger or more sophisticated. Obviously, the military, including marines, reports to the Regents through Admiral Spencer. There are three fleets. Home Fleet and Second and Third Fleets. Third Fleet is headquartered at Fortuna and under the command of Admiral Namath."

"How many ships do you have?" Frank asked.

"Unfortunately, that is classified. I can say, not enough yet to have a successful final conflict with the Arkon," replied Raynaldus.

"So, that's why Namath is looking for more shipbuilding capabilities?" Van asked.

"While we were not told why we were headed here, that would make sense," said the *Triton*'s captain. "We are very efficient, but with only about a million people, we are necessarily constricted."

"Where do you live? I mean the Host in general," asked Rebecca.

"The location is classified, as you might imagine," replied Raynaldus. "But after a long search, our grandfathers found a planet very much like Earth, which they chose to call New Belton after our ancient home planet. The majority of us live there. The exceptions are those on Fortuna and the deployed ships and one or two small outposts."

"You mean Fortuna is one of a kind?" Van asked.

"We have orbital shipyards at New Belton, but yes. Fortuna is unique."

Things were slowly falling into place for Van, so he decided to take a risk.

"Basil, did you know Tafaris is an AI?"

Raynaldus put his wineglass down so quickly it nearly broke. "What did you say?"

"Tafaris is an AI. We discovered it during your last visit. We have an AI we call Harry who was the Caretaker for the Host depot sites on Earth two hundred years ago. Harry detected the true nature of your ambassador."

"That explains a lot," Raynaldus said absentmindedly as he stared at nothing in particular.

"There's more you should know," Van continued. "You know *New Horizons* came equipped with an AI, correct?"

"Yes, I heard that."

"What you may not know is that the AI, we call it Jennifer, was in communication with *Triton* and/or *Kara* before and during the Arkon attack on Zarminia."

Raynaldus leaned his head back in the sudden realization that his suspicions were confirmed.

"I see by your reaction," Van said, "that you knew about this."

Recovered, the Host captain said, "When I was reviewing the ship's communications and sensor logs, I did see the type of transmissions you mentioned. It was in a code, however, that neither I nor my crew could break. But some things are starting to make sense."

"What do you mean?" Van asked.

"I probably shouldn't tell you this, but since you've been so open, I will. When we were en route to Zarminia, *Triton* detected a disturbance, which gave the appearance of combat at a distance — but the admiral chose to ignore it. Later, when I accessed the communications logs, I also looked at the sensor logs and discovered it was a battle between an Arkon force of undetermined size and several small ships accompanied by an old Host cruiser. I think you now call her *Reliant*."

"And you didn't help?" demanded Frank as he rose from his seat and then slowly sat back down.

"To my regret, no," said the contrite captain. "We took our lead from the admiral, and the detailed identification of the fighters was apparently suppressed at the time. But getting back to the strange communications, I had a discussion with a friend I trust and it occurred to me that *Triton* may have entered your Arkon battle at the very last minute on purpose."

Now Van was at a loss for words. He and Dick suspected such might have been the case, but to hear a Host officer say the same thing sent a shock from his head to his toes.

It was Rebecca's turn to speak. "So, let me get all this mess straight. Your admiral, Namath, along with an AI impersonating a human as a Host ambassador, flew secretly to Zarminia and intentionally ignored an Arkon attack on Host-friendly ships and then surreptitiously timed his entry into a life-and-death struggle with the Arkon and us so he could be seen saving the day?"

Nobody spoke as they absorbed the thought. Raynaldus couldn't or didn't want to answer.

Finally, Van spoke. "That's my conclusion, Rebecca, and I think I know why."

"Please explain," Rose said. "I don't."

"Namath wants the help of the alliance to increase overall ship production to meet the Arkon, given our reduced threat timeline. He was on his way here to bargain with us. When he saw the *Reliant* battle, he ignored it, knowing the aftermath would make us more receptive to help.

"Then, learning the Arkon were attacking us in Zarminian

space and we were losing, he timed his intervention to again reinforce the value he could bring to the table and throw the allies into a panic for any help they could get."

"You mean all that was in preparation for an advantage for his negotiations?" asked an incredulous Frank.

"I don't think he had negotiations in mind, Frank," Van said. "What he hoped would happen is that the allies would be so eager for help that he could dictate terms. Ignoring the *Reliant* fight and his dramatic intervention was just icing on the cake."

"But based on your recount of the discussions today, his ability to dictate terms has taken a hit with the allies balking at the control he wants," summarized Rose.

"Exactly," Van said.

"So, what will he do next?" asked Rebecca to anyone who would answer.

All eyes went to Raynaldus, who squirmed with discomfort.

"I would continue to negotiate to get the best terms possible. Knowing the admiral as I do, however, I would not rule out the threat of force to get what he wants," Raynaldus said, concern showing in his knitted eyebrows.

"And how would you and the *Triton* react to such an order?" Van asked, placing the officer in a difficult position.

But Raynaldus didn't answer.

Seeing the conundrum facing their guest, Van asked another question. "What do you think your Regents would do in this circumstance?"

"That's my problem, Van. I can't see our Regents going to this extreme. There's no reason to that I'm aware of."

"But I predict tomorrow the allied representatives will stick to their guns, so to speak, and say no to the level of control Namath wants," Van said. "If Namath resorts to force, I have a strike force ready to respond and another on alert. *Triton* could be the deciding factor for the Host. She is more powerful than many of our ships together. With the addition of the *Kara*, a fight could be brutal. What will you do?"

Raynaldus rose and stepped away from his seat. "If you all

will excuse me, I have to return to my ship. My thanks for the dinner and the pleasure of meeting you all."

Seeing they had laid enough on the unsuspecting captain, Frank also stood. "Of course, I'll walk with you to the flight bay."

CHAPTER 50

"WHAT DO YOU MEAN *TRITON* is gone?" the angry admiral asked the *Kara's* captain, who was interrupting Namath's breakfast.

"I mean, sir, she is gone. Sometime early this morning she eased out of orbit and went to FTL. She was gone before we had a chance to ask any questions."

Namath threw his napkin down on his table and stood, knocking over his chair. The major portion of his force was now gone, and a threatening allied military force stood off about a thousand miles. He had planned to give an ultimatum to the allied representatives today with *Triton* and *Kara* as backup. Now, *Triton* was gone and where to was unknown. He went to his desk and took stylus and pad in hand and scribbled out a message. Then he handed the pad to the *Kara's* skipper.

"Send this to *Ditona*, launch her to Fortuna with all possible speed, and have her transmit this message as soon as she is in range."

The captain glanced at the pad, which read in part, *Bring all available ships to Zarminia immediately.*

"Yes, sir," said the captain as he turned on his heels and left the presence of his admiral.

"Captain!" Namath called before the man passed through the hatch.

"Yes, sir?" asked the man, nearly falling over as he stopped.

"Inform the allied representatives I have fallen ill and will rejoin them as soon as possible."

"Yes, Admiral." The captain disappeared.

"Where do you think Raynaldus went?" Rose asked as they sat eating lunch the next day on the mess deck.

"Not sure," Van said, contemplating the news. "But if it were me, I'd be either heading home or departing for parts unknown."

"No, you'd head home to chat with the Regents," Rose said, looking at him over her coffee cup.

"You're probably right. And I hope he does. Right now, Namath is vulnerable, but my bet is *Ditona* went for reinforcements."

"And what will you do?"

"The only thing I can do. I sent a message to Stan to bring in Strike Force One and stand by."

Rose put down her cup in surprise. "You'd really fight the Host?"

"I don't want to, but we have to be ready to stand up for the allied rights to self-determination."

"You feel that strongly? Even if it meant possibly losing to the Arkon as a result?"

"I do, but more importantly, the allies do."

On board the Sonaran orbiting shipyard, James Harris and Dick Carson had just finished giving Majel a tour of the facility, along with a description of their challenges.

"So what do you think, Majel?" Dick asked.

"You mean about this facility or about your alliance?" Majel asked in return.

"Both."

"Your construction facility and methods are primitive, and I don't see how you can meet your proposed timeline, the help of the Host notwithstanding."

"That's encouraging," Harris said.

"I'm not trying to belittle you, but those are the facts as I see them," responded Majel.

"How about the alliance?" Dick asked.

"The alliance is more interesting. I have substantial knowledge on how difficult it is to form and maintain such alliances. To have come as far as you have in so short a time is impressive. I am also impressed with your stance on maintaining a position of autonomy when faced with the combination of advantages and force presented by your Host friends. But do you think it wise to take so firm a stand that it might lead to violence? Wouldn't that be counterproductive?"

Harris chuckled a little before answering. "It may be, Majel. But as you learned from Van, the culture of the allies is entrenched in independence and self-reliance. To give even a portion of that up is antithetical to our basic history as humans. Of course, we hope it doesn't come to violence, but we have to be prepared and we are willing."

"Yes, I remember 'the speech,' and I see some similarities in our own history. But we grew out of the violence part."

"But only after obliterating all your enemies," Harris reminded the older man.

"There is that," was all Majel would say.

Two days later, a large force centered on another Host cruiser appeared in Zarminian space. *Kara* maneuvered to join them.

Frank sat in his command chair aboard *New Horizons* and asked for a count of the new ships. This time his golf club was out of its holder and stretched between his two hands as he unconsciously rolled it between his fingers.

"Two cruisers counting the *Kara*, Captain, five destroyers, six frigates, and four corvettes. And they are splitting into two groups, each with a cruiser in the center," answered the sensor operator. "Also, Strike Forces One and Two are closing their distance to Zarminia."

"Interesting," Frank commented. "Helm, ease us out of here to get behind Strike Force Two. Sound general quarters."

"Roger that, Captain," called out the helm officer, after which the automated system rang out.

"General quarters, general quarters. All hands, man your battle stations."

With the flag bridge now manned, Van assumed his command seat just in time for his communications officer to alert him.

"Commander! Zarminian gunboats are coming up and joining the strike forces. Also, there are two Zarminian corvettes requesting to join us."

"What a difference a few days make," Van commented to no one in particular. "Split the gunboats between the two strike groups and send the corvettes to Strike Force One. And open a channel to the *Kara* and Admiral Namath."

"Yes, Commander," replied the communications officer. "I have the *Kara* on speaker now. Should I open this channel to all our ships?"

"Yes," Van said.

"It's done, Commander, and the admiral is live on the line."

"Admiral Namath, I see you've got friends."

"Call it moral support, Commander. Are you and your allies ready to continue discussions?" asked Namath with just a hint of sarcasm.

"You know just as I do, Admiral, negotiations with intimidation is not a good mix."

"Not intimidation, Commander. Consider it another demonstration of the sort of help and technology we can offer."

"Is this the entire Third Fleet?" Van asked.

"Ah, you must have been talking with Raynaldus. He has broken security, and I'll have to chat with him about it. But to answer your question, this is not all of Third Fleet or of the Host forces as a whole. Just a small entourage. Are you ready to resume negotiations?"

"That sounds a lot like an ultimatum, Admiral," Van said.

"Call it what you like, Commander. I am ready to take my shuttle to the surface. Can I count on seeing you there?"

Van thought for a brief second, eyes squinting as his mind raced. Then he said, "No, not while your forces are here. Send them back home and we can resume."

"Then I'm truly sorry, Commander," said the trailing voice of the admiral as a green ball of plasma from *Kara* raced to intercept *New Horizons*. The blasts impacted the *New Horizons'* shields, sending them to dangerously low levels.

"Stand down, Admiral Namath," came a new voice over the network as the *Triton* materialized between the two forces. Then another and another Host ship appeared as stealth systems went off-line.

"Is that you, Raynaldus?" asked Namath with irritation. "You are under arrest for dereliction of duty."

"I'm afraid it is you, Barton, who is under arrest. And no, this is not Raynaldus. It is your old friend and Host commander, Admiral Spencer. Until you fired on *New Horizons*, I couldn't believe you had gone so far. You are relieved, and a shuttle is on its way to pick you up and bring you here. You will stand trial before the Regents when you get home."

There was a loud noise and then nothing. A minute later, the captain of the *Kara* came on the line.

"I'm sorry to report, Admiral, that Admiral Namath has taken his own life. *Kara* and her forces are standing down and await your orders."

"Take your forces and retune to Fortuna, Captain. I will see you in a few days," said the admiral with sorrow in his voice. "Now then, Commander Childs, would it be acceptable for me to join with you and the allied representatives on the surface?"

Van relaxed in his chair and gave a sigh of relief. "Absolutely, Admiral. Would one hour give you the time you need to get to the surface?"

"One hour it is. I will see you there." The connection ended.

CHAPTER 51

E VERYONE FROM THE NEGOTIATING GROUP waited anxiously for the new admiral to arrive. No one, including Van, knew what to expect. Harry, as usual, was in the room, and this time Majel also had a seat.

The door to the big room opened, and a short but fit man with wavy white hair walked swiftly into the room.

"Thank you, gentlemen, for accepting my request. I only wish our first meeting could have been under better circumstances."

"Glad to have you here, Admiral," Dick said and then made the appropriate introductions before everyone took a seat. "Before I launch into why we have been gathered here for over ten days, what do you already know, Admiral?"

"More than I want to, I'm afraid, Mr. Carson. In a nutshell, we determined Namath was hoping to build a force strong enough to assume command and control of all Host forces and launch an attack on the Arkon. He apparently had an exaggerated view of our overall capabilities if he thought he could be successful. He needed your shipbuilding capabilities, resources, and labor support to make his plans happen. He did a good job of hiding what he was doing until Captain, or I should say, Admiral Raynaldus came to me in *Triton* with his fantastic story. I had to come myself to see what Namath was capable of. I am beyond sorry for the troubles he caused.

"That being said, Namath had a point. The Arkon attacks on you have come much earlier than we expected. Even with our capabilities combined with yours, we are not ready for them right now. It makes sense that we work out a deal to combine our efforts to build our forces faster. Even then we are all at great risk."

This was a surprise to just about everyone, and Van let the admiral know.

"If everyone in this room is like me, our collective heads are spinning," Van said. "Rightly or wrongly, we always carried the thought that the Host would be our ultimate salvation. We knew we would have to help, but we assumed you, the Host, were far more prepared than we. How many ships do you have at present, if you don't mind my asking?"

The admiral eased back in his chair, contemplating how or if to answer. Then he leaned forward and said, "Just a little over four hundred combat ships and about one hundred auxiliaries."

Silence shrouded the room. Only four hundred? Not nearly enough, everyone thought at the same time.

"What do you have at present?" asked the admiral.

"Not enough to make a difference, Admiral. All allied hulls, combat and auxiliaries, come to about thirty-two, including hulls under construction."

"Hmm," the admiral mused. "Our estimates are the Arkon can easily mount a thousand ships or more. We know their maintenance and repair is terrible, but with those numbers they can easily overwhelm us. But we can only do our best if we can all work together. I don't care who is in control, just as long as it is coordinated. I have appointed Admiral Raynaldus as the new commander of Fortuna and Third Fleet. Can you work out something with him?" the admiral said, looking straight at Van.

There were smiles all around as heads nodded in affirmation.

"It looks like we can, Admiral, and we're happy to do it," Van said. "But given the build rate I just calculated in my head, we are a long way from getting to a thousand ships."

"Yes, I know," said the admiral grimly. "We just have to hope the Arkon give us some breathing room."

"Maybe not," came a new voice from the table. It was Majel. All heads turned to him.

"What did you say?" Van asked.

"I said maybe not. Meaning, you may be able to have your thousand-plus ships sooner than you think."

"How is that possible?"

"We have some."

"But you haven't been in battle for nearly a thousand years. What could you have?" Van asked.

"I told you we defeated our enemies and assumed a peaceful life those many years ago. I didn't say we got rid of our ships," said Majel, enjoying the puzzled looks around him.

"But they'd be a thousand years old. What could they do?" Dick asked.

"Yes, they are old by your standards. But they still exceed your technology levels. And they are perfectly preserved in space, where no damage or significant deterioration could take place. They were serviced and sealed, and they are still there."

"And how many are there out there?" Van asked, bracing for a disappointing answer.

"Six hundred and forty-nine," was the brief response. "And I believe my fellow Naskapi would offer them to you."

"That would be most gracious," Spencer said. "And we would greatly appreciate it."

"No, Admiral. I don't think you grasped my meaning. I was speaking to the commander. He is the one who passed our tests and whose values we trust. It is to him we offer these ships under the banner of Guardian Force."

Oh shit! Van thought, frozen into inaction. *This is way more than I bargained for.*

EPILOGUE

GULV'S TALK WITH REEB SUGGESTED that Daan's attack had been successful. However, nothing had been heard from his kinsman and his force in too long a time. It now seemed obvious that something had happened to his forces either in Zarminian space or elsewhere. Regardless of what had actually happened or how, the majority of Red Sector 20 forces were gone and presumed lost, along with their commander. More distressingly, the supreme leader commanded his presence in the great hall. He paced his quarters, knowing that few people summoned by the supreme leader in this fashion lived to see another day.

I have to have a plan, he said to himself, still pacing. Of course, he would have to plead ignorance and claim Daan had screwed up all on his own. But if he were to survive the audience, he had to know what needed to be done next. And he did have an idea. A bold one, but it just might be possible.

Two hours later, Gulv stood outside the great wooden doors of the audience chamber, his red crest and his knees quivering. Then the doors began to move. Slowly at first, but they picked up speed and banged into the chamber walls with a terrifying sound that reverberated throughout the now open chamber. He stood as straight as he could and walked purposefully forward.

END

ABOUT THE AUTHOR

A graduate of the U.S. Naval Academy, Annapolis, Maryland, Mike was a career naval officer, decorated combat pilot, and served in senior positions on staff in Washington, D.C. Following his military service, he embarked on a career as an aerospace systems engineer and executive with several Fortune 500 companies.

With a desire to help others develop as leaders, Mike earned his PhD in Organizational Leadership and started a leadership development consulting firm, specializing in executive coaching and development.

Mike's passion for writing, developed throughout his career and in his doctoral studies, resulted in his writing a non-fiction book, Leaders Are Made Not Born. That writing and publishing experience fueled Mike's desire to try his hand at writing fiction... which he finds an even greater challenge.

When he's not writing, Mike spends as much time as possible saltwater fishing with his wife, Lynne.

Sign up for his newsletter www.michaeljfarlow.com to get access to updates, new books and events.

CONTACT MIKE:

Author Website and Blog: www.michaeljfarlow.com
Facebook: https://www.facebook.com/MichaelJFarlow/
LinkedIn: https://www.linkedin.com/in/
michaeljfarlow?trk=nav_responsive_tab_profile
Goodreads: https://www.goodreads.com/
author/show/6550141.Michael_J_Farlow

If you enjoyed this book, please spread the word. AND,
you can help other readers find this book in these ways:
RECOMMEND it to you family, local library, friends,
online forums, discussion groups and book clubs.
REVIEW it on Amazon, Goodreads, or any other review site.

COMING NEXT

DARK ENEMY
Book 5 in the Host Saga

In this action-packed thriller, Galactic Force and allies increase their capabilities with help from both old and new friends. These new relationships are not without problems and unexpectedly pit Van and his force against friends in and out of the alliance. While still struggling with these issues, an opportunity arises to take the offensive against the Arkon who experience problems of their own. Do they fight or do they wait? Don't miss what happens next.

Genre: Science Fiction
Audience: Ages 18+
Publisher: Wolf Press, LLC

OTHER BOOKS BY
THIS AUTHOR

Best Science Fiction Series Award by the
Texas Association of Authors
Future Discovered: Host Saga Book 1 This
book was revised in July, 2018

"*Future Discovered* will have you questioning the use of
advanced technology and the future of humanity. This
is a unique, compelling and intriguing combination
of science fiction and thriller. A must read."

— *Bob Mayer, New York Times Best Selling author*

Van Childs's accidental discovery of an alien cache of advanced technologies thrusts him into the role of reluctant guardian of the human race. Upon learning of an extra-terrestrial space-faring population, the Host, who visited Earth some two hundred years before, Van is forewarned of an impending invasion by the Arkon, an expansionist race with a history of destruction. Childs's mission to prepare Earth for the Arkon's coming invasion meets with opposition by a powerful human adversary with conflicting goals. Who will win?

Genre: Science Fiction
Audience: Ages 18+
Publisher: Wolf Press, LLC
ISBN 978-0-9973121-0-2 — Trade Paperback
ISBN: 978-0-9973121-1-9 — eBook (ePub)

Immortal Guardian: Host Saga Book 2

"*Immortal Guardian* continues the engaging and
thought provoking Host saga. A great read."

— *Bob Mayer, New York Times Best Selling author*

In this second book of the Host Saga, Van Childs faces a new and more difficult decision: to either continue the path he reluctantly started, a path there's no turning back from, and face a lonely future of immortality; or opt out and allow mankind to fend for itself. With his previous enemy defeated, it is possible to continue to prepare mankind to meet the Arkon if he chooses. But as Childs's ally, the Host Caretaker, continues to unearth new Host technology that could be used either to help or hurt the human race, Van doesn't consider the possibility that individual, state, and even extraterrestrial forces might act against his efforts — and the interests of mankind.

Genre: Science Fiction
Audience: Ages 18+
Publisher: Wolf Press, LLC
ISBN 978-0-9973121-2-6 — Trade Paperback
ISBN: 978-0-9973121-3-3 — eBook (ePub)

Search for Help: Host Saga Book 3

"In *Search for Help*, we realize the galaxy is immense and so are its problems. Intrigue, betrayal and combat keep the hero and his strong supporting cast of characters on their toes and readers glued to the story. A must read"

— *Bob Mayer, New York Times Best Selling author*

Van Childs continues his mission to ready Earth for the Arkon invasion. He now realizes that his own interplanetary Guardian Force's and the Earth Federation's combined ability to prepare for and defend against the Arkon is not enough. If they are going to be ready in time, Van has to gamble Earth's—and his own—safety and embark on a desperate search for help in unexplored parts of the galaxy. But political upheaval in the Federation and a traitor within the Guardian Force ranks threaten to derail the mission, and at the crucial moment when help is within their grasp, an attempt on Van's life forces them to return to Earth—and face an enemy he never could have anticipated.

Genre: Science Fiction
Audience: Ages 18+
Publisher: Wolf Press, LLC
ISBN 978-0-9973121-4-0 – Trade Paperback
ISBN: 978-0-9973121-5-7 – eBook (ePub)

*Leaders are Made Not Born: 40 Simple Skills to
Make You the Leader You Want to Be.*

"...straightforward, zeros in on key leadership skills,
and exceptionally practical. I like this book."

*— John Ryan, President and CEO,
Center for Creative Leadership*

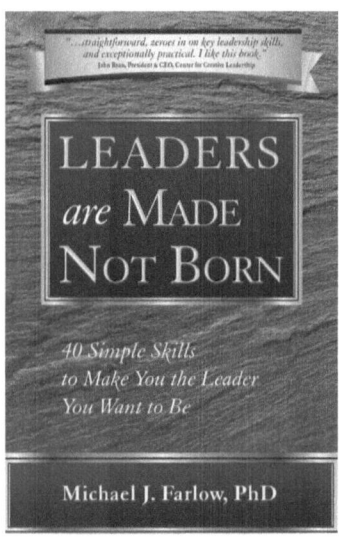

There is no such thing as a leadership gene. What you need instead are the forty principals and easy-to-apply skills in the book. Clear, concise, yet comprehensive, *Leaders are Made Not Born* provides the skills; you do the rest.

Genre: Business/Leadership
Audience: Ages 18+
Publisher: LinkUp Publishing
ISBN 978-0-9826746-8-0 — Trade Paperback
ISBN: 978-1-4835348-5-5 — eBook (ePub)

Quick Tips for Leaders: To Make a Difference

For those of you who are on the go and want a quick, short reference for building your leadership skills, this is the book for you. Drawn from *Leaders are Made Not Born,* this book summarizes fifteen useful tips for those who want a quick look at leadership. This is an easy read and offers special notes for entrepreneurs. It will grab your interest and desire to know more.

Go out and make a difference!

Genre: Business/Leadership
Audience: Ages 18+
Publisher: Wolf Press, LLC
ISBN 978-0-9973121-6-4 – Trade Paperback
ISBN: 978-0-9973121-7-1 – eBook (ePub)

www.ingramcontent.com/pod-product-compliance
Lightning Source LLC
Chambersburg PA
CBHW030700120726
47905CB00001B/295